Livid Blue

By

Jason Blacker

PUBLISHED BY:
Lemon Tree Publishing
Copyright © 2013 by Jason Blacker
JasonBlacker.com

Visit Jason Blacker on the web at www.JasonBlacker.com

Editing: Dragonfly Editing

ISBN-13: 9781927623190

Table of Contents

I

"No one knows me, Peter."

"Come on, Janko, I know you for God's sake."

"Yeah, you and that bitch out there who thinks she's trying to be helpful, but she's fucking not."

"How come every time I come and see you, you act like a spoiled brat? How long have we known each other…fifteen, probably twenty years, and I've never seen you as grumpy as you are now…"

"Yeah, Peter, twenty or so fucking years and this is the shit you make me put up with. I'm dying here, with fucking tubes stuck up me every way they can, and you've got to point out to me how fucking grumpy I am. Twenty fucking years, Pete, and you won't give me an ounce."

He looked at me funny, like he sometimes does. His one eyebrow was raised like an accent. He stood at the foot of my bed, looking down at me as if he was my judge and jury. Fucking guy, I've hardly ever seen him sit down.

"Hey, Jan, I know what you're thinking. You know why I look at you like this, because I can see right through you. You're a fucking shallow piece of shit. You want me to sit down and berate you some more, I will. Okay?"

Jesus Christ. Twenty years and maybe I should give him a break. He's stuck with me through a lot of shit.

"What are you smiling at?"

"Sorry, buddy, I'm just thinking I should give you a break. But who else do I have to bitch to. Nobody comes to see me anymore…Fucking nobody."

"That's not true; you've told me about a few of your other friends that have come to see you. And what about that doctor that's coming to help you soon…what was his name?"

"Michael, I think, Michael Malichem. And he's not a doctor, he's a fucking shrink. I don't need a shrink, Pete, I need a miracle."

"Well, they say that modern medicine offers the miracle cure…"

"That's not even funny, okay. That's not fucking funny."

"Hi, Janko, are you okay?"

"Yes, Maria, I'm just getting upset, thinking of why no one ever comes to visit me."

"Dr. Malichem will be coming tomorrow. You'll like him, he's a kind man and empathetic, too."

She smiled and then turned and left. The last thing I need is the syrupy condescension of strangers.

"She's got a nice ass, hey? What I'd do to spank that puppy."

"In your dreams, Peter, in your dreams."

He's been coming around once a day or so to visit me ever since I came home to die. That's funny, coming home to die. A lonely place, this shithole that I call home. But it beats dying in a hospital, racing against all those old folks, smokers and alcoholics seeing who can kick the bucket first, and then us all talking about them, like they're heroes. Jealous that they got to go before us. Every one of us seeking that sweet solace of death, but so terrified to die that we're clinging to this frayed rope of life. Shit, I'm way better off here at home, if you can call it that. Hovel more likely, but at least it's mine.

"This is nice what you've done with this place, Janko. It doesn't feel like a hospital at all."

Jesus Christ, that fucking guy always seems to know what I'm thinking.

"That's because it isn't a hospital. You've got to give me some fucking dignity in death. I mean, please…"

"Come on, Jan, I'm serious; it is nice. You've kept it like it was before you got sick. I'm just trying to help. You don't want to go out like this do you?"

"How would you know how I want to leave? You don't think I've got enough right to be a little pissed off considering the shit that I've been through. Fuck, you've been there for me through most of it, Peter, you should know."

"Yeah, and that's why I don't want to see you go out like this. I think you should make use of this shrink guy to help put your mental affairs in order. Work through all of that shit that we've been through…"

"Hey, now, I went through all of that shit, okay. Not you."

"Yeah, I know, Jan, but I was there for you…I'm just saying as your friend. I just think you owe it to yourself. You don't know what is out there on the other side. I mean, just prepare for the journey. That's all I'm saying."

The pain was getting to me. I hate the fucking pain. A body ache all over; my lungs filled with fluid and every breath a gasp at life. A life of what? Fucking pain is all I know now. And Peter's right. I'm taking it out on the only few people who have stood by me through thick and thin. I'm lonely and loveless. Love's the only thing that got me this far, and where is it now?

"Maria…Maria."

Maria came in. God, I love those white uniforms. They don't wear them in the hospital, but what a sight for sore eyes. I bet it would boost the spirit of my sick colleagues.

"Yes, Janko."

"Please give me some more morphine. My bed sores are killing me…"

I had to laugh. It's not the fucking bedsores that are killing me, but that'll have to wait until later.

Maria smiled shyly, like she might hurt my feelings.

"You know what I mean. They're hurting like hell."

Such a soft complexion she has. Not much younger than me, but so much life and vitality in her that it kills me. Fuck, I've got to stop saying that, there is only one thing that is killing me, and it's nothing like her youthfulness. I just wish I could reach out and touch her face. It's been so long since I've touched the warm, soft skin of a woman's face. So long…so, so long.

"I'll put some in your I.V., okay?"

"Uh huh."

"You ever been in love, Maria?"

She looked at me for a moment. Not sure if I was serious or just bugging her. I looked back at her. What deep brown eyes; I know the answer she will give to me. A woman like that doesn't go through life without love.

9

"Sure I have. Haven't you, Janko?"

"I dunno. That's a hard question. I mean what is love? In my state I'm questioning everything. I mean, everything is up for grabs now. At the end of my days, what I thought I knew about life, I'm just not sure about anymore…"

I thought that maybe I was rambling, that she might think I was rambling. But it didn't last long. On your deathbed, if you'll pardon the cliché, although for me it is perfectly real, you care less about what other people think. Fuck, at my stage, life is too short, just way too short. And there's another fucking cliché.

I looked at Peter, but he was lost in Maria's white uniform. His eyes all over her. He's kind of lewd like that in some ways. But I forgive him, he's my oldest friend.

"But to answer the question, I think I have been in love, maybe even a few times. But I can't be sure, I mean, I have no one now, do I? I always thought that love would last forever. Isn't that what they sell you in Hollywood? And I guess in many ways I still think maybe it does. And if so, where is my love that has lasted. Well, it's not here, is it?"

"Well, I guess so. Although I still believe in true love."

Maria was being sincere, of course she believed in true love. If I was a healthy man and not dying, I'd still believe in true love—looking into her deep eyes. Wouldn't any man?

I always like morphine, it makes me sleepy, and sleep is the only respite I get from the pain. The emotional pain, the mental anguish, too. So much pain in just thirty-three short years. So much pain, and yet even though the end is near I'm still scared; I'm fucking terrified. I always thought it'd be easier to die. It seems a lot of people convince themselves that it's no big deal. No big deal until the time comes, and then they're pleading for a few extra days, some months to put things right. I've had many months and yet nothing is right. How can you put your affairs right if you're not right yourself? And I'm like the rest of my ilk. The rest of the deatherer. I made up that word myself, because it rhymes with ditherer and that's what we are. We're living on the cusp of dying and we're taking our time about it. Too scared, and so are you, even if you think you're not. You're scared too, and I'll tell you it's scary, you ought to be scared. Fucking quaking in your boots. Because I am. I'll tell you that much. I'll tell you a lot more; a dying man's got nothing but truth to tell and tell it as quick as I can.

"Looking in your eyes, Maria, you're almost making me believe in it again."

She blushed I think, and turned away. Maybe I was making her uncomfortable. But fuck it, what can I do to her. I can barely get out of bed to go to the bathroom. I'm no threat to anybody.

"I don't mean to make you feel awkward. I know we've only known each other for a few short weeks. It's just that I've got to talk about it. I've got to say what's on my mind. I don't have much time, I've figured that much out."

I tried a weak smile. It was easier than I thought it would be. The morphine is great. Just fucking great.

"It's okay, Janko. You're not my first patient. I like to hear what you have to say. You seem much wiser than your years."

She smiled at me and it warmed my heart. They certainly know how to choose these nurses. The ones that deal with the likes of me, the terminally ill, the deatherers, or as she puts it, the 'patients'. Yes, I guess I am patient. You can only be patient when death comes calling. I never thought I'd find myself at thirty-three years old and dying. Maybe it's best I never knew my fate, if it is fate at all. But then again, if I had known maybe I could've done more, been something with my life. You'll see; my story is kind of a sad one. I never amounted to much. Not that I solely blame myself. My path has been steep and hard, and fuck it, I couldn't do better than I've done. Though God knows I tried my best. I really did try my best.

"You're really good, Maria. I bet they give you special training on dealing with people like me. People who are dying. You know I came up with a word for people like me, I call us the deatherers. Because we're trying to die, but we're taking our sweet time about it. Too scared to let the body go."

Peter was still leering at her. I tried to give him a look, but he wasn't taking his eyes off her. Maria didn't seem to mind, I don't think she really even paid much attention to him, or even really took notice of him. I don't blame her. I think he can give women the creeps. But I had to talk to him about it. He was making me fucking uncomfortable. But he'd always been like that. A little bit of a misogynist.

"I've never heard that before, Janko. I like it though, even if it is…um…a bit morbid."

"You'll be surprised at what you find humorous when you're dying. I think humor helps take the edge off the fear. I think we all fear death. Don't you?"

She didn't say anything right away. She was still fixing with my intravenous. All these fluids dripping into me, trying to make me more comfortable. Preparing me for my journey to the netherworld. We look at the Egyptians and think how quaint it was of them to send their dead with belongings into the other world. I think we do the fucking same. These tubes and drugs and businesses taking care of me. Making sure my journey is a smooth ride. Making a killing off the dying. I won't name names, but think of any of the pharmaceutical giants. The more AIDS patients, the better their stocks. The more cancers, the more drugs to sell, the better their stocks. Fuck, am I really that cynical now, as I lie in wait. I hope not.

"Yeah, I guess humor helps, doesn't it? It brings people together under a common understanding. And why not during death, too?"

She looked away quickly. I think she caught herself saying the word "death" as if it were a bad thing. I think not. I like it. Bring it on, I say. Let's get fucking real about what's happening here. Can't sweep this shit under the carpet. Not like the other things in life that have been swept up and out of the way, sanitized to keep us numb to the realities of living. The macabre and incestuous courtship of brother death and sister life.

"Yes, and why not death? Aren't we all dying the moment we come out of the womb? Maybe the moment the sperm hits the egg. Maybe that's when it all starts going downhill."

I thought I was on a roll now. Maybe I could get her talking some more. I liked her company, and besides she smelled like a meadow. Soft, sweet flowers. I couldn't name any by name. I mean I could say "rose" or something equally trite, but she didn't smell exactly like a rose. Softer, less pungent, if you know what I mean? I've never had more than a passing acquaintance with flowers. And I mean, literally a passing acquaintance, as when I pass by a florist I catch a whiff of a bouquet. I don't think I've ever been given more than two or three bouquets in my life. And maybe I've bought myself a couple bouquets more. I've been more into flowers for their shapes and colors than their aromas…

"I don't know, Janko…if you don't mind me saying, I think you're kinda cynical sometimes."

"I don't mind you saying. And yes, I am kind of cynical. It helps me make sense of the shit that is my life…at least was my life."

Peter had stopped staring at her now. He was looking down at his fingernails, pulling at the quicks, or giving himself a manicure or something. I didn't really care. As long as he wasn't eyeballing Maria then maybe she wouldn't get all freaked out and leave.

I live down on Bowness Road. I'm not gonna tell you where exactly because then you might get all fucking interested and come down after I'm dead and gawk at where I once lived. Once sighed, and once spewed my guts out to strangers, doctors and nurses. No, thanks, my life isn't that much more interesting than yours. Hear my story, but then let it go. Let the dead worry about the dead. If anything, you go on living; there's lots to do. Maybe you'll see that once I've finished my wailings here.

Well, I like Bowness. People like me fit in here, not that we're welcome, but we can stay and mind our own business. There're all types down here. We've got bikers and real rich people too. You should come down and check it out sometime. It's not the shithole people thought it once was. I don't think it ever was that way; people get the wrong impression about a lot of things.

"How are you feeling, Janko?"

"Pretty good, thanks, that morphine works like a charm."

"Okay...I think I'll head out into the living room for a bit. I've got some paperwork to fill out before I leave."

"Oh...okay."

Maria turned around and walked out. Both Peter and I watched her ass as she left. My God, if only I was a healthier man. Fuck, who am I kidding, I'd never meet a woman like that even if I was a healthier man. You'll find out why soon enough.

That's probably my problem. I get to rambling in my head too much. I always have been a dreamer. But people get nervous when conversation ends, or there's a long pause. They get fidgety, and start talking to themselves inside their heads. Everyone does it, only most folks don't like what they start to uncover. So they go off and get busy, keep their minds focused on mundane shit. Like Maria, she up and left because of the hole in the conversation.

Happens all the time with people, you should watch sometimes. But look at Peter and me, we can sit and hardly say shit to each other for a long time. I mean he didn't once interrupt the conversation, did he?

But that's because we're both comfortable in our own minds. We don't mind wandering the sewers of who we are; uncovering the muck and grime in our dingy little heads. I bet you're scared to see what lurks in those recesses.

Anyway, I'm disappointed she left. I could've used more of her company. Fuck, time is so precious to me now; each minute worth a year of living. I can't harp on that too much. You'll see, especially if you get to die slowly, knowingly. You'll see.

"Fuck, I'm feeling tired, Peter. This morphine is working just like a charm."

"I can tell, Jan, you were getting kinda animated with Maria there."

"Yeah, well, I wasn't the one eyeing her like she was a piece of meat."

"Hey, don't get sore buddy, just 'cause I could get it on with her if I wanted to."

"Fuck you…fuck you, Peter, you're not funny anymore."

He was smiling his little sly smile. I had to grin inside, too, but I couldn't let him see that. I've been grumpy too long to give it all up. Maybe soon, especially if he keeps at me like that. The bastard. Although he's a great friend. He really is.

II

"Okay, Bethaney. I'm going home now. I won't be in tomorrow until later in the afternoon. I'll be visiting my newest patient…What's his name again?"

"Janko, Janko Reinhard, Mike."

"Yes, that's right…Janko, that's a pretty unusual name isn't it? Sounds to me like it could be Eastern European or something. Especially with the last name too, although that sounds more German than anything else."

"Quite possibly, I'm sure you'll ask him and find out. Do you want me to get the file for you now?"

"No, thanks, Beth. I'll hold off on that for a little while and let my intuition lead for the first bit. Keeps things more interesting, and dare I say, more honest that way."

"Yeah, I guess so. But you know, Mike, you're one of the more eccentric doctors I've worked for."

"Well, I'll take that as a compliment…Bye now."

"See you tomorrow."

I like Bethaney. She's only been with me for a few years, three actually, I think. She's honest, and I like that. Most of the other assistants play you for what they think you want. Not Bethaney, she puts it out there. Refreshing, very refreshing…Shit where did I park my car again. I've got to try and stay on top of those things. Now I'm going to spend a few minutes looking for it. Oh well, I'll count it as part of my exercise regimen.

"Hi, honey, I'm home."

15

There was no answer. Not particularly unusual, but usually my wife is home before me. I put my briefcase down and walked into the kitchen. I'm hungry and there's no sweet smells of food cooking. Not that Margaret does all the cooking, I'm pretty good that way, and we share the domestic chores. But tonight I could use a meal right away.

There was nothing on the stove, so I looked into the fridge for some left over pizza and grabbed a slice. I think she's probably downstairs in the laundry room. Margaret is pretty finicky that way. Maybe because I ruined a couple of her pieces of lingerie.

"Hi, honey."

"Jesus, Mike, you scared me."

She did grab at her chest and do a little jump when I snuck up on her. She was putting a load of whites in the dryer.

"Your whites are the brightest in the neighborhood, honey."

"You just say that so that you don't have to do the laundry."

"No, not really, although I think it helps, doesn't it?"

I put the last piece of pizza in my mouth. It was a big piece and I couldn't speak with it all in there. I grabbed Margaret around the waist and kissed her. Margaret was pretty much my college sweetheart. We met in first year psychology, debating Freud's theory of penis envy. She figured he was a closet homosexual, that's why he came up with the idea of penis envy. At that time Margaret thought that gay men, in particular, reviled women. I never understood where she got that idea, still don't, however she has changed her mind since then. She was my first, and I guess only, true love. I'd had two other girlfriends before then, both of whom I don't like to talk about too much. But hey, I was young and foolish. At least nothing monumental happened with either.

"I was just thinking of our times in university when we, or should I say you, debated and I listened to your arguments about Freud's penis envy theory."

She laughed at that.

"I know, wasn't I awful back then? I thought I was a real know-it-all. Crazy, you get so much information and you try to make so much sense of it. All this freedom of thought and expression. And some of us became quite combative with the profs didn't we."

"Yes, you did…and combative with your friends too."

"I wasn't that bad, was I?"

"No, not really. Although it was one of those things I fell in love with. Your fiery temperament."

I kissed her again, and this time she kissed me back. Her mouth warm and moist against mine. We hugged each other tight. Her body was warm and firm; I couldn't believe how well she had kept herself in shape all these years. Maybe because she'd never born children she was still firm and supple like a woman twenty years younger. I on the other hand had developed a small, soft belly. A stubborn thing that I continued to fight.

"What shall we have for dinner, hon?"

She pulled away from me a little and bit her lower lip in contemplation. God, thirty years and I still loved this woman.

"I dunno, why don't we order in?"

"Yeah, that sounds great...Any thoughts."

I was thinking of anything. I was hungry enough to eat the moss off of a cold stone.

"I don't know. Why don't we get some curry delivered? I could use a little spice I think...How about you?"

Curry sounded great.

"Yeah, curry would be awesome."

We both went upstairs. I liked watching her climb up ahead of me. That bum of hers wiggling a little from side to side. I've got to be one lucky man.

Margaret made the call. She ordered us some buttered naan, a chickpea curry and a vegetable curry. Margaret was vegetarian, had been since shortly after we met. An old vestige from our college days that she stubbornly wouldn't give up. I didn't really get it, but I had long ago stopped teasing her about it. As a matter of fact I'm pretty much on her diet when we're at home. I sneak meat a few times a week when I'm out of the house or ordering food just for myself. I admire her for her determined stance on it. I'm just too weak, I think. I enjoy all sorts of food too much to give up a whole category.

"I'm thinking a nice red wine would be wonderful for the meal, hey, hon?"

Margaret nodded as she put down the phone.

"Would you prefer a cabernet or a merlot?"

"I think a merlot would be preferable."

I took one off of the wine rack, opened it, and poured us each a generous glassful.

"Cheers to you, honey…and to us."

"Yes, my love, cheers to us and to you."

We looked at each other over the rims of our glasses as we took sips simultaneously. After all these years I still enjoyed coming home to Margaret, it made me feel good. I'd like to think it was because I am a psychiatrist and can read her well, but truth be told I think it is mostly because she is so easy going. With me in particular.

"Let's go sit in the living room and put on the fire."

We both walked into the living room and I turned on the fire. Then we sat down together on the love seat. Margaret had her legs tucked up underneath her. Her slender feet clasped by their socks.

"How was your day, love?" she asked.

I thought for a moment, taking another sip of wine.

"Not too bad. I've been thinking a lot about this new patient I'm getting tomorrow. I don't know much about him, but what I do know makes me quite curious. Just from the little bit I've uncovered he seems quite unusual."

"How so?"

"Well, he's a young guy in his early thirties. Quite sad really, in that he's dying from complications related to AIDS, and he's decided to spend his last few weeks or months dying at home. I don't think he has many friends, or at least if he does then I guess they come and visit him at his apartment. I don't know, I think it would be better for him to be in a hospice. I'm sure the care would be better…"

"But shouldn't that be something for him to decide, to be able to make that final determination about the last days of his life? Surely you have to grant him that much?"

I stood up and moved towards the fireplace. I was staring at the fire, thinking about how passionate Margaret is about these things; fighting for the underdog. I am, too, it's just that sometimes I don't think the underdog knows what's good for it.

"Yes, but what if there is a complication which requires the services that a hospital or a hospice could offer that you won't find at home?"

"I've always loved that about you, Mike. Your passion for saving lives and minds. But didn't you say this young man only has a few weeks or months to live. Maybe he doesn't want the misery to be extended. Maybe he is ready to die, to put an end to this life. Perhaps that is why he has asked for you. Has he been seeing anyone else, lately?"

"No, not that I'm aware of."

I moved back to the loveseat and sat down. I kissed Margaret on the lips.

"Yes, I can see your point. I guess it is the physician in me that wants to extend life and heal illness. But maybe you can't, maybe as you say, the only person to decide when the end is right, is the person doing the dying. It just seems so counter intuitive to what I've been taught all those years of learning I've done."

"I know, love, but even with all that schooling, you can't decide what is best for another individual. That is one of the basic tenets of our democracy, the right to freely choose the course of our lives…and perhaps our deaths."

"Well I don't know about the right to choose our deaths."

"It boils down to our freedom of choice, our freedom to be left alone if we want. Maybe that is why he wants to live the last few days of his life at home…privately."

I didn't say anything; I was looking at the fire thinking about how much more liberal Margaret is than I. I could see her point; I just couldn't completely accept it.

"Isn't your first duty to do no harm?" she asked.

I looked at her. She liked to argue, or should I say debate.

"Okay, okay, I give up. I don't want to argue about this small point. The fact of the matter is that I'm intrigued to meet this young man tomorrow. That's all I wanted to say."

Margaret looked away. I looked into the fire. It was comforting and helped settle my thoughts. I just wanted to talk to her about this patient of mine, not argue about whether he should be allowed to die at home or in a hospital. Jesus, it was a moot point anyway, he was dying at home as he wanted.

"Sorry, love, I guess that is the lawyer in me coming out. I just like to debate and play devil's advocate. I don't doubt your sincerity for a moment. I know you have his best interests at heart."

She stroked her fingers through my hair. I liked that, her hands were warm and soft.

"Tell me more about him, Mike. I like to hear about your patients, I sometimes think they are more colorful than my clients."

I looked at her and she was smiling, a twinkle was in her eye, she was back to being playful. I looked at our glasses, they were almost empty. I took hers.

"Let me get some more wine. Dinner should be here soon, hey?"

"Mmm…hmmm."

I returned and handed Margaret her glass. Then I sat back down next to her. I valued her input, but I usually didn't tell her much about my client's personal problems. I've found that too much salt can sometimes spoil the broth. It wasn't a fast rule, but something that I had mostly upheld, unless I needed a fresh perspective. And before you go pooh poohing me, Margaret is like a colleague, a confidant, better help than many of my peers that I do discuss cases with. Besides, she never meets any of my patients and has the greatest integrity of anyone I've met.

"His name is Janko, Janko Reinhard. Very interesting, I'm eager to find out his heritage, not that it makes a difference, but you never know. Sometimes culture can really mix up the emotional baggage. Sounds to me like it would be Eastern European or something…What do you think?"

"Yes, that would be my guess. Perhaps German or Slavic. Mind you it's so hard to tell nowadays with the global village and people moving around so freely. He could just as easily be Irish, I guess."

I smiled, and saw Margaret smiling too. I was Irish, if you consider having grandparents being born on the rock makes you Irish.

"Yes, I suppose he could be Irish."

I took a large swig of wine. It was good, but I suddenly realised that there wasn't much left in the bottle and that I had better go easy if I wanted some with dinner. Margaret had barely touched hers.

"Yes, I suppose he could be Irish, just like me."

"You know what I mean, Mike. You're just being silly now."

I smiled at her, and gave her a wink.

"Anyway, I don't know much about his mental state at the moment. I imagine he'll be depressed, probably angry, too, unless he's had a chance to deal with all of that over the last few years. At least, I imagine he's been slowly dying at least for a few years, if he has AIDS."

"I don't know how you do it, Mike. Dealing with people dying all the time. I mean, you never see your patients get better do you? Eventually they all die, and leave you in a way, don't they?"

"Yes, I suppose they do all leave me and die. But I've never looked at it that way, honey. If I can be blunt, I've always seen myself as a broker. A death broker perhaps, helping people make the transition to the other side. It's like soul scrubbing, I'm helping them clean their souls in preparation for heaven or nirvana or whatever is out there. I find it very rewarding when I've helped them exorcise the demons from their lives. I think a big reason people are so scared of dying is because they are so attached to this life. And what I mean by that is that people have not gotten over the hardships from their pasts. The difficulties, the hurts and grudges, and even hates that anchor them in the past."

I stopped and looked at Margaret, she was taking a small sip of wine. I looked at the fire. It was a live serpent, hissing at me. Flickering its warm tongue into the flue.

"When I've helped these people come to terms with these demons that torment them, torment us really, and to heal their hearts and souls, I find it wonderfully uplifting. At the end of the day, we are all going to die, but it is the process of dying, not the death itself which can be so traumatic. I try and help ease that process."

"You are truly wonderful, love. No wonder I fell in love with you. You are such a wonderful human being."

I looked at Margaret and she was smiling at me. I smiled back and thought her eyes were a little moist. The doorbell rang. I got up to get it and kissed her on the forehead as I passed by. I paid for the food and brought it into the kitchen. Margaret joined me and served us. We took our plates back to the living room and sat back on the loveseat. It was warm by the fire. I liked it.

"Good choice, honey. This meal is excellent."

"Yes it is…they always make good curries, and at a great price too, hey?"

"I'd be happy paying twice the price," I said.

We ate in silence for a while. I think we were both very hungry. I got up and brought the rest of the wine back, where I emptied it into our glasses. I was feeling an ever so slight buzz. It was warm in my veins.

"But how do you cope, Mike, with those times when you aren't successful in helping your patient come to terms with their life?"

"Yeah, I must confess, you've got me on that one. I've never quite been able to get a handle on those cases. Sometimes it doesn't bother me. Sometimes I get a patient who just won't open up. That is usually the problem, they just won't open up. They get angry at me and antagonistic, and I find that I am then unable to get that emotionally involved with them. So when I am let go, as they will often refuse to see me anymore, or on the rare occasion that they die before firing me, I know it wasn't me. It was all about them. Nothing I could have done to help them."

I grabbed a chunk of the naan and mopped up the curry sauce with it. I stuffed it into my mouth. I was going to need seconds. The wolf in my belly was still hungry.

"On the other hand, I've had patients who are scared to shine a light into the darkest recesses of their lives; hose ugly little spots where the mold grows from neglect. You keep working with them, but they are never quite able to get to those places. And then one day, it is too late. They die and I keep thinking if only we had a few more days or weeks then perhaps we could have come out winners. Those are the hardest patients to lose, because they could have come to grips with their lives. They could have cleaned that slate and died peacefully. But they don't, they die still carrying that fear in their eyes. It's terrible really, pointless and unavoidable."

Margaret looked at my plate just as she had finished the food on hers.

"Can I get you more, love?" she said.

I nodded and watched her walk into the kitchen. The wine was making me lascivious. I looked back at the fire and tried to imagine this Janko Reinhard. What an odd name. I imagined him as a tall thin fellow with gaunt features, maybe more so from the AIDS than the genes. I saw him as a skinhead, a punk rocker if you imagined one as a classic hooligan. Maybe it wasn't fair, not that I was trying to prejudge him, but so often I've found that my patients are often the masters and mistresses of their own demise. Not all the time, but often enough that I could generalize that way.

"What are you thinking of Mike? So pensive."

I didn't notice Margaret there. The fire was so mesmerizing. She was holding out my plate with another pile of food on it. I took it and looked at my glass. It was all but empty. I finished the last of it.

"Oh, nothing really, just thinking about my patient, Janko. It's silly, but I was wondering what he looks like. I'm not very good at it. Every time I've tried to imagine what these DJs look like I seem to get it ass backwards. Usually, it's no different with my patients."

I felt like some more wine.

"Shall I open us up another bottle of wine, honey?"

"No thanks…speaking of DJs, I don't seem to get them right either. But then again, their voices don't often match their faces even when I've seen them."

I wanted some more wine, but I wasn't going to open up a new bottle just for myself. I got up and went into the kitchen to get a glass of water. Margaret was still working on her wine.

"So what does he look like, do you think?"

"Your average hooligan. Kind of like a punk rocker, and thin. But maybe I'm just putting his disease into this idea of what he looks like. I could be totally wrong, probably am."

"So he's a rebel without a cause is he?"

"Maybe, I don't know, I'm just letting my imagination get away with me. I'm sure he's no James Dean, though."

Margaret smiled. She had always had a fondness for James Dean. Young man cut down in the prime of his life. She loved the underdog, the brooding rebel, the unappreciated artists like Van Gogh. These were her people, the people she felt for and understood.

I could understand it. But then again, these were classic examples of people at the helm of their own ships. If James Dean wasn't driving so recklessly fast, if Van Gogh hadn't put a bullet in his belly, they might have seen great success while they still lived. You have to take ownership of your own life. You have to come to terms with the decisions you make. Margaret would disagree, I know. She believes that environment influences our lives more than I believe. She'd say that the pain of rejection, of frustration and the emotional toil of art were too much to bear for Vincent or James. I think they should have shouldered more responsibility themselves rather than carrying that plank in their eyes. That's what I try to do. Get people to take responsibility for their own lives and the decisions they've made that have created their present. It works pretty well. Acknowledge it, mourn it if need be, and then move on. In my patient's case, move on to the after world.

23

LIVID BLUE

III

So there I was sleeping like a charm. Or at least I thought I was. I guess I must have been tossing and turning. I woke up in the middle of the night to take a piss. Rolled over with much effort and leaked into the bedpan. Fuck, that felt good. About the only good feeling I get nowadays from a bodily function. That and shitting, only I only shit once, maybe twice a week if I'm lucky. I don't remember what an orgasm felt like. Or at least, I pretend I do, but I can't be sure. So long ago. Norma was her name. Norma Jones. Fuck, love can be cruel.

Anyway, I was minding my own business taking a piss when I turn back over onto my back to look out the window. To see the lights shining up on the hill, on Canada Olympic Park, when out of the corner of my eye I see Norman Osbourne. Norm's a friend of mine, but a fucking asshole, though.

"Jesus fucking Christ, Norm, how long have you been there?"

I don't know who would have let him in. I'm pretty much alone from midnight until five in the morning. The nurses have gone home, but I've still got a panic button that puts me straight through to Emergency Medical Services. I don't get it, I could still die in the three or four minutes it would take them to get here. But I gotta tell ya, I like it. The only peace and quiet I get. And I'm trying to die, anyway.

"Hey, Jannie, buddy. Glad to see you, too. You know I have my ways of getting into places. I just came to see how you're doing. Thought you might need some company. Didn't mean to wake you."

"You didn't, but Jesus, can't a guy take a piss in private."

"Sure you can. I didn't see anything, and besides you're not my type. You look ugly bro'."

"Fuck off…so did you break into my place?"

I was still feeling quite groggy from sleep. Probably from the morphine, too. At my end stage they don't mind giving you morphine. Especially when it helps ease the pain, and it does. Just about the only thing that does. And I've tried a bunch of shit too. I make sure they leave a little dose in my IV when they leave for the night. Gets me through the night, all right. Yeah, it's all right.

"Now, why you asking me shit like that. Everything I've taught you. Fucking everything I've shown you and the shit that we've been through together. And you're getting uppity about me breaking in to see my buddy. Fuck you, Janko. You can't sit there and judge me. Shit, you've been in more shit than I have, anyway."

Norman was getting ugly now. I didn't like his ugly side, he was liable to go off at anything, and I'm in no state to fight him. Even back in the day he'd whip my ass most times. Funny how that is, I always thought that the name Norman was for a pussy. Some geeky kinda guy. But Norm over here put a rest to that for me quite quickly. He sure showed me a trick or two.

"Okay, buddy. You're right; we've been through tons of shit together. It is good to see you, but Jesus you can't just show up at a guy's place and not give him a fright."

"You see how easy it is, Jannie. I've been here over an hour, and there you are sleeping like a baby. I could've slit your throat. Had you grinning from ear to fucking ear."

"Come on now, Norm. There's no need to talk like that."

"I'm just shitting with you. You know you're my bro'. But speaking of B and Es, there are some sweet properties just back behind you, against the river. I bet those rich fuckers have some sweet goods we could pillage. Are you up for a shake for old time's sake."

"Fuck, Norm, look at me. I can barely get out of bed for fuck's sake. Jesus, you should visit more."

He looked at me kind of sad. He's like a child sometimes; he doesn't take these things seriously enough. He got up and went and looked out the window. Looking up at the ski hill. I looked at my alarm clock on the bedside table. The blood red numbers said it was around three thirty in the morning. Norm turned around and came up to the bed next to me. He was tall and lanky. I'd put him well over six feet, and so would he, though he'd never tell me exactly.

"Jesus, bro', it's sad to see you like this. Wilting like a fucking flower. I never took you to be a pansy."

He started laughing at his own joke. Quite the card.

"Fuck you, Norm, you're always picking on the weaker ones, aren't you? Haven't changed in all these years. You need your fucking clock cleaned, is what you need."

I reached over to the panic button just in case Norm had any ideas about hurting me.

"Look at you talk, Jannie, fucking all thin and shit and ready to die. Fuck, I bet if I just blew you, you'd die."

Norm went back and sat on the chair he was originally in. Just off to the side of the curtains. I looked out at the night-lights of the city.

"Ah, shit man, I'm just tired and bored. I've been sitting here keeping an eye on you and now that you're awake, I thought we could get up to our old shit. Are you really that fucked up, bro'?"

"Yes, I am. I'm dying, Norm. I'm dying of fucking AIDS, and I only wish I'd gotten it from sex."

"Well, I knew that, but you looked pretty good last time I saw you."

"Sure, that was over a year ago. And in the last few months it's gotten a lot worse. I can feel my body slowly shutting down. My lungs are leaking fluid and sometimes I feel like I'm drowning."

I started crying. I don't know why. Sure, I was fucking sad, so would you be if you were dying slowly, painfully. It was no good, really. Norm wouldn't really give a shit. He wasn't one of my most caring friends. It's just the pain is so overwhelming sometimes. And not just the physical pain. The physical pain you can isolate and remove yourself from, mentally anyway, if you focus hard enough. It's the pain in the spirit; it's the pain in my head. My mental, emotional pain. That's when I really feel like dying. Like now, when the pain just wells up inside me. Life's been shitty for me. I don't have very nice friends, mostly, and I've never really felt love. I'll tell you about that if you remain interested in my story. And I hope you do, if only because it means something to me, that someone maybe, cares in a way.

"Are you crying, Jannie?"

I didn't answer him. Fucking idiot question, couldn't he tell.

"Are you ok, bro'?"

"No, I'm not, Norman, I'm sad. I'm really sad, if you really must know."

Norm came up and sat on the bed. He put his hand around my shoulder and pulled me in for hug. I felt the warmth of his body next to mine. God that feels so great. I can't remember the last time I felt a hug. I shook the last cry out of my body and then lay my head in his shoulder. He patted my back all the while.

"It's ok, bro'. I'm here now to piss on you and make fun of you like old times."

He took himself away from me and went back and looked out the window some more. I could have used more of his hugs. But Jesus, what he gave was more than I could have hoped for from him. He's mostly an asshole, I think I've told you that.

"Fuck, it's sad to see you like this, Jannie. I remember the good times when you were strong and arrogant. When we did stupid shit together. Now look at you, you're sad and pathetic."

He was still looking out the window. Staring into the dark blue sky, the yellow streetlights and the snow on the ski hill.

"Why do you have to be like that, Norm. Always been the fucking asshole to me. One minute you're giving me a hug and the next you're berating me. I don't know why you put me through this shit. You've always been a cruel and mean bastard."

"Yeah I know, I can't help myself. I remind you of someone don't I?"

"Yes, you do remind me of someone. Of lots of the fucking bastards that have been in my life actually. I don't know why I have you as a friend. You're useless."

Norman turned around and glared at me. I could see better now, and I also had my bedside light on. It was on a subdued dim setting and he looked kind of menacing. Had looked like that often. But shit, in my state, I don't care much now. And I'm not scared of him, anyway.

"You keep me as a friend, you fucking moron, because you can't live without me."

"Fuck you, Norm, of course I can live without you. You're just fucking crazy."

"You've got that wrong, Jannie, you're the fucking crazy one."

Norm went and sat back in the chair. It had a blanket on it, which he took off and covered himself with. I think I'm done with him. I'm on borrowed time and I'm trying to right my life. I don't need his influence on me. I've made mistakes, like he mentions, but now I'm trying to set the record straight. He's not going to be helpful to me.

"You can leave anytime you want. Actually, I'd like you to leave right now."

"Well, you can forget that, Jannie. You're in no shape to be bossing me around. And don't you forget who's the boss, anyway. I'm hungry and I'm tired. I think I'll crash here tonight. What do you have to eat?"

"Does it look like I eat a lot of food? You'll be lucky if you find any bread and jam in the fridge."

"Well maybe that's your fucking problem, Jannie. Maybe you should eat up and then you might not be so fucking stupid. Then maybe we can go out and do some crazy shit like we used to."

I folded my hands on my lap and closed my eyes. I was sick of listening to him. He sounded like a child now, whining and complaining. He got up and went into the kitchen. I could hear him rustling around, looking for something. He wasn't going to be happy with my supplies.

IV

Margaret took the plates away. The wine was tingling my brain. I was also feeling the warmth in my loins. She had never wanted kids, and me, well I had always been indifferent. I sometimes wondered what it would be like to have a child. Have a little bambino wandering about the house. On occasion I think it could be kind of nice. And besides, I'd like to knock her up, see that growing life of mine in her belly.

I got up from the couch and turned off the fire. It was anaesthetizing me. That along with the wine and I'd be out cold before I could make love to my wife. I kept thinking of names I'd call my child or for that matter children. Certainly not something as odd as Janko. Janko Malichem, nope, that just wouldn't work. Maybe that's why I enjoy being a psychiatrist. People with emotional and mental disorders are really like children, aren't they?

"Hey, honey, should we go upstairs?"

Margaret was scrapping the food off the plates and putting them in the dishwasher. I wrapped my arms around her waist and kissed her on the nape of her neck.

"I know what you're after, Michael."

I thought I saw her smile.

"I'm always after that, hon. I like to love you a long time. Let's go make babies."

She looked at me sternly.

"Don't start that again, Mike, we've beaten that one to death…a long time ago, too."

"Sorry, I don't mean anything by it. It's just a phrase, honey. Let's go make love. Or would you prefer it if I fucked you."

She looked at me sternly again. I wasn't getting anywhere, so I went upstairs to get ready for bed. It might be an early night for me without any love. I brushed my teeth, more out of hope and aesthetic appeal than for oral health. I got into bed naked, the eternal optimist.

"Come to bed, honey."

I wasn't going to give up without a good effort. I heard her come upstairs and go into the bathroom and close the door. I closed my eyes and started feeling sleepy, so I opened them again. The toilet flushed and Margaret came into the bedroom. I watched her undress and expose her nakedness. Even after all these years I still got a thrill from seeing her naked.

"Come to daddy, honey. Come to daddy."

She came to bed and we kissed passionately. We played with each other's bodies for a while, exploring the maps of each other that we had travelled along many times. Then we made love and if felt so good to be alive.

"Do you ever think about the minutiae of life?" I said.

We were naked, glowing and warm in the love we had shared. We were facing each other and I was looking into her eyes stroking her hair behind her ears. I could see the creases around her eyes. The laugh lines, the roads of happiness we had travelled together.

"What do you mean, love?"

"Well, the billions of us all here, yet each one unique. But so many of us, are we really sacred?"

"Of course we are, love. Don't you think so?"

"Well, yes, I suppose I do. But so many of us, sometimes I wonder how special we are. I mean what makes me unique from the next ten husbands, psychiatrists or men for that matter?"

"Well, you've got me don't you. And they don't."

I smiled at her. I was trying to be serious. I rolled over onto my back and stared at the ceiling. My left arm was behind my head. Margaret moved in closer and placed her head in the crook of my neck.

"Okay, Mike. Seriously, you are kind and gentle and gifted in helping people come to terms with their emotional and mental problems. Not everyone has that gift, Mike."

"Yes, I suppose not everyone has that gift. But I bet you hundreds, no probably thousands of other men and probably more humans if you count women have those same gifts. I mean aren't we all trying to be kind and gentle and loving and helpful? We are, and some of us are succeeding better than others. But lots are succeeding as well as me, I'm sure of it."

I thought of asking Janko these same questions tomorrow. You'll be amazed at the sane clarity and truths that you can get from the insane sometimes. They had often helped me see life's existential dilemmas in a clearer light.

"True love, but no one has the exact same experiences and life path as you. That is what makes us all unique, isn't it? We may, many of us, be doctors or bus drivers, but not one of us has lived the same life as the other. And because of that we are all unique and bring to each moment in life our very own experiences that have shaped us and formed us into who we are."

Margaret paused for a moment and stroked the hair on my chest. Running her hands through it often made me feel my manliness. I held my body hair in high esteem, not like many of the male models in the current fashion magazines. Androgynous if not a little effeminate. Could you really trust a man who wasn't sure of his physiology?

"Yes, I suppose you are right. But sometimes the futility of life seems so heavy. So, infinite. I mean, here we all are struggling along this tightrope of life for what? What happens at the end of this journey? Do we die and turn to dust or do we have to come back and have another go?"

"Well, aren't these the eternal existential questions, love? I think that just being alive is enough. We are here and that's it. Just trying to do the best we can. Try to love one another and help ease each other's burdens when we can. Isn't that what many of the religious leaders have sought to teach us?"

"I don't know. I just sometimes think it is all so futile, so pointless. Does any of it really matter? All the billions of us, all the billions of planets around the billions of stars in the millions of universes. Maybe this is a bored God's sick joke; to watch us try and make meaning of our total insignificance. I mean, look at all the pain. Look at some of the real hardships people are born with. And I'm not talking about their own self-made misfortunes.

For example, that baby who was placed in the hot bathtub and scalded on purpose by her mother's boyfriend, which was in the paper today. There is a totally innocent infant suffering, for what?

Through no fault of her own, she has to suffer at the hands of that fucking guy. For what? There is no purpose to that."

I sighed. That type of sickness really got to me once in a while. Most of the mentally ill, although crazy, were generally harmless. It was the sane people that worried me the most. Not the paranoid schizophrenics. Maybe they knew something we didn't.

"Well, at the risk of sounding indifferent, it could be that baby has chosen to come back into this life for lessons to learn. Now that is not to say we remain unconcerned, and perhaps that is the crux of our goal here. To help each other with this journey's burdens. To make sure that that baby doesn't have to go through something so horrendous ever again."

"I don't know, honey. I mean, what could that baby have done to deserve anything close to that."

You'd think as a psychiatrist I'd have figured out all the existential dilemmas by now. But maybe because I was a psychiatrist I hadn't. I'd been searching all my life for the reasons to the suffering mostly, but also to the purpose of being. Sometimes I bought into Margaret's ideas, other days I struggled.

"I know, it is so difficult to really understand. And I don't pretend to know it all. Maybe if I did I would be in Nirvana already. Not enjoying making love to my husband and explaining to him the meaning of life."

She smiled at me and kissed me on the cheek.

"You know, love. At the end of the day the most each of us can do is to love and to live. To live everyday as if it were the last. To do good every day and shy away from meanness. To help each other and to love each other. It sounds kind of trite or corny but it isn't really. That's why some things are clichéd, maybe because the kernel of truth in each cliché has stood the test of time…if I can use a cliché to explain one."

We both smiled at that. Margaret had a wonderful way of taking away my edginess and smoothing my grumpiness. I felt a lot better, but yet I hadn't bought it hook, line and sinker. And I was tired. I had an early start in the morning. I kissed Margaret on the lips.

"Good night," I said.

"Good night, my love."

V

I woke up at around eight-thirty in the morning. The sky was brushed with pink. The sun was going to come up soon. Salima, she's another nurse, was poking and tugging at me. Fucking people, I wish they'd let me sleep. She was taking my temperature in my ear and bumping my IV, which tugged at my arm where the needle was. I looked at her, groaned and frowned.

"Sorry, Janko."

"Uh huh."

Funny thing about Salima is that she wasn't even East Indian, and I always thought that name was an East Indian name. She was so white, snow white, but not as pretty.

"How are you feeling today? Dr. Malichem is scheduled for about nine-thirty this morning. I think you'll like him. He's very good and kind."

I didn't say anything. I hated mornings. It was like I was fucking saddened to be alive, to have to go through another day of hell. I was trying to look at it differently. I was trying to count my lucky stars. And it was helping. I only had a sense of dread for the first half hour or hour in the morning. My days were numbered, and I didn't want to go out a miserable son of a bitch. I was hoping Dr. Malichem could help me with that. Everybody had said nice things about him. That was unusual. All my life, people had hardly ever said nice things about me especially, but about most things too. It's hard to buy into it, but at the same time it's kind of contagious.

"What would you like for breakfast, Janko? How about some nice warm oatmeal?"

I smiled.

"Yes, that would be nice."

Everything was so nice lately. All these fucking people, so nice. These last few months everyone was nice to me. That was a change. But why did it have to be now, when I was dying, when I was on my way out. Were they sorry for me? Were they feeling guilty, even though none of them had done me harm? Were they paying the price for all the cocksuckers I'd suffered in my life? Or maybe they genuinely cared.

"How is your pain today?"

Salima was bending over me, holding my hand, inspecting my face, my chest, all my bedsores.

"Manageable I guess."

"Do you need any more morphine?"

"No, not for right now."

I squeezed her hand. I was sorry to be grumpy. It's just seeing Norm last night pissed me off. He's such an asshole. He wasn't around, anymore. Typical, he was never much of the social butterfly. Always leading me down the wrong path. I was always getting into shit with him. Fuck, I wish I could be done with him. But it wasn't that easy. He was never one to respect the wishes of others.

"I saw my friend last night. Norm."

"Oh yeah…How could he have gotten in?"

"He probably broke in or something."

"You don't like him much, right?"

"No, he's a mean bastard. I'd rather not see him anymore, he brings out the worst in me."

"Well, maybe Dr. Malichem can help you with that. I'm sure if you tell him about Norm, he'll have some tips and advice on how to get rid of someone like that."

"Maybe."

"I'll go start your oatmeal for you, okay?"

"Sure."

I need people. I need to find my place with them. I'm feeling an urgency in connecting, in building fucking relationships before it's too late. And yet what is the point. If I'll be dead within months, what is the fucking point?

Do you ever feel like that? Feel so alone that the pain is worse than anything you've physically experienced?

I guess I've felt it all my life, but only recently have I begun to know it intimately. In my younger years I guess I was able to block it out, to ignore it by hanging around with people. And not even with people who gave a shit about me, either.

I looked outside and wished I could take a walk out there. Even though it looked cold, I'd give anything to take a fucking walk outside. Feel the fresh air on my face, hear the sounds of humanity buzzing around. People going about their important business, that isn't all that important. I'd go out with my IV if I could, but I get too fatigued now. And besides I look like shit. Like absolute shit.

I got up and sat on the edge of the bed. My lungs wheezed and I coughed for a while. I grabbed a tissue and spat the blood into it. My lungs were on fire. The morphine only helped to tone down the pain. Make it a manageable noise rather than the ear shattering hell it would be otherwise.

I went to the washroom to take a shit. My IV jiggling next to me. A coat rack I'd start hanging my dirty laundry on now. Seemed like it was the fucking excuse I needed or at least the permission. I didn't take a shit more than once a week or so, and it was hard to. But it felt good, gave me an excuse to get out of bed.

I was finished with that in time to get my oatmeal. I made it into the living room and fell onto the couch. It was so fucking hard. So fucking hard just to move around this little bit. I could feel the sweat prickling my forehead. My pajama pants sat limply around my waist because I was so fucking thin. My foster mother once used to kid me about wasting away because I never ate much. But now I am wasting away for real. One hundred and twenty pounds on an average man. I've finally gotten a fucking six-pack, but a rack of ribs too.

"Should you be walking around, Janko?"

"Well, I've got to do something, Salima."

"I know, but you're perspiring and panting."

"I know, could you open the patio door a little please, and I think I left my cigarettes in the room. Could you get those?"

Salima opened up the patio door and went into my room to get my cigarettes. I liked American cigarettes best. And with only a few weeks left, I figured I'd treat myself. Think what you will, but I'm fucking dying and it's the least of my fucking worries.

"You know, Janko, that Dr. Malichem is not going to be happy with that. And your GP has told you as much, too."

"Yeah, I know, and now you're fucking hounding me about it, too."

"I'm just saying it's not going to help you."

"Okay, okay."

I lit up a Camel and blew smoke rings towards Salima. She gave me a look. Not a harsh one, but a look, nonetheless. I picked at my oatmeal with my spoon. Food hardly had any appeal. It all tasted bland and filled me up so quickly. The cigarettes, well, at least they warmed my insides and gave me something to do. I was so cold lately. I had my place cranked up to seventy-eight and still I'd be cold sometimes. I'd think it was the breath of the grim reaper or maybe his bony arms clutching at me, trying to hug me in his deathly embrace. Soon enough, you fucking bastard, soon enough you'd have me.

I was looking outside at the traffic go by. It was quite busy. Cars zooming by, mostly just one person to each. So important these people are, so important.

"Do you ever wonder what these fucking people do?"

Salima was sitting behind me at the kitchen table, which wasn't in the fucking kitchen, but still, it was no dining room table either.

"Are you talking to me, Janko…what was that?"

"Yes, I don't see anyone else here at the moment. Do you?"

Salima didn't go for that. I don't blame her; I was being a fucking asshole. Just enjoy my cigarette is what I should do. Maybe she doesn't want any chitchat.

"What did you say, Janko?"

"I was just wondering if you ever thought about any of the people out there. There they go zipping by to work or whatever, maybe off to rob someone, maybe off to die in a car accident. Do you ever think about that sometimes?"

"Sometimes, but not quite as morbidly as you do."

"Yeah?"

"Uh huh."

I sucked on my cigarette and exhaled ring after ring. I'd see how far I could get them before they toppled into a cloudy mass or dispersed into wisps of smoke. I also liked to spend a ton of time trying to see how many rings I could get to pass through each other. I'd never made it more than two.

"Well, what kind of things do you think about?"

"I prefer to think about good things. Like, take that man over there waiting at the bus stop with the briefcase. He looks happy enough. I'd like to think he has a loving family and wife, and maybe he got laid last night too…"

I had to laugh out loud at that. He looked like he'd get less sex than me, and I'd also rather not think about him getting it on with anyone.

"Well, you never know, it's better than thinking he'll die stepping off the bus or something equally morbid…"

"I'm sorry, I wasn't laughing at you, I just thought it was quite funny thinking about that old guy across the road there getting it on…please, tell me more."

"Well, maybe he's got two children, a boy and a girl and they're both honor students. She's a cheerleader and is dating the football star and the son is a hockey star, and handsome, too. That's what I think about it."

"Wow, that's pretty good, although I don't get where you think his kids would be good looking."

Salima laughed.

"You never know, Janko, it could always skip a generation."

The bus came and took Mr. Handsome-and-successful-porn-star away down the road. I squashed my butt out in the ashtray. The cold oatmeal had congealed and lay thick, like vomit, in the bowl. I was getting cold.

"Salima, could you please close the patio, again?"

"Sure."

I watched her push the sliding door closed. Her ass was perfect in her little white dress. If I could, I'd go give it a pinch. That's a bad, bad bum. Besides, I get a kind of perverse pleasure from bossing these women around. Sure, I could get up and do it myself, although it would take a lot out of me, but I'd rather watch these women (I was going to say whores) move to my beck and call. You see, that's part of my problem, I've got lots of problems, but my lack of respect for a lot of people, especially women, is something I'm trying to overcome. Obviously, not doing so well so far. Fuck it; maybe I should forget about it now, the end is so nigh. And a life of despair can't be undone in a few short weeks. A few short weeks, if that. Ah, Jesus, what the fuck am I going to do?

I took the blanket off the couch and pulled it over me. My thin little arms were pimply with goose bumps.

Fuck, I was cold. Why the hell did death have to be so damn cold. Everything was cold, the fucking emotions I'd experienced from people, the slow demise of my life. My own mind, cold to me like a dead fish. I was looking forward to seeing Dr. Malichem. Even with his fucking odd name and all. I grabbed the remote off the coffee table and turned on the radio. Some rock station with idiotic DJ's who were ignorant but funny were on. My arm got tangled in the fucking IV. Jesus Christ, all the small things here to break my fucking back.

Five for Fighting came on with their song "100 Years." I guess I was lucky to get a third of that. Such a beautiful song. My fucking eyes got all misty. I'm a fucking mess. Jesus, I've got to get my shit together. I've got to save myself from myself, somehow. Please. For God's sake, please.

I decided I'd go back to bed to wait for the good doctor.

"Everything, ok?" she asked.

"Yeah, I'm just going back to bed. I can't shake these fucking chills."

"You know Dr. Malichem will be here shortly?"

"Yeah, thank God."

I smiled feebly at her as I passed by. An old man in a suit of young skin. I was hunched over, my fist wrapped around the IV trolley like a dear companion. An old fool I felt like, with a whirlwind of emotions storming inside me.

"I don't want to see any of my friends if they come, okay?"

"Sure, Janko, if I see them I won't let them in. Mention that to the doctor, too, okay?"

"Sure."

I don't know what the fuck that meant. What was Dr. Malichem going to do?

I climbed into bed shivering and pulled the comforter and blankets up tight around me. Fucking IV got tangled up again, around my arm and blankets. Jesus Christ, the fucking small things aggravating me today. Sleep, which was such a tease, was my only solace to my mental and physical prisons. I wanted to jump out of my body, run as far away from it as I could. I was done with this ride. Stop, I want to get off.

VI

I found the place easily enough. Bowness is one of those communities it is easy to get around in. He lived in a crummy looking apartment complex in the wrong side of Bowness. The far side of the river. My heart went out to him already. It was the poor who so often got themselves, or somehow got involved, in the difficulties of life's mental mazes. I folded the paper with the address on it and pushed it into my pocket. Janko lived in number three-oh-one. I pushed the buzzer and a soft woman's voice answered and let me in.

She greeted me at the door. Her name tag read "Salima" and she was in a quaint white nurse's uniform. That was weird. They usually wore scrub type uniforms, now. But, who am I to digress about that. She took my hand firmly in a shake. I liked her, she was pretty and brunette, and young too. Probably younger than my patient.

"Hi, Salima, I'm Dr. Michael Malichem. Please, call me Michael."

"Thank you, Michael. Janko seems quite anxious to meet you."

"Good, but first I'd like to have a few words with you, if I could. Somewhere semi-private would be best."

"Sure, come on in."

I took off my shoes and entered the apartment. It wasn't bad for a small place. Only looked like a one bedroom with a large galley kitchen. It was neat and simple. I liked it. People's surroundings always spoke to me so loudly about whom they are. Mind you, this place was seeing a lot of professional people lately. Helping to clean it up, make meals, etc.

Salima sat by the kitchen table. It was old fake wood with metal legs and chairs, four of them. It came right out of the seventies.

"Would you like to see his file?"

"No, thanks. Not just yet." I said.

"Would you like some coffee?"

41

"Yes, that would be great."

Salima got up and went into the kitchen. I stood by the patio door. Janko's apartment looked out onto Bowness road. Traffic had lightened up. The number one bus went by, half full of people. I'd ridden that bus occasionally. It made for great people watching. From the west to the east of the city, from one shining shithole to the other shining shithole.

"Here you go."

Salima handed me a mug full of coffee.

"There's cream and sugar in the kitchen if you like."

"No, thanks, I take mine black."

We sat back down at the kitchen table. He was poor, that I could tell for sure. The apartment complex, his old furniture, the sparseness of the place. But at least it was tidy, and I liked that. Reminded me of my own place during undergrad days.

"So, I take it that Janko is not doing too bad, then?"

"Well, actually, he is definitely end stage. His primary care physician has given him no more than a couple of months, if that."

"Really, well, what's wrong with him, then?"

"We're not one hundred percent sure, as Janko won't let us do too many tests on him, anymore. He's tired of that, he says, and ready to die. From what we can tell he has Kaposi's sarcoma coupled with Cytomegalovirus and pneumonia, probably amongst other things, and his T-cell counts are extremely low."

"Jesus, and here we are walking around in an environment of germs. Does he know the risks?"

"Yes, his doctor has spoken extensively to him about them. As I said before, he is ready to die and I think he wants to die. As you'll learn, he has many difficulties that he needs to overcome, and I think he sees his physical problems as the last of his problems."

"Okay. But that all seems very odd to me."

"I can understand that, Michael, but if you have a look at his file, it may make quite a bit of sense to you. Are you sure you don't want to have a look?"

"No, thanks, and don't tell me too much, either, unless I ask. The first session or few I like to form my own opinions of my patients. I don't like sullying the waters from the start. It can create a bias, I find."

"Yes, I suppose. And you do come with your reputation preceding you. I think that if anyone can help Janko, it will be you. But, I confess, I don't think either of you have enough time."

"I think there is always enough time if one is motivated."

I sipped my coffee. It tasted awful. But somehow that seemed appropriate. The bitter dregs I was sipping from this cup; the bitter dregs that perhaps Janko had sipped from the cup that was his life. All people's lives created difficulties to be endured. Some of us overcome them better than others. Some of us never do, without help. I was looking forward to helping Janko. I knew I could. Now was the time for the young man to walk with me along his path to self-forgiveness, I think. Self-forgiveness: that is the key to leading fulfilling lives.

Salima surely had her own problems and she has obviously managed them sufficiently well to obtain a good education and a comfortable life, no doubt. Yet she didn't have a ring on her finger. Maybe her social life was a disaster where her demons mocked her. Perhaps. Perhaps she never ventured far enough in a relationship to figure that out. That can sometimes be a way of coping. Living superficially to avoid confronting the demons that rattle in the closet of our minds during the quiet times, when our lives are still. That's why we live such busy lives, most of us, we don't want to sit and be still. Look into those darkened closets of our past. Don't see, don't acknowledge. Ah yes, ignorance is bliss for a shallow life, a short life. But in my experience it catches up with all of us eventually.

"Is everything okay, doctor?"

I noticed myself staring at Salima.

"Yes…sorry, I didn't mean to stare. I was just deep in thought. It's fairly quiet here, isn't it? Is Janko around?"

"Yes he is, he's in the bedroom, but I think he may be sleeping. Perhaps if we made a little noise we could wake him up?"

Salima smiled as she said this.

"No, that's okay, we'll give him a little while. I blocked off my whole morning for this. I can give him some time to sleep…Is he sleeping well at least, or fitfully? Do you know?"

Salima tugged at an earring.

"No, I don't think he is sleeping well at all. Though there aren't any of us around from about midnight to six a.m. But I've heard him complain of it often. He often takes naps during the day."

I finished my coffee except for a small gritty bit at the bottom of the cup. I was glad to be done.

"Would you like some more coffee, Michael?"

"No, thanks, it isn't that good if I can be honest."

Salima laughed and nodded her head.

"I know, it's awful. I think of bringing in some of my own, but I keep forgetting. Janko usually orders good coffee whenever anyone is out picking up some things for him. But it we've run out I'm afraid. I should've warned you."

Salima got up and took my cup to the kitchen where she washed it. I watched her. She was young and perky and nubile. As much as I loved my wife, I still had an eye for attractive women. Particularly young ones.

"How long have you been working here Salima?"

She finished washing and returned to her chair.

"It's been about a year. Before me was Maria Cobain. She's the longest serving here. I think she's been looking after Janko for about eighteen months or maybe even close to two years. There are four of us all together. Besides Maria and myself there is also Veronica Drake, who has also been around for about a year, and most recently Rose Joplin, who has only been around for about six months or so."

"And you are Salima?"

"Oh, yes, me, Salima Hutchence."

"So, is Janko in a lot of pain? Does he require anything for it?"

"Yes, apparently the pain is excruciating. We have him on pretty high doses of morphine, and we put some in his drip before we sign off at night to help ease the pain so he can sleep. Other than that he won't let us give him anything else. This is part of the problem. His physician comes in once a week. His name is Dr. Manfred Rowles, but primarily he checks up on him and makes sure that his pain is being managed successfully."

"Very interesting. And that is all he requires for pain management?"

"Yes, but pretty high doses of it, though. It's not at a level that you'd start a patient off."

Salima looked off to my left shoulder. I think she saw something outside that drew her attention. I looked behind me. All I could see was a man walking along the side of the road, on the other side.

"Anything else you think I should know about Janko without giving away the farm?"

I couldn't hear him at all. If he was awake or if he was sleeping he was very quiet. No snoring. No murmurs. Nothing.

"Well, he told me that a friend of his came by last night. Apparently he broke in, but I can't see how. I think he's sick of this particular friend coming by. You might want to ask him about that."

"And what is this friend's name?"

"Norm, I believe he said."

That was often an impediment for my patients in getting well. You need people who will nourish you, nurture you in your path to wellness. You couldn't afford to have negative people around. I felt the same way about food. If you put poison in your body you'll be poisoned. If you hang around with thieves you'd likely become a thief. The same could be said for guarding our mental doors. Maybe the most important. If you listened to hardcore negative rap music, or you watched gratuitous violent movies, it would affect you badly. Negatively. The same with porn. You consume quantities of porn and you'd become not a porn star, but driven by that insatiable need. Every woman would be a whore. Every woman would just want to be fucked like a bitch.

VII

I woke up to a man's voice. And a woman's. I recognized it as Salima's. Made me fucking grumpy, because I figured they were talking about me. I got up slowly and rattled my way into the living room with my IV. The good doctor was there. He stood up and reached out to grab me. I gave him the cold shoulder. I noticed he was wearing socks with little gnomes on them. Red dunce caps and portly bellies covered by a green shirt. Or something like that, there's probably a better name for it than that.

He was fairly tall and nice looking, in a way. With a short trimmed beard, and round glasses on his nose. His hair was dark and he was slim, except for a belly on him. Too much good living I figure. This guy couldn't help me. He hasn't seen the inside of a shithole, let alone come across a few pebbles on his smooth path. I bet his fucking life was a bed of roses, the thorny stems woven to make the fucking mattress I sleep on every fucking day. Jesus, I'm pissed off, and I'm not sure why.

He looked like death warmed over. Janko was definitely end stage and looking very grouchy about it too. He looked like a concentration camp survivor. At least from the pictures I've seen. He was stooped over, clinging to his IV for dear life.

"Hi, Janko. I'm Dr. Michael Malichem. Please, call me Michael."

I offered him my hand. He took it limply.

"Hello."

"If you'd prefer, I'll pop out for a coffee break or something and leave you two to talk…How is about an hour, Michael?"

I looked at my watch. It was ten thirty.

"An hour would be fine."

I sat on the couch. The sun was bleeding into the room, the runny yellow spilling all over the floor and onto my feet. It was warm, like urine. I liked it. The good doctor took my granny chair off to the side. We looked at each other for a while and then I looked outside at the blue sky. Wisps of condensation were leaking out of the chimneys across the way. Ghosts of the recently deceased, I figured.

God, he looked so frail sitting there hunched over and thin. He wrapped a crocheted blanket around himself and shivered a bit. I followed his eyes outside but I didn't see anything that caught my attention. It looked cold. Inside his apartment it was hot. I took off my sweater and unbuttoned the top two buttons of my shirt.

"So, Janko, is there anything pressing that you want to talk about?"

"No, not really…actually, would you mind getting me my smokes from the bedroom?"

"Sure."

I went into his room, which was more cluttered than the rest of his place. A stained bedpan that I almost stepped in was on the floor. A dressing gown was tossed at the foot of his bed, and the curtains were only half open. His cigarettes were on the bedside table with some matches. I brought them in to him and fished one out. He pinched it in his lips and sucked on it like a straw as I offered him a light. His cheeks puckered and he closed his eyes.

"You look angry, Janko. Anything you want to talk to me about."

He looked at me with fire in his eyes. I could tell he was seething about something. Probably me. I think he was unhappy to see me. Often you'll find patients who say they want help get combative when that help finally arrives. I'd seen it plenty of times. But he looked like one of the angrier ones.

"No. I've got nothing to say to you, I don't even fucking know you, yet."

"True, but you did request a psychiatrist and here I am. Costing somebody close to three hundred bucks an hour…Three hundred bucks whether we sit and cuddle quietly or whether we have a fistfight. I'll get rich, and you'll get closer to the end."

I thought maybe I was overdoing it a bit with him. But I figured he needed to see my stern side. I'm not all mushy and empathetic with all my patients all of the time. Sometimes, you've got to give them tough love. They've hardly ever had it, but like children, they respond very positively to it.

Fucking guy. Sits there in my granny chair. The chair my granny, if she really was, gave to me. Invited into my fucking house, and there he sits giving me the piss. But I like him, I think he means well. A pussy cat trying to be a tough guy. That's funny.

"Three hundred bucks, hey. Where do I get a gig like that? I hope you're worth it."

"Oh, I'm more than worth it. You won't die unless you've cleaned out the demons in your closet."

"Really?"

"Really."

I sucked on my cigarette. Blowing smoke rings between us. Seeing them grow into a halo around his face. Or maybe a noose. We looked at each other. Me, all hunched up, him sitting there with his fucking Buddha belly, all smug and shit. Like he could really give me the pink slip to die. Fucking arrogant asshole. Very much like Norman. But I figure he's really here to help me. I guess. I looked at the ceiling. It was kind of stained a little yellow, from the smoke from my cigarettes lying against it. Defying gravity. It's face all pimply with white heads. I wanted to squeeze them. See if they'd ooze yellow nicotine puss. Maybe have some drip down onto the good doctor, here. See if he'd be all smug, then.

The sun was creeping into the room and spilling onto Janko's feet. The coffee table's shadow had jumped up into his lap. He kept smoking and trying to blow the cigarette smoke at me. We were too far apart.

"Salima tells me that you had a friend come by this morning?"

"Yeah...do you find that so hard to believe? That I could have friends. I probably have more fucking friends than you do."

"Come on now, Janko, I never said that. I'm just asking. If you're going to continue to be belligerent, I'll leave and we can try again another day."

He stubbed out his cigarette in the ashtray. It was the old glass kind. Square and clear. There was already one bent up stub in amongst the ash.

"Okay. Don't go just yet…Yes, I had a friend come by. He's a fucking loser and his name is Norm. He breaks into places, and he broke into my place this morning. Scared the shit out of me when I woke up. He was just sitting in the chair in my bedroom."

"So, you don't like him very much. Why is that?"

"Well, because he's a fucking goof. He's always been mean to me and goading me and making me do stupid shit, dangerous shit, too. That's when I've been in most of the trouble in my life. When I've been hanging out with him. Breaking into people's places and getting beat up by cops and other shit bags."

"And so, how did he get in today?"

"The same as he always has. He fucking broke in somehow. Probably climbed up the balconies to get here. He's harmless. To me, anyway. And besides I'm not going to call the cops, so why does it matter how he got in?"

"No, you're right. I'm just trying to get us talking, Janko. This is no big secret. I'm here because you want me to be. If you don't want me to be here, I'll go. I'm not a cultist trying to get you to change your views on anything. I just want to try and help you along your path to enlightenment, if you will."

I could tell that he was going to be a tough nut to crack. He kept talking so tough, and yet bent over as he was. So frail. So desperately frail and lonely. I could tell that easily. It was no secret as to why he was so lonely. It was written all over his mannerisms. The false bravado like a big red warning light.

"If you'd like, we can probably install some extra security measures, if you're concerned about your friend breaking in, again."

"No, that's okay. But maybe you can give me some ideas as to how better to handle him in the future?"

"Sure."

If I'd ever had a real fucking father. This good doctor might be a candidate. But fuck, who needs fathers with the kind of shit foster parents I've had.

"Why the big furrowed brow?"

He was looking at me, the good doctor. Maybe he can read my fucking thoughts.

"Maybe you can tell me?"

"Well, for one thing, you've got an exorbitant amount of anger pent up. And not necessarily at me either. I think we'll have a lot of work to do."

"And that's worth three-hundred bucks?'

The good doctor leaned forward on his elbows, trying to give me the evil eye. Looking all stern and shit. He didn't wear it well.

"Janko. I've got over a dozen patients who enjoy my time. They make use of my expertise and could use this time that I'm spending with you. Please understand, another outburst from you like this and I will leave. That is not a threat. It's a promise."

I looked at him and felt myself grow small. The fucker. Making me feel small. I didn't need that shit. I feel small enough without his fucking help.

"Now, I know I can help you. And I want to help you. But you have to let me. You have to give me the chance."

My eyes got wet a little. I felt so fucking hopeless and lonely. Here he was, probably just looking for an excuse to leave me like all the other fucking people in my life have done. I looked at my feet under the table. They were blurry. Fucking baby, Janko, get your shit together. No need to go and fucking cry just because the good doctor hurt your feelings.

I just kept my eyes open. I figured if I closed them then the tears would drop down. I didn't want him to see me vulnerable. People feed on that shit. They'll tear you apart if they see you're vulnerable. I'd had enough of that shit.

"I'm sorry, Janko. I don't mean to upset you. I really want to help. But you have to let me."

He was still leaning on his elbows. Only his eyes were kind again behind his glasses. I had to turn away. The tears were coming. The fucking tears. I couldn't help myself. I pushed my hands into my eyes. I wanted them to stop.

"It's okay, Janko. It's okay to cry. As a matter of fact it's good to cry. Let it out. I know how much pain can be in a person. You keep it balled up tight like a fist in your belly.

And it gets bigger, pushing up against your heart and it hurts. It gives you heartache. And sometimes you've got to let the pressure off a little. Let the steam out. Let it roll out hot on your cheeks. Burn up the pain, Janko. Let it out. I'm here to help."

I came and sat next to him. The poor boy. So much like a vulnerable child. My heart went out to him. I put my arms around his shoulders and squeezed him tight. So much pain. So much of my own pain mirrored in his. I knew of emotional pain. Red hot heartbreak.

"Let it out. Let it out, son."

He seemed so fragile. Jesus. This was the hard part of my job. I hated to see the suffering. The pain. The pain from what we do to each other. Words like viruses left to eat a person up. A careless word. So often just a mean and nasty word. And this is what you have. A shell of a human in such agony. Such suffering. Janko shuddered and moaned and sobbed. The tears came hot on my hands and arms.

"So much pain, doctor. So much pain I can't manage it anymore…so much pain. My heart hurts. My fucking soul aches doctor. I'm dying and so much pain. So much heart pain. So much soul pain."

"I know, Janko. I know. I'll help to ease it. I'll help you carry it."

And more sobbing. And more tears. My shirtsleeves were wet with his pain. My muscles tight and aching, supporting his pain. Poor boy. Poor young man. But I was getting to him. This was the first step. A big step to be sure and I was going to carry him if I had to. Despite only having met him for such a brief time I felt a connection with Janko. I felt a need to help him. I wanted to and I knew I could. This young man could be resurrected and healed before his death. Before his crucifixion, this young man could rise again. A phoenix. My phoenix.

He settled down and I got up and got him a tissue from the bathroom. A couple of tissues, which he used up and crumpled into the ashtray. I stood by the window and looked out onto Bowness. The sun was beating down on a thin layer of snow and ice. It was cold outside. Yet the sun felt so hot from the heat in his apartment. It was too hot. For me, anyway.

"I love the bright sun on cold winter days, Janko. So hopeful, so uplifting. It's a wink of what spring will bring."

I smiled at the good doctor. He was standing there looking out at the sky. His hands wrist-deep in his trouser pockets. The bald spot on the back of his head tilted horizontal. I could guess him smiling into the outside. Smiling at nothing. Smiling, I guess because he'd still live to see spring.

"Hope springs eternal, I've heard. But I guess for me, my fucking hope has dried up like the dead leaves on the ground."

He kept looking outside. At something. At nothing. Who knew and really, I didn't give a shit either. But surprisingly I felt a bit better than I had in a long time. If there ever was a guy I could've look up to. A father figure or mentor that I could've used. Well, I was looking at him. Looking at him with his hands thrust in his pockets, smiling to the outside world. On my deathbed, on my fucking deathbed, I find my hope.

"You have a nice balcony out here, Janko. I bet you've made use of it a few times. I'm surprised, though, that you don't lock your balcony door. I think Norm probably could have climbed up the balconies below and then entered your place."

I turned around to look at Janko. He had a bit of color in his cheeks and his eyes were bloodshot. Still he seemed healthier than he had since I first laid eyes on him.

"Yeah, I have used it sometimes. And I have usually locked the balcony door. I think that probably one of the nurses must have forgotten to close it."

"Okay. I'll speak to Salima when she gets back, which should be any minute. Anything you want to talk about before I have to leave?"

"No, I don't think so. I'm so drained, doctor. I don't know whether to trust you or hate you."

Janko looked away and reached for another cigarette from the table. He lit it and inhaled deeply. Spluttering and coughing after. His breath was shallow, probably from the pneumonia.

"I can understand that, Janko. Listen, I have a sense of urgency for us. I think we can do some really good work. But I think we need to work quickly on it."

"How can you say that, when you haven't even found out what is wrong with me? Aren't you being a bit presumptuous?"

"No, not really, Janko. I can look at your chart anytime I want. But I'd sooner have your side of the difficulties you face. And besides, you've already told me lots about yourself without even having said much."

He puffed on his cigarette some more. Such a terrible habit. Should be the least of my concerns. I mean, it wasn't going to kill him, at least. He kept on trying to blow the rings at me. And he kept missing. They tumbled and fell like hollow promises. Hot air. I think we were still blowing smoke at each other. Dancing, skirting around the meat of the matter. Beating around the bush and fencing. Well, that was okay for now. Next time I'd need more from him. I'll get more from him next time, by either his charts or preferably from his mouth.

"It's okay, Janko. You're scared and I can accept that. I'll earn your trust. I'm not going anywhere. I'm not going to let you down. Maybe I'll be the first person in that respect, and perhaps I'll be the last. But it'll be worth it. You'll see. It will be worth it."

He kept looking at me, so I turned around and slid open the balcony door. I put my hand outside and waved it around. It was cold. Refreshingly cold from the oppressive heat in his apartment. I'd be leaving soon, but next time I'd come at least for the whole morning.

We both heard the key in the door and then Salima came in. She smiled at us both. Her cheeks were rosy and she looked so naïve, so Mary Poppins-ish. Somewhere over the rainbow was the pot of gold for Janko. That wasn't from Mary Poppins, but what the hell, it came on its coattails.

"Well, Janko. It was nice to meet you. I'll see you again next Tuesday. Bye, Salima."

Just like that the fucking good doctor left. I watched after him. I might have said goodbye but he didn't wait long enough. I spat imaginary tobacco at him, at his memory. Well, maybe it was my own fault. Maybe I should have opened up more. But I hardly know the fucking guy, yet. These things take time.

"Well, did you have fun with Dr. Malichem?"

What kind of fucking question was that? This bitch is a moron. Comes in here after her happy little coffee break, all chipper like a little bird at the first sign of thawing snow. Meanwhile, the blizzards are just around the corner. Shit. And they call me crazy.

"No, we didn't have fun. This dying and trying to tie up loose ends isn't fucking fun Salima…okay?"

"Okay."

Then she humped off into the kitchen. Shit, I'm being a miserable bastard. I got up after stubbing out the cigarette and went to bed. To sleep. To dream perhaps.

"Sorry," I said after myself.

I don't know if she heard, but it almost choked me coming out. The good doctor had left me raw. I didn't want to rub the wounds, but he'd left me fucking raw, nonetheless. Maybe some zzz's would put me in a better mood.

I sat down on my bed. The fucking IV was just driving me nuts, the tubes getting tangled up, and all in the way all the time. I wanted freedom. I wanted to be left alone from my misery. Left alone from my pain; the physical pain and the emotional pain. The emotional pain being the worst. The demons in my head so anxious to torture me. This is how I spend my days. Trying vainly to sleep them away or watch them wither and die. Nothing to show for them.

I started crying. I couldn't help it, okay. Maybe after you've found out the shit I've been dealt maybe then you might give me a little slack. My face pricked and flushed and the tears ran down my face and dropped off onto my thin hands. The drops landing on my IV, my rubbery veins, and wetting my pajama pants.

"Are you okay, Janko?...I brought you some chamomile tea."

I didn't see her there. And now I was embarrassed.

"Yeah, I'm okay."

I lied to her. We are always lying to each other in one way or another. I didn't look at her, either. Shame faced. So much shame just for wetting my face. It's fucking stupid, isn't it? But it's never been easy for me. Not to express the "bad" feelings, anyway.

Salima put the mug of tea on my bedside table. The steam rising up out of it reminding me of the chimneys I'd seen earlier across the road. She sat on the bed and put her arm around me. Not too intimate, just a warm gesture was all. She didn't say anything. Her arm was warm and meaty on my bare back and shoulders. She rubbed my shoulder and back a bit before putting her hand back on my shoulder. I thought I'd die from the warm feeling it gave me.

"I'm sorry I was mean to you...It's just that...It's just that life's been so hard for me. It's much easier for me to build walls than to tear them down...I'm sorry."

I still couldn't look at her. It was like, if I looked at her then she'd disappear and this warm human contact would be just a spiteful dream. Like the dreams of my childhood. Like the people I'd experienced in my childhood, always dismissing me, me and my dreams.

Salima turned and looked at my profile.

"It's okay, Janko. Despite what you might think, and despite your previous experiences, we took on your care because of what we saw in your file. The person who you are underneath all the difficulties you've experienced. The good soul that we all know you are."

I looked at her through blurry eyes. She wasn't lying to me. She was telling the truth, and telling it to me to my face.

"Yes, you are, Janko. You are a good soul. And maybe that belief has been beaten out of you. But all five of us know it. And we aim to help you come to see it, too."

I put my hand on her knee. And I cried some more. She put her other hand around my neck and hugged me. I cried into her neck.

"Thank you, Salima. Thank you."

VIII

"MJ...how the fuck are you?"

"Shh."

I got up with effort and closed my bedroom door. I hadn't seen MJ in weeks. Probably months. I was smiling at her. I couldn't stop grinning. She was my best friend. I loved her and wished we could have been boyfriend-girlfriend, but it never was. Peter was a pretty good friend too, but MJ was the best.

"How are you, MJ?"

"I'm good J...really good. And you don't seem too bad, yourself. I snuck in past the nurse."

She had a mischievous grin on her face.

"And I've missed you, you know?"

"No, I don't. You've hardly been around."

"Well, that's only because you've been hanging out with that idiot Norm mostly. You know how I don't like him. And he turns you into such an asshole, too."

"I know. I saw him this morning, as a matter of fact. But I've seen my doctor and I've told the nurses I don't want him coming around here anymore."

"Good, because he doesn't do you any good anymore. I'm sure I don't have to remind you of that one time you and he were out breaking into homes and you got caught by the cops. Do you remember the beating your old people gave you when the cops took you home?"

I winced. I didn't need to be reminded. I still had some scars across my back from that beating.

"No thanks, MJ, I'd rather not think about that anymore, okay. And besides they weren't my folks. I don't have any folks."

57

"I know, J. I'm sorry, I don't mean to upset you. It's just that I like you and I don't want to see you get hurt, which you seem to do every time you hang around that idiot."

"Let's talk about something else, okay? I haven't seen you in such a long time, and I don't want to waste the time thinking about Norm. I've just finished dealing with him from this morning."

Salima came in. Unannounced, without knocking. It'd be nice if she just fucking knocked.

"Is everything okay, Janko? You sound upset."

"Yes, everything is fine. I think I've just had a bad dream."

She looked around the room. She didn't see MJ, she was just inside the bathroom.

"I'm making some lunch. Some lentil soup. You must try and have a little bit okay?"

"Okay, Salima. I'll try a bit."

She walked back out, without closing the door behind her.

"Salima," I yelled, "could you close the door please."

The door closed and MJ came back out of the bathroom.

"You don't have to stand back there, MJ. They're not going to kick you out or anything...unless I want them too."

I smiled at her. But she wasn't smiling.

"You know Peter had been here, and they don't seem to mind him. They don't pay him any notice, mind you, but they don't mind him anyway...you remember Peter, don't you?"

MJ came in and sat on the chair where Norm sat. She was twiddling with the blanket. Fondling it without paying much attention. She had such lovely hands. Long slender hands. And thin, too, with nice nails, just plain but clean and a little longer than the tips of her fingers.

"Yeah I know Peter, he's a nice guy. At least he seems nice enough. Although he looks at me a little weird, sometimes."

"I know, he did the same with the nurses. I think he's just horny. He's pretty harmless. A lot of talk, but pretty harmless, unlike Norm."

I smelled the onions and garlic frying in the pan. I loved that smell. It reminded me of one of the few times in my life that were pleasant. When I was living with some foster people and for a change they were nice.

They were Italian and it seemed like just about every night we ate something with onions and garlic. My mouth watered, maybe I'd be able to eat something for a change. I was hungry, that was for sure. I grabbed my mug of tea. It was a kid's mug, yellow with a smiley face on it. I wanted to put a fucking bullet hole in it sometimes. Only sometimes, now I was happy. MJ was here, and I was always happy around her. The tea was cold and smelled of flowers. Funny how smells are so intertwined with memories. Thankfully most of my smell memories are good ones. Mostly.

"What's on your mind, J?"

I looked up at her over my yellow mug. The smiley face was smiling at her. I wasn't.

"I was just smelling this camomile tea and thinking about how smells remind me of things, places and shit like that. Funnily enough, most of my smell memories are friendly. Can you smell the onions and garlic that Salima is cooking?"

"Yes."

"Well, they remind me of that foster couple I was with for about six months. Do you remember them?"

"Mr. and Mrs. Diablo?"

"Yeah, that's right. I think I was only around ten or something…"

"Or eleven, I don't really remember them that well."

"Yeah. I don't remember you being around much when I was with them. But I've known you that long, haven't I?"

"Oh, yes, but you didn't seem to hang around with me much then. You didn't seem to hang around any of us then. You had your other friends from school."

MJ was looking sad. She was rubbing the blanket some more, looking at her lap. Her eyes were distant. I put the mug back down on the table.

"What's wrong?"

"Well, that was just a sad time for me, J. We didn't see each other much then. It was like you didn't need me much. And that made me sad."

"Well, you were always in my heart, MJ. But that was one of the few good moments in my life. Why are you trying to make me feel bad about it? Why can't you be happy for me, instead?"

"I'm sorry, J. You're right. I should be happy for you. It's just that when I get to thinking about it, you only ever seem to need me when times get tough. It's like, whenever things are going good you don't want me around or you don't need me anymore."

Jesus Christ, why couldn't she just be happy for me? My best friend and she has to bring this up. You'll see why she wasn't part of my life during the brief times when things were going well. I'll tell the good doctor about it and then you'll see. In the meantime, don't judge me too harshly. I bet there have been people in your life that you don't see anymore, or don't care to see anymore. And I still care to see MJ, okay? I bet you've had people in your life that were there and served a purpose. Helped you during some crisis or two. And maybe now they aren't a part of your life. It happens sometimes, doesn't it? Not everyone is meant to be in our lives for all times. Only the very few, the lucky few. And only a few lucky ones of us get to have lifelong friends. I guess I'm lucky in that respect. I have MJ and Peter, and maybe Norm, if you want to count him. Maybe you're lucky enough to have a few or even one fucking friend that'll see you through thick and thin. So don't judge me too hard just yet, okay? Wait until I've told my story and then see if you don't think I did my best under the circumstances. Maybe at the end I'll have earned my redemption. I'm not going to hide anything, not like most of us. The good doctor, he'll hear my whole story. So give me some slack, okay? I think I've earned it.

"Jesus fucking H Christ, MJ. Will you quit it already? It's not like we are ten anymore okay. We're supposed to be fucking adults, okay? I like you, you know I do. I don't have a lot of time left. Please, let's enjoy it, okay. Let's talk about something else okay?"

She looked up at me, still sore.

"Okay" she said and bit her lip at me.

"I remember you loved the smell of the wild rose. Do you remember the time when we were out in the field together down by the river here? Do you remember I picked you a rose and it smelled so good, but it pricked my thumb and the drop of blood smeared the petals, but you took the rose and kissed my thumb, anyway?"

I looked at her. She was smiling a little now, at the memory. So was I, such a nice memory. So few of them, they would take up hardly any space in this book if I told them all.

"And remember how you smelled the rose and my blood left a smudge on your nostril. And you looked at me and said how much you loved me?"

"Yes. I remember and I also remember how you said you loved me, too. How you'd always love me. The only girl you'd love. The only girl who was in your heart."

"I do love you…I mean did…I mean I still do. You're in my heart MJ, always."

She smiled at that. It was awkward, it had always been fucking awkward for me to talk about my feelings. Nobody had ever showed me how. I mean, it was easier for me to talk to my friends, especially MJ, about it. But that was because she was so non-judgemental. Everyone else, well, everyone else wasn't like MJ. They'd been mean and cruel and, well, it just hadn't been easy because of that. The fucking people I've had in my life who have taught me nothing but pain and misery. For fuck's sake, I was just a boy during most of it, okay? A little boy and the things I had to go through. It'll make you sick. It really will. You'll hear about it in good time. Don't rush me, I'm pacing myself, okay? I can only rehash so much of this shit at a time.

"Are you okay, J?"

MJ had come up to me and sat beside me, putting her hand on my knee. I guess she'd seen the pain in my eyes. Always the fucking pain in my eyes. Do you ever see how people's eyes mirror their souls. I mean, if you really look at a person's eyes you can see the pain, or the peace or even the joy if they're that lucky. Me? Every time I look in the fucking mirror I see sad eyes. Sad blue eyes. Watery with pain.

"No, not really, MJ. I'm sad. So fucking sad lately I just don't know what to do. But I'm dying already, so it's not like I can kill myself anyway."

"Don't talk like that, J. You know how sad I'd be if you died. Let's not talk about your death. Let's talk about the good times we've had together, okay?"

Sweet MJ. Sweet, beautiful MJ. I wish I'd have known more MJs in my life. Like, if my mother had been MJ and my girlfriend and my sister maybe. Shit, if I'd just had more friends like MJ I could've been a lot better.

Maybe I wouldn't be here telling you my story. Probably because it'd be nice and boring, like most of your lives, instead of this fucked up life I've had. Like a bad accident people can't help to look at because they're so fucking grateful it isn't them. That's how I feel. Like that person slowly dying, injured and bleeding in that car wreck. I don't aim to be bitter, but you'll see. The shit I've had shoved down my neck. Well, I don't think you can blame me, really.

"Do you remember the first time we met, J?"

"Yeah."

I sipped some more tea. It was cold but it was good. It was something to do. I need things to do lately to keep a certain sense of mental calm. I guess that's why I tried to sleep so much. It was something to do to keep me from my past. Keep me from the shit heap.

"You remember you were out in the field. The one down there by the Bow River where we used to hang out a lot together?"

"Yeah, I remember."

I smiled at her. They were good memories. I could see the golden dry grass now in my mind. The warm summer sun. The sand under our feet by the river and the foot long grass swaying in the warm summer breeze. Fuck, that place just used to team with bugs and crickets and birds. I loved the birds. I loved their songs in the summer. So chirpy and happy and gentle on the ears. I can hear them now. I don't know what kind of birds, but such a nice sound. So much nicer and rhythmical than a human's voice. The voice just loud and hurtful and harsh. Give me a bird song any day over the slurred scraping of a man's voice. Or even the harsh shrill of a woman's screams and shrieks. You'll know what I'm talking about soon. You will. I'm not lying to you. I'll spill my guts soon enough.

"You were so sad at that time. Just sitting under the bridge hugging your knees and crying. I think you were about eight years old or something. You had on a dirty shirt. It was grey from dirt and grime and you had on a pair of blue shorts. I remember your sneakers were torn at the toes and I could see your big toe sticking out the one shoe. You weren't wearing any socks."

"Yeah, I remember that. I remember why I was unhappy too..."

"Don't think about that now, J. I want us to think of the good memories of the meeting. When I came up to you and put my hand around your neck and sat next to you."

I did remember. It was probably the first real memory I've had of human kindness. And it came from a fucking stranger. What does that say about us? That we can't treat those closest to us as nicely as strangers do. What the hell does that say about us? I don't understand it. So many times, those people who were supposed to love me the most have loved me the worst. The milk of human kindness has always come from strangers. But it's the bitterest dregs I've tasted as my daily fare. From those who should've cared.

"I remember, MJ, I remember how I cried. How your love and caring burned hot in my chest and I cried. I hadn't felt that tenderness in such a long time. I wept like a baby. And you held me closer. You weren't ashamed of me. You weren't scared off by my pain. You embraced it and absorbed it and rocked me gently in your arms."

I looked at her now and the tears were streaming down my face. Like a fucking baby. I was crying and I couldn't help myself. My dying was causing me to relive all the pain, all the sorrow that had been locked up in my heart. Stored away in my soul. The shit I thought I had dealt with was coming back now to haunt me. Maybe it was good to get the shit off of my chest. It's just so sore is all. It's all just so sore. Can you fucking understand that? Have you had your sorrows? Have you wept when the pain was awash in your heart? When you've been all alone. When you've felt lonely. Do you know the pain in the chest? The heartache that knows no rest? I suppose you have, I suppose we have all suffered to some degree our own pains and burdens. Forgive me if I don't commiserate with you. My own is too much of a heavy burden to bear. This cross we carry, and I'd just as soon be crucified already for God's sake.

Mary Jane held me close and hugged me. Just like she had done those many years ago. It felt so good. I wish I could've had more of that from my foster parents, teachers, ministers. Jesus, anyone really. It's just not enough from MJ. I need more, like I'm an addict. My old folks, my foster parents and teachers, they never spoiled me. They never spared the rod. They used it more than a towel to dry themselves off. I've still got some marks, some scars from the beatings. I don't mind them much anymore, except that they remind me more of the loneliness, the sadness, the overall fear rather than the physical pain.

Can you understand that? Can you understand the shit that an eight, nine even ten year old boy goes through when he's beaten worse than a dog.

When that supposed sanctuary, that fucking warm home and hearth is a place of hell. Where only the cold impersonal outside world is a safer place for a boy. For a small child. Can you understand what that does to a small person? I was just little, okay. I was only a boy, okay. Maybe as I tell the good doctor about it you'll understand me a little better. Offer me that patience and understanding, hell, compassion would be nice too, that I'm asking for.

I put my head in MJ's neck and cried freely. It felt good. It was good. I had hardly had the opportunity to do that. And you know what? It was making me feel a little bit better. It was helping me cope just a little bit. Surprising what a small token of appreciation, a small hug, a gesture of love, can do. It can change the world I'm sure, because it can change people.

IX

I was finished for the day and I was off to see my friend, Joachim
Gebs—with a soft 'g'. That's what he told everyone. Not the 'g' like in
golf, but the soft 'g', like in Geoff.

Bethany had gone home early after my last appointment of the day.
I don't think I'd done the rest of my clients any good. I couldn't stop
thinking about Janko. I just knew we could do some good work together. I
felt fired up about working with him. I still hadn't really looked at his file,
but it seemed so easy. The answers were just right there. But would he be
willing to put in the effort? That was the key. Would he allow me to lead
him from his difficult past to living in the present? And that was especially
important for him, because he surely didn't have a future.

So I was stepping into the Sandstone. A nice, swanky bar at a new
hotel downtown. They had leather wingback chairs, and the dim, smoky
lights that hearken back to the old speakeasies, but with more class. I liked
it. Sometimes I am a bit of a snob. I've worked hard to get where I am, and
I like to enjoy it, sometimes. It helps with the stress of dealing, day in and
day out, with other people's messes. Lots of lawyers, oil barons, and
business tycoons hang out there after hours. You should go; I think you'd
like it. But if you're looking for the eclectic mix, the Janko's of the world.
Well, they just ain't gonna be there.

Another thing about Joachim. It's a soft 'j', more like a 'y' as in
yoke, and not like the 'j', as in Janko. His name is pronounced like yoke
with an 'm' on the end. I have to tell you all this, because it is indicative of
Joachim's personality.

I wondered what kind of parents could name their kid like that. But
the thing is, it is a name he gave himself. He's had it legally changed, too.
It's on his driver's license and his passport. He's shown me both, because
at first I didn't think he was serious.

I still don't understand why he'd give himself a name like that. And they're both made up. His last name and his first name. His real name is Reginald Montmarte III, and his parents weren't happy that he changed his name. I don't think he's spoken to them since then. That was many years ago, just as he was finishing med school when he changed his name. I can understand his father being upset. You've been named after your own pa, you've named your son after yourself and your pa, and he goes and changes his name. That has to be a slap in the face. I've never met his parents, but I think that naming children after you and your father, etc., speaks loudly of the perhaps pompous and arrogant nature of such people. But hey, that's just me.

Anyway, this is my friend Joachim who I've known since med school. He's gone on to practice anaesthesiology and makes quite a fortune at it, too. Not that he's shallow, but he definitely doesn't like to reflect upon himself, or anything else for that matter, to any depth. But I digress. I was telling you about Joachim and his name to give you a sense of the person he is. He always gives everyone the same spiel when he meets them and introduces himself. I think it is to remind himself that he is a self-made man, which in many ways he is, rather than being a chip off the old block, so to speak. That's just my interpretation, as I've said, I've never met his parents and he doesn't talk too much about them either.

"Hey, Joachim, how are you?"

He was standing at the bar ordering two martinis. I like them, straight alcohol not cut with anything and yet so smooth. The other thing about Joachim is, he doesn't go for pet names or nicknames. Just Joachim. He'll tell you that, too, if you try anything cute on him.

"Dr. Mike. How are you, buddy?"

"Good, really good…Is one of those for me?"

"Of course, but you can have both if you want them."

"Don't tease me."

We looked around to find a seat. It was just after five and already the place was getting busy. We sat at a small table with two comfy chairs up against the wall, which was windows out to the outside mall. People were wandering by, huddled against the cold looking at their footsteps. Not looking at each other.

I pulled out the olive, the three of them, and tossed them onto a napkin. I hate olives. Little green rotten eggs is the best way to describe them.

Joachim sat back in the chair and lit a cigarette. The smoke curled up and around him like it was a belly dancer twisting her body towards the ceiling. He had his legs crossed over at the knee. His oxfords were polished shiny and expensive. Probably calf leather.

"How is the somnolent business?"

Joachim's eyebrow above his left eye was twitching ever so slightly. He had those nervous twitches often. Ever since I've known him, and mostly around the eyes too.

"Well, Mike, it's tiring me out."

I knew he wasn't serious. He loved it. He'd often tell me how many books he read while sitting in the theatre waiting for the surgeons to finish up their dicing and slicing. I smiled at him.

"No, seriously."

"It's the same, Mike. Never really changes you know. I put people to sleep. I'm such a bore…and then I wake them up, again."

He was rocking his left foot back and forth. The light slipping all over the top of the toe of his shoe. He was also massaging his left eyebrow and eyeing his martini. Mine was half gone already, so I set it down to let it sit for a while. My belly was already nice and warm.

"Although, I did have a close call this afternoon. This guy was in for an appendix removal, and we almost lost him on the table. His heart stopped for a bit. But we got it going again. It was right in the middle of this exciting book I was reading. No wonder my insurance premiums are so high. Drives me nuts."

"Yeah, I can imagine. I don't know how you can do it. Not so much the stress but the boredom, the monotony."

"Well, Mike, I drive a new bimmer every three years and I live up there in Mount Royal. I figure the sixty hours or so a week is worth the lifestyle it buys me. I've never figured out how you decided to go into psychiatry. Dealing with people's mental shit all the time. There's more to life than trying to make it a better place, Mike. I mean really, it's not like you're going to change the world anytime soon."

"Well, perhaps not. But I might change a person, and that might change the world."

"Ahh, Jesus, Mike, still the eternal optimist. But you know that's what I love about you."

A pretty young waitress in tight black polyester pants came to take our order. We ordered more of the same. I was thinking she probably gets pretty good tips looking like that. We guys are suckers for a nice ass in pants. I had forgotten to ask her to hold the olives. I'd have to put them with the other three on the napkin. Create a nest of these little green rotten eggs, if you will.

Joachim watched the waitress sashay all the way up to the bar. Jesus, we could have done it ourselves and saved a few bucks in tips. Didn't matter though, I think Joachim was enjoying the show. I wonder sometimes if this is how women whore themselves out sometimes. I mean, I got taken advantage by it at one point. Firm ass in tight pants, got me in trouble, once. But I digress.

"You still seeing Michaela?"

"Nope," he said.

"I'm sorry to hear that."

"Don't be, she had it coming. I mean, these damn women I'm getting involved with keep getting too hard to maintain, if you know what I mean?"

"Well, come on, Joachim. Don't you think it has something to do with the type of women you attract to yourself? I mean, blonde bombshells done up to the nines, in my opinion, are only looking for a sugar daddy. And especially when you keep telling them about your big house, your expensive car. Shit, Joachim, you can't expect anything else."

"I suppose. But I'll tell you, Mike, I love a good looking babe. And these blonde bombshells are so subservient. I mean, they'll suck your cock anytime you want, no questions asked. And I love that shit."

"Yeah, well, who doesn't? But they're whoring themselves out, buddy. And as soon as they figure your well is dry, or you aren't serious about taking care of them, they're onto something better. And what about you, where's your self-respect that all you want out of women is a sexual object and a sparkling bauble on the end of your arm. I thought you had a little more self-respect than that?"

"Come on, Mike, just because you've been with Margaret for umpteen years, and you're miserable, doesn't mean you have to rain on my parade.

"You can tell that to yourself if you like, Joachim, but I'm happily married to my wife, and we've been together thirty years. I don't think you could understand the commitment and depth of understanding and love that occurs over such a long time. But that's okay, I think I've hit a nerve with you, but unfortunately I think you'll get over it, rather than think about what I'm saying…"

The waitress came by with our drinks. The three olives were in my martini like ugly specimens pickled in formaldehyde. I quickly took them out.

"What's your name, honey?" he asked her.

"Candy."

"I bet you are…hey, listen, what time do you get off tonight?"

He was old enough to be her father. But I was mildly amused by the banter. I don't think he'd even heard my last comment. If he had, he'd already forgotten about what I'd said. He never changes. Maybe a lack of growth potential, but I think that is why I keep seeing him. He's amusing and somewhat shallow, but I keep believing in that kernel that I believe lies in all of us, that pushes us to be more than we are. I'd like to think he's just not found his kernel yet.

And give me a break, a name like Candy. She was just his type, or should I say he probably thinks she's just his type. Blonde hair, tight ass, but her boobs were a little small.

"I get off late, very late."

She batted her eyes. She was smiling at him all the time.

"Well, when do you work here next? I'd love to buy you a drink."

"You'll usually find me here on the weekends and sometimes on Monday nights, too."

"My name's Joachim Gebs. Joachim as in yoke and Gebs with a soft 'g' like Geoff. I'm an anaesthesiologist up at Foothills."

"Very interesting."

She was picking up our glasses. She was smooth. Probably used to drunken idiots trying to pick her up all the time.

"Do you want your olives?" she asked me. I shook my head.

"You know what, Candy?" he said, "I'd love to take you for a ride in my bimmer. I just got it a few months ago. It's a 540, and has an awesome sound system in it. I bet you like house music?"

What a loser. He's my friend but he's such a loser sometimes. I wasn't buying it, I don't think she was buying what he was selling either, and yet old Joachim thought he was all that. I kept looking at his twitchy eye. I couldn't see if she noticed it, too. Joachim was sitting back in his chair, light still slipping on and off his shoe as he wagged his foot at her.

"Actually, I prefer country. But you're very generous."

All smiles, dripping sincerity. She was good and my good buddy was just eating it up.

"Listen, I have to go check on my other tables. But I'll be back soon, okay?"

She gave me a knowing look and I nodded at her.

"OK, honey," he said.

She sashayed off, back to the bar. This place was busy, but not nearly full.

"Hey, buddy ol' pal. You see I've still got it. I bet you she'd bury my bone in the back of my car. Chicks love that shit."

"I bet she wouldn't."

She was talking to the bartender. He looked over here, nodding at her. She was good, smarter than I had given her credit for. She was no whore, but yet at the same time, women have to put up with this kind of shit, in these kinds of jobs to make a decent living. They've got to flaunt the flesh, sashay the sex, to make a living. Doesn't seem right to me. Yet, culturally, they aren't given many choices. I mean, even Margaret has had to work harder than a man in her position to get to where she is. And good for her, I thought, the way she handled my buddy. Lots of class.

"Well, how can you say that? I mean look how invitingly she listened to me."

"Joachim my friend. The only reason she didn't tip your martini over your head is because she's working and trying to make a living. I bet you she has to listen to this kind of shit all night, every night. She's used to it. And just because a woman has blonde hair, doesn't make her a bimbo."

"Ahh, shit, Mike, you're just sore because she wasn't paying as much attention to you as she was to me."

"No, that's not it at all. And besides I'm very happily married, as you'd recall."

We both nursed our drinks for a while. My first was finished and I was well into my second. This is where I'd probably stop. Joachim was looking out onto the avenue. It was fairly dark by now. He was picking at the red plastic sword that had just recently speared three olives. He was using it as a toothpick in his teeth. I was looking around the bar. The subdued amber lights lent a warmth to the ambience. But mostly I was looking at Candy. She was a looker, that's for sure. I could see how a guy like Joachim could get caught up in someone like her.

"Anyway, Mike, there's this really hot nurse at the hospital who likes me, I think. She's asked me out a couple of times. But I'm playing hard to get."

"What's her name?" I asked just to stoke the conversation back to life.

"Rowan."

"Mmm. That's sounds like a good Irish name, I think. She's not a blonde is she?"

"Nope, she's a redhead. But I'm not sure if I'm crazy about her."

"Why is that?"

"Well, I think she may be a little outspoken. A bit too boisterous…"

"Then you can't complain about all these other women who become too hard to maintain. Sounds like she might be intelligent and honest, with integrity. That'd be a change for you, Joachim."

"Jesus, Mike…How much do I owe you for that psychobabble? I'm just saying I'm not sure if there is chemistry there."

"Oh, okay, I misunderstood."

I smiled at him. We bugged each other once in a while. He was a good egg, just a little misaligned, I thought. He probably thought the same about me, though. No matter. We only got together once in a while, about every month or so. It was enough, but we still had a lot of history between us that kept us bonded. Besides, I did like the bugger, in spite of himself.

Joachim took a break from his martini. He put it down on the napkin and put his plastic sword in it to sterilize, I think. He looked over at Candy, who was moving around up by the bar. The two little dimples in her lower back showing and quite lovely too.

"So, Mike, tell me about the latest project you're gonna save?"

I looked at him, he smiled at me.

"Well, his name is Doer, Try Doer…as in go for it my friend."

"No, come on now, Mike, I'm serious. I'm interested. You know I only like to bug you about that."

"Yeah, I know, and I like to bug you back."

I sipped some more of the martini. It was a generous serving.

"He's an interesting guy, my latest patient. I'm excited that we could do some good work. But he's got a lot of baggage; that is for sure. He's also terminally ill and might only have a few months left, if that. That, I see as the biggest hurdle in helping him. And also that he is a little belligerent at the moment. I don't think he trusts anyone. I don't think he has been able to trust anyone in quite some time."

Joachim crossed his legs over the other way. He was now wagging the other foot at me with its shiny, slippery toe spilling light. I noticed he had on thin, charcoal grey socks matching his charcoal grey pants. He had taken to picking at his teeth with the red plastic sword, again.

"Have you looked at his file, Mike. Or are you winging it, like you usually do?"

"Well, seeing as you put it that way, I'm winging it like I usually do."

"I could never get away with winging it at work. Putting people to sleep requires deft skill and exactness. I've never understood why you operate that way."

"Well, with you Joachim, you need that exactness and skill. You are after all administering substances to people to put them in a coma to some degree. The graveness of any errors you make cannot be disputed."

"Yes, you're right."

"With me, on the other hand, I've found that if I do delve too deeply into the patient's file before I've met with them, I lose my objectivity. You can get sullied without giving them a fair shake. You must know what I mean. If I told you that a guy you were going to meet was the biggest loser, he'd cheated on his wife, embezzled from work, and was lazy, fat, and ugly, you'd have an idea of the guy which would taint your first acquaintance with him. Do you know what I mean?"

"Yes, I do."

Joachim was looking at another woman across the bar. She was sitting at the bar. I followed his eyes. She was wearing a dark blue pinstriped suit with stiletto heels. Her hair was long and straight and dark brown. Very attractive.

"Are you going to have another?" he asked me.

"No, I think I'll be okay after this one."

"Oh, okay…So tell me more about this Doer fellow?"

He smiled at me. Then he looked back at the brunette. His foot still wagging up and down. I waited, sipped my martini, until he looked back. Like a child he is, in many ways. His attention flip-flopping here, there, and everywhere.

"Well, he's young, around thirty-three, I think, and frail. But that is mostly from his disease I think. He has very few friends and the one he's told me about broke into his place the other day. He has nurses that stay with him for most of the day and night. There isn't much to tell, really, except that I think we could do some really good work…"

Joachim was looking off at the brunette, again. She was sipping a cocktail of some sort and peering around the room furtively. Waiting for someone, maybe getting stood up. Unlikely, anyone would be a fool to stand up a beautiful woman like that.

"Hey, Joachim. Jesus. Are you even listening to me? Do you even care?"

Asshole.

"Come on, Mike, yeah I'm hearing you. He's thirty-three, you think you could do good work with him…"

He looked at me and smiled again. He stopped wagging his foot and placed both feet on the ground. He leaned his elbows on his knee and looked at me.

"Go on," he said, "I can't help it, Mike. I'm listening but my eyes are still wandering."

I picked up my martini and finished the rest of it. I was feeling relaxed.

"Well, I was saying I think we could do good work, he and I. I don't know what it is, I'm just excited about the opportunity to work with him. I'm sure he's got similar issues to many of my other patients, but in many ways I think he is going to be quite unusual too. Also, the fact that he is dying gives an urgency to our work."

I was looking forward to getting home to talk to Margaret about Janko. It wasn't quite the same with Joachim. Firstly, he wasn't really listening carefully to me, and secondly I don't think he really understands what I'm all about.

"Can I get you guys anything else?"

Candy had come by and picked up my empty glass. Joachim finished his drink and ordered another.

"I'd also like your telephone number, too," he said.

"I'm sorry, but I don't give out my telephone number to customers."

"Not even to anaesthesiologists?"

"Sorry, no, not even to handsome anaesthesiologists like you."

She smiled and walked away to get Joachim his third drink. I was counting his drinks for some reason. Why, I don't know. I was just about to be leaving soon, anyway.

"You know what, Dr. Mike? I think you're wrong. I think she could grow to like me."

"Okay, Joachim, you keep dreaming…we'll see."

My eyes were caught by the brunette at the bar. Maybe she was getting stood up. If I was a single man, I might gather the courage to go and talk to her. God, I hope Joachim doesn't give it a try. I looked outside, it had started snowing a little and it was dark. The snow was sparkling down, leaving little crystals of itself on the pavement outside. It was soft but small. Little feathers from heaven's pillows.

"I think I'll be leaving, soon."

"Sit with me while I finish my drink, Mike. Be a sport."

I did. I sat with Joachim for a while and looked outside intermittently. At the snow gathering itself together like iron filings. It was a melancholic scene, echoing my feelings for some reason.

Joachim and I spoke of a few things before I left. He asked after Margaret and told me about this new BMW he wanted, and would be buying next year. We spoke of the weather and this conference he went to in New York for anaesthesiologists. He also bored me about the many women he'd bedded recently. I didn't believe half of what he told me. He lies about a lot of that, I'm sure.

We walked outside together and said our goodbyes. I was happy to leave him, and sad, too. People really can be so much better than that. I walked back to my car and the cold, dry air cleared my head. I stuck my tongue out to catch some snowflakes and by the time I was driving off home I was feeling a lot better.

X

It was light when I woke. And I woke up grumpy as all hell. I slept okay, but I didn't remember any of my dreams. That happens a lot to me, I hardly ever remember any of my dreams. So I'll blame my grumpy mood on a shitty dream I've had. Maybe it had something to do with the good doctor. Probably not, I'm just not sure how to deal with him. Or how to deal with myself, really. Maybe that's the fucking truth. I can't deal with myself so how can I deal with anyone else properly. Anyway, I'm glad you're still with me. I'm trying, honest to God, I'm trying to get it right. Thing is, I've never had any real fucking mentors except maybe for the Antolini's, they were good people. They treated me with respect, but by then the damage was done.

Jesus, thinking about this shit wasn't helping. I got out of bed and threw a blanket over my shoulders. I went into the washroom to piss. It was strong and almost brown. I looked at myself in the mirror. A regular Auschwitz victim. I rubbed a bony hand over my ribs. I could stick my fingers under my rib cage and feel the inside of the ribs. Smooth and hard like warm rubber.

I walked into the living room grabbing my cigarettes and trailing my IV behind me. Maria was on shift. I looked at the clock on the microwave, it was seven thirty seven. Maria looked up from the table at me. She was reading Cosmo.

"Good morning, Janko. How are you this morning?"

"Okay, I guess. I wake up and I'm never sure if it's a blessing or a curse."

I went and sat down on the couch and pulled the blanket around my shoulders. This is the way I spend my fucking life. Watching other people living theirs.

I lit my cigarette and inhaled deeply. I loved the first cigarette of the day. Sure, it'd kill me eventually, but I'll be dead before then, anyway. Give me a break, okay. It's a small vice in the bigger picture here.

"Could I get a cup of coffee please, Maria?"

I could smell the coffee. It smelled freshly brewed. I had them buy only whole beans for me. The expensive shit, and a dark roast too. It was a small treat that I enjoyed.

"Sure, Janko. How about something for breakfast too?"

"Yeah, okay. Toast with marmalade."

I blew smoke rings at the balcony windows. I watched the people come and go and I imagined where they might be headed. I wondered what it'd be like to go to work, spend time with people each day, and to be paid for that. Maybe sit around a big office and push paper and shit around. Go to meetings and meet even more people. Sounded like the good life to me. Maybe it wasn't. Maybe I'd get tired pretty quick of doing that. If I had to do it every day. Maybe it was with people I didn't really like. But I don't know. It sounded pretty good to me. I mean, I've never had much of a job in my life. Sure I had a paper route once, and I've worked at a couple of fast food places. But never long enough to have it matter. I couldn't stand it. Sitting over that hot grill and having this fucking juvenile delinquent, someone like Norm, telling you what to do. It's bullshit, it really is. But maybe a nice cushy office job would be better. I could wear a suit and tie. Look really smart, look at the women in their smart suits with their asses hard as apples straining the fabric. Sounded good to me.

I looked over to Maria. She had a nice white nurse's dress on. But her ass wasn't hard as apples. More like a pillow. But it was nice, though. Still nice. I turned back and sucked on my cigarette. I couldn't afford thoughts like that. They were too expensive. I mean, what would I do with them? They'd just fucking depress me, is all. Looking and not being able to touch. It's like being a starving man at a restaurant and not being able to eat. It is. You'd choke on your own saliva.

So I looked outside at the living breath of Mr. Pornstar, strangling him as it left his nostrils. He had arrived across the road at the bus stop.

The number one bus stop, the first and last, the alpha and omega. You know what I mean, from one shit hole…Bowness, to another shithole…Forest Lawn. In the middle it passes through the city of oil, black gold, as they say.

From poverty through money to poverty again. That is the number one bus. Anyway, I'm getting carried away. Pornstar was standing across the road looking at his feet. He had rubbers on his shoes. He was swaying slightly and clutching at a briefcase, which he held in front of him. His one hand was over the other and showed a silver watch. Why am I telling you all of this shit? Because my eyesight is about the only thing that hasn't deserted my body, yet. And because he looks like an interesting dude. And because it's about the only fucking thing that keeps me going, keeps my mind from my body. From my decay, okay? And because I haven't lived a charmed life, a life that would be worth dwelling on in your final hours. I'd sooner imagine what could've been. Like, maybe if things had been different, I could've been Mr. Pornstar across the road there, living the good life, the fucking happy life. Maybe I could still be feeling the love of a good woman now. Even if I am dying. So what, maybe I could still have the caring caress of a wife or girlfriend. Maybe, just maybe, okay? I can dream can't I, it's about the only fucking thing I've got left, okay? There's nothing wrong with it, okay?

"Is everything alright, Janko?"

I hadn't seen Maria sit down in the armchair. Hadn't seen her put my toast and coffee in front of me. Okay maybe I did, but I didn't have an awareness of it. I looked over at her and pointed to Pornstar with my fingers. The cigarette curling gray ash to the floor.

"I was looking over at Mr. Pornstar there and wondering what kind of life he lives."

"Who?"

"Pornstar, the guy standing at the bus stop."

"How do you know he is a pornstar?"

"I don't. It's just a joke that me and Salima shared the other day. What day is it today?"

"Wednesday."

"Well, I guess it would've been yesterday, then. We saw this guy over there and Salima thought he'd had a good night, maybe got it on with his old lady. I don't know why she thought that, but she did. So, then I called him Mr. Pornstar. We thought it was pretty funny at the time, anyway."

Maria kept looking at him across the road. Her forehead was furrowed.

"So what do you think of Mr. Pornstar? Do you think he's a lucky dog?"

Maria looked at him a little more and then back at me.

"Yes, I think he is a lucky dog. Because you gave him a lucky nickname."

I smiled at that. Then I put sugar and cream in my coffee, and a little more sugar. It was sweet and creamy.

"And also," she continued, "he looks like a professional man. He keeps himself in shape, from what I can see, and he looks smartly dressed. Yes, he's one lucky dog I should think."

I sipped my coffee and watched Maria. She was watching Pornstar still. Then she took a bite of her own toast, which also had a thick spread of marmalade on it.

"It's fun, Janko, isn't it? Imagining the lives that other people lead."

"Maybe that's why the soaps are so popular."

"Probably…So what do you think about his life?"

"Pretty much the same that you do. I do that a lot about other people. I imagine mostly good lives that people lead. I don't often think about sad lives. My own was sad enough for a hundred lives, I guess. I just like to imagine what could've been. Maybe what might've been."

"Well, Janko. You know, a lot of people live sad lives. Or lives of quiet desperation, as Thoreau put it. That is something that has always amazed me over the years. People are not always as happy or as content as they appear. Oftentimes there are great burdens within the souls of those we bump into on our daily grind."

I had a bite of my toast. Sweet and tangy and I could taste the orange. That brought back good memories. I always had good times with oranges. Stealing away with an orange into the backyard or up a tree or to a playground, and ripping its skin off and tearing at its flesh. I had a soft spot for oranges more than for most people, I guess. Sweet and juicy and so fragrant. An assault on all the senses, really, except for maybe hearing. But you could hear the skin rip from the flesh sometimes if you paid attention. If it was quiet enough and you wanted to savor the experience. At least, I heard it once in a while. Try it sometime, you'll see.

"Are you listening, Janko?"

"Yes, I am, just enjoying the toast…thanks, by the way."

"You're welcome."

We sat in silence for a while. I ate one piece of toast. It was tasty but I couldn't put another piece in my belly. My appetite had forsaken me, and most of the enjoyment in food had left me too. I ate now to stave off the inevitable. To see maybe if I could die from something other than starvation. That seems like such a waste. And I don't mean to be punny.

I got up and poured myself a fresh cup of coffee. When I came back Maria reprimanded me.

"I can get that for you, you know?"

"Yeah, I know."

And she was right. I was bagged just getting up to fetch some more coffee.

"See, I was going to go and get myself some more and I could've gotten you some, too."

With that she got up and went and poured herself a fresh cup of the dark brew. I watched Pornstar get on the bus and drive away. I don't know where he sat; he was still walking down the aisle when he left my view. I sparked up another cigarette. I needed to kill time. That's all I have, time to kill before it kills me. A murder suicide.

I thought about being outside. Being in that cold, crisp air. Fuck, it would be refreshing.

"Maria, could you open up the balcony doors?"

"Sure."

She opened them with one hand. The other gripping the mug of coffee. She opened the doors a crack. Or maybe a couple of inches, then she looked at me. I nodded at her. I could feel the draft. It was cool and crisp and I shivered a little. I put my cigarette down and grabbed the blanket that was on the arm of the couch and wrapped it around me. That felt great.

"If you're cold, Janko, maybe I should close the doors."

"No, I like it like this."

We both sat in silence for a while, sipping our coffee which curled condensation up towards the ceiling like a belly dancer. I remember seeing a belly dancer once down at Stephen Avenue Mall. Probably would've been before I was sick, and I thought she was the most beautiful woman in the world. The way she shook her belly and jiggled her hips. Jesus, I can't fucking afford thoughts like that.

"When is the good doctor coming back?"

"Tomorrow...and you know, Janko, he really is a good doctor. Probably one of the best that this city can offer. You're lucky to have him. And I think he's very willing to help you too."

"I know, and I do like him in a way, too. I just don't know if you can understand how difficult it is to talk to someone you barely know. Especially about shit that makes you feel vulnerable."

I finished my coffee and lay out on the couch. Fucking IV was getting in my way, again. I cursed it and thrashed my arm about a bit until the cord unwrapped itself from my arm. I felt like a fucking fetus attached to the IV bag like an umbilical cord. In many ways it was my lifeline. Prolonging my slow demise. I wonder what it must be like for people to view death in slow motion. Like, to view me dying before their eyes. Slowly, badly, in a way. Suffering. Yes, suffering indeed. And in more ways than one.

"You know, Janko, Dr. Malichem really does care. If there is one psychiatrist that I believe truly cares about his patients, then it would be him. This might be hard for you to grasp, but you have to try and trust him. Trust his expertise to help you. I mean, if you really consider it, you don't have very much to lose, right?"

"I suppose."

And she probably was right, too. All these people who are fucking right. What about me. Jesus, I'd like to be right once. Maybe if I listen to them, maybe that would be right. Shit, I don't know. Sometimes the fatigue of thinking is just too much.

Maria got up and went to the kitchen taking our plates and mugs with her. I closed my eyes to rest a little. But I had a lot on my mind.

"Maria, I've got a question for you."

"Sure, Janko. What is it?"

"Well..." I hesitated, "I guess it's not really important."

"No, don't tease me like that. Tell me."

"Shit, why the fuck not. I wanted to know what it is like to see someone dying right before your eyes. Slowly, wasting away. The ugly mask of death slowly revealing itself. What is that like?"

Maria turned from the sink to face me. I had opened my eyes to look at her. I didn't know how she'd take my question. She frowned a little, holding her yellow gloved hands out in front of her like the branches of a tree.

"I'm not sure I understand," she said.

"Well, like me. How is it to watch me die slowly right before your eyes? As I waste away here I wonder about that. I mean I know what it feels like for me. But what does it feel like for you?"

"Janko! That's a little macabre, don't you think?"

"Yeah, I suppose. But I'd still like to know."

Soapy water was dripping off the tips of her yellow fingers as she kept her arms outstretched like branches.

"You really want to know? I mean, do you want the truth?"

"Yes."

My eyes were still closed. I was trying to rest, maybe take a nap, but I was too interested in hearing what Maria had to say. Macabre yes, but that's all I'm fucking dealing with at the moment. The macabre. My macabre life, maybe that's what I should call my life story. "My Macabre Life: Living to Die" or maybe "Dying to Live," sometimes I just don't know which one I'm most interested in. If that makes any sense? But so far the living is winning. So far.

"Well, if you must know."

Maria took off her gloves and came and sat in the chair. My granny chair, as I call it. I was still lying on the sofa.

"Could you close the balcony door please, I'm getting cold, now."

She closed the sliding doors and sat back down, leaning her elbows on her knees. I cuddled myself in the blanket. My eyes still closed. Maybe not wanting to hear what she had to say. Have you ever done that? Not seen something in the hopes that just hearing it will make it sound less harsh. I've been using this technique for years. I really think it works. Especially when you're small and adults are berating you. Fucking yelling at you up and down. It helps to close your eyes. You can think of other shit then. Like, now I was thinking of the Vancouver coast. I went there once when I was around ten or twelve. Swam in the warm waters of English Bay. The sun was warm, the sand was warm and dry. People were laughing and other children were squealing with delight. I remember hearing them. Listening to them, watching them from a distance. Yeah, there I am. I can see my skinny self in baggy swim trunks now. Watching. And happy, too. I was happy then. Shit. Another one of the few moments when I was happy. And it was with the Antolinis. Good people. Fuck, probably the only good people I've ever known...

"Well, Janko, it doesn't repulse me if that's what you mean. I've been around a lot of death, you know."

"Yeah, I know. But still, you've been spending a lot of time with me. Close personal time with me. It must be different from the other times?"

"Yes, it is. But to be honest, I'm not saddened for you. And I don't say that to be cruel or mean. I mean, I empathize with you and I sympathize for you when I can see the suffering and pain you go through. But no, I'm not saddened by your demise. I guess probably because I believe we all go at some point. And even though I don't understand why you have to go so young like you are, I guess I believe that your purpose here has been fulfilled. Your mission, if you will."

She stopped kind of suddenly. I craned my head around to see her. She stared at her clasped hands dangling like sausages over her knees. Then she looked up and outside. Not at anything in particular, I don't think.

I closed my eyes again.

"What mission? What purpose? Just doesn't make any fucking sense to me. I don't get it. Maybe it's just fate, maybe it's just random acts, random events. Or if you want to be cynical it all could be orchestrated by some cruel fucking God. I don't know."

"Well, I don't know if I would go that far, Janko. I know you're angry. God knows I'd probably be angry, too, if I were dying. But try not to swear too much, you just end up feeding the anger and making it worse. Besides I don't like it."

"Jesus, Maria. I'm dying here and you're upset that I curse a little bit. Come on, give me a break."

"Just because you're dying doesn't give you the right to curse. You don't gain any privilege by dying, Janko. Hopefully you'll gain perspective, hopefully we all do when the end comes, but you don't gain privilege."

I turned to face the couch and drew the blanket around me tighter. Fuck. I know I'm dying, but how about a little slack for God's sake. That'd be nice. A little slack. A little emotional elbow room could do wonders.

Maria got up and went back to the kitchen. I could hear her washing the dishes again. I turned around and fumbled for the remote for the TV. I turned it on to a music station. The volume was low and I tried to lull myself into sleep. A sleep perchance to dream, I had heard it said once. Yeah, dreams instead of nightmares. That'd be nice. I could like that for a change.

XI

I was sitting up in bed smoking a cigarette. The lamp on my bedside table was on its lowest setting. It was dark but with a warm, safe, yellow glow from the lamp. It was snowing lightly outside. The sky had a kind of grayish purple hue to it. And the snow was twinkling past the streetlights like shards of glass. The streetlights had a similar yellow glow to them as my bedside lamp, only a little more orange.

I sucked on my cigarette. The red amber snaked down the shaft and the gray smoke, the color of ash, danced up to the ceiling. It was warm and safe in my room. I was alone but not lonely. Rose had come and gone. The radio blinked a red two-eighteen. It was quiet. I couldn't hear anything. I tried harder but all I could hear was some trickling water in the pipes.

My lungs were hurting. Smoking wasn't fucking helping, for sure. I fiddled with the IV for more narcotic to subdue the pain. The funny thing about pain is, when you're dying, it acts like a benchmark of your life. Life is full of pain to some extent. Some of us get more than our fair share, others less. But we all get a dose to some degree. And the pain of dying, the constant pain I feel stokes the memories of historic pain. The pain I've had, but it also helps aid my memory of some of the good times I've had. However few they've been. And of course, most importantly, as long as I'm feeling pain I'm alive. And sometimes that is sweet. The sweet pain of living.

But it's a delicate balance. Too much pain and I just want to die. It consumes me with its intense focus. Other times it is manageable, like the throb of a dying headache. That's how it was now. But with it being so quiet, even a low-grade pain was too much for me to bear.

I'm sitting here thinking about Maria and what we were talking about. Sometimes I don't sleep very well. I often suffer from insomnia, actually.

Anyway, I'm sitting here and thinking about what she was saying about watching me die. It is a waste. It's a fucking terrible waste of my life. That's the fucking kicker. My fucking life. Nobody else's. I guess I'm feeling a little sorry for myself. Sometimes I can't help but feel that way. Okay, it's a small thing. You'd understand if you were dying. So I was thinking about that shit, and feeling sorry for myself, so I started thinking about the good doctor. I mean, I was thinking good things about him. Despite myself, I couldn't fucking hate the guy. And I know deep down I need someone like that to help me make amends with my past. My sins and transgressions that haunt me. But also my fucking punishments okay, for shit I never did. Punished for nothing other than being born. And the great fucking irony is that now I'm being given the biggest punishment for having been born. I've been given a death sentence. And not a nice "go to bed to sleep and never wake up" kind, but the shitty kind filled with pain and agony. The demise and deterioration of my fucking body. The thing is just packing up on me. Crumbling and falling apart as I watch with mental fucking clarity. Can you imagine what that is like? Being trapped in a fucking body that is being eaten away from the inside as you watch and wait. It is a horror show, okay. A fucking horror show.

Jesus, I'm going off on tangents. Sorry, I'm trying, I really am. So I'm sitting here in bed, cosy and warm, smoking a cigarette and trying to think happy thoughts. Trying to psych myself up for the good doctor, when I hear this noise coming from outside on the balcony. All I can think of is Norm, that bastard. And I bet I didn't, or Rose didn't, lock the balcony doors.

I hold my breath and listen some more. Sure enough, I hear someone sliding open the balcony doors and slip in. I think I should try and pretend that I'm sleeping, but I know that Norm will smell the smoke. And he wouldn't care anyway. He's just an asshole, as you've figured by now, and he'd just wake me up. Jesus, I wish I'd locked the fucking balcony doors. He's the last person I want to see now.

I knew it'd be him. Nobody else would jump up two balconies to get to me. I don't have any shit worth stealing. He'd be one of the few people out on a night like this anyway. I cleared my throat. I couldn't help it. And I thought I heard him clear his too.

I poured myself some water from a carafe that Rose had left. It was blistered with dew from the heat in my apartment. And fuck it was heavy. Shouldn't have been, I guess I'm just weak. A feeble weakling dying a feeble death, visited by my archenemy. Jesus, could I get a fucking break, please?

There he is. He sauntered in like he lived here. Gray workman pants and an evergreen tree colored heavy sweater. There was no snow in his hair and he didn't even look like he had struggled to get in. Jesus, just the sight of him makes me despise him sometimes, and sometimes I fear him too. But lately that isn't happening often.

I watched him walk over to the window, obscuring most of my view. He sank his hands into his trouser pockets. Big meaty hands for a thin, average guy. Tough as nails he is, with those mitts of his. I saw the back of his head. A full head of mousy brown hair. Like mine used to be, and even though he's my age, he seems a lot younger. But he's not dying, he's living. I grabbed another cigarette. I only had two left. I'd have to get Maria or one of them to pick me up some more. I couldn't help but notice the damn rubber cord of the IV snake around as I sparked up my smoke. I felt like some hideous alien creature.

I blew the smoke at the back of Norman's head. Wish it was acid or fire or something like that.

"Hey, Jan, how the fuck are ya, buddy?"

He didn't look around. He kept staring outside, maybe retracing his steps to how he got in here. His hands twitched in his pockets like he was juggling something. Maybe coins, maybe something else. The pervert.

"I'm okay. At least I was until about five minutes ago."

"Come on, now. You're hurting my feelings."

He still stared outside. I could see the reflection of his face in the window. He had that usual smirk on his face. I sucked on my cigarette and folded my arms. Waiting for the fucker. He couldn't sit in silence. I think it deafened him. He had to be doing shit or at least talking. Maybe that's how he kept thin, doing stuff all the time. Getting me in trouble all of the time.

You know, Jan, it seems so long since I've seen you doesn't it? But it hasn't been that long at all."

I didn't say anything. I sipped some water. Blew more smoke at him. Always refolding my arms. He turned around and walked up to the edge of the bed. He stood there with one hand in his pocket the other one caressing my fucking IV.

"Should I pull this out for you, J?"

That fucking smirk.

"Don't you dare, you fucking asshole. I can still push my panic button and help'll be here in minutes okay?"

"Yeah, but you could also die by then."

I reached for my panic button, but he grabbed it first. Taunting me with it.

"Is this what you need?"

He was pulling at my IV tubing.

"Stop it, that hurts."

"What's a little pain, baby. You're riddled with pain, just look at you, and you're complaining of me tugging gently on this little IV. Pussy."

"Stop it, okay…just stop it…please."

Fuck it. I was crying now. He's such an asshole, always trying to bring me down. I threw my cup at him but it missed.

"You fucking little shit," he said as he hit me across the top of my head with his hand.

"Stop it…please just stop it."

"Stop it, please stop it. You pussy."

I tried to stop crying and sucked on my smoke.

"Why do you always have to harass me? Beat down on me?

"Because it's so easy, Jan, so fucking easy. You're still that pathetic little kid I knew since we were eight. I'm still the one trying to protect you, trying to put hair on your chest and make you into a man. You never ever fucking stood up for yourself against those adults who beat you and ridiculed you and treated you worse than a dog. You're still a big pussy. Always have been, always will be."

"Fuck you, you bastard. If I wasn't sick I'd kick your ass."

But he was right, though. I hadn't stood up to those people. But Jesus Christ, I was only a kid and they beat the shit out of me.

"Come on then, go for it."

He was standing next to me so I tried to hit him in the belly but I'm slow and weak and he just moved out of the way. Then he hit me over the head again with his hand.

"Stop it…Why are you doing this to me?"

I was crying again. I couldn't help it, okay. I'm dying and this guy knows how to taunt me. Has since we were small. It's not that easy to be brave all the time. Especially when you've been beaten down dozens of times, okay? It's not easy to stand up for yourself when you've never been shown how. When you've been stepped on and kept down. It's hard for a boy, okay. It's hard when you're eight years old and these giants are yelling at you and telling you you're a no good piece of shit and that they'd all be better off if you were dead. And then they'd beat you so badly you'd hurt for days after. Just try to imagine, okay. Just try. I was eight fucking years old when it started. Eight years old only. Small okay, small.

"Hey, listen, Jan. I'm only shitting with you. Remember when we were young and you'd come and hang out with me and we'd get up to shit? When your folks had been rough on you. Remember when we used to hang out and I'd try and teach you to box, and how you were able to beat up that one bully in school 'cos I was there by your side, and you finally gave him a licking after those years of him teasing you and being shitty to you? Do you remember that, J?"

"Yes, I remember."

He came and sat on the bed next to me and patted my knee. Then he got up and stood by the window again, looking out into the distance. I dried my eyes and snivelled. Shit the pain was awful. My heart ached, my chest squeezed it hard. When had my heart not ached like this? So few those times were. So plenty the pain. He was right in a way, too. He had tried to help me, in his way, to toughen me up. But that's not what I needed. I needed love. I needed companionship, compassion. I needed to be liked and respected by those people who were in charge of me. And instead they let me down. Well, enough of that shit for now. You'll be sick of it when I'm done telling the good doctor my story. And by then, hopefully, you'll not think too badly of me. Maybe then you can understand a little about who I am. I hope you'll extend some compassion, maybe a little slack to me. That would be worth a lot.

"I'm worried, Jan. I'm scared that you're leaving me. We used to be so close and now we barely see each other anymore. I'm your oldest friend, Janko. I deserve a little recognition and respect for that."

That wasn't entirely true. He was my second oldest friend. MJ was my first and Peter was my third. But I get his point.

"Well, Norm, we are drifting apart. I'm dying and I'm trying to make amends for my life. You know it hasn't been the easiest for me. Yes, you've been there for me in the past. But I need something different now. I need to learn to love, if I can."

"I love you, Jan. But, you know that. At least you should know it."

"Well, maybe so, Norm. But it seems like a sick kind of love. It doesn't feel like love should feel."

"Who's gonna love you, Janko? Who? That doctor, those nurses?"

He had turned around and was looking at me now. Leering at me was more like it. His hands still twitching in his pocket. I didn't say anything right away.

"Well…yes, maybe. Maybe the doctor will show me real love…I feel like I need it. My heart needs it. My soul is aching for it."

"Jesus, Janko. You don't even know this doctor. Who says he just doesn't get some perverted pleasure in listening to people's sad lives. Maybe he gets off on being in a position of authority and power over his patients. Maybe he's no different than Dirk and Janet Roebels. And I don't have to remind you about them, do I…"

"He's not like them, okay. He's not anything like them… Fuck you for bringing them up, okay. He's nothing like them. Besides, I'm an adult now, and no one is going to beat me like that, okay. I'd tell the cops, okay, I'd call social services on him, okay."

I was yelling now. That bastard always knew how to get my goat. Why bring up the worst foster parents I ever had. I still have the fucking scars on my back from where they whipped me. Shit, why'd he have to bring that shit up now? Bastard. Why?

"Ha, I got your nerve there, didn't I? But listen Jan, I'm not saying he's exactly like that. I'm just saying that as Dirk and Janet got off on their power trip by beating you and seeing you beg for forgiveness and mercy and all that other shit, maybe in a sick way, Dr. Malichem gets off by getting you to be all vulnerable by telling him your deepest and darkest secrets? Maybe he goes home or to the office and tells his wife or his colleagues about this stupid fucked up loser that he had to listen to all day. Imagine them all laughing at how stupid and how big a loser you are…"

"Fuck you, just fuck off, okay. I'm not listening anymore. And he's not like that, okay. The nurses have told me he's the best in the city. You're just scared because someone else cares for me in a good way, in an appropriate way... I don't care what you think. You're just scared because you're losing me. And you should be, because you are losing me."

He came up and leaned against the bed. He was holding my knee, squeezing it. Kind of in a friendly way. Almost a caring way, as best as he knew how.

"Come on, J, Don't be like that. I love you. I know you. We've been through so much shit together. Don't turn your back on me now. Don't you dare turn your back on me now. Nobody can care for you as much as I do. I've been through thick and thin. When you had nobody, I was there. When you were nobody, I was there. I've been through the fucking fire with you, J, you owe me more than this. I never once let you down. Not once do you hear. Not once."

He went over and sat in the chair in the corner of the room. He crossed his legs over each other, propped his elbow on the arm of the chair and tucked his chin into it. He was looking outside. And for the first time he looked small. He looked vulnerable. He looked scared.

And the thing is. He was right. He was the only person there during some of my worst times when I had nobody. Not even MJ or Peter were there all the time. They were there a lot, almost all the time. But occasionally it was just Norm I had to lean on. Jesus, it's just so hard. I just don't know what to do. I mean do I owe him a place in my life now? When he kind of sticks out like a sore thumb. It's so sad. He looks so sad. And despite it all he's my friend. He's still my friend.

I fumbled for another cigarette. I needed something to do.

"Do you want a smoke Norm?"

He just shook his head and kept staring outside. I still wasn't tired.

"Norm?"

He wouldn't look at me.

"Norm..."

He still wouldn't look at me.

"Norm...you're right. You have been through the fire with me. You have been there for me often. Okay, maybe all the time. But things are different now. I'm not that boy anymore. I'm trying to move on now and put my affairs in order before I die."

"I know," he said, "I know you're dying."

89

A tear trickled down his cheek, but he still wouldn't look at me.

"You okay, Norm?"

"Yes, I'm fine."

"Are you crying, Norm? Is something wrong?"

"Yes, I'm fucking crying."

Another tear dripped onto his thigh. I sucked on my cigarette. Fuck, it wasn't supposed to be this hard. My throat was tightening. My eyes were burning and brimming with tears.

"What's wrong, Norm? Please tell me."

He looked at me then. Tears thick like oil on his bottom lid.

"I love you, Janko. Okay. I really do. You think it has been easy for me? It hasn't been easy for me. It's been fucking hard. It's been hard for me too, you know. Seeing you beat by those fucking people. And there's nothing I could do about it except try and be strong and brave and tough and hard on you. That's not easy. I'm just a person too. I've got feelings too. When they beat you, Jan, it was like they were beating me. I only wanted to help you be stronger. Help you get through it better. I only ever tried my best J, the way I knew. I only tried my best."

He looked outside at the flaky snow. He dabbed at his eyes with his sweater. He looked like the mirror image of my own pain. I felt a hot tear sear my cheek.

"I know...I know, Norm."

What could I do? It's like the blind leading the blind. I'm a wreck and my friend, who I thought was as strong as iron, is an absolute mess. Jesus, I've got my own shit to deal with. I can't carry his too. I looked out at the night sky. Fuck. I just wanted to be one of those little flakes of snow. Just to be blown about by the wind. Have not a care in the world as you float to and fro. Not a care in the world. I wonder what that is like?

"Okay, Norm, I'll leave the balcony doors unlocked. You can come and visit me anytime. But I have to ask you a favor, though. And you've got to promise to do it or else the deal's off, okay?"

"Okay."

He smiled at me, a little smile. Not a smirk, and his face was softer, warmer.

"You've got to let me give Dr. Malichem a chance. We're not boys anymore. We can't keep living in the past with the same attitudes and anger.

You've really got to help me move forward, Norm. I can't stay stuck like this, I can't be moving backward, okay? I'll need your help with this more than ever before. But it's a different kind of help, okay? You've got to try and be kind and generous like you were just now. Deal?"

"Deal."

I put my hands out. The rubber tube of my IV smiling from me to him. He came over and we hugged. And he kissed me on the head and then he went back to the chair. Yeah, it was awkward, but it felt better than fighting.

XII

I met Margaret for dinner at an Ethiopian restaurant in town. I took my seat and waited for her. She was a little late. While I waited I watched the other diners. There was a group of five Ethiopian men sitting around drinking coffee and arguing in a lively way. No one getting very upset, but all of them animated. I could smell the frankincense fill the room, burning thickly from a small cube on the coffee tray. It was thick and gray and infused my nostrils with its sweet pungency. I wondered if I was looking into the lives of rural Ethiopia. I imagined these men sitting around some table in some village debating the important questions of the day. Perhaps that's what's missing from our own lives here in the west. Community. A sense of belonging.

At another table was a young couple. I'd put them in their early twenties. They looked like university students, only because they were wearing the casual dress of the liberal arts major. He was in canvass sneakers with jeans and a seventies style long sleeve shirt untucked from his pants. She was wearing a long flowing spring dress, is how I'd best describe it, with long johns underneath and a wool cardigan over top. He was holding her hands in his and they were staring into each other's eyes. Young and in love. They reminded me of Margaret and I during our student days. Even though they were only sitting two tables over, I couldn't hear their conversation. Their voices were hushed as they huddled, embraced in the cocoon of their love. He let go her hand and sipped at some water. But his eyes never left her. It was sweet and beautiful really. That's what fills me with optimism. The vibrant expression of love, which is life, really. That's what this living is all about I'm sure.

The waiter, one of the owners of the place, came and asked if I needed anything. I ordered half a litre of wine. Margaret would be here any minute. I'd already looked at the menu, but I'd let Margaret choose the dish. I didn't mind eating vegetarian tonight. And besides, Ethiopian vegetarian food is pretty good. I heard the bells jingle as the door opened. I looked over and there she was. My beautiful Margaret. Don't mind me going on about it. It's just that I'm often so happy, so pleased and still so attracted to her. She smiled at me and her eyes sparkled. I took her winter coat, kissed her on her cold lips, and hung it up. She sat down and then I followed.

"Hi, love, how are you?"

"Super, and you?" I asked.

"Ah, so busy at work. I could use a holiday I think. Maybe I will take a few days off next week."

She pushed her hair out of the way and took the menu and started to look at it. Her brow was furrowed.

"Why don't we, honey? Why don't we take a mini break from here? Let's go to Mexico to an all-inclusive and just relax. Escape this winter and get frizzled in the sun?"

"Sure, maybe."

She was still looking at the menu.

"Okay, I think I know what I'll get."

"I ordered us a half litre of red wine. Is that okay?"

"Just perfect...I don't know about Mexico, love. Maybe we should talk about it a little later. I'm just a bit frazzled at the moment. I just want to sit and relax and unwind over a nice meal with you."

The waiter came by with the wine and poured us each a sip. Really, that's all it was pretty much. I took the bottle once he had put it on the table and topped us up. Now, that's better.

"Have you decided, love?"

"I thought I'd let you choose, honey?"

"Oh, okay."

Margaret looked back down at the menu and then ordered the vegetarian combo. An assortment of quite tasty stews.

"And a glass of water, too, please?" she said.

I took her hands in mine. Taking a page from that young kid's book.

"Tell me about your day, honey? You seem harried."

She squeezed my hands and then sipped some wine, humming after.

"Oh, love, it has just been one of the worst days ever. I had to deal with a horrible incident that happened with one of my clients. Absolutely horrible."

"Tell me about it."

I sipped some wine and Margaret sipped some more. I could smell the strong, sweet smell of fermented grapes on the table. I don't get all the smoke and cherry and woody undertones nonsense. It is fermented grapes. Tasty sure, but really that's all they are.

"Well, this young woman. She's a university student. Probably just left home for the first time and maybe nineteen years old. She's on student loans and in debt up to her eyebrows I'm sure. The other thing is, she's from a small rural town. Caroline, I think she said. Anyway, she's been renting an apartment in Brentwood. It's close to the university and close to the Safeway where she works sometimes. She lives by herself and has been in that apartment for only a couple of months. Well, a couple of nights ago, on the weekend I believe it was, she woke up around two-thirty in the morning to the apartment manager fondling her breasts. You can imagine how creeped out she was, and she screamed bloody murder."

It's that kind of ignorance and disrespect that drives me nuts. I really lose my patience with that kind of thing.

"Can you imagine what that was like, love?"

"Yes, I can. I surely can. That stupid idiot. Why would he do something like that?"

"Well, apparently he totally backed off, and pleaded with her not to call the police. Can you believe he said something about coming in to check on the place because he thought he heard screaming and fighting and wanted to make sure she was okay? I mean really, what a lame excuse. Well, she called the police and they didn't buy the story and charged him with sexual assault. I feel so bad for her. I mean this guy has keys to all the apartments, what if this is his modus operandi? How many other women has he tried this stunt with? And how many have not said anything because of fear or embarrassment or something like that? Did you know that only one in ten rapes are reported?"

I nodded. Here we go again, God love her.

"Well, at least she's done the right thing, honey. She called the police, the guy has been charged and hopefully that will be the end of it."

"True, but now she lives in fear of him coming back for revenge or to do something worse to her. I mean he probably still has the keys to the apartment complex."

"Does he own the building or is it a company? Because if it is a company then I'm sure they'll at least suspend him until the outcome of the trial right?"

"I think the complex is owned by a corporation. But still, love, he could have made copies or duplicates of the keys. She's the one that is going to have to move now, not him. And that is not right."

I squeezed her hand and had some more wine. I poured more into our glasses too. It was good wine for a house wine.

"What did she want from you?"

"She wanted to know how she could leave the apartment building quickly and if she would be legally responsible for any missed rent in not giving notice. And also she wanted to know if she could get her security deposit back. She really needs the money."

"Well, I certainly hope she could leave without penalty. Wouldn't be fair otherwise, I don't think."

"Yeah, she'll be fine. But she could certainly have a battle in trying to get her security deposit back. That is so challenging in these sorts of cases. You'd be astonished at how many of these companies try to keep that money back from their clients. And they do it illegally and underhandedly, too. Really makes me mad because they know that these students and young people are intimidated and unmotivated in pursuing legal recourse through the courts. It is just so wrong. And this poor woman, just trying to make a future for herself and then she has to deal with this crap. It is not right and not fair. She will most likely need counselling to overcome this."

She made a growling sound to express her anger, but it sounded more cute than angry. I almost couldn't help myself from smiling.

"Why do you think this has affected you so much, baby?"

I was going to use some of my skilled training on her. Nine years of psychology had to come in useful once in a while. I knew where this was going. I was going to needle it out of her if I had to.

She looked at her glass of wine for a moment. The color of blood as it dries in the air. She took a good sip and put it down again. I looked over to the young couple.

He was trying to feed her a piece of injera with stew on it which fell out onto the table. She pulled away giggling at him and he stuffed the piece of injera in his own mouth. She tried the same with him and was more successful. At this rate he'd be eating most of the food.

"I don't know. Maybe just the injustice of it all."

She was looking at her wine all this time. A wistful look on her face. She didn't look at me and I think it was because she didn't want to have to admit it.

"Well, baby, I think I have an idea if I might venture?"

She grabbed the wine glass at its stem and was twirling it with her fingers.

"I know what you're going to say, and maybe you're right. Still doesn't make it right though, the way this guy behaved."

"I know, baby. But you don't have to own it. It wasn't about you. It wasn't your professor using his position of authority over you and fondling you. It was someone else. And as much as it makes you mad, this woman did the right thing. She called the authorities and he's been arrested and will hopefully go to jail. I know she has been hugely inconvenienced by having to move, but a lesson like this came with perhaps a small price."

"What do you mean lesson, Mike?"

"Well, I don't know. Perhaps that was a bad choice of words. I'm sorry. I mean that it could have been a lot worse for her."

"Yes, it could have, Mike. It could have been a lot worse, she could have died. And why do you have to bring up my assault from so long ago? What the hell has that got to do with anything?"

Jesus, where the hell did that come from? I guess my training didn't help. My hands were lying shamefully alone across the table. I pulled them to me to hide the embarrassment and used the one to drink more wine. Then I added more to my glass. Not hers.

"Baby, I'm just trying to help. That's all. I think that your assault is maybe why you feel so strongly about this. I'm not accusing you of anything; I'm just trying to help."

"Leave it alone, Mike, okay? You don't understand."

She huffed at me under her breath and then emptied her glass of wine. Drinking it, not pouring it all over me, thankfully, and then she emptied the carafe into her glass. We'd probably need some more.

The waiter came with our food, placing the big round tray in front of us. It was a communal meal and I didn't feel too sociable at the moment. He entreated us to enjoy it and I gave him a half-hearted smile. Margaret ignored him completely. I also ordered another half-litre of wine. Margaret ignored me too.

I looked over at the happy couple again. They were still smiling and trying to feed each other. It didn't look so nice anymore. As a matter of fact it looked pretentious and out of place. She looked at me smiling, and I looked away. I couldn't bear her happiness. I tore at the injera and squeezed at some stew. I wanted some meat just to piss Margaret off. But I'd get over it in time.

We sat in silence in for a while. Eating stew and injera. Washing it down with wine. Not looking at each other. Careful not to look at each other. The food didn't taste as good as I remembered. I called for some water. Margaret asked for some, too. The group of Ethiopian men got up to leave. Cigarette smoke intermingling with the remnants of frankincense. That annoyed me too. I hate having to smell cigarettes when I'm trying to enjoy my meal. They lingered for a while around their table, waiting and taking their time to say goodbye to the host/our waiter/the owner I guess. I wanted to talk to Margaret about the things that were on my mind. Mostly Janko, really. But the wedge between us was widening and I didn't think that I should be the one to have to apologise. I hope you're not siding with her, either. Are you? I mean, give me a break, I was just offering her my perspective and I don't think she needed to get all uptight about it like she did.

More frankincense was ordered by the young lovers. They had ordered Ethiopian coffee and with it came the fragrant scent of church. That's what it reminded me of. The long boring Sundays spent in church. Especially around Christmas time when they fog the church with frankincense. The clanging of bells, the sparkle of brass and the gray smoke smouldering from coals of passion. Fond memories really, but boring as hell for a young boy, especially one dressed up in the white starched cotton of an altar boy.

And no, I was never molested. We'll get that right out of the way. My mother, in a very laid back sort of way, maybe hoped that I'd become a priest. So I became an altar boy just to please her, in a way.

And also to test-drive the occupation if you will. That way when I didn't become a priest maybe she'd at least believe that I gave it a serious nod. It's just that I couldn't buy into all the dogma. Maybe that's why I became a psychiatrist. I really believe in free will rather than destiny. We are the masters of our domains, the captains of our ships, the pilots of our planes. I always did get a kick out of that bumper sticker that read something like my karma will run over your dogma.

I had finished eating. I wasn't enjoying my meal anymore. But the wine was better, it was oiling my bitter feelings. I filled my three quarter full cup and Margaret's, too. A small gesture of condolence.

She looked up at me and took my hand.

"Sorry, love," she said, looking at me shyly.

"I'm sorry, too."

Though in truth, I wasn't sure what the hell I was sorry for. But that's the way you have to play it, isn't it? I suppose I was sorry for her hurt feelings. The way she had taken this poor girl's plight so hard. But I wasn't really sorry for what I had done. I didn't think I had done anything wrong, anyway.

"Aren't you going to eat any more, honey," I said.

"No, I think I'm full. What about you?"

"No, I'm full too. Besides, it didn't taste so good after a while."

I smiled at her and she smiled back. I looked over at the young lovers. He was whispering something to her, leaning right across the table with the smoke from the frankincense curling around his neck like a noose. She was giggling, putting her hand to her mouth and fluttering it about like a butterfly. Trying not to spit out the contents. He leaned back again, took a sip from his thimble sized coffee cup. Pleased as punch with himself no doubt. She reached over the table and gave him a good-natured tap across the arm. He turned away from her in mock defence.

I sometimes think half of what I do is about observation not so much discourse. The body language of my clients so often shouts over what they are actually saying. The police use it all the time during interrogation to learn if they are on the right track. And if you know what you're looking for, it is highly accurate.

But you can't let your ears deceive your eyes. The eyes are the windows to the soul and if you let the soul see what it needs, it can give you an extraordinary amount of knowledge about the souls of others.

Or, their character, if you prefer a clinical word for soul. And hey, not that I'm perfect at it. It's just a valuable tool in reacting to people. Not rocket science. We all do it all the time but mostly without paying much attention to it. I just try to put it into practice a little more is all. Especially when I'm with my clients. For example, I'll often hear one of my patients telling me that everything is fine. They'll bore you to tears telling you how good everything is. How hunky dory they are. But if you muted them for a moment you'd probably get a different picture. Their arms are most likely folded. They're bladed towards you with their legs crossed and their expression is often defiant. Looking at you from a head tilted slightly up. These are the kind of clues I look for. And most often it happens when we've begun to dig deep, when we're getting close to a kernel of dark coal. Their most vulnerable and darkest place. The place where their problems are more than likely born from the dark coal of fear. But my job is to help them polish away at that coal, put it through the heat and fire of passion and exploration and unearth the diamond that they are underneath it all. But you've got to be able to read past their lips. Lying lips.

"You're right, love. I know you're right. It's just that sometimes I get so upset about the injustice, my own injustice that I suffered. This woman reminds me of that. And it's also not fair that she has to suffer the same indignity as I did."

I nodded.

"I just don't know how you do it, love. How you cope with hearing the pain and anguish from other people. How you cope with that. I just don't think I could do it. I'd probably get so personally upset that I couldn't focus on helping them."

Margaret was looking down at her glass of wine. Twirling the stem like before.

"Well, that's the key really, honey. If I did get personally upset about it I'd be no good to them, and that wouldn't help anyone. But that doesn't mean that it is easy. For the most part, the difficulties people experience are not born out of a sense of healthy self-esteem but rather from places of fear and insecurity. And how does that happen?

Well, from being dishonored, neglected and let down as children. And I mean gross negligence and abuse. You know how many patients I've counselled who have been physically, emotionally, sexually ad infinitum abused?

It is horrendous. Imagine what happens, as an example, to a child that is told over and over that they are worthless, no good and that the world/their parents would be better off if they weren't even born. Now add to that physical and/or sexual abuse and you get a lost soul. No, I should say a damaged and battered soul. Fragile, yet still beautiful. Unfortunately, not all people are able to bounce back from that. A lot of my patients are, and those are the ones I hang my hat on. Those are the people from whom I get my strength to continue on and to listen and absorb their pain in order for them to find their beautiful souls. It is hard, honey; sometimes I despair that I might not be able to do it. Continue the work I do. But I manage. You help me immensely with your insights and support. You help bear my burden, and for that I love you."

She looked up at me and smiled. I leaned over the table and kissed her.

"And you are also a beautiful soul, my love. That's why I married you."

We finished our wine and went outside to brave the elements with warm bellies, fiery blood in our veins and dry yeasty breath. I loved wine. Oil of the soul if you ask me.

XIII

I woke up grumpy as shit. I was half upright. I must have fallen asleep propped up while Norm was here. I looked at the chair. The blanket thrown over its back was still nicely folded. It was like he hadn't been here. Sometimes I second guess myself. Like, sometimes you're not sure if you're dreaming or if it's in real life. I've sometimes confused television for my own life. Have you done that? Maybe it's just because I'm living such a fucking lame existence. Real life doesn't seem so real anymore. I mean who wants to believe that they are really dying. Give me a break. I'd much rather be yakking and laughing with my "real" friends in a coffee shop. Everything's always so fucking nice on TV. Everybody's so good looking, so happy, so rich. There'd never be a character like me on TV, not unless it was a sympathy role. And besides, they'd still look damn good. Make up and a tan and probably a full head of hair. Not my gulag fucking look. No sir, that wouldn't cut it on prime time. Not while people are trying to eat their TV dinners and wash it down with the same pop that the actors are drinking. No, not in my fucking lifetime. Hell, not in a real person's lifetime, really. Okay, I'm bitchy, I'm sorry, okay? My mouth is an ashtray and I've got no more smokes even though I thought I should have one left. And I've got a horrible crick in my neck and the fucking sun is interrogating me through my bedroom window. I feel hung over. Like death warmed up. That's a joke, okay. I'm trying to shake off this pissy mood.

"Hello?"

"HELLO?"

Surely someone was here. It was daytime already. Where the fuck was the hired help?

"Yes, Janko."

Veronica Drake was standing in the doorway. She made me feel good about myself. A tall, awkward woman who reminded me of a giraffe. Her orange hair was in a knot at the back of her head. Kind of like an old school madam or something. I don't know, she just wasn't very attractive, with a bit of an overbite, too. I felt almost good looking next to her. And I was knocking at death's door. She had her hands perched on her hips like she was going to give me a lecture. Awkward social skills too. Not very personable.

"Can I get some cigarettes and a glass of water?"

"Okay. You know you shouldn't be smoking, Janko, in your condition."

Jesus would they all just fucking quit it about the smoking already.

"Yeah, I know. Would you just go get them for me, please."

It's gonna be one of those days. In a way I'm glad the doctor is coming.

"Okay. Suit yourself. Do you want the water first or when I get back?'

Shit. You see what I mean? The woman has no idea.

"Before"

I got up to go to the washroom. My bladder was heavy. Like carrying a fucking grapefruit in my belly. I sat on the edge of my bed for a few minutes, leaning on my hands. I looked at my thin, pale arms, the rubbery veins like worms sneaking around them. I closed my eyes tight. They felt like I had salt in them or something. I'm miserable okay, I'll admit it. Today's not my best day, okay. Just bear with me, the good doctor will be here soon and we'll all be happy.

I went and sat on the toilet seat. I couldn't bear to stand. I felt the cold sweat of a pending fainting spell prick my forehead. But I held it back. I felt like vomiting, too. I clutched at the IV stand. The splash of urine in the water sounded like pissing on glass. But it felt good. It felt really good. Ever had that kind of pleasure from a piss? So close to orgasm, but then I barely remember what that felt like. I don't want to hear about it, okay? It was a rhetorical question.

I needed something to eat. I got up and the nausea hit me again. I heard Veronica leave. No fucking water. Jesus, did I have to do everything myself around here. I much preferred Maria and Salima. I should have gotten her to make me some toast or something before she left.

JASON BLACKER

I wobbled into the living room and collapsed on the couch. I had no energy, I felt like the end was so near. Cold sweat pricked at my forehead again. I got scared. I didn't want to fucking go out like this. Not alone, not without hope, not without any confession. It's funny, in a way, how just when I feel I am ready to die and then I think I'm about to, I get scared. It's lonely, okay? To die is lonely, and all I've ever known is fucking loneliness. I just don't want that to be my last experience here. Just to have someone around when I die would be nice. Even Veronica, for God's sake, even she would be better than no one. Maybe you can't understand. I mean I know we come in alone and we leave alone. But that's different from dying lonely. Lonely and alone are two different things. Maybe you'll find out one day. Though it's not something I'd wish on my worst enemy. Okay, maybe my worst enemy but that's all. There's nothing in the world like the prison of loneliness. The harshest and most barren wasteland of the soul. I can't really tell you what's it like. Just so much heartache and pain.

"Hey, Janko."

It was MJ, God I was happy to see her. I never heard the door open in my space of fear.

"Hi, MJ. Thank God, you're here."

I started to cry. Fuck, fuck, fuck. I just want the end of this pain, this suffering this loss and loneliness. She came up and stroked my head. My fuzzy, prickly, mostly bald head of hair.

"Hey, baby, it's okay. Why are you so sad?"

I looked at her with wet eyes.

"I thought I was dying, MJ. I thought I was gonna die all by myself. All alone. And I was scared. I was really fucking scared. Thank God, you're here."

I grabbed at her hand. It was all I could do. She sat down on the edge of the couch with me and held my hand in both of hers.

"You're sweating, Janko. Are you okay? Do you want me to call the nurse or something?"

"No…you've been so good to me, MJ. So good. Thank you so much."

"You've been good to me too, baby."

She was caressing my head again. I loved her, I loved her so much. The only other woman I had truly loved. Been able to love. The only two women who had been feminine softness and compassion and love to me. Unlike all the other women. So unlike the other women.

"No, MJ, I was an asshole to you sometimes. Especially after I'd been with Norm, but you were always so kind to me. So patient with me."

"Well, it's okay, J. Let's not dwell on that now. All that's in the past, we don't have to talk about that stuff now. Where is the nurse by the way?"

"She's gone out to get me some smokes. It's Veronica. I don't like her very much. Too severe and disciplined. I don't know why she's in this kind of work. I don't think it suits her at all."

"Yeah, I don't think she likes me very much, either."

"Why do you say that, MJ?"

"Well every time I'm around she looks at you funny like you're crazy or something for hanging out with me or something. I don't know. She just gives me the creeps."

I had to laugh. It was good to laugh. MJ makes it so easy for me to laugh. I wiped my eyes dry and placed my head on her lap. I looked up at the ceiling, the stubbled ceiling stained yellow. This was heaven. I could die now and not be so scared. With MJ caressing my forehead. I could die and not worry about blown out dreams and shitty lives. At moments like this I'd almost like to die, so that I'd be finished with the fucking pain. Funny that at these happiest moments I'd almost wish I was dead. But you probably wouldn't understand. When you could count on both hands these precious moments, then maybe you'd understand wanting to be taken away during one of them, not having to endure the pain that follows. Five minutes of heaven for years of hell. That's not much, but it's enough to get you wishing for death. But I never did it, did I? I never could take my own life. And God knows I tried. I just guess my heart wasn't in it. Maybe I was too scared, maybe it was the fear of hell and damnation beaten into me. I don't know, I just couldn't, okay. Does that make me weak? Or does it make me strong? Maybe it makes you pity me. But to me it just makes me sadder. I never decided to live but I never was determined enough to die. Fuck. Fuck, it just doesn't make any sense.

"Why the furrowed brow, Janko?"

"I'm just thinking about how happy I am, MJ. I feel so happy when you're with me. So peaceful, too. I could lie in your arms and just die, and it wouldn't be so bad, you know? It's moments like these that I'd like to freeze and capture forever. I've just never had many like this. You know that, MJ. You know my life, my childhood."

She looked down at me and smiled. I closed my eyes and felt the heaviness of bliss. My body felt soft and warm. For the first time in a long time I couldn't feel any pain. I couldn't feel the rain. Rain always reminded me of pain. The pain of having to suffer the physical abuse and remain indoors without escape into the outside world. No escape under the bridge by the river. Rain meant I had to lick my wounds and skulk around narrow hallways like a beaten dog. But, enough of that. Let me try to live for just this moment. This precious moment of which there are so few and for which I have paid so dearly. And now as the sun sets over my wreckage let me enjoy the view. Is that too much to ask? I don't think so. It's the least I can fucking ask for.

"I don't want you dying just yet, Janko. I'd rather have you around for a long time still to come. Why do you always have to be so morbid? It upsets me, J, I thought you knew that."

"I'm sorry, MJ. But, let's face it, I'm dying and it's kind of on my mind right now. Can you blame me? I mean, I don't think I have that long left to live. Maybe weeks, maybe months. I'm just trying to make every moment count. Especially the ones with you."

"Okay then, what can I do to help?"

"Just be yourself, MJ. Just be yourself. Your kindness is a gift that I need so much right now, if I'm going to be able to overcome the inner turmoil in my spirit."

"Okay, J, if that's what you want. I can't say that it's going to be easy for me though, okay? I mean it's hard enough to see you wasting away like this. It's like it's me dying, Janko. And that is so hard for me to deal with...I love you...don't you know that?"

She laid her one hand on my shoulder and the other one on the arm of the couch. She looked out the balcony doors. Her eyes were blistered with tears.

"Please, don't be sad, MJ. It breaks my heart to see you so sad. I know you love me, and I love you, too. You're one of only two women I've ever really loved, MJ, and you're still with me. That's important. I'm so happy when I'm with you, MJ, please don't be sad. I need the happiness, I have too much sadness to carry, and I can't bear yours too."

My eyes were prickling with tears too. Fuck. Enough of the pain already, please. Time is so short.

MJ looked down at me and dabbed at her eyes with the sleeves of her blouse.

"Okay, J. I'll try."

She squeezed my shoulder and looked out into the day again.

"I'd love to take you out for a walk out there."

"But it's cold and look how thin I am."

"Well, it's not that cold out there. We could bundle you up, wrap you in this blanket and take you out for just a little fresh air. This apartment is beginning to smell more like a hospital all the time."

I looked outside. It was a clear day now. Puffy clouds like cotton balls on blue skies. The sky looked like the backdrop for a baby boy's room. Like I've seen in pictures. Not like I've ever experienced. It didn't look that cold, but there was still snow on the ground and the heat from the houses across the road was condensing out of gaping chimneys. It was a tempting idea. I was thinking we should go for it. But Veronica would be back so soon.

"Yeah, MJ, I think it would be a great idea."

I smiled at her and she giggled at me.

"Let's."

"I want to, but I think we should wait for another time. Veronica could be back any minute and I don't want to get us in trouble."

"But how long do we have, Janko? You keep going on about how time is short and that you have only weeks maybe months. I mean, come on, you could be dead before we get this done."

"Come on, MJ. I really want to. It will be like old times by the river, just me and you exploring. And we will do it. I promise. The next time that the nurse is out of here we'll go. How about next week at the same time. I'll even send her on some errands to give us more time, okay?"

MJ wouldn't say anything. She kept looking outside. The occasional car went by and, even more rare, was a person walking by. I looked at her and she didn't seem mad. And me, well I was feeling warm and cosy again in MJ's lap. A grin melted on my face and I felt even better.

MJ slid my head off her lap gently. She cradled it back on the couch and was headed towards the door.

"I'm going to take that as a promise, Janko, okay?"

"Yes."

I watched her leave, a big smile on my face. Shit I felt a lot better just spending those few minutes with her. Things weren't looking too bad to be honest. I had kind of worked things out with Norm and I was feeling good about MJ. Now I'd just wait for the good doctor and I'd be right as rain. It was about time. I'm sure you can agree. But fuck, I was getting hungry. What was taking Veronica so long? Well no sooner had I said that and seen MJ out the door when in came Veronica. Uncanny.

"Did you see MJ as you came in?"

"No, I didn't see anyone."

She went into the kitchen and unpacked some stuff. I was waiting for my cigarettes. She brought them to me. I sat up still feeling very weak and lethargic.

"I really don't like getting these things for you, you know?"

"Yeah, I know. Thanks, anyway. Can I have some toast with margarine?"

"Okay."

"And coffee."

"All right."

Man, she was downright miserable.

"Why don't you have some, too?"

"Have what, Janko?"

"I dunno, fucking anything to get you out of that pissy mood."

I smiled to myself. I wasn't that upset. I wasn't going to let her bring me down, try as she might.

"Now, now, Janko, that's not a very appropriate way to talk to me."

I ignored her and lit my cigarette. I left it on the ashtray to smoulder.

"When is the good doctor coming?"

"In about an hour."

She was talking to the back of my head and I was talking to the street outside.

"Okay, what's the time now, then?"

"About eight-thirty."

I slouched back into the couch. It was going to be a long hour. Veronica came by and settled the toast in front of me. It was brown bread. I must ask them for white, but its surface was wet with fat and it smelled good. She fiddled with my IV, attaching a new one and fiddling with the dose.

"Tell me if you feel light headed or queasy."

"Okay."

She went off and came back with coffee. It was in my favorite mug. It was an astrological one. Aries, that's me and this is what I'm like apparently. Ambitious, impulsive, adventurous, and a lover of freedom. I am open to new ideas and open to challenges and also I make a good leader but poor subordinate. Bullshit, I say. But this mug was a gift from the Antolinis. It is about the only thing I have that I salvaged from my shitty childhood. And another thing I learned about Aries. We are supposed to have a great sexual appetite, often leading us astray. Yeah, right, I can count on less than both hands how many times I've had sex in my life and they've all been with the same woman. Norma Jones. I'll be speaking more about her to the good doctor, I'm sure. So 'hah!' I say about sexual appetite. But fuck, I would have loved to have had more intimacy with a woman. Not necessarily screwing around, but just to have that physical intimacy. I mean, I can still remember what it was like. Such a good place to be. If there is a heaven, and I'm not so sure, then basking in the afterglow of sex is it.

I had some toast. It was good. Even without my appetite I still enjoyed food. The little bits of it that I could have. And coffee, well coffee was like the elixir of life for me. Toast, coffee and cigarettes. Now, if you ask me, that has got to be a recipe for Xanadu. At least, my Xanadu, anyway. When you're down to the wire, it's the small things, I think, that bring you happiness and peace.

Maybe the small things always can, but maybe we just don't recognize it while we are too busy with living. Maybe it's only in dying that we get to recognize the core of what is important.

A shitty deal if you ask me, I'm just offering a suggestion. At least that's what happened to me. But then, you can't count my living as an example because it's been too hard. Too brutally painful in many ways. Anyway, all I'm saying is that this dying has opened my mind up to what should have been important during my more sombre moments of living.

I craned my head around and saw Veronica sitting behind me at the table. She was having a coffee too.

"Hey, why don't you come and sit on the comfy chair here?"

"No, thank you, I'm quite comfortable here."

Jesus, this woman I just didn't get. She hasn't always been like this. When she first started working for me, or should I say helping me out, she was way friendlier. But the last six months, or more even, she's been downright miserable. I tried to have her moved so I could get someone more pleasant in. But they wouldn't hear about it. For fuck's sake, there's only space for one bastard here and that is me.

"What are you doing?" I asked her.

"Having a coffee the same as you."

I could keep this up for about an hour I'm sure.

"Yeah. Do you have it sweet with cream?"

"Yes. Cream and sugar."

"Hey, why don't you come and sit over here so we can have a fucking conversation?"

I still wasn't really upset, but definitely getting annoyed. I felt like I was pumping a dry well and I don't have the energy.

"Certainly not, if that is the way you're going to talk to me."

"Okay, I'm sorry. It's just that I don't get you. I mean you seem to be getting more and more miserable, and that's hard when I'm trying to get more and more content with dying. You're just not helping me. Maybe you're my nemesis."

Shit, I loved that word, nemesis. Sounds like a super hero's arch villain. I'd played with the idea of making up an arch villain called Nemesis. I don't know, somebody to kick Superman's ass. I mean why do the fucking super heroes always have to win?

All the "good" people in my life were always beating the shit out of me, I needed a villain whom I could count on to make things right. Anyway, he was going to be Nemesis, beating up the arrogant super heroes and their allies.

He wasn't going to be an asshole and a cruel, mean guy; he'd just be a guy who had taken a couple of knocks, you know. Maybe having been raised on the wrong side of the tracks. Well, needless to say, it never got off the ground. But still, I think it would have been a great fucking idea.

I smoked some more of my cigarette. I think I smoke sometimes to be rid of the boredom. To pass time. Something to do. I mean, there is only so much self-reflecting that I want to do. I blew a jet stream of smoke up to the ceiling.

"Come on. Come sit next to me. We can talk and be friends, maybe."

I was being facetious of course. I heard a big sigh and then some noises, clanging of mugs and stuff. And then she was sitting in the chair holding her coffee mug on the arm rest. I smiled at her. She looked away.

"You know about my background, I'm sure. All of you nurses are nosy, well maybe you need to know it. So anyway, you know my excuse for why I'm such an asshole. What was your childhood like?"

She kicked her legs out and crossed them in front of her at the ankles. She leaned back into the chair and held the mug in both hands. It was hiding her lips. Horse lips, I thought.

"Why do you want to know, Janko?"

"Well, I'm trying to have a conversation here, maybe kill the hour we have left. Besides, I'm going to be dead within weeks probably, months at the best."

She just looked outside and thought about something. I was thinking that maybe her childhood was as bad as mine. That wouldn't be so bad, at least not so bad for me. I mean, misery does like company. I reckoned she was probably in her late forties, maybe doing this kind of work was killing her. But she's got it all wrong. It's killing us, her patients. I'm joking, okay, I'm trying to keep my sense of humor here.

"How old are you, V?"

She looked at me slowly. A fucking horse, I swear to God, that's what I see every time I look at her. She put her steely gaze on me, only it wasn't that steely.

"Forty."

Jesus, she's had a hard life, then. Looking probably closer to ten years older than she actually is. Mind you, I'm a fine one to speak. I look like a decrepit old man and I'm only thirty-three. Watch this, here it comes.

"How old are you?"

"Thirty-three."

Now it was my time to look outside and do some contemplating. I sucked on my smoke to help disengage my mind, but it didn't work very well. I started thinking about all the shit I've been into. How fucking haggard I look myself. I could vaguely see my reflection in the glass sliding doors leading to the balcony. It was forgiving, but that wasn't saying much. My skin was sallow and thin like rice paper and marked like it, too. Only, I had bad wrinkles around my eyes and forehead. Picture this if you can. This is the charming picture of death. Pleased to meet you, did you get my fucking name. See, this is what frustrates the fuck out of me. I just can't sit still for an hour, no, make that forty-five minutes, in a good mood. Some poison in my mind has to start seeping in and making me pissy and grumpy. Fuck it, death has got to be a lot better than this shit.

"You don't look bad for thirty-three."

I thought I saw her smirk ever so slightly. I smiled. I mean if you can't smile at yourself you've got no sense of humor. I've had to smile at myself a lot during this life, just to get by.

"Thanks, V, you don't look too bad yourself for thirty-three."

Now, she really smiled.

"You're flattering me. What do you want?"

I smiled at her and said nothing. I looked out the balcony again. It was sunny, another sunny day. That's one of the nice things about this place. You can count on the sunny days in winter or summer. Probably one of the sunniest places in Canada and that was so important to my mental well-being. I'd probably be fucking dead by now if I lived without sun for much of the year. It is hard enough to have the short days in winter; I couldn't imagine them being short and overcast.

"Actually, you could get me some more coffee please."

I took the last swig and reached my cup out to her. She took it and went to the kitchen to get some more.

"Have you ever been married, V?"

I liked that, calling her V. I think it might start loosening her up. I mean I'm doing it half in jest, but it puts me in the right frame of mind in dealing with her.

"Yes, I was married, once."

She was talking to me from the kitchen.

113

I heard the clinking of the coffee carafe being replaced on the hotplate of the coffee machine. She returned and handed me my coffee. A bunch of sugar later and it was much better.

"So, what happened? Are you still married?"

"Wow, Janko, you've never been so interested in what I have to say."

I didn't say anything. I didn't know what she meant.

"No, I'm not married, anymore."

"Do you smoke?"

I'm not sure what I'm doing. Sounds like I'm trying to pick her up but I'm not, swear to God. Just trying to make conversation. I picked up my pack of cigarettes and lit another one like the cool actors do in movies. Or should I say, James Dean. He was one cool dude, and I think he made smoking cool. I think that's one of the reasons I started smoking was the way he smoked. All hipness.

No, I don't smoke. Never did, and if I did, I wouldn't anymore. Not as a nurse. You know that stuff will kill you, Janko."

"Yeah, I know, but I'm dying already."

"That was just a little attempt at humor. Sorry."

"No, that's okay. That's good. I didn't think you had a sense of humor. It's gonna take me a while to get used to it, I think."

My last piece of toast lay limp on the plate. It was no longer glistening. It looked like a dog had drooled all over it. Tanned, wet, brown bread. Not very appetizing, but I probably couldn't have eaten it even if it had been appetizing.

"Have you ever been married, Janko?"

"No. Does it look like a guy like me gets the girl?"

"You never know. I believe there is someone for everyone out there. Maybe you just never found her."

"No, I think I found her, once. But I don't think she wanted me. She left for another guy."

Enough said. Jesus Christ, here I go blabbing off again to Veronica and I barely know her, and she probably doesn't really care, anyway. Maybe Salima or Maria, hell maybe even Rose, would be more interested.

"What happened?"

"Do you really care, Veronica? I mean, we haven't had the friendliest relationship, have we?"

114

"Well, the answer is yes, I do care and yes, we haven't had the best relationship, yet. Mostly, I think it is because you are so combative and belligerent and I can see through that to the helpless vulnerability that hides behind the façade. And also because I haven't wanted to get too close to you and end up hurting when you do die."

She stopped then, when I think she was really just getting going. I looked at her for a while and she just stared out the balcony at the blue sky. She didn't look too horsey then, kind of soft, actually. Or maybe it was my eyes getting all blurry. But I didn't cry. No tears for me, I need to save them for myself. Besides I'm just getting to know Veronica. I don't have the emotional investment in her that would bring out deeper sympathy. Mind you, this side of her sure catches me by surprise. I cleared my throat and sipped my coffee, sat back and inhaled my cigarette. Awkward moments. Why the hell can't we all be more authentic? Say what we mean, when we mean it. Too much life is wasted on beating around the bush and not being direct enough. If you love someone, say it. It you care deeply for someone, say it. If you'd be sad to see someone go, then say that, too. I mean, we're too quick to hate and give voice to that, but what about the love that we hold silently behind zippered mouths? God knows I could have used love in my life, and I could have used hearing it too. Now, an almost stranger is choking on saying the same thing, and it's touching, it really is. But she can't say it. She won't say it. But then again, neither would I. I've never been given good examples of expressive love. Maybe that's the problem for most of us. No examples to fall back on, no tools to use to express our feelings.

"Why do you care, V?"

She looked at me and sipped her coffee.

"You tell me what happened with your girlfriend first and then I'll tell you why I care. You're pretty good at avoiding my questions."

She smiled at me. Teeth. But not ugly, not horsey. She was looking better and better to me all the time. Fuck, now I had to be intimate with her. Awkward. So damn awkward I feel scared just trying.

"Well, it's kind of a long story."

"We have nothing but time, Janko. Dr. Malichem is not going to be here for a while. And I'm all ears."

She smiled at me again. Lots of teeth, some gum too. But still not as ugly as I had often thought she was.

"Where to begin. I guess at the beginning."

Just start it already, for fuck's sake.

"Her name was…is Norma Jones. I mean is, because I think she is still alive. Most likely, anyway. But then I haven't seen her in over ten years. I guess she was my high school sweetheart. We met when I was in grade ten, just turned sixteen. Actually it was like, three weeks after my birthday that I met her. I remember that birthday because it was the first one in a long time that I actually got a card from my mother. I thought she had forgotten about me. And there was actually twenty dollars in it. That was the most amount of money I'd ever been given by anyone to just spend how I wanted."

My throat was getting a bit stuck. Something was squeezing it, so I sucked on my cigarette some more to open it up. Then I crumpled the cigarette up in the ashtray. The blue sky looked like a backdrop to a play I had been in once at school. Same kind of baby blue. Peaceful blue, I really like that color.

"That was probably pretty good change back then?"

"Yeah, it was okay. Not a fortune, but it did me all right. I actually hadn't spent it by the time I met Norma. Jesus, I was so fucking scared to ask her out I couldn't believe it. My throat went all dry and my legs were shaking. I had never asked a woman out before and I was shit scared she'd turn me down. I mean, my life has been a marathon of rejection, but you probably know that."

She nodded.

"Anyway, I had this one friend back in high school. My only friend back in high school, I guess. His name was Curtis Peppermans. Anyway, he told me to go for it, so I did. I still remember what I said. I said 'Hi, I'm Janko' and then I froze. I'm still not sure what she said but I think she said something like she knew who I was, but I was waiting to hear something like piss off, you moron. Then she stood looking at me for a while and I was just totally dazed. She eventually had to ask what I wanted and I then asked her if I could buy her a soda or something. She said yes."

I was smiling. It still brought such joy to my heart to think of Norma and how pretty she was and the sound of her voice saying that yes, she'd like to go out with me. I can still hear it as if she was saying it to me now, right next to me. Right here. And I guess she is right here. In my heart, anyway.

Maybe you don't know what I'm talking about. I mean, she was one of the few good things that ever happened to me so I remember that. I cling to that. It's helped me through some hard times. Really hard times. Maybe if you've been blessed with lots of good memories then maybe you don't cling to them, maybe then you can get choosey about which ones you want to hold onto. I wouldn't know about that, though. I cling to every precious memory I've ever had. I guess because there haven't been that many. No not many at all.

"So, tell me about your first date."

I looked at Veronica, I had forgotten about her for a moment.

"Well, on Friday I knew that my foster parents would be out at bingo or boozing it up wasting all the money that they got from the government for us. At that time I was one of three kids they had. All of us orphans and me the oldest. Fuck, that place was awful. I left pretty soon after this date. Anyway, I knew that I didn't have to get home before ten, so I knew I could take her for a soda. We went to this corner store down in Bowness which was close to the high school we both went to. Bowness High. I still remember she had ginger ale and I had a cream soda and we took them to a park close by and sat drinking and swinging on the swings. I could tell you exactly what kind of day it was. It's like it was still yesterday for me."

I stopped then. The memories that came shortly after that were painful. Not immediately, but that was sure as hell where the conversation was heading. I mean we had quite a few more good times together. Some months actually, but then shit happened, again, and I was left alone and abandoned with the same old miserable bullshit to deal with. Only, that's when I went on my own. And that was no better. Not in many ways anyway. I lay back down on the couch. I wanted to keep to the happy memories. I mean can you blame me?

And I was tired, too. So tired. Mostly from all the shit that I've had to deal with. It seems I can't talk about a happy memory without some shit coming up from my past to suck the fucking life out of it. I wonder what it's like to have more happy memories than sad.

Must be fucking great, I reckon. Maybe one day you'll be able to tell me what that's like. Shit, I just remembered, I'd be dead by then.

Don't worry about it. But maybe whisper it out into the air. Maybe it'll be carried to my ears here and I can hear what it's like. Maybe that'll give me some comfort. Tell me. Tell me that the world is a nice place. Tell me that people are good and kind and caring. I'd like that. I'd like to hear that because most of my life, I'm just not believing it.

"Is everything okay, Janko?"

Veronica had come up to check on me.

"Yes. Everything's just fine. Hunky dory."

"Are you sure?"

"Yes, I'm fucking sure. I'm tired and I want to rest, okay?"

I didn't mean to yell. I mean this is part of my problem. Too much fucking anger directed at the wrong people. At least I'm aware of the problem okay? I'm trying. I really am trying, okay? You don't know what it's been like, okay?

"You see, Janko. That's the problem with you, you blow hot and cold. Maybe that's your way of keeping your distance so you don't get hurt anymore. But, you know what. We're all here to the end. All of us. Me, Maria, Salima and Rose we all made a promise to stay with you until the end, okay? So this is not going to work with us. We know you're background. We know and we won't do the same to you that others have done."

I looked at her and she looked right back at me.

"Okay," I said, "I'm sorry. But you don't really know what it does to a person. This shit life that I've had. You couldn't really know."

I turned over and covered myself with the blanket. Fucking IV was getting in the way again.

"No, you're right. We couldn't really know, unless you told us instead of getting all pissed off at us. You don't have much time, Janko, and in spite of yourself we all like you. You're going to have to try and trust us. Especially Dr. Malichem. If there is someone who can help you, then he is the one. You should think about that. You should think about how you want to spend your last days. Do you want to keep stuffing those emotional bags full of garbage or do you want to try and lessen the load. Make the end journey lighter and freer. I'm talking about your soul, Janko. Yes, you've had a tough life. By any standard. But how you end it now is up to you. Don't let those ghosts from your past haunt you into your dusk."

With that she gathered the plates and mugs and went off into the kitchen. I heard her dump my soggy piece of toast into the garbage. She was right. I knew that. I don't need you to tell me, too. But how does a leopard change his spots without becoming a different animal. I need help on that one. That's the key. I need help on that. I closed my eyes to see if Sandman could offer any help. Not that I'd get to sleep, but maybe I could shut my brain up for just a bit. A moment's peace.

XIV

It was a great day. I'd checked in at the office with Bethaney. There weren't any pressing concerns. My morning would be spent with Janko if that is what he wanted. I felt like we could be doing some good work now. We'd laid the foundation. I'd had my "fatherly" talk with him. I think we understood each other. Margaret and I had a very nice amorous evening. We had really connected at a deep level after our little spat at the restaurant. Boy, I loved that woman so much. I'm sure you know what that's like. Nothing in the world like the love of a woman to make a man feel alive. If I was a kid I'd be skipping. As it was, there was a bounce in my step. Not too much, mind you, I was carrying coffees for everyone and I didn't want them to spill. I couldn't stand the coffee Janko had at his apartment, or at least the stuff I had been offered when I was there. I should have bought him a bag of beans. Good dark roasted beans. Maybe next time. In the meantime this coffee would be just right.

I rang the buzzer and was let right up. Right on time, almost to the second. I pride myself in that. It's important I think. It shows respect for other people's time and I know I hate it when people are late with me.

I balanced the tray of three coffees carefully. All black. I couldn't remember how Janko liked his and I didn't know who was working with him today and how they liked theirs. Me, I liked mine black and sweet. I knocked on the door. That common one-four-two wrap that so many people do, and which I only seem to use when I'm in a good mood. I usually do the one-one-one knock. Business like, serious but not depressing. Authoritative. The one-four-two is sprightly, almost cute, but pleasant for the mood I was in.

An odd looking woman answered the door. I immediately thought of a giraffe but, on reflection, maybe horse was more apt.

She was tallish but gawky, somewhat awkward and she wasn't smiling. I did, I gave her a big beam. My mood was expansive, I'm sure you get the picture.

"Dr. Malichem. Michael Malichem. But please, call me Michael or Mike."

I held out my hand and it was tugged at by a warm, floppy fish.

"Hello, doctor, I'm Veronica Drake."

She smiled then. A toothy grin, with too much pink and not enough white.

"Michael…please, call me Michael. Coffee?"

"Oh, yes please. Thank you."

"Anyone," I said to her gesturing my tray towards her keeping my index finger curled around my coffee.

She took the tray and brought it inside with her. I indicated which one was mine. I entered the apartment, took my shoes off, and saw Janko curled up on the couch. He looked asleep but I wasn't sure. I gestured towards him.

"He's just resting, I think. We had a pretty good talk earlier. Emotionally difficult for him, though."

I nodded. We each grabbed our coffees and Veronica splashed some milk and sugar in it after inquiring if I had sweetened them.

"Can we pop outside for a bit?" I asked her.

Just outside the door in the hallway, in hushed voices I asked her how he has been.

"Pretty good, actually. His pain medication is somewhat consistent. He hasn't been asking for that to be increased much at all."

"I meant, actually, his mental outlook."

"Oh, right. Well, he's doing better, I think. In little bits. As I said we had a good talk today about his childhood sweetheart. Norma Jones I think was her name."

Veronica looked up at the ceiling with her fingers on her lower lip. On another woman that would have been endearing, if not cute. But on her it looked awkward. Poor woman. Not her fault, but in a way, I felt sorry for her. I don't know why. So homely I doubted she was married or in a serious relationship. Are the plain people, even the ugly people more lonely? You'd think so.

"Yes, I think it was Norma Jones, indeed."

I couldn't help thinking about the loneliness of being ugly. I don't mean to be critical or nasty. But looking at Veronica, I couldn't help to think that she must be more lonely than I am. Not that I'm a big hunk either. But being average is all about the bell curve isn't it? Lots and lots of others to choose from. Being gorgeous gives you even more people to choose from, but being plain or ugly leaves you at a disadvantage, doesn't it? Could you go so far as saying it was part of the evolutionary process to increase the attractiveness of humanity? I'd say that I married up in the looks scale. Margaret is definitely more attractive than I am handsome. So that probably makes it worse for an ugly woman as opposed to an ugly man. He might have other things going for him. And I'd argue that men are more attracted visually than woman are.

"Doctor...?"

Where was I looking, I think I might have been looking at her chest. Not on purpose, but by accident because I was so deep in thought.

"Yes."

"Norma Jones. That was the name of Janko's girlfriend."

"Right. Thanks. I was just thinking about my high school sweetheart, too. Did you have one?"

This wasn't going to go anywhere.

"Yes. But you were asking me about Janko. Have you read his file?"

"Yes. I mean, yes I was asking you about Janko, but no, I haven't read his file yet. Soon, though. I just like to get a flavour of my clients before being colored by their files. People are so much more than a paper opinion."

"I'd definitely agree with you on that one. Especially, when it comes to Janko. I, we, all think he's pretty special once you get over, under or around his flippant and belligerent persona."

"I think you're right. So, how is his mood, then? Pretty approachable?"

She looked at me as if I hadn't been listening to her at all.

"Your conversation with him about his girlfriend Nora Joe, did it leave him angry, resentful or what?"

"Doctor Malichem, his girlfriend's name is Norma Jones and I think it was difficult for him, but I'm sure he will get over it. I had to give him a bit of a lecture about being so angry and uptight. Which I think he took rather well."

Or pretended to. I found her mannerisms and social skills less than desirable. A bit abrasive actually.

"Please, Veronica, call me Michael."

"Okay."

She had her hands on her hips now like she wanted to give me a lecture or something. That wasn't about to happen.

"Shall we," I said as I ventured back into the apartment past her.

We went back to the table and I grabbed my coffee and Veronica took hers. I took Janko's and placed it on the coffee table. He turned around, then, and looked at me.

"Doctor."

Sounded like a question but I wasn't sure.

"Yes, hi, Janko. I didn't wake you, did I?"

"No, no, I was just resting. Biding my time before you came."

"I got you a decent coffee," I said as I gestured towards the paper cup on the table, "I must confess that I wasn't wild about your coffee the last time I had it."

He smiled and then with some effort pushed himself up to sitting. He rubbed his eyes and looked at the coffee. To me he looked tired. Very tired and weak.

"Does it have sugar in, doctor?"

"No, Janko, I wasn't sure how you liked it. And please, call me Michael."

"V, can I get some sugar?"

Veronica brought the sugar over and Janko dumped a lot of it in his cup.

"How is the coffee?" I asked Veronica.

She smiled at me and nodded.

"A nice change."

"You know, I've actually been wanting to ask you guys to pick me up some decent coffee when you next go shopping for me."

"I'll see what we can do, but you're on a pretty tight budget, Janko. That's the only reason we don't splurge."

"Fuck, man. A dying man can't get a decent cup of coffee because the fucking government is penny pinching."

He was grumpy, obviously, but he seemed to have hardly any fight in him.

"Okay, Janko. I'll do my best," said Veronica.

"I'll make sure you get decent coffee for around here," I said, "as a matter of fact I was going to pick you up some, but forgot in my rush to get here."

"Thanks, doc."

"Michael please, Janko, Michael. It'll make our sessions a lot easier."

I liked the good doctor. Now he was earning my trust. And he was going to get me some good coffee, though the nurses had been getting good coffee for me regularly. Not sure what Veronica's problem with good coffee is. V sat on the opposite side of Mike. She took my other granny chair. At least it looked like a real "granny" chair. I don't know what it is really called, but you probably have a pretty good idea of it anyway. The good doctor was sitting in my real granny chair with the crocheted blanket on it. I liked him in that chair; it made me feel more at ease. But I'll tell you one thing. I'm not gonna be saying shit to the good doctor if Veronica thinks she can take part in the inquisition, that's for sure.

I lit a cigarette again. Stop counting, okay, I'm dying anyway as I keep telling you. Besides, a cigarette and a cup of coffee are like bread and jam, just made to go together.

"Thanks for the coffee, doc."

"You're welcome, Jank."

What the hell was that about? He shouldn't be so particular about his bloody name.

"I'll try, Michael, it's just that it sounds weird."

"You'll get used to it."

He was looking around my place, like it was the first time he had been here. Cradling his coffee like it was some precious baby in his arms.

"Veronica, would you mind giving Janko and me about a half hour alone to chat. The library's not far."

"Sure. I have some errands to run, anyway."

"Is that okay, Janko?" the good doctor asked.

I nodded at him. Moron, it was more than okay, it was the only fucking way he was going to get anything out of me. I sipped my coffee. Damn, it was so nice to have a cup of coffee shop coffee. He was trying to butter me up I'm sure. And it'll work, too.

Veronica got up and left quietly through the front door. She didn't seem upset, and maybe she could've been. I mean, I had kind of opened up to her a little before the doctor came. But that was just chitchat. The doctor is business and he's also the professional. It's different. I stared at my coffee table and my coffee. The doctor got up and walked over to the sliding doors.

"This is a pretty nice place you have here, Janko. Kind of reminds me of the first bachelor pad I had. I like the view too. Bowness road always has something going on. How long have you been here?"

"I don't know. A few years, I guess."

He did have a nice place. And it was kept pretty clean thanks to us taxpayers. Which is only fair, really. It is probably costing us less keeping him in his own place than in a hospice or certainly a hospital. Besides, I think people do better in the comfort of their own homes amongst family and friends. That's probably why hospices have become so popular, give the dying a down home comfy feel to the experience, or more importantly, give the spouses and family a break from having to clean up after the dying. And there's a lot of clean up involved with that. You'd be surprised, horribly surprised.

"You know, Janko, I love this time of year. Cold outside and yet so crisp and fresh and so blue and sunny. This place is always so sunny in the winter. I love that."

I turned around to face him. He was slumped over his cup of coffee sipping it every once in a while. Smoking his cigarette every once in a while. The smoke was like a tendril snaking up to the ceiling. Kind of like a vine. I don't see what people get out of smoking. Some people, though, are just self-destructive perhaps.

"Yeah, the sun is nice. Makes the cold more bearable, although I'd like the warmth a lot more. I feel too cold too often now as my life leaks away."

"Have you ever thought about quitting smoking, Janko?"

"Fuck, doctor, will no one give me a fucking break about smoking? I mean what is the God damn point. I'm dying already. Probably will be dead before spring and everyone's gotta give me gears about smoking. Jesus Christ."

I came and sat down again. I leaned in towards him resting my forearms on my elbows. He was looking at me, then at his cup, then at his cigarette, then outside and then back at me.

"Have you thought about quitting cursing, too, Janko?"

He didn't say anything. He looked at me. Leaned back on the couch, inhaled some smoke, tossed his head on the back of the couch and exhaled towards the ceiling.

"Before you get all upset, just listen to me, okay. I believe that your smoking is intertwined with some of the difficulties, emotional difficulties, that you no doubt experienced as a child and which continue to bear prickly, thorny fruit for you now. It is a method of beating yourself up. And yes, I know that you might be addicted now, but the mind and the will are more powerful than any addiction. I've seen that first hand. But people continue to abuse themselves, of which smoking is one form, because they do not love themselves holistically. They are still carrying the barbs and slings of what others have launched against them, or what life has dealt them."

"I don't think I quite understand what you are saying, doc. I mean, Michael."

"Okay. Let's say that as a child you are made to feel worthless, if you allow yourself to carry that with you into adulthood you might take on habits that help to fulfil that belief. I'd suggest that smoking is a way of making yourself feel worthless. It's a reminder of how people made you feel and how you continue to let them have that hold on you. As long as we continue to berate ourselves over what others have said, we will continue to give them more power over us than they deserve."

Wow, I was off and running. I should probably pace myself a bit better.

"So, are you telling me, Michael, that I'm smoking because I hate myself?"

He was still talking to the ceiling, his hand with the cigarette hanging limply in his lap. The veins in his forearm looked like surgical tubing. One had broken out and was the IV, or so it looked.

"Well, those are strong words, Janko. Only you know how you feel about yourself. But I'd hazard a guess that you smoke because you've come to value yourself poorly."

Now he looked at me and brought his chin onto his chest. He let out a big sigh.

The good doctor might be on to something. But Jesus Christ, if he doesn't come shooting out the gates so quick.

"Okay, Michael. I'll give you that. But that's no fucking secret, okay. I mean you only deal with the shit of humanity, the people who've been kicked to the curb in one way or another. It's not rocket science."

He was looking intently at me. I put my cigarette down on the ashtray and lay back on the couch. It was more comfortable that way, once I'd gotten the fucking IV unstuck from under me. That fucking thing drives me nuts. It is such an obvious eye sore of my predicament. I can't stand it. But yet, it does offer me the release from the pain.

"What about the cursing, Janko? Would you think that you use that as a way to distance yourself from people?"

"Probably."

"Yes, I'd think so, too. Why don't you try for just the remainder of this session to not curse, okay?"

"Sure, I can try. Might get pretty quiet in here."

"That's okay, I can talk the tail off a donkey."

I looked at the doctor and reached for my cigarette. He was still leaning in at me. I spluttered a cough on the inhalation of smoke.

"Are you okay, Janko?"

I nodded at him through my spasm. Fuck, my side hurt. Right by my ribs. The doctor got up and got me a tissue. I spat up some blood on it. Foamy, red blood. Yuck.

"I've heard that you won't take any medicine for your symptoms, Janko. Are you sure about that?"

"Yes, I'm sure, okay. I don't need you and my family doctor busting my balls about that, okay. I take pain medication and that's enough. I wish I didn't have to, okay. This might be the end of my life, but it is about the only time I've felt alive. I wish I could manage feeling the pain, okay. I've never felt so alive as I do now, when I can feel my suffering, my pain. Do you have any idea, doctor, how it is? How it is to live locked up in yourself because of the shit...stuff that you've had to endure as a child just to make it from week to week? Do you have any idea how many times people have either wished I was dead or threatened to kill me? It's been lots, okay. Tons. Can you imagine how deeply you hide inside the shell of who you are?

It's so deep and dark in there, you have no idea. But it's better than anything else. You numb yourself, you become a machine so no one can hurt you. You don't feel anything except the physical pain…and that is so horrible you wish you could escape it, but it's the only pain you can't. And you don't have any friends because you're so numb you can't relate to anyone. And you don't want to, you don't want to have to be able to relate because you don't have any space left in your life, in your heart, in your soul. You can't afford to open up a small part of your spirit to be trashed again, okay. That would kill you. As it is, you feel like a walking zombie, okay. But that's all you can manage. So allow me a little breathing room if I want to feel myself die, okay. I've never had so much pain, so much heartache, so much soul sadness in my life. It's all brimming up to the surface and cascading over now. And it feels great in a way, okay. It's hard for sure, but I feel alive like I've never felt alive before, and that's why I've asked for you. I need you to help me manage it. Manage these feelings, this pain, this sorrow that are my constant companions, okay. I want to live if I'm going to die soon. I have barely any life left, and yet I am desperate to live it. Even if it is the hardest part of my life I'm having to live. Can you understand that, Michael? I'm dying and I'm suffering and I'm bleeding and I'm wounded emotionally, spiritually, physically, but I'm alive God damn it, and I want to die at least having lived at the end, okay? Having tasted just a small bit of life. Even if it is only the bitterest dregs. And maybe, maybe if I'm lucky and you can help, if you're as good as they say, then maybe I might taste a hint of happiness. That's my gamble, Michael. I'm throwing it all on this last roll. I want to feel the pain, because by feeling the physical pain I'm getting in touch with the other pain too. It's hard and I'm tempted to take medication. I'm tempted every fuc..frigging day to take my own life, okay. It takes all I've got to get up in the fucking morning, sorry, and just have to live. But there is sweetness in it. A bitter sweetness, but the taste of real life like I've never had before. Can you understand what I'm saying, doc, Michael? Can you help me?"

I turned my head towards the ceiling and started to cry. I was sad. I was sad and also relieved. Unloading like that was such a huge step for me. Maybe to you it's nothing, but to me it was huge, okay? And I wasn't sure how the good doctor would take it.

I needed, like, a mentor or a father right now. Not a professional, clinical asshole. But the tears burned hot on my cheeks and the one track of tears slipped into the corner of my mouth and it tasted salty. Tears taste like blood, I don't know if you've ever noticed. All pain is just varieties of the same flavor.

Boy, I didn't know what to say. I was stunned, for sure. This monologue of Janko's took me by surprise. I'm doing my best to get him to open up, but I wasn't expecting such a huge and quick closing of the chasm between us. This is huge. Even though he hasn't gone into details about his difficulties, he's opening the door a crack and letting me see inside. Just a bit, just a little bit, but I'm very encouraged. The pain is written all over his face. His tears and his eyes are filled with pain. But it's good, because he will get to taste the sweet bits of life, if only momentarily. As the cliché goes, there is always sunshine after rain, joy after the pain. Poor boy, desperately poor boy but he's so brave.

"Janko. I won't say another word about your medication unless you discuss it with me."

I got up and went over to sit on the edge of the couch. I took his veiny arm in mine and patted his hand. It was very strange how paternal I felt towards him. I'm usually more clinically predisposed, but I sensed that he needed something more. A friend, God forbid, maybe even a big brother or father figure.

"You're right, Janko, it is good to feel the pain. Forgive me, I just feel that you've had more than your share and I feel somewhat protective of you. It is a professional indiscretion. But you're right. Feel the pain, because I'm sure you'll taste happiness soon."

He looked at me and smiled. I got up and got him some tissues from the bathroom. I also brought him a glass of water.

"Michael, could you open the balcony doors please. I feel hot all of a sudden."

I opened the doors and inhaled the crisp, cool air. The sky was clear, sunny and baby blue. Across the road I could see a few house sparrows flittering from limb to limb in a big bare tree. Large patches of white snow covered the ground and I felt good. I turned to Janko and smiled at him.

"Yes, Janko, we will do good work. I will help you peel back the layers of pain to the sweet kernel that is under there. You'll see, I'm sure, by the time we are done that life is good and your natural state is a happy one."

He looked at me through tear stained eyes. Blood shot, misty eyes. Deep wells of sorrow. I really get energized when I see such progress. Don't misunderstand me. I'm desperately sorry for his pain, his sorrow. But I'm looking into the future and seeing him overcome that. He's going to get to a peaceful place before he dies. That really fires me up. This is what I live for. This is where I feel my calling, where I feel at the peak of my talents and skills as a psychiatrist.

"You've made a huge leap of faith here, Janko. I don't know if you really know that, yet. But what you've done by accessing this pain of yours, by just opening up a little bit to me, is a huge step. I know you were probably scared to try at first. But it's not that bad though, is it?"

He shook his head, grabbed a tissue and blew his nose.

"We need some practice on the cursing, but that's really the easy part."

I smiled at him.

"Shit, doctor, I'm sorry about that."

He laughed at me. Generously. I went back to the balcony doors and closed them again and then sat down across from him.

"I could use another good coffee I think, Janko. How about you?"

"For sure, Michael. But I don't think we have any. Should have asked V to get some while she was out."

"You're right. But I'll bring some good stuff next time. That way I can be certain you'll be looking forward to seeing me. How about some tea?"

"No, thanks doc, I'm kind of tired. I just want to sit and chill."

"Okay, I'm going to get myself some tea, though. And share a little about myself with you."

I got up and went to the kitchen and rummaged through the cupboards. I found some green tea which was a pleasant surprise. I put the kettle on.

"Do you want anything while I'm up, Janko?"

"No, thanks."

"Well, I'll start from the beginning. I was born in Dundurn, Saskatchewan. I'm not sure if you're familiar with it, but they have this provincial park just about next door called Blackstrap Provincial Park which is named, I guess, after Blackstrap Lake. They have this mountain there too; well actually it is a hill called Mount Blackstrap which I understand is manmade. I spent a lot of time there in the summers in my youth. It was a wonderful lake. Pretty warm in the summer, considering. And the sky, big blue sky like it is out there right now. I could lose myself in that park for whole days at a time. Have you ever been to Saskatchewan, Janko?"

The kettle boiled and I poured some water in my mug and went out to the living room, again. I sat back in the chair and blew the steam away from the rim. Janko was lying like a corpse on the couch. His hands flopped into each other over his waist. He was looking at the ceiling.

"You know, it's funny you say that, Michael. I was actually born in Dundurn, well actually Saskatoon, but my mother was from Dundurn and I went back there after I was born."

"That is very interesting."

Janko closed his eyes. He looked ashen and sick. And yes I know he's sick, but sometimes he looks sicker than he is. Or maybe I forget that he's sick and perhaps sometimes this comes as a reminder. Nevertheless, sick is how he looked now. I sipped my tea, it was too damn hot. I blew at it some more.

"Doc, I'm gonna try and take a rest if you don't mind. I don't mean to be rude, but I just feel so tired. You can go on talking if you'd like, and I'll try and listen."

He looked at me and smiled. Then turned his head to the ceiling and closed his eyes. It didn't take long before his jaw slackened and he was breathing slowly, deeply on his way to deep sleep. He looked more like a corpse then, than he had before. Some people think that sleeping people look so peaceful and charming. Maybe babies, infants and children. But certainly not dying adults. They look like they slip into the grave every time they fall asleep. It's not peaceful at all. I sometimes wonder if the grim reaper doesn't cover them with his cloak as they drift off to never, never land.

XV

After the good doctor had gone I lay down for some more sleep. I was more comfortable in my bed and I also needed to go and relieve myself. The coffee had worked its way through me. I sure hope he keeps his promise of bringing some good coffee with him next time. Veronica had obviously returned. Not that I couldn't be on my own. I wasn't sure if I'd know when I was about to die. Sometimes people say they know when they're going to die. I certainly didn't have that sense. I could've been left alone the whole day and I wouldn't have keeled over, if I was to go by gut feelings or premonitions. But then I don't feel so certain about my death radar. I mean I might be a deatherer, but I don't think I'm really on my own schedule. I get a sense that something or someone else is really in charge. And besides, I don't think the good doctor was going to let me go to sleep without someone close by. But I mean, come on, if I'm going to die then I'm going to die whether someone is here or not. The only difference is they might find me quicker. But I'm liable to die quietly, anyway. At least I hope so, just kind of fall asleep. That's my goal anyway.

So, anyway. I went to sleep and had one of the most relaxing and peaceful sleeps I can remember. Although I woke up to a pretty weird dream. I'm kinda embarrassed to talk to you about it. I was young I guess, around eight or nine years old and I was in diapers like I was a baby or something and I was being rocked by an older man. I was sucking on a pacifier and it tasted like pink cough syrup. Horrible.

He must have been eighty or ninety, or so he seemed, but he was much healthier than that. Anyway he was sitting on a swing and cradling me in his arms and rocking me at the same time. The swing was on a beach and this old man was singing "Have no fear for daddy's here", over and over.

133

Now I've never met my father, but the funny thing was this guy reminded me of the good doctor although it couldn't have been him because he didn't look like Michael at all and this guy in my dream was older. Anyway, I felt sort of scared by this guy but not enough to do anything about it. And all the time he is singing this lullaby to me the tide is creeping up until we are drowning in the ocean but he's still singing to me and I'm hearing him as if we were on dry land, and I'm not really scared any more than I was before we were drowning. Well, that's when I woke up. But I felt relaxed and peaceful. Maybe from the sleep and not so much from the dream. It was just sort of weird, that's all. Weird, and I'm not sure why I'm telling you this all. The dream doesn't seem to have any relevance on anything, except maybe it means I'm getting comfortable with the good doctor. Which I am, but it also seems that maybe I don't trust him that much which could be, too. I mean, I've opened up to him a bit, but I guess I don't feel fully comfortable with him yet, either. Anyway, it's just a stupid dream and probably doesn't mean shit. Oops, am I going to be able to swear again? The doctor has got me thinking about that now, too, fucking guy, swearing is like a habit for me now. He can't be allowed to ruing everything can he? Anyway if Michael's into dream interpretation like Jung he might find it interesting. I wonder if I should tell him?

Okay, so you're probably wondering where I'm going with this rambling. Nowhere really, just got off on a tangent, hope you'll allow me the courtesy. But when I woke up and lifted my woolly head off the pillow I thought I saw an apparition. I don't know if you've ever been in that state where you're just waking up and you feel totally awake but at the same time you're seeing things. Well I saw my friend Peter staring at me from the end of the bed. At first I didn't recognize him, but after blinking a couple of times I realised it was him for sure.

"Hi, friend," he said.

I nodded, still groggy from sleep. Don't get me wrong I was happy to see him, but my friends just keep showing up whenever they feel like without giving me any notice. It gets tiresome after a while. I'm sure you wouldn't want to be having your friends just show up at your place whenever they wanted. Or worse yet, just peer at you from the end of the bed as you lie sleeping and then you find them like that when you wake up. It's a little unnerving, okay?

"You've been out cold for a while."

"Uh huh," a long pause, "I take good sleep whenever I can get it, Peter. How long have you been watching over me?"

"I don't know, maybe about an hour. Did you know you snore sometimes, too, and you mumble in your sleep as well?"

"I do not."

Peter was dressed in new jeans that looked like they were old. I didn't get that kind of fashion, and he had on a red t-shirt with dark blue trim around the collar and the end of the sleeves. He must have been cold outside.

"Weren't you cold outside Peter?"

"No, my sweater's over there on the chair. It's hot as hell in here, Janko, I took it off. Besides, it's not that cold outside. Warmer than it looks, actually."

I saw his sweater on the chair. My room was a pigsty. I needed to get it cleaned. Maria was good at that; I'd have to wait until she was on shift.

"Did Veronica say anything to you when you came in?"

"Are you kidding me, J. I snuck in so quietly she wouldn't have noticed me; she was in the kitchen doing something when I snuck past. But you guys shouldn't be keeping the door unlocked; you never know who could get in."

"Yeah, like you."

I smiled at him and he smiled back. He thrust his hands in his pockets and turned around to look out the window. I closed my eyes and looked at the inside of my eyelids. Dark red. Very dark red. I wonder if that is what death is like. Eternal dark red darkness. Death as staring eternally at the insides of your eyes. Kind of macabre but interesting, nonetheless, don't you think?

I stopped that because I was beginning to feel claustrophobic behind my eyes. Trapped in my own body and feeling claustrophobic, now that's fucked up. Anyway, I poured myself some water from the jug on my bedside table. I don't remember it being there, but I love it when things are just within arm's reach. These nurses are awesome. Mostly on top of everything. Maria especially, although Veronica probably placed this jug of water on my bedside table. Serendipity, even the sound of that word sounds sweet and syrupy. That's what I think it is having things just in the right place or happen just when you want them to, or need them to. Like the stars being aligned.

Peter mumbled something to the window but I couldn't hear him.
"What's that, Peter?"
Repeated mumble.
"Sorry, Peter, I can't hear you."
"I said I'm sad, Janko. I'm very sad."
He still wasn't looking at me. Looking far outside into the distance, maybe at the mountains. I think you might just be able to see them from my window on a clear day. His hands were stuffed deeply into his pockets. He was toying with some change in his left pocket. I could hear it tinkling like bells.

"Why are you sad, Peter? I'm not, I'm happy you've come to see me, even if it is unnerving waking up to you staring at me. You know that freaks me out."

He turned then to look at me and he had lines of tears streaking from each eye. They sparkled like zirconia. Not diamonds, well maybe diamonds, it's just that I've never had the chance of actually seeing real diamonds, but I have cubic zirconias and they sparkle pretty good. Actually bought my girlfriend, Norma Jones, a cubic zirconia ring once. Had to save my money for like three months before I had enough. Which is kind of weird considering that's how much a diamond is supposed to cost you, isn't it? Three month's salary?

"Come on, now, Peter, why are you sad, my friend? Would you prefer I cursed and argued with you like last time?"

I smiled at him but he wasn't in the mood. He looked at me with those sad eyes and then looked down at his feet and a wave of anguish gushed shakily out of him and he cried openly. All of a sudden I felt very sad, too. His sadness was affecting me deeply. My oldest friend who had been a rock for me. My hope and guardian angel, was now as fragile as an autumn leaf. I felt hopeless. Hopeless and fucking sad. I'm in no shape to be anyone's rock. If anything, I need my closest friends to be my rocks and support. Shit, I'd already had to deal with Norman and, in a way, MJ, although she had held it together better.

"My guardian angel, don't let me down now. Peter, tell me why you're so sad. You're making me sad, and I was happy to see you until just a few minutes ago."

He walked off into the bathroom rubbing his eyes on his shoulders. He blew his nose and then came back out.

"You're dying, J, and it's killing me."

He went and sat on the chair. First time I've seen him sit for quite a while.

"We're all dying, Peter. We're all dying."

"Come on, Janko, that's idiotic. Of course we're all dying, but look at you. You're what, thirty-three? Jesus, you shouldn't be dying at thirty-three. I mean after all we've been through these twenty odd years. It's just not fair. It's just not right."

He sighed and dabbed his eyes with the front of his shirt. He looked at the floor for something. Maybe inspiration, maybe something else to think about. Hell, maybe even a spider.

"Yeah, I know, Peter. It's kind of funny though, both you and Norman, and even MJ, are all more ripped up about my dying than I am. Maybe I just want to die, you know the kind of life I've had to live, Peter. It hasn't been an easy one. It's been hard, fucking hard really. You know that, I mean you've helped me through most of it. I mean you guys have been like family to me, you were my family really. I never had a real family Peter. No family really, except for the Antolinis and that was short lived. I mean, for God's sake, I hardly knew my mother and I've never known my father."

He looked at me through his bloodshot eyes and sighed again. Then he came over to the bed and sat down beside me. He rubbed my forearm through the blanket.

"Do you really want to die, Janko? I mean I know your life has been hard. God knows I wouldn't have been able to cope with what you've had to put up with. But has it been so bad that you really want to die. What about tomorrow?"

I looked at him. He meant well, but he just didn't have a fucking clue. Maybe you don't either, though I'd like to think that if you've come this far with me you've got an inkling, a hint of where I'm coming from by now.

"Yes, Peter, sometimes I'd like this game to be over. Sometimes I feel like the brunt of some sick, fucking joke, okay. I'm sorry, but that's how it feels sometimes. And as for the tomorrows, well they've been just like the todays lately, okay. A life of pain and misery and having to try and rehash the painful past. I sometimes wonder what kind of help that is going to give me, I just don't know, Peter, I just don't know."

I sighed myself and then looked down at my lap. Yeah, sure, I'd had a good session with the doctor but that's exactly what I'm talking about. It's hard having to open up like that and confess my sins. The sins that have been put upon me by others. I'm not as brave as I think I am sometimes. I get scared having to look back at my troubles. I thought I'd escaped once before.

"How can I help, J?"

He held my hand through the blanket. I felt warm, but unsafe, if that makes any sense. I could hear Veronica in the kitchen rattling at pans or pots or something. Maybe she was making lunch. I couldn't smell anything yet, but I could hear water running in the sink, too.

"Be brave for me, Peter. I get scared sometimes, trying to dig away at the dark pile of my history. It's lonely work and it's scary work, and I'm scared, Peter. I feel like that little boy who was eight years old and beat on and cursed at and belittled. It's hard Peter, you know, you were there for me for most of it. I still don't know how people can do that shit to a little boy. I couldn't hurt anyone. I was small then, okay. Weak and vulnerable, and impressionable. All I wanted was love, that's all children want isn't it, love and a safe place called home? I had neither of those. Why would people do that to me, Peter? Why would they do that to anyone?"

I was crying again. Hot tears on my cheeks, my throat thick and burning. When will the pain end? Will it end before I die? God I hope so, I need something to help lift me up. Maybe this is just the storm before the calm. Is it? You who have lived a life and felt love, will it come to me? Will there be a few happy days before the end?

"It's okay, Janko. I'll be brave for you. It'll be all right, I know I can be brave for you. Don't cry, please. I don't want to see you sad. You've had it so hard all these years, now is the time to put that all behind you. But maybe you need to explore it one last time with the doctor. You aren't that small child anymore. You are a grown man and they can't get you anymore. You can climb this mountain with my help and MJ's help and Norman's help and the doctor's too."

He was hugging me tight to his chest. He was rocking me gently and my tears were melting on his shoulder. My eyes were stinging and my nose was blocked and mucousy and my throat was a hot pipe.

"You are braver than you think you are, J. What you've been through would have destroyed many other people, but you're still here and you're fighting. Through the pain and the sadness and the grief you are still fighting it out. By yourself, too. Even though we're here to support you, you are still fighting it out by yourself. You're the most courageous person I know, J. I'm sorry, I will be brave for you. But I love you and it's hard for me, too. But I'll say no more of my sadness, I'll be here for you. Don't be sad anymore, my J, don't cry anymore."

His kind words just made the tears flow more. But after a short while I had done enough crying and I hugged him. It's amazing how tiring being sad can be. And yet it seems like so many people are way too sad all the time. I don't get it. Maybe they have the right to be like me? I think I've earned the right to be a little sad, if you don't mind. But maybe some people just like being sad. It sort of gives them direction in life. Something to do. But probably their sadness is not a deep well, maybe just a mild disappointment in something gone wrong. Maybe they've never really fallen into that deep well of sorrow that drowns so many men. And women too, you probably know what I mean. I'm just tired of having to be politically correct, okay. Jesus Christ, can't we just say what we mean and be understood for it? Anyway, it's the fucking posers that get to me. The people who mope around but aren't really sad. Just because things don't go your way doesn't give you the right to be sad. You have to earn that honestly. I mean, I've been happy with very little. But I guess when you don't have much you get excited by very little. A bowl of soup can make you very happy when you've had nothing to eat for days. Trust me on that. But I don't get these people who aren't happy with caviar. When cordon bleu is passé, and a sirloin tip is so yesterday. Cry me a fucking river. These kinds of people haven't earned the right to bitch and moan and mope around so sad like their lives have been hell. I'll tell you about hell if you bear with me long enough. Anyway, enough said. I'm sorry, okay, I go off on a tangent sometimes. I hope you understand. I'm trying, I really am trying, okay?

I leaned back on my bed. My life is so fucking tiring sometimes. This emotional roller coaster. I used to think I was doing pretty good. My life was going well when I wasn't sick. I had a shitty job sure, but it was a job anyway and it paid the bills and I had a roof over my head and food in my belly and cigarettes in my pocket. Okay, maybe I wasn't happy, but I was getting by.

Isn't that the best we can hope for? Maybe not for you who have so much. Maybe if I'd had a different life like yours I might be happy or expect a contented existence. But I can't speak about that because I don't know about it. Maybe you can tell me one day if it's true. Maybe I'm being unkind to you. I'm sorry if you're offended, but I've only known a shitty life, okay? So maybe I think that some people are luckier than I am. Maybe I'm jealous of you, if that's the case. But for Christ's sake, you've gotta give me a fucking bone. I mean humor me a bit, okay. I'm no threat to you; I'm just trying to make sense of my life. Anyway, maybe my life was going just hunky dory until I got my sickness. What I'm saying is that I was getting by. Not sad, not happy just goldilocks okay. Just getting by like most people. Sure I was just doing time but it was so much more sweetly mundane than this shit. I mean look at me. I'm a wreck, an emotional wreck. Forget about the physical disaster my body has become, my mind is a train wreck and my emotions are a roller coaster ride, okay. There's something to be said for the mundane. I mean especially now when I don't really think I'm getting ahead. I sit around moping and then weeping and then getting pissed off and then getting scared. I mean Jesus, if only I was getting ahead in some way, but I'm not and I'd rather have my old boring, soul numbing life back compared to this. Okay, maybe I won't say that later, but for now. Fuck, for now, just give it to me back or take me away somewhere where everything's forgotten. Where only bubbles break, not bones. Where only roses are red and not skin. So tired, so very tired I am of life. This life that I've so often thought is hell. Maybe another planet's hell. Have you ever thought about that? Maybe we fucked up somewhere before and now we are in hell, and with karma we'll keep coming back because it isn't gonna change. I think about that sometimes. About how this could be hell. This planet Earth that sometimes intoxicates us with its beauty is only a hell for some other place. You know, like me and you, we've done some bad shit somewhere and now we're paying for it. At least I feel that way. If I had a million dollars and a gorgeous wife and a big house with a white picket fence and a bouncing happy kid on each knee, make it a daughter and a son and a totally hard body, then yeah, I might be thinking I'm in heaven. But that ain't me. That's not my story, if I can go on for a bit about my life. Please bear with me, I'm trying to make it through to the other side, and with your help, your interest, feigned or sincere, I hope I'll make it. Don't judge me too hard, please, okay? These are just my rants, my ravings. Call me a madman if you like but stay with me, please. Okay? And probably that thought is the only thing that keeps me alive, sometimes. That maybe this could be hell and if so, then where do you go? Hell's hell? That scares the living shit out of me sometimes if I think about it too hard. So I try not to, and maybe that is why I'm hanging on so hard to this fraying filament of my life. I'm scared and I'm sad and I'm lonely and all I want is love.

Peter went off to the bathroom to blow his nose or something. I looked up and out into the big world. A cold world today, but with a baby blue face. Veronica walked in.

"Everything okay, Janko?"

She looked at me again down her nose with her hands on her hips, elbows as arrows pointing in opposite direction. No clue where to go. I looked at her and nodded.

"It's just that you sounded upset. Were you crying? Are you sure you're okay?"

I saw Peter skulking in the bathroom just off to the side, not wanting to get caught like he was playing hooky from school or something. Which we did a lot of, him and I.

"Thanks ,V. I just don't want to talk about it, okay?"

She looked at me and smiled her gummy smile. Looking at this woman, so socially inept but trying her best, makes me feel good about myself, sometimes.

"Okay…I'm making some nice lentil soup for lunch. It'll be ready in just a few minutes. How many slices of toast would you like with it?"

"Just one, thanks."

And then she smiled again, trying her best to make me feel good and turned away and walked out.

Peter came back grinning.

"She scares me in some ways, J. She reminds me of that awful teacher you had in grade six. Ms. Nisliski or something?"

"Yeah, I remember her. Hadn't thought of her until now. She was crazy, looking down at us all the time from her reading glasses, and her mouth pulled back exposing her horsy teeth. Do you know, Peter, she used to talk to herself sometimes. I caught her once."

"Oh, yeah? What was she talking about?"

"Couldn't tell. It was more mumbling than anything else."

He went and sat down on the chair at the end of my bed.

"She's not all that bad really."

"Who?"

"Veronica. The nurse who just came in. She's not really all that bad. I was trying to talk to her earlier, and she's not that bad, really. I mean if you look at her, just her physical appearance you can probably get a sense of the tough life she's had."

"Yeah, I suppose," he said nodding but looking at the floor.

"What's on your mind?"

Peter looked up at me, his hands fiddling fingers in his lap.

"Not much. Just wondering how long we might have together. It's been a long time that we've had our friendship, and yet I feel desperate now that the time is coming to an end. Do you know what I mean?"

"Yes, I do. I was thinking of that myself. I have such a sense of urgency to finish up this unfinished business of my life."

He smiled. A sad smile, but sweet. He was holding himself together.

"We've been through so much all these years, I'm hopeful I guess, that we can come through this together."

"Yeah, Peter, me too. I've had some really good heart to heart talks with my friends. You and MJ and Norman. Especially Norman, if you can believe that. I saw a side of him I haven't seen before. He was genuinely concerned and saddened because I am dying, after we got his temper and shit out of the way."

Peter shook his head and frowned. He was looking at his hand.

"I don't know, Janko. I mean, are you sure. You know what Norman is like, I mean, sure I know he is your friend, but he's also been an asshole all these years and I just don't know if that can change overnight."

"I think he has. Maybe not changed totally, but come to an understanding that I'm not going to be like him, as hard as he might come down on me. I think he understands that now. I mean, if you put yourself in his shoes, he was really the only one who tried to physically protect me, to stand up for me against all who bullied me back then. And in a way I'm still being bullied by all those people. Look at me, Peter, I'm scared to go forward and yet I can't die being stuck in this muck.

Anyway, I think he's starting to see that there is no point left now for him to berate me even if he means well by it, because I've got so little time left, anyway. If you can believe it, he was actually crying when he finally told me how he felt.

142

I was very moved, Peter, he reminded me a lot of you at that moment. I really think he is changing or trying his best, anyway. Besides, Peter, you of all people know that I've never had many friends except for the three of you mostly, and I could use all the friends I can get right now. I need all of you. You, Peter, my compassionate friend. MJ, the girlfriend I never had but wish I did, and Norman my rock. You guys have been, and are, all so valuable to me. Can you understand that Peter?"

"If you say so, J. If you say so."

Veronica walked in and stood at the doorway. Peter looked at her but she just ignored him.

"Lunch is ready, Janko."

"Thanks, V, can I have it here please? I'm tired and in no mood to get up out of bed."

"Sure."

And she strutted out. I could smell the lentils. It smelt good and I felt hungry, but God knows how much I'll be able to eat.

"Do you want some, Peter? I can ask Veronica to bring some extra for you."

"No, I'm okay."

He was looking outside into the blue sky. From where he was sitting I don't think he could see much else other than the sky, maybe the tops of some buildings. He looked kind of blue.

"You ok, Pete?"

He looked at me and then at his lap. His one leg was swinging over the other. The foot a see-saw on the fulcrum of his knee.

"Yeah, I'm okay. I'm just worried about you and Norman, that's all. Maybe we'll all be able to get together and I'll see for myself how he's changed. It's just that I'm not so sure he was ever very good for you, Janko."

"I can understand that. I mean, maybe he's been my most dysfunctional friend. But still, he has been a friend I've needed at times and that I've leaned on. Or maybe, Peter, maybe he's needed me more than I've needed him. I mean that could be, right?"

"Yeah, I think that is probably closer to the truth...But do you really need him, now?"

Veronica came in with the lentil soup and a slice of toast buttered pale yellow on its face. The soup was muddy brown but smelled really good. She placed it on my lap. There was a glass of water on the tray too.

"Thanks, V."

"You're welcome. Just call me if you need anything, okay?"

I nodded and smiled at her. The soup was steaming but I slurped a little spoonful into my mouth.

"It's really good, Peter. Are you sure you don't want any?"

"Yeah, I'm fine thanks. But, what do you think about Norman?"

"I'm thinking, Peter. Yeah, maybe he does need me more than I need him. But I feel like I need you all with me now at this crucial time of mine. I'm totally scared and then I'm angry and then I'm lonely. It's shitty Peter and I just think that all three of you are crucial for me to get over this. And to be honest with you, I feel a certain sense of obligation to all of you. I mean, all of you guys have been there for me and the least I can do is be there for you guys at the end."

I had some more of my soup and took a bite of my toast. It tasted good, at least what I could taste, anyway.

"So, maybe, actually we need each other the same now. I just don't want to die alone, Peter. I just don't want to die without being loved. Like, really loved."

A fucking tear dropped into my soup. I reached over to the bedside table and grabbed a tissue. Peter got up of the chair and came and sat next to me careful not to spill my tray. He gave me a hug.

"I don't want you to die alone either, J. I love you. Don't you know that I love you?"

I looked at him through my blurry eyes. Yeah, he was a good friend. A really good friend.

"I know, Peter. I know you love me, but that's not what I mean. I need to be loved by the doctor or my nurses, someone who doesn't know me or who hasn't been in my life like you guys have been. Can you understand that?"

He nodded, leaned back and put his hand on my knee. Veronica came in.

"Janko, are you sure you are okay? You're crying…is the soup not that good?"

I laughed.

"The soup's good, thanks. I'm just a fucking mess, Veronica. I mean, look at me. My body is unrecognisable to myself and my emotional and mental states are chaotic."

I was crying again. Dabbing at my eyes as I went.

"I mean, right now I'm scared to death…excuse the pun. I'm just scared of dying, but this life isn't worth living, either. Maybe this is what purgatory is all about? I don't know how much you know about me, Veronica, but I haven't had a good life or an easy life. Most people I've known have been mean to me. Especially the people who should have known better. I've never known real love other than once from my only girlfriend, Norma Jean, but that didn't last, and maybe a lot of it was my fault, I just don't know, anymore. I just don't know what the meaning of all of this is. I'm lost, so, so lost and I don't know how to find my way."

Veronica came and sat on the bed and held my hand. That didn't help the tears go away.

"I want to be loved, V. I want to know that maybe life is good, that it can be good, that people are kind and caring. I've never really known that and all I want now is to experience maybe a few weeks of love. To taste how it could have been before it's too late. And I don't mean in a sexual way either. I don't mean sex, I mean an authentic love. Being valued and cared for because of who you are, your faults and all. And I know I have plenty."

"I don't think she's gonna say it, Janko," said Peter.

I looked at Peter. Veronica ignored him, but I knew what he was thinking and no, I wasn't expecting her to gush about loving me. Sometimes he doesn't get it, either.

"Well, Janko, a lot of us nurses have chosen to be here taking care of you. Mostly because of what we read about you in your file. Yes, you've been through a lot in your short life, but we all seemed to sense a kernel of goodness about you that we hope to help you make shine. And with you telling me this, that is a huge step. It can't be easy for you to open up like this with me. With anyone, for that matter. We do care for you and we want to help hold you up. Hold you up to the light so that you can see yourself as you are, a child of God and one deserving love and care and compassion. But you have to help people to learn to love you, to care for you. And I think you do that by opening up to them and allowing them to get near to you. Yes, you take a risk by doing that, and by all accounts you haven't had the right people up until now to help you with this journey. This is what we are all hoping we can help you do. Especially, Dr. Malichem, he is really good, Janko, and he'll help you with that, too. Don't be sad, because I am encouraged by your openness to me, now. This is really a big step, an important step in healing, Janko. It truly is."

She got up then and rubbed my shoulder.

"Now, finish up your lunch. You need your strength."

I nodded and picked up a spoonful of soup as she walked out the room.

"She's not as cute as the other one, is she?" said Peter.

I ate my soup.

"You know, Janko, I'm getting tired of being ignored by these nurses. She's the second one to ignore me."

"Well, you can't blame them, Peter. I mean you ignore them too and they're really here for me and not for you."

He looked outside again, frowning a little.

"And another thing, Peter, they're not here just to fucking please you. I mean why is it that every woman that has come into my life you look at like a piece of meat? It's all about their cuteness to you or their physical attraction. You know what, Peter, that's lame. It really is fucking lame and it would sure help if you could stop that, okay? You talk about trying to help me, well that is one way that you can, okay? I don't need that kind of distraction. I need to start valuing people for who they are. I mean, Jesus Christ, that has been my own burden all these years. People haven't allowed me to be myself and to blossom and become who maybe I am."

I ate more of my soup. Peter looked at me half amazed and somewhat dazzled.

"Who pissed in your soup?"

"Nobody. I just don't need that shit anymore, Peter. Come on, maybe when we were fifteen or sixteen it was cute and even macho. But come on, we're in our thirties now, surely we should be doing better than that. Surely there are things more valuable in people then their physical attraction. I mean look at me for God's sake. Not that I was ever a model, but lately I look like death warmed over. And you stick around me despite it all, so I know there is that goodness in you, otherwise you probably would have ditched me long ago. It must be hard to see me disintegrating in a very morbid way, and I respect you for being there for me. Let's extend that goodness. Let's milk it for what it's worth."

My soup was getting cold, I was acting cold and I didn't mean to. It was feeling frigid in my damn apartment and I was tired. I wonder if all this laborious work is going to be worth it.

"Point taken, Janko. Point taken."

We sat in silence for a while. Not mad at each other, but contemplative. Exhausted perhaps from the emotional rawness of my life.

XVI

Margaret was pouring me a glass of Chilean Merlot. Dark red like clotting blood. I love this wine. I was smiling all over her. She looked at me out of the corner of her eye and smiled at me back. Man, I was feeling fantastic. This first real connection with Janko had me terribly pleased.

"Cheers my love," I said to her as we clinked glasses.

"To me and to you, honey. Boy, you are in a really super mood tonight. Looks like you caught a mouse."

I laughed.

"I guess you could say that. Actually I had the first really terrific session with Janko. You remember him? That young lad who is dying from AIDS? Anyway, he has been exceptionally difficult to deal with. Very uptight and brash and aggressive and belligerent. Well, for the first time I was actually able to get him to access his pain in an ever so small way. But it was important. Crucial really, because I don't know how much time we have and I have a sense of urgency in trying to help him, to get him to a place of peace and understanding and forgiveness."

Margaret was scraping scrambled eggs onto buttered toast. We were eating a light repast. Margaret wasn't interested in cooking up a big meal, and tonight was her night for cooking so I wasn't about to complain. I just needed my wine and I was happy.

"That's great, honey. Anything you want to talk about?"

I took our plates to the kitchen table and set them down. Margaret came and sat next to me.

"Thanks for dinner, love…well with Janko, he was just able to access some painful memories that's all. He cried a bit, and I think that was hard for him to do. He started off brash like he usually does, but when I sent the nurse out he opened up a bit."

I took some hot sauce and poured it onto the eggs. They were well cooked, I didn't like them runny. Too close to nature. The spicy, vinegary smell of the sauce wafted up and nipped my nose.

"You know something very interesting, though? I was talking to Janko about where I was born and raised in Dundurn. Turns out that he was born there too. Well actually in Saskatoon but lived in Dundurn for a short while. I figure it must have been shortly after I left that he was born there. Quite neat, I mean when you consider that Dundurn is so small."

"And do you think that means anything?"

"Well no, not really. Coincidental but still sort of fortuitous and, if anything, a good omen that we have something in common. Common ground, if you'll excuse the pun that we share. I think it might just help bond us a little quicker. Or at least get him to feel more comfortable with me, rather sooner than later."

Margaret was picking at her food. Taking a bite here and a bite there. She smiled at me and looked at her glass. The wine swirling in it.

"I've got him trying to stop swearing. That might be one of our biggest struggles. He curses a lot, really quite a lot. Mostly because I think he uses it is a mechanism to distance himself emotionally from people. Quite an effective technique too, at least for outsiders. But I'm onto him and I think it will help him to gaze deeper into his soul."

"Do you really think it'll make a difference? I mean God, I deal with splitting the meanings of words into infinitesimal bits. I sometimes think it is just posturing, just a game. Sometimes it works to get my clients off, sometimes prosecution splits it better than I and they get jailed. But, Jesus Mike, it's just a game. I sometimes wonder what I'm doing practicing law like this. Really, it is so silly, what is the benefit? Where is the better social good, if it is about the wrapping rather than the substance? I just don't know, anymore. So confusing. Anyway, I just don't know that language really is that powerful. It's just fluff to cover up our bullshit, our insecurities. That's what I think sometimes."

She had a sip of her wine. Picked at the egg on her toast with her fork. She looked sad. Her eyes were deep and troubled. I didn't know where this had come from. I gulped the rest of my wine and filled up both our glasses. I think I need help with this one. My tongue immediately felt looser.

"Are you okay, love? Tell me about your day."

I looked at her. She looked back at me and smiled sadly.

"I had a tough day, Mike. A really tough day."

"What happened?"

I went back to my eggs and toast. The hot sauce was hot. Too hot, I had been too generous to myself. I drank deeply from my wine.

"I don't know. I just don't know anymore if the law is any good. At least I feel like I'm losing focus on why I started practicing law. I look at you honey and I see that you are so passionate about what you do. You genuinely care and you seem to make such a difference in people's lives. That's what I wanted to do with the law, but it just doesn't seem so anymore..."

She drifted off. She drank some wine, gazed at the glass, her fingers and thumb twirling it around, the wine catching the light and sparkling like rubies.

"Was there anything specific today that happened. Anything that you can put your finger on as to why you feel this way now. You usually enjoy the law, love, I don't often hear you this upset with it."

She looked at me and smiled, but her eyes didn't.

"Well I've been working on this horrible case. We've been working on trying to defend this man who killed his wife and two small children. He almost killed the wife's new boyfriend too. He seemed so evil, I mean, he knew what he was doing. It had been planned. He had been abusive to his wife when they were still together and that was why she left. It had become awful. You have no idea, Mike, torturous really and belittling too. It makes me sick to even think about it now. I mean, the small little kids, Mike. They were only four and six years old. Can you imagine the evilness in this man's heart, the cruelty required to do something like that? This is what I mean about the law. What is the good that can come from defending the most despicable human behaviors? At least you are lifting people out of that, moving them to a place of peace and fulfilment."

"Tell me what happened with this guy. Did he get off?"

She looked at me and furrowed her brow.

"Yes, he most certainly did get off. Have you even been listening to me, Michael?"

I didn't go near that one. Margaret sipped more of her wine. I filled up our glasses again, this time emptying the bottle. We both needed help.

"Yes, love, I can understand how difficult that would be to see a guilty man get off," I said.

"Not just a guilty man but a despicable human being. What am I doing Mike? What am I doing with the law if this is what my career has amounted to? I used to believe that everyone deserved a fair trial, to be judged based solely on the facts. I believed that justice was blind. That only the guilty would be jailed and the innocent set free. Now it doesn't look so easy anymore. This vile man got off because of a technicality. And we all know he is guilty. God, honey, he even knows he's as guilty as sin. What good will come of this? Now that this man is roaming the streets freely. He could easily find another wife or girlfriend or, God forbid, have kids and do this again. What's to stop that?"

This is what I loved about her. Her sense of justice, but it gets so frustrating for her sometimes. And I can see how easily it could too.

"I guess there is nothing to stop this man from remarrying or finding a new girlfriend or even from starting a new family. But you did your best. You chose the work you do love. Is it not better for a hundred guilty men to go free than for an innocent man to be thrown into jail? I think you might have said that to me once."

"Yeah, but I don't know if I believe it anymore. In theory it sounds wonderful but the practice of it is making me weary. Where is the accountability, honey?"

"There is the ultimate accountability from which none of us can escape. I truly believe that he will be called to the bar and made to answer for his choices. As we all will. I am convinced of that. I'm sure the repercussions for his choices will be severe and swift. I know mine have been."

"But how can you know that, honey. I mean really, how can we be so sure? I mean it sounds fine in principle, but it seems like just another platitude."

"Well love, just look around you. Look at how nature operates. As you sow, so you reap. Remember in the summer we planted some green beans and we cared for them and tended to their needs and each bean grew us a hundred more. The same can be said for the weeds and the thistles. If we hadn't carefully pulled the weeds out, and been vigilant over our little garden plot, those weeds would have been just as prolific as the beans, eventually outstripping them and choking them out. You could use that vegetable plot as an allegory for our lives. If we don't tend to the beans and carefully eradicate the weeds, the plot and hence our lives will become overcome with weeds and bear few useful fruit.

We are daily making choices, my love, that are bearing fruit for us in the future. The choices we make will determine the fruit we dine on in the years to come. This man is arguably sowing the seeds of bitter fruit. His future will not be one of sweet feasting. You my love are working with the law in an authentic and compassionate way. Just because you are defending people like this, does not make you kin to people like that. I think you could be well advised not to forget that you came to practice this area of law because you had and still have a keen sense of justice. The system needs to work properly and how can it do that if you or others like you won't defend the worst of humanity. Never lose your sense of justice and integrity, love. I know how hard it can be to see evil set free. But it is never set free from the shackles of universal and infinitely encompassing justice."

I got up and grabbed our dishes and took them to the sink. On my way there I kissed Margaret on the head. I know how hard it can be for someone like her to live in such a fallible world like this. Her sense of integrity and compassion and justice is part of what made me so attracted to her. Lots of people are attracted to her for that. There is no bullshit with Margaret, and I think people like that. But it can be scary at times because she calls you to account to be better than you are, and sometimes that is hard. The hard way is often not the first path that people wish to take.

"It's not easy for you to live in this world, sometimes. I know that, love. But never give up on yourself, okay?" I was talking to her as I washed the dishes. She came and leaned against the kitchen counter, twirling her wine, deep in thought.

"Yes, it is hard, Mike. Sometimes I wonder if it is worth it. Why don't I just take the easy path like everyone else does? Maybe I should go into corporate law and make twice as much as I am now? Maybe I'll feel better about everything because at least I'll be living a selfish and abundant life."

I had to laugh, I couldn't help myself.

"Oh honey. You have to be kidding me. I don't think you'd last a month in a corporate law firm. You know you wouldn't. Besides, the extra money isn't going to contribute to a much better lifestyle for us now. I think we do pretty well at the moment, actually."

I thought I caught a small smirk as I glanced at her. I finished washing up and took off the yellow latex gloves all bearded with white soapy water. I went up to her and embraced her.

"I love you. I love you especially because of your sense of justice and your integrity. When I'm with you, honey, I want to be a better person. You help me reach beyond myself just by being you. And I know it is true with all of your friends. You have a natural way of helping people be more than they are. Please, don't lose that. It is a gift my love, a divine gift bestowed only on the chosen few."

I squeezed her tight.

"Why don't you come to the living room with me for a kiss and a cuddle? And I can tell you all about my problems...at least my hopeful problems. I could use your advice on my newest client, Janko. I want to get a sense from you if you think I'm being too emotional and not rational enough. Hey, let's even put on the fire and open up another bottle of wine."

I pushed away to face her and winked at her. I held out my hand, she took it and I led her to the living room, though I had the bedroom on my mind.

"I don't think I need any more wine, honey. I've still got half a glass and it's making me sleepy."

"Oh no, I was hoping I might be able to take advantage of you if I got you drunk enough."

"You know you don't have to get me drunk to take advantage of me, Mike. When it comes to me, you've always had the advantage."

I turned on the fireplace and then sat close to her. I put my arm around her neck and stared at the fire.

"I'm wondering if I'm seeing clearly, or should I say professionally, when it comes to Janko. I just don't know. I feel this tenderness, this compassion, toward him that I can't quite explain. Maybe because of his fragility and frailty. It could be that I feel this way because of the short time I know we have together. I can't recall many other patients that I've had where we knowingly didn't have much time for all the work that needed to be done. I'm just not sure, and I want to be sure, because for him especially I want to be the best I can to encourage his growth in the short time we have together."

The fire was licking itself. Flickering up the flue. Mesmerizing me.

"Maybe you see him as the son you never had and maybe would have wanted."

Margaret was also looking at the fire, entranced by it.

"I don't know. I haven't wanted to have a child for a long time now. And so many of my clients are too much like children. The constant care and attention they need. Their egos and spoiled dispositions. So, maybe he does remind me of a son I would have wanted a long time ago, but I don't know, Marg. I mean he is gravely ill in both body and mind. I don't think he'd be the kind of icon I'd be looking for when considering a son I would have wanted."

I leaned over and kissed her on the cheek. I was warm and getting sleepy. The wine was only encouraging it.

"Perhaps. Or maybe there is something about his frailty that is bringing out your most compassionate self. Could be that maybe you two have known each other before in a different time, in a different existence. Maybe in many ways he represents a part of yourself that you had to struggle with. Maybe you see yourself in him as he struggles with his own demons. Could it be that you recognize that struggle as one you went through with your own demons? Your own struggles."

I sipped some wine. Margaret mirrored me. I was feeling anaesthetised by the heat and the alcohol. I couldn't get my eyes away from the fire. I felt helpless in a way.

"You mean my own mental illness, my schizophrenia?"

"Yes."

"Well, I've dealt with that a long time ago. I barely think about it anymore except now and then when I'm taking my medication. And besides, probably seventy, maybe seventy-five percent of my clients are schizophrenic to some degree. It is fairly common, as you know."

Margaret nodded her head and sipped some more wine. I mirrored her this time and looked back at the fire. The wine was warm and I was feeling thirsty. Really thirsty. I got some water for both of us from the kitchen.

"I'm just trying to offer some different opinions."

"I know, honey, I'm just trying to figure it out with you, that's all," I said.

"I think I have a good one here. Seriously. Could it be that like us, Janko has had some real struggles in life. Not just his mental illness, whatever that may be. Not just his physical disease, either. I'm talking more about his life. The theme of his life from what I've gathered from you, love, is one of hardship.

You and I have both had to work hard to get where we are. We weren't born with a silver spoon in our mouths, and I bet Janko wasn't either. I'd argue, and I'm pretty certain that you would agree with me, that if you haven't had any real struggles then how can you intimately appreciate the difficulties that others have had to face. I know many of my colleagues, for example, don't cast their minds to the issues of homelessness or of poverty or of famine, because it is so foreign for them. This is not to say that you have to have starved or lived on the streets to appreciate the difficulties of the homeless or the hungry. But I do think that if you have been handed everything then it skews your perspective. Hardship is an excellent and honest teacher, isn't it, Mike. Maybe that is why we have chosen our fields, because we know what hardship can be like, and we wish to help ease that burden for others."

She is a really smart woman. And she makes perfect sense. I kissed her fully on the lips.

"I think you are probably right, honey, many of my clients have lived soft lives, if I can put it that way. They haven't known hardship. But then not everyone who has known the value of work or of suffering or of hardship has been softened by it. Some of them have become downright miserable."

"That's true, Mike. But those people whom life has softened are the beautiful, the tragic people. It is in those people that we can recognize our souls, our own vulnerabilities and helplessness. Those weathered spirits who have been tossed about on the stormy waters of life, who have been bruised but not broken; they are the ones that show us how to be our best, who call us to our best and highest states of being. Janko does it for you, I'm sure…"

"And you do it for me, too…"

"And I'm not saying that people who have lived charmed lives are mean or cruel. They are, most times, decent and nice people. But they don't have the same insight. They don't have the same breadth and depth of soul, or well of sadness from which to share in the sorrows of humanity."

She stopped suddenly and drank more of her wine. She looked at the fire and her face glowed in its yellow hue.

"You are an angel, honey. No wonder I have loved you all these years. Will you come upstairs with me and send me to heaven?"

I winked at her and squeezed her shoulder. She turned to me and smiled.

"Heaven is waiting for you, bad boy."

And we went upstairs.

XVII

I woke up in a terror. I seem to be having obscure dreams again about the good doctor, and for some reason I find them frightening. I looked at my bedside clock and it was all threes. Red, bloody threes. My age as a multiple of ten. Whatever, I was wide awake and trying to digest my nightmare, though you might not think it is a nightmare, it still left me with the same feeling.

Outside it was a dark, passionate purple. The kind of purple that you might see on a priest's robe if it's dark in the church, around lent. The sky was dropping cold dandruff on the scalp of the earth. That's what it looked like to me, anyway. Basically it was snowing again, big fluffy bits of snow that feel like dog's tongues, if you've ever had them land on you. That's the kind of snow I loved as a kid, still love. You can build the best forts and snowmen with it. And you can have wicked snowball fights with that kind of snow. I remember one time getting into a snowball fight with these bigger kids from school. Well, actually they were bullies. It was me against them. It started off friendly enough, except they kept laughing as they threw the snowballs at me. It was kind of weird, but they kept missing and I kept dodging. Except this one big snowball, probably the size of a softball, hit me above my left eyebrow. Those fuckers, sorry, I'm trying not to swear too much. Maybe you can help me with that, kind of point it out so I'll be more in control the next time I see the doctor. So anyway, this snowball hit me right above the eye and it split my eyebrow open. Those bastards had put a stone in the middle of it. I ran home crying, I was only about nine or ten, okay.

That was when I was living with the Antolinis. She cleaned up the wound and he drove me to the Children's Hospital and I had five stitches to close it up. It was over an inch long.

I think it was the amount of blood that scared me the most. That and also my feelings. I was really hurt that they would do that to me. It was yet another example of people treating me meanly, this time by relative strangers. What I remember the most about that incident though, is something nice. Mrs. Antolini walked to the corner store while mister and I were gone to the hospital. When I came back she had some liquorice for me, and a chocolate bar. It was a Snickers, I think. Well, that was one of the few tender moments I can remember from my life. Can you imagine that, a life of thirty-three years and I can only remember a few tender moments? Can you understand that? You probably have a tender moment every day, maybe at least once a week, or if you're desperately unlucky maybe at least once a month. I'm sorry to be dumping on you, but I guess if you've come this far with me then you're used to it. Maybe even immune, though I think my doses have been greater than therapeutic. I know I should be saving this for the good doctor, and he'll get his share for sure. It's just that I'm awake now, and I'm lying here a little scared and I need to vent. I need to get this shit off my chest. Give me a little leeway, have some patience. And thank you for that, I know that if you're this far in you've had some patience, haven't you?

Anyway, I see I'm getting ahead of myself; I want to tell you about my nightmare before it fades. Does that happen to you? Dreams seem so vivid until you try and recall them or until some time goes by and you start to forget them. That happens to me quite a bit. Mostly it's good, like now when I've had crappy dreams. But sometimes it's bad, like, if I've had a good dream. You know, something sexual. Because, God knows, I've only known that a few times in my life and how sweet it was. Yes, indeed, how sweet it was.

Fuck, sorry, I'm getting lost. My dream, I'm going to tell you about my nightmare, dream, whatever. You decide.

I was maybe around five or six. Yeah, probably. That was the time I first really started thinking about why I didn't have a dad. I mean, I didn't have a mother really either, but at least I'd known her briefly. Shit, it was at about that time that she left me to the state.

What I'm saying is that I really was around five or six when I started thinking about why I didn't have a dad. I was the only kid in my class who didn't know his dad.

Sure there were other kids whose parents had split up, and there were kids who hadn't seen their dads in months, but I was the only one who didn't actually know his father. Anyway, I was also around five or six in this dream of mine. I was called to the principal's office, and I hadn't even done anything wrong. In my dream it was like I was walking on a horizontal escalator, except I was walking against it and it was taking me forever to get to her office. I still remember her name. It was Mrs. Lipchuk, back then most of the elementary schools had female principles. She was awesome, really treated me nicely, maybe because she knew the shit that was my life. Sorry, I'm swearing again, I know, but I'm really trying to stop, okay. Really, I am.

Well, I finally got to her office and she invited me in and closed the door behind me. It was a huge room, at least it seemed very big. And it wasn't as I had remembered it in real life. It was more like the boardroom of an office building. There was a whole bank of windows on one side and her large desk, a glass desk, spread from one side of the office to the other. Two chairs faced her desk with a coffee table in between them. But on the coffee table was a potted plant. It was a bean vine because I could see the bean pods hanging off from the stalk here and there. This plant had me mesmerized as I kept watching it. It wasn't attached to anything, but was growing up straight and thin by itself and moving like a snake. It had this leaf at the very top and it kept turning around and peering down like it was looking at me. So weird I know, but it's a dream okay. So, because this plant was growing up from this pot on this coffee table, you couldn't put anything else on the table at all. Not even a small coffee cup would fit on the table. So Mrs. Lipchuk asks me to sit down across from her. This huge desk, at least that's how it feels. So I sit down and I can barely see over her desk to see her. She's leaning her elbows on the table and looking at me with real kindness in her eyes, and the strangest thing is that she is my mother. I mean she is the principal and all, but she looks like how I remember my mother looking, and she is acting like my mother used to act. So frigging strange, because she isn't being very motherly to me. She's being nice for sure, but not as nice as your mother would.

I keep looking up at this plant which keeps growing up and is soon touching the ceiling and then spreading tendrils out across the ceiling. All this time the plant keeps looking down at me. Well, not really looking because it doesn't have any eyes, but you get what I mean.

I'm intrigued by this whole thing, but not freaked out. I feel a little like Alice in Wonderland. Not that I knew about that story when I was five or six, but now I'm interpreting my dream through my adult mind.

"I've got really terrific news for you, young man."

This is Mrs. Lipchuk talking to me now. My mother if you can believe it, but all of this shit...um stuff is not weird to me in my dream.

I'm not really looking at her; I'm watching this vine and wondering why it keeps looking at me. I know you're thinking this is some freaky Jack and the Beanstalk motif, and I get that, and I want to start climbing up it, except as I say, it is so thin and that leaf is staring at me menacingly, if you know what I mean.

"Janko...Janko, I have really good news for you."

I steal myself away from the plant and I look at my principal. She's still looking at me from across this glass ocean of a table. Her elbows and forearms stretched out in front of her like pink peninsulas.

"Your father's coming to get you. Isn't that exciting?"

I'm looking back at the vine and the leaf is shaking from side to side at me like it's telling me no. Answering Mrs. Lipchuk's question. Now I start getting scared, and I can't tell you why. I mean, I know I've never known my father, so this should really be excellent news. But I have a sense of foreboding about this for some reason and I guess it's mostly because that fuc...that plant is shaking its leaf at me.

"Janko...Janko, look at me...That's better. Well isn't that good news about your daddy?"

I shake my head at her but I don't say a word. I'm back looking at the vine and it's growing down the walls now and all over the ceiling. Soon pods of beans start falling from it. It is like it's raining bean pods, but they fall slowly like snow. But I think they look more like big fat worms. And the funny thing is they fall totally straight. I mean not moving or wavering at all, and I don't know about you, but I'd expect them to move a little, maybe whirl even or something. But they don't, they fall perfectly straight and slow.

And it's raining thickly with these bean pods, and that one damn leaf keeps looking at me. And as thick as the bean pods are falling none are touching me and it's like they melt into the floor because there isn't a single one on the floor.

Mrs. Lipchuk is oblivious to this, or she can't see it or something. She's still looking at me and talking and asking me if this is great news. I'm still looking up at this plant, this vine and shaking my head. But now it looks like I'm shaking my head at the beanstalk, at this leaf that keeps looking at me, because I have this sense of foreboding about this whole event. It is so bizarre, but scary now, too.

"Your daddy's coming, your daddy's coming, isn't that great?"

This is Mrs. Lipchuk breaking into song now and doing a dance on the other end of the table, holding onto two shoots of the vine. She's kicking her legs up and out to the side like a Vegas show girl. Singing and singing that bloody line over and over again. Now I'm looking at her with shock and awe, and as she's kicking her legs out she's kicking bean pods all over the room but they're still going super slow.

This is where the dream gets really weird. I mean I know it's been weird already, but now it gets weird in a kinda real way. This vine starts changing into a man in a grey suit, the same guy on either side of Mrs. Lipchuk, each one holding one of her hands. And these guys are smiling so nicely at her as they become human from this plant.

By now the vine has disappeared. It's finished raining bean pods and the guy on the right of Mrs. Lipchuk has vanished into thin air, leaving only his twin. He's still grinning at her like he's besotted with her and she's looking at me.

"Janko," she says, "say hello to your father."

She turns to him and curtseys and he bows and turns to me.

"Hello, son," he says with this big stupid grin on his face, "remember me?"

And guess who it is? It's the frigging good doctor. Yup, Dr. Malichem. But in my dream it didn't seem weird, but natural. Only, I didn't want him to be my father, I didn't like him. And I was getting up to leave and he stretched out his arm and grabbed me, like the vine was doing earlier towards the ceiling. He pulls me into him and starts hugging me hard and I melt into him and become him. Then I'm looking at Mrs. Lipchuk and thinking sexual things and getting an erection when I wake up. No happy ending for me.

I don't know why I'm telling you this. I should really be keeping it for the good doctor. But he's not here, you are, and I guess by now I feel comfortable telling you this stuff.

It just helps to get it off my chest, you know. Is that okay? I guess so, especially since you've been with me for so long already.

You know what is unusual about this whole thing. In my dream I wasn't happy to have the doctor as my father and then I became him. And I have no idea what that shit, sorry, stuff is all about. But anyway, I've been thinking about the doctor and I figure he must be a pretty good dad. I mean, he has put up with a lot of my shit and that's probably a lot. If I was to be a kid again, I guess I could do worse than having a father like him. Compared to the kind of "fathers" I've had, he'd be really great. Anyway, I have no idea what it might mean. Could be nothing or maybe it suggests some deep seated paranoia I have with Dr. Malichem. Yeah, I like that one.

Well, I'm not going to bore you to death, anymore. It's dark outside still and the streets are quiet. I can hear the pipes creaking as they heat up my apartment. I'm warm, but my bladder is bursting and it's just after four. I feel sick to my stomach too, it's probably the morphine. It happens that way sometimes. And, God, I'm so tired, I need to try and get some decent rest. I'm going to get out of this warm bed and go to the washroom. I want some peace, okay. I need some help and some peace. At least none of my friends are here to bug me. A night of solitude and I can't frigging sleep.

XVIII

Someone was tugging me. Maybe like a child would tug at you, only they were pulling my vein out of my fucking arm…sorry, I'm just waking up and I've got this weird sensation of someone pulling on my veins. I opened my eyes slowly. It wasn't sore, just damn annoying.

Well, there wasn't anybody there, just the frigging IV taut against my forearm and the bed sheets. A rubbery noose stretched around my arm. I freed it with my other hand and got up onto my elbows to see what was going on. I mean, now I was awake. It was light out and I could hear the pleasant sounds of someone in the kitchen. I could smell coffee and hear the lulling of a soft voice singing, "I am, I said". It had to be Rose, she was often singing and had a pretty good voice with it too.

My blinds were open and the sky was blue and deep and seemed to go on forever. I couldn't see a cloud from this corner of my room. My elbows got weak and I flopped back onto the bed. I'm so damn weak nowadays it drives me fucking nuts. I'm sorry, okay, it's just that sometimes there isn't anything like a good swear to get your meaning across. I mean, you can probably feel it, right? Instead of all this bullshit frigging and sugar shit. You couldn't take me seriously with that, could you? Hell, I couldn't take myself seriously talking like that. But I will try with the good doctor. I really will.

I closed my eyes again because I felt pretty tired and I wanted to see if I could get some more sleep. I couldn't, but I could hear Rose Diamond in the background crooning to herself. Or to me, though I doubt it, I think she was trying to keep it down, but the rhythm of her voice was a gentle breeze keeping me awake. And besides, she had a nice voice.

I lay down in bed on my pillow, my head a large egg in its nest. You'll forgive me I'm sure, but you've got to have fun with thoughts sometimes when that is all you have.

I was staring at the stippled ceiling, seeing all manner of shapes in it. There were faces, lots of different faces. Lots of ugly, devilish faces, but a few fat and cherubic faces that I was trying to concentrate on. But my focus was on Rose's voice. I liked Neil Diamond and I liked "I am, I said", you probably can figure out that it reminds me a lot of my own life. Maybe everybody's lives in some way, that's probably what has made it popular.

I was hoping to see the good doctor again today, and I think it was today he was scheduled, although I didn't have a fucking clue what day it was. Not important to me anyway. I'd only been given a couple of months, and how depressing would it be to be counting them down. Maybe I should be marking them off on the flesh of my forearm. But why, I'm trying to move on here in a positive way, not count down the days to my death. And okay, I know I've wanted to die soon enough at points. You've come this far, you've heard me bitching about wanting to get it over with, but in cheery moods like this I can focus on the work at hand, at the work that the good doctor and I need to do. And come on, give me a break, I am doing good work, you've got to hand me some credit, right? I think maybe even in this short time you've got to recognize the strides I've been taking. I mean shit, it hasn't been easy, you know. Gentle reader, if you've come this far you know it's been a struggle and hard work for both you and me. Not to say it's gonna get easier necessarily, but I'm more open to working with Michael. We're building a rapport, wouldn't you agree?

I mean, I don't really want to go into lurid details about my abusive past. Frankly I don't want to relive that crap, and I'm sure it'll disturb you. Fuck, it'll likely disturb me, too. But bear with me, I might have to, for the good doctor's sake if he thinks he needs the specifics in order to help me heal. I'm hoping that won't be the case, but just be prepared, I'm trying to prepare myself, too. Shit, this stuff is getting depressing, isn't it?

I reached for a smoke from the table. I pushed it between my lips and lit a match to it. I love that first inhalation of a freshly lit cigarette, that's also when it smells its best too, in my opinion. I coughed though, a phlegmy, bloody cough that I swallowed back down. Sorry, okay, I'm sorry, but I didn't feel like getting out of bed just to spit a bit of phlegm in the toilet. The way I'm wasting away I need to hold onto every last bit of myself I can. Really.

Then I started having a fucking coughing spasm. Jesus, can I not enjoy a good cigarette. I mean, come on, I'm dying anyway, let me enjoy my last few vices.

"Everything okay, Janko?" said Rose. She had popped her head in the doorway.

"No," I said between spasms of hacking, "I need some water."

She came back with it pretty quickly, too, and I gulped a couple of large sips from it. Immediately I felt a lot better. Shit, if only everything was that easy. I tugged on my cigarette again and this time it went down a lot smoother. Thank God for American tobacco.

"I'm going to put some coffee on to start, Janko. Dr. Malichem brought some of the good stuff in, I see. Let's try it. Also, would you like some toast or cereal or oatmeal?"

"Just a slice of toast with jam, please."

I had to smile at Rose's comment about the good coffee from the good doctor. He had promised to bring some in. I'm glad he did. But to me, I don't have the luxury of waiting on good coffee. It's all good when you can probably count the number of cups you'll have left in this lifetime. Give me Arabica or give me bat shit, I'll take it all, so long as it is sweet and milky.

I lay in bed some more, the day getting brighter outside. Not a lot just a little more clearly bright. A more transparent, hotter brightness, if you know what the fuck I'm trying to say. Sometimes I don't, but I'm trying my best to explain it. I blew smoke rings at the gnarly faces on the stippled ceiling pretending they were Star Trek phasers that were annihilating them. The sweet faces I pretended were being smothered with smoky, heart shaped kisses.

I thought about that, I mean why is it the heart that hurts when you feel emotional pain. I mean it does really, doesn't it? I get that tight, leaning weight right over my heart, my chest, just bearing down on my poor vulnerable heart. It hurts like hell, I'm sure you'll agree. I've felt a lot of that in my life. But I've also felt the odd joyous happiness. And I guess, in all fairness, that makes your whole body feel light, your heart is a buoyant balloon, isn't it? I'd like to do away with all the shitty emotions. The sadness and sorrow and hatred.

Get rid of that whole bunch of them and give me peace and joy, happiness and love. That's what I'd like. Impossible, you say, well probably, but let a dying man enjoy his momentary madness. His happy hallucinations. I know that without sorrow you can't experience joy etcetera, etcetera, but it'd be nice just to try wouldn't it? At least I'd be up for the challenge. I'd like to try more happiness, more joy. You would, too, if you'd had the buckets of shit I've had to deal with, okay? You would, too.

"The coffee is ready, Janko. Would you like me to bring it in here for you or are you going to come out and socialize with me a little bit. It's getting boring having to sing to myself."

"Nah, I'll come out and socialize. Besides it's better to people watch from the living room. More traffic going along Bowness Road. Hey, is Michael coming in today, or am I ahead of myself."

I looked at her while blowing smoke rings like halos around her head. She was smiling at me. Her black hair a short waterfall over her head, frozen over her collarbones.

"Yes, he'll be here today. Probably in only a couple of hours," she said looking at her watch.

"Do you want me to help you out of bed, Janko?"

She had come over to me, ready to get her hand under my arm.

"Sure, thanks. Could you get me my bathrobe first, please?"

She got it from the chair that had carried the weight of Norman on many occasions. It looked like a sad chair, oppressed. I felt empathy for it. I got up onto the edge of the bed, the smoke dangling from my lips like it used to for Humphrey Bogart. Only he never looked as crappy as I. He had a good, full head of hair to start with. I've got the cool, modern, escaped convict look that's so popular with the kids today. Rose helped me into my robe. It was soft, I think it was a nice fleece robe or something. I didn't have my right hand in it obviously, because the damn IV would then be sticking up out my neck, tugging on my wrist. No, thanks. Though I have taken the IV container off the trolley and held onto it as I've put my arm in. But I was too lazy for that right now. And besides, I wasn't that cold anyway. Sometimes I've detached the rubber from it, but you've first got to clamp it by the bag and then wait until it's dripped through, but it works.

I hobbled into the living room with Rose hanging onto my left arm. I wasn't sure if she was helping or hindering, but I was too weak to care. The smoke from my cigarette snaked and trailed behind me as if I was really boogying, but I wasn't. It also sometimes got into my nose and eyes and seared them with its acridity. I fucking hated that from cigarettes. That was my one pet peeve. I almost felt like spitting the damn thing out on the carpet, but I didn't of course.

I was sucking in lungfuls of air when I got to the couch. I took the cigarette out and rested it on the ashtray. I flopped onto the couch an exhausted man. Exhausted from just a dozen steps. Can you imagine that? A dozen steps finish me off. A thirty something young man. That is not fair, gentle reader. Not fucking fair at all. I took a moment and lay there, my chest heaving. After a while I reached for my cigarette, you can't smoke when you're dying for air. And oxymoron, I know, but it's true. Those of you who share this filthy habit with me know what I'm talking about. The last thing you want, the last thing you can enjoy is sucking on tobacco smoke when you're really craving air. It'd be like drinking a shot of whiskey when you're parched and thirsty as hell. The only thing that'll do it for you would be sweet aqua. A nice tall frosty pint of Adam's ale.

"Here you go, Janko. Sugar, milk and a nice mug of hot coffee. Good stuff, I might add."

Rose was smiling at the tray as she put my coffee and stuff down. I peered into the milk jug. It looked like it was half and half. At my stage of the game, I'm enjoying it all. To hell with low fat, no fat, full fat or any other kind of dietary restrictions. I'm going for it all. Might as well enjoy it while you can I figure. You would too, I know you would. You know coffee tastes better with cream than it does with skim, with two spoons of sugar rather than one. Well it does to me, so here's to me.

"Thanks, Rose. Where's yours?"

"In the kitchen. I'll go and fetch it."

Coffee and cigarettes, nothing better I can think of to start a day. A day that could be one of my last. But good reader, I'm sure you don't want to be reminded of my demise. Might hit too close to home, hey? I mean, we are all dying, but how many of us are really living. I didn't make that up. Although I wish I would have, at least I could be remembered for some pearl of wisdom.

The guy who came up with that probably will be remembered for that. But I wonder if he was dying when he said that, or was he just contemplative. Or maybe he had just had an orgasm with his partner and was lying there on his back smoking a cigarette getting all mentally creative in the afterglow of sex. Indulge me, please, okay, I mean a guy's gotta wish. I know I couldn't perform if it came down to it, but I can sure wish and wonder, can't I? You won't deny me just a few pleasurable thoughts. That'd be cruel. Fuck, it is cruel even thinking about it. Who am I kidding? I've only felt that kind of tenderness or love just a few times in my long life. Becoming one with a woman, Jesus, that has got to be the best experience in the world. Well, for me it is anyway. Nothing else I've experienced even comes close, not drugs, not sleep. Nothing. Absolutely nothing. I'm going to have to talk to the good doctor about that. I think he's a married man. He'd have some good thoughts on that, I'm sure.

"Ahh, it's nice to sit down here and have some coffee with you, Janko. You're looking pretty good since the last time I saw you. You've got some color in your cheeks."

"I think it's called overexertion from walking this long way to the couch from my bedroom."

She smiled and looked at me for a moment. Thinking about something, you know. Like when you look at someone just a little longer than you should. I mean it was a nice look. Tender, but there were thoughts behind it. Then she took a sip of her coffee and cradled the mug in both hands and looked outside. I followed her gaze and saw a blue sky, not much snow, but some heat escaping from chimney tops.

"You know, Janko, it would sure be nice to be able to take you outside soon when the weather clears up. I mean, look at the lovely day it is outside. Granted it looks a little cold but look at the blue sky. You just want to reach out there and pinch its little cheeks."

I laughed at that. The image was bizarre. I put my hand out towards the sky and pinched at the air with my thumb and index finger.

"Look at you, you pretty little blue sky. Awww sooo cute."

"Very good, Janko. Are you mocking me? Doesn't matter anyway because you are so damn funny."

We both laughed at my silliness. I reached down towards my coffee and my cigarette. I took a sip of my coffee and sucked on my cigarette which was just a little stump anyway.

"Cheers," I said raising my mug of sweet, milky coffee to the ceiling.

"Back at you, Janko. Boy, you're in a good mood today."

"Yeah, I am, aren't I. I think it is because the good doctor is coming by, and I feel like I can begin to trust him, you know. Like he just might accept me for who I am and not be shocked or repulsed by my shit."

"He won't be, Janko. He is a good doctor and he has been practicing a long time. He's seen it all and won't be put out by any of your demons. None of us have, and we all have intimate knowledge of your difficulties. We've all had to become familiar with your file. And as you know, we all chose to sign up for this case, because of what we saw. Because of who we believe you to be. Your authentic and natural self. Sure it was difficult in the beginning and we've all had some troubles with you," she smiled when she said that, "but we're working it out. The key is for you, with Dr. Malichem's help, to come to see yourself and to understand yourself as the beautiful soul that you are."

She took a sip of coffee, a long sip. I put out my cigarette, bending it carefully over itself. A hamstring stretch if it was a person. Rose smiled at me before continuing.

"In my opinion, Janko, the goal for you is to clear your spirit of the baggage that this life has heaped upon it. And to be fair, Janko, this life of yours as I've come to see it, has heaped a heavy dose of baggage upon your broad soul. And I say broad because I've come to believe that you have been up to the challenge. All of us, Salima, Maria, Veronica and I have come to admire your courageous spirit. You are still here, still fighting to the end as your life wanes. Your spirit is seeking clarity and lightness so that it can leave unencumbered to the next world, whatever you believe that to be. And it encourages me to see you beginning to accept that. This is growth, Janko, this is real, palpable growth that I can see you undergoing."

"And what if I don't believe in the next world. I mean shit, I don't even believe in this one."

Rose looked at me steadily for a moment. A small smile creased into her cheeks.

"Well, then, all the more reason for you to let go of your baggage. At least then you will leave this world peacefully. It all wouldn't have been in vain.

This world is a good world, Janko. I know it doesn't feel like that for you and you have a right to question that, but it is. There is goodness all around us. There is love all around us, we just have to look with open eyes to see that beauty. And despite what you might think, this world believes in you. It believes in all of us. Life wants for us to succeed."

I sipped the last of my coffee. Careful not to take the dregs, the coffee sand, into my mouth. I hated that last sip. The dirty grind.

"Could I get some more, please?"

Rose got up and fetched me some more coffee. I'd be needing the toilet soon. But what the fuck, it was a small price to pay for the joy of coffee, seeing as I couldn't be having the joy of sex. I was thinking about maybe getting a catheter. That way I wouldn't have to hassle about getting up to go to the bathroom at all, and I'd always have someone fondling my cock. Okay, I'm sorry, okay. I'm just joking, Jesus, can't a guy joke, pretend at least that he might have enjoyed physical intimacy if only things had been different, if only he'd been whole.

"Thanks, Rose. Thanks for the coffee, and thanks for the words. They help."

I made my coffee right. Sweet and milky. Testing it to make sure.

"You're welcome, Janko. How is it?"

"Really good," I said over the brim of my mug.

"Can I ask you a personal question, Rose, seeing as you guys know all about me?"

"Sure, but I might not answer it."

"That's not fair. I'm an open book to you guys and I know next to nothing about what you all do."

I smiled weakly. I was kind of joking, but not really.

"Go on, Janko, ask and don't take it personally if I don't feel like sharing, okay?"

"Well, I was wondering if you were married, because I've been thinking a lot lately of love and the tenderness of women."

I was clutching at my mug, keeping it at face level, like a barrier, a fence, or a wall between me and her. I was nervous as hell, okay.

"Yes, I'm married. Why do you ask? That wasn't so bad was it?"

Rose was looking outside, watching the traffic go by, the sky, the clouds who knows.

"I dunno, I just think about women I would have liked to have been intimate with, that's all. I guess because I haven't known many women who have been kind to me, I feel a tenderness for you. Crazy I know, feels like love if I've ever known love, but then again, I don't know."

Shut up, you fucking moron. Just shut the fuck up. I had no idea why I was being such a retard. Jesus, can you believe it? Such weakness and crap and grovelling. If Norman was here he'd be all over me.

"That's sweet, Janko. And I think you are a great guy and would have made some woman somewhere very happy."

She looked at me briefly and then turned to look outside, again. I think there were birds out there somewhere. If I looked hard enough I'm sure there were birds out there somewhere.

I sipped on my coffee some more. It didn't taste nearly as sweet and creamy as it just had.

"I'd like to believe that Rose, I really would."

"What would you like to believe, Janko?"

"In love and goodness and that stuff, but I just can't seem to buy into it. Maybe the doctor will be able to help me see that. Maybe if you've had a good life, been given opportunities, then maybe it makes sense. Maybe then you can believe in goodness and love. But if you've only known anger and violence how can you rely on that? How can you believe in it with a conviction that will move your soul?"

The door buzzer went off. I looked at it and knew who it would be. It was the good doctor coming to see me. I had to ask him this question. I needed to know how I could come to believe in this goodness, this life as love rather than pain and suffering.

Rose got up to answer the buzzer and let him in.

"I think we all know who that is."

XIX

"Hi Rose."

I looked past her towards, Janko. Jesus, he looks worse and worse every time I see him. Or maybe all my other patients just look so good next to him. Whatever it was, I have to get going on our work here.

"Hi, Janko. How are you feeling this morning?"

I walked in and took a seat in the armchair with the blanket draped over it.

"Were you sitting here, Rose?"

"Yes, but that's okay, I should probably go and run some errands, anyway."

"Hang on just a minute, please. I wanted to talk to you about that," I said. "Sorry, Janko, how are you feeling today?"

He looked at me with sad, weary eyes.

"Okay, I guess. I've been looking forward to seeing you, and I've been having some really heavy questions laying on my mind for some time now. Rose and I were just talking about some of it, actually."

Rose asked if I wanted some coffee and I said, yes. Janko asked for some more, too. She went off to get it.

"Listen, Janko. I wanted to ask your permission for something. It is not common practice, and frankly not something I've ever done before, but I think it would work well for us."

"What is it, doctor?"

"Well, I'd firstly like you to try and call me Michael, but that's not what I'm asking. I'd like to include your nurses in our conversations. I think we could get a lot of helpful insight that would be useful. These women have known you longer than I have and I know they care deeply about you, Janko.

They came highly recommended and as you probably know, they all wanted to work with you. They've shown me a lot of initiative and stamina and patience and they are also intimately knowledgeable of your situation and history. I think it could really help us expedite things nicely."

I sat and waited for a moment. Rose came and gave us our coffees. Janko looked at her for a long moment, searching for something. She held his gaze.

"What do you think?" Janko asked Rose.

"I would like to, Janko. I feel like you've come to trust me over these months. It would mean a lot to me and to the others, for sure. We've always just wanted to help you and this really would be your hand reaching out to us that would be held firmly and loyally."

I liked the way Rose put it. I watched Janko sip his coffee, add sugar and then cream to it. Sip it again and then add more sugar.

"Yeah, I think that would be a good idea."

Rose smiled broadly as did I.

"Great news, Janko. Great news," I said.

"But, Michael, I curse and I can't help it. It helps me express my anger and it's something I've done for so long I'm not sure if I can stop. I mean, I've been trying but fuck, it's just too hard."

"That's okay, Janko. Just keep trying. Keep thinking about it and why you need to explore your anger that way. I'm hoping we can explore your anger in a more appropriate manner. Your emotions are critical in understanding yourself and in overcoming the pain and anguish you must feel. And we will need to explore them and bring them to the surface and let them froth and bubble over. But I hope that over time, your anger will give way to forgiveness. Not that we forget or that you allow yourself to be misused or ill-treated again and again, but to forgive so that the soul can explore its true beauty and find in that forgiveness the love that is abundant within you and which is all around us."

Janko smiled and I wasn't sure at what.

"That's funny, doctor, because that last bit is exactly what Rose said."

Rose nodded her head and took a seat in the armchair opposite mine. We were flanking Janko, supporting him, I liked to think.

"But do you understand what I'm trying to get at?"

"Yes, I do. I really do. It's just so hard doctor, Michael. It really is. And I want to believe in this love, this goodness that is there. Shit, I need to believe that it is right inside of me itching to come out and show itself. I'm hoping that is what we can do. I feel desperate, doctor, I really do."

Janko put his head down and started to cry. Slowly at first and then it came shuddering over him like a storm and his coffee was a brown squall splashing over onto him. He put it down as Rose went to get him some tissues.

"I'm sorry, doctor. I just feel so much pain. I thought I had gotten over it, but I guess I was just numb before. But now the pain...the pain is so hard, Michael. I'm desperate to find this love...love that I need."

I went over and sat next to him and hugged him to my chest. He shook even more then, and hugged me back, letting the pain flow freely through his tears. Rose came back and sat on the other side of him and rubbed his back and held the tissues out towards him for when he might need them.

"It's okay, Janko. This is good. Let it all out. Let out all the dark places, the lonely places and the sad, painful places. Then there will be space for the light. Then love will come and live brightly in you. It's light will fill you up. But first you have to get out the dark places first. Let it out brave, young man. Vanquish your demons, soulful warrior. Let the light shine in."

Rose's eyes were getting glassy. I smiled at her softly. She gave me a weak one back, all the while patting Janko's back.

He sobbed again as if taken by another large wave of emotion. It might have been the words I was saying. I hoped so, I wanted him to be able to cry freely. With that you can move past the pain, eventually, and more importantly he can learn to trust me, us, Rose and me.

"I've never even known a father, Michael. I've been thinking of you as my father, kind of wishing you had been my dad and then I might not have ended up like this. Fuck, it's embarrassing, I know, but I wish things could have been different."

I didn't know what to say. It was common for patients to fall in love with their psychiatrists, it was one of the risks of the job, but a manageable one if you kept your wits about you. Of course you could understand how such things happen.

We help our patients to learn to trust again and to heal. Without sounding arrogant, and it is a gift, but you are come to be seen as a savior when actually all you've done is helped them channel their own healing powers to heal themselves. But right now, Janko had caught me off guard. He was at a very vulnerable place and his reaction was uncommon. Usually my patients confess such things from a clearer vista, when lots of good work has been done, and they feel stronger and on the path to self-worth. This was unexpected and I didn't know what to do with it.

"I'm sorry, doctor," he said pulling away from me and looking away, "I'm such a fucking idiot."

"Come on now, Janko, that's unfair. You're being too hard on yourself. I think that is someone else speaking. Be kind Janko, be kind to yourself."

Rose and I went back and took our seats flanking Janko again. I drank some of my coffee, not knowing what to say.

"Would you like the tissues, Janko?"

Rose was handing them out towards him, not sure what to do, also just trying to be helpful. Things had taken a bit of a bad turn.

Jesus Christ, you know. Fucking doctor, in my moment of weakness sits back in his own chair and sips his coffee. I'm sorry if you're offended, doctor, about my feelings for you. Fuck. I shouldn't have said that shit. I took some of the tissues that Rose was handing out. I didn't know what else to do. Jesus, what would you do?

"I don't have any children of my own Janko, but I think you would have made a great son if I'd had one."

So now he says it. Now, when I don't believe him.

"Honestly, Janko. That is the truth. I can't afford to lie to you. I won't lie to you. We need to build this relationship on trust. We've got lots of good work to do, and we can't afford to lie to one another."

He didn't seem to be buying it, but what I was saying was the truth. I had very warm feelings towards him and he would have made a great son. I see potential, that's why I want to work with him. I see huge potential.

"Okay, Michael, if you say so, I'll believe you. I mean, it makes sense. And I was thinking about it because we come from the same neck of the woods. Dundurn, Saskatchewan. I mean, I've been thinking a lot about that, Michael. And also Mount Blackstrap which I've visited a few times. I mean it isn't outside the realm of possibility that you could be my father."

He looked at me carefully. Dammit, this wasn't a road I wanted to go down with him. It wasn't helpful.

"We need to be careful, Janko, that we don't wish for things that could not have happened. We need to be careful that we focus on what we can really change. It is an interesting idea you have, Janko, but honestly I'd know if I had ever fathered any children. And I haven't. I'm sorry, Janko, but I haven't. If you'd like though, I can try and find out who your father is. If you have no idea who he is."

"Of course I have no idea who he is, if I did, I wouldn't be fucking around with this lame idea, now would I?"

I raised my eyebrows.

"I suppose not."

"Maybe," said Rose, "that you thinking about Dr. Malichem as a father speaks to something deeper, a need for a father figure. Someone you can look up to and use as a mentor."

She was speaking to Janko, and I think she had a point. He was looking at her steadily.

"Maybe. But maybe it just could be true, too."

He looked at me then, expecting some sort of reaction.

"You know what I will do for you, Janko? I'll make some inquiries to find out some more about your father. I know this is something important for you, so I'll be happy to try and help you get some closure on this. But honestly Janko, I can't be your father. I would have known. We have to move away from that idea."

Janko looked outside. Nothing to see, but I'm pretty sure he had a bunch of images sliding past his mind's eye. Maybe about Dundurn, maybe about what he did know about his father, if anything.

I sipped my coffee and looked at Rose. She smiled at me and sipped her coffee, too.

"Tell me about what you do know about your father, Janko."

He bit his lip, looked down at his mug, picked it up and drank from it. Then he fumbled with a cigarette and lit it.

He inhaled deeply, exhaled through his nose still biting his lip and rested the elbow of his smoking hand in the palm of his left hand. The IV tube looped down his forearm and then up to the stand. It made a J. All this time he stared out the window.

"I don't know, doctor. I don't know much about him at all."

He still looked outside at the blue, cold sky.

"I sense some sadness, Janko, about this. Is this causing recollections of painful memories?"

He didn't say anything for a while, still chewing his lip. I looked at Rose, he looked at Rose and she smiled at him.

"Well, doctor, I just don't know much about him, okay. I mean, I hardly knew my fucking mother, okay. She dropped me off at a church when I was six fucking years old. Do you know what that's like? She told me to go inside and pray. I had never been to church before…"

Janko's eyes were welling up again and a tear crested his lid and slid down his cheek. He wiped at it, swallowed hard and inhaled on his cigarette again.

"'Go and pray, Janko, for good things for me and you,' those were the last words she said to me. Go and pray for fucking good things. And you know what, doctor, I haven't had many good things since then, and I prayed, okay. I fucking kneeled and prayed for hours. I prayed that my daddy would find me and come to love me. I prayed that my mommy would hurry up from the store because I was getting hungry, and she had told me she was just quickly going to the store and she'd be right back. Dear Jesus, I prayed, please bring me a bicycle for my next birthday. Please bring my daddy back to love me. Please bring my mommy back to love me so that I can love her, too. On my knees I spent those hours praying and then crying and praying some more. All on deaf ears, my pleadings falling on deaf ears, doctor. Okay. I was small, okay. Six years old and fucking abandoned by the one person who is supposed to take care of you. Abandoned by my own fucking mother, after having been abandoned by my father."

He was crying now, easily. The tears really like two streams glistening down his cheeks. I was finding it thick and hard to swallow now, too. I looked at Rose and she had bright, wet eyes. The sorrow, pain, and sadness were big, hulking guests in this room. Like some large monster that we couldn't see but kept brushing up against.

He looked at me before he continued. He looked at me and he was unashamed. And through this difficulty, this pain, I was proud of him. He had nothing to be ashamed about.

"And my knees, doctor. My knees were sore. I remember that, I had hardly ever been to church that I could remember, and my knees were bruised and red and sore before the sister finally found me later that night. I waited hours, doctor, like a good boy, because I was a good boy, okay. I was praying like I had been taught, okay. I was on my knees and my hands were pressed together in front of my chest and my head was bowed and my eyes were closed. That is how you're supposed to pray, right? And that is exactly how I was praying. But I couldn't stay like that forever, okay, I was just a little boy and my hands were going numb, and my knees were aching and I was hungry. But I was a good boy, Michael."

He turned to Rose. His nose was running now, too. He wasn't sobbing much, but occasionally he did, and the mucous would stream out of his nose. Almost clear like his tears. Body fluids as icons of pain.

"I was a good boy, Rose. I never gave my mother any reason to abandon me. I didn't hardly cry when she sent me off to school and I was alone and wearing second hand clothes and I didn't have a fucking lunch, okay? I never let my mother see me cry, okay, because I was her big, brave boy. I cried when she turned away and walked to the bus, but for her I was her big, brave boy. And I was only five then and scared. I didn't have nobody, okay? I didn't have a damn father. No big brother, and no friends that I knew who were going to the same school as me. So I went into that fucking church with a hungry belly and the belief that my mother was just going to the store to pick up some stuff for dinner. And I know what you're thinking. You're thinking why wouldn't she take you to the store with her? But you know what, I was an obedient and good boy and I did what she wanted me to and I waited and I prayed.

And I never once thought that she wasn't going to come and get me. Sure, I got scared and I was crying after a while, but it wasn't because I didn't think she was going to come and get me, but because I was worried something had happened to her and I was hungry and there was nobody in the church, if you can believe it. It's true anyway, even if you don't believe it. Okay? So you're asking about my father when I hardly even knew about my own fucking mother. I mean, you think you know someone, right? Like your own mother.

You're living your life feeling as safe and secure as you can in a single parent household. Wait, worse than that. A single parent household that is poor, where you're never certain if you're going to get three squares a day, and most days you don't. You know what I remember eating the most. Bread and macaroni with cheese and not even real cheese, but that shit that comes in the box. That was a good day too, because maybe I would've had some oatmeal for breakfast, too. Hungry and poor, Michael, but I had my fucking mother, okay? And then she abandons me like that in a fucking church. How does it go…suffer the little children? Well, I'm sick and fucking tired of suffering, okay? Too much pain all my life. The emotional kind too, not the physical that'll heal nicely, maybe leave a scar that you can remember it by, but the emotional pain that scars your soul, your being that rubs at you like a stone in your brain, okay, all the time not letting you heal."

Janko stopped then, suddenly, and I think he had lost his thoughts. He grabbed some tissue and blew his nose, crumpled it up and sat in on the table. He took some more and dabbed at his eyes and wiped at his chin where the tears dripped from and he wiped at his cheeks, too. His cigarette had burnt down a couple of inches and the ash was an impotent curve, a sad mouth. Janko sighed looking out the window and inhaled from his cigarette, spilling the ash onto his lap. He was oblivious to this. I looked at Rose as she reached for some tissue to dab at her cheeks too.

This was good work, we were doing some good work. Don't get me wrong, my heart was heavy and I was weary, but I was gaining ground with Janko. I felt for the first time a certainty that I could help him through these difficulties. A big part of it was just allowing someone to talk and to listen to them. Really listen, without prejudice and especially without judgement. If a person felt heard and safe they could let go a lot of the pain just by talking it out. The communion of souls I call it. One of the most effective methods of healing.

"Thank you, Janko. Thank you very much for sharing that. I can only imagine how difficult it must have been for you."

And it was difficult. I could tell and Rose could tell. She reached over to him and patted his knee, smiling at him. All the while he looked outside and he was still and he was no longer crying.

A little house sparrow flew across the balcony and away from us towards the other side of the road and Janko followed it with his eyes. I couldn't help but think how allegorical that image was. Set your pain free, Janko, just like that bird. It's not trite, it's sincere and appropriate and on point, too. Perhaps he was getting the idea. I sure hoped so.

Rose was patting my knee and it felt good. I didn't dare look at anyone, I was tapped out. I didn't want to change anything. I was tired and drained but it felt good in a way, if you can believe that. I don't know why, all my life I guess I've tried to remain that big, brave boy and never let out the pain. Never talk about it and maybe it'll go away. But you know what? It doesn't go away. Because wherever you go, there you are, and the shit eats you up. Look at me; I'm thirty-three years old and dying mostly from a broken heart and a broken mind because of all this shit in my past. Take a page from my book, okay, it's not worth it. And remember how you treat people, too, okay? Especially the small people, the children, the ones that suffer so much. They need special care and consideration. Protection and love and loyalty above it all. I suppose it goes for all of us, but the children don't know how to ask. They need without knowing how to ask, and that's okay, that's gotta be taken care of, okay? Otherwise you're left with adults like me, all broken up and cutting themselves on the pieces as they try to stick themselves back together. It could've been better, it should have been better, and here I am trying to put myself back together. Like humpty fucking dumpty. The pain, okay, the pain is the hardest fucking thing to visit and I'm trying to visit it and heal it. But it's hard, so damn hard.

Rose was still patting my knee and I just wanted to drown into her lap. Curl up like a cat on her bosom and be rocked and cradled like a baby. Peace and understanding. Can you understand that? To be held and nourished and protected and loved. That's what I wanted, but all I had was the shitty end of a cigarette that was growing smaller. That, and coffee that was growing colder. I sucked on my cigarette and sipped on my coffee.

"Can I get you some more coffee, Janko?" asked Rose.

"Sure, thanks."

"Doctor?"

He nodded and she grabbed his mug too.

"I'm very pleased, Janko. I'm very proud of you," he said when Rose was in the kitchen getting us more coffee.

183

I looked at him and he was smiling just a little, and his eyes were creased and wrinkled a little in the corners and I liked it. For the first time he looked to me like he was also vulnerable. Like he was also human and that made me feel a lot better. A helluva lot better. He didn't hold all the power over me; he was just a man trying to help. Maybe, maybe he was, if I could believe that, and I think I did just a bit and I felt more relaxed. A lot more relaxed and almost peaceful. Peaceful in a way I hadn't felt in months, at least.

"Thank you, Michael. It feels good to get it off my chest, but scary too, scary as hell, to be quite honest."

"But I think the hardest part is behind us, Janko. Making that first foray into the dark places, into the hurt and pain that's all hidden up and rotting in there. That is the hardest. Because before you look into that part, you never know what lies underneath it all. How ugly is it? But giving it voice, letting the light come on in to shine on it takes away the fear and the trepidation. Light clears out the darkness, Janko, it incinerates the shadows and cleans the dirty. And what we've found isn't that ugly, is it? It's just a pile of hurt from a long way away in history."

Rose came back with the coffee carafe and filled all three of us up. That was the last of the coffee. If this shit kept up I'd have to be peeled off the ceiling. I couldn't be drinking so much damn coffee while getting shit off of my chest.

Rose squeezed my shoulder and then went and sat back down, sipping her coffee. I poured milk and sugar in mine. Stirring it, tasting it, adding more sugar. It had to be just right.

I looked at the good doctor.

"I like your analogies, Michael. The light and the dark. I just feel like I've been living in the fucking dark all my life, you know? I just want to be basking in that light you talk about. The warmth, like the sun. I mean, is that even possible? I'm not a young man, Michael, and I don't know if I've got enough time."

I sat back and cradled my coffee. I felt exhausted. This unloading was way harder than I would have imagined it'd be.

"It is possible, Janko. I believe we have enough time. And not only that, but you're a young man, too. Don't forget that. Look at me, I'm a lot older than you are. Your youth is always an asset, even if you might not have much of it left."

Michael reached in for his coffee and sipped it, looking at me over the rim. I could still see the creases around his eyes. It looked like he was cracked, broken. Just like me, and maybe we all are. Maybe, as the good doctor says, that's how the light gets in.

"You are still a young man, Janko," Rose was offering her pearls before swine, "and I know you sometimes feel pretty old, your body has been taking a beating, but you have no idea how happy I am to hear you talk about your feelings here today for the first time. I am so encouraged, just like Dr. Malichem. I just know that you are going to find the peace you are looking for, and I'm certain we have plenty of time for it, too. I am so proud of you, Janko. Truly I am."

We all sipped our coffees for a while staring at the great big outside sky. It was like wallpaper really. Like if you peeled it back you could see something more there, something dark, sinister maybe. Maybe this blue backdrop was just a nice façade to keep us reaching, keep us happy, unaware of the dark places in the universe. And maybe it was just the same for each of us. Maybe behind each bright, sunny smile was a world of hurt, a whole body full of darkness.

"Michael," I said, "I want to ask you something."

He looked at me, and Rose too. He was holding his coffee mug, sitting back comfortably in his chair.

"Sure, Janko, anything at all."

I lit another cigarette. Not a word, okay? I know I'm smoking a lot, but as I said before I'm dying and it helps me think. Gives me something to do, helps me hold onto something when I need some courage to ask the tough questions. Not such a bad crutch when you consider that I'm dying anyway, okay? Please, let me be…just about this, okay?

"I was just looking outside at the nice blue sky. Cold sure, but nice isn't it?"

He nodded, not knowing where I was going.

"Well, it just seems that I can't escape the fucking negative. Excuse me. I just can't help but to pull things apart until what was beautiful lies cut up, bleeding and ugly. I'm not sure why I do it, and I don't really like it, but it seems like the natural thing that I seem to do to good things.

Like, I was thinking of that beautiful blue sky and thinking that if you peeled it back like it was some sort of sticker or wallpaper or something there'd probably be blackness and darkness behind it.

A whole universe of dark, blackness. I guess in a word, negativity. And so I got to thinking about people, too. You see so many people smiling with happy faces and I was thinking maybe that underneath that happy façade is some miserable son of a bitch. Maybe all these people are bodies full of darkness and corruption and stuff like that. Just like most of my foster folks. I don't know. Does that even make sense?"

I felt like I was rambling again. I mean maybe I just wasn't making sense and the good doctor was getting tired of listening to me. But then again, for fuck's sake he was getting paid to listen to me, wasn't he?

"I think you're asking three questions, Janko. I hear you asking firstly as to why it is that you pick good things apart until all you are left with, the last bits that you see, are the negatives about good things. I think the second question that you ask is whether your analogy is correct about the universe being a dark place. And the third question which is very similar to the first is whether human beings who seem happy and sunny on the outside are truly happy, or are they hiding behind that. The second question I think also incorporates much about the third question. And that is, is the universe malevolent or benevolent, and as such, is this life meant to be a hardship or a joy. I think the answer to the second question could help us point to the answer to the third question. But is that a pretty accurate reflection of the questions that you are asking?"

Rose was listening intently to the good doctor as was I. I'm not sure what sort of psychobabble he was on about, but he had heard me correctly. I tapped the ash from my cigarette into the ashtray before inhaling again.

"Yeah, that would pretty much sum it up, I think."

Janko had raised his eyebrows at me. That was part of the problem. He saw too much negative experience in everything. And no doubt with good reason, too. I would wager that he saw the universe as malevolent instead of kind and nurturing. I was planning on overturning that outlook.

I looked at Rose and then back at Janko. I smiled at him as he exhaled smoke out his mouth like a veil across his face. Hiding. Maybe this was all about hiding behind pain, untruths and anger, and about not being real.

"Excellent, Janko. The answer to your first question is easy. I think it is with good reason that you pick the negative out of all experiences.

I have still not had an opportunity to review your file, or should I say, I still have chosen not to review your file, but I will be doing that before our next visit. From what you have shared with me already and from what I can gather of your early life, it has been horrendous. You have just now given me the example of your foster parents. And it seems that most of them have been unkind, if not downright cruel. It would take an exceptional human being, a saint, to overcome such hardship and not look for the negative in all situations. This, I think, will be our greatest work and where I think our efforts will be best spent with the best results. I believe that helping you to see the good in life, the positive in experiences, will help you to see your other two questions in a different light."

I took a sip of coffee, put my mug down on the coffee table and reached forward, leaning elbows on my knees.

"The second question being whether the universe is a dark place is both allegorical and real, I think. In reality, the universe is mostly black and dark. Allegorically, though, I believe the universe to be kind and benevolent. If you were flying in a spaceship through the universe, you could choose to focus on the empty space, the darkness, and you would likely wander and get lost and confused. Alternatively, and this is the view I like to take, you could focus on the stars, on your destination, on the points of light, and you would reach the stars and the light. I see the universe as a bright place full of stars and twinkling jewels. Just as when I look at the night sky I see the thousands of stars and not the darkness, rather the beauty that the darkness allows the stars to bring forth. It is a matter of choice as to which you focus on. I'm hoping that I will be able to reach you with some light, some bright star that you may focus on and hold onto. I believe the universe to be a good and beautiful place. A bright, sunny and happy place. A place full of love and peace and joy. And sure, it is not without its dark moments, but I prefer not to focus on those. Keep your eyes focused on the light and soon enough you don't see the darkness so much. It does make a difference, Janko. It truly does, and I think the universe responds in kind, too."

He might have been buying it, but I wasn't sure. He was smoking his cigarette, drinking his coffee and shifting his gaze from me to the blue sky and then back again. I think he was trying to imagine, and that is what it would take to get it. To shift his outlook.

"Your third question I think is probably answered by the second. Some people might be putting on a façade when they look happy. But is anything really wrong with that. The old cliché 'to fake it till you make it' has validity. But on the other hand, a lot of people are genuinely happy, and a lot of people are genuinely happy in some of the most horrendous situations. As a matter of fact, there appears to be more disenfranchisement and disillusionment and unhappiness in the developed world than there is in the developing world. Sociological studies have shown that and proven that. Above having one's needs like shelter, food, clothing, etcetera, met, more money or possessions does not necessarily increase our happiness. It makes sense to me, Janko. Happiness, to a large degree, I believe to be a choice and is an easier choice if your outlook on the world, in God, whatever you choose him or her to be, or the universe is one of compassion and peace and love rather than darkness, hate and struggle. It is a matter of looking at life and the problems that come your way and focusing on what could be the positive aspects of it instead of the negatives. It is as easy as the answer to my next question. How much coffee do I have left?"

I took a big gulp from my mug leaving about half of the coffee left in it. Janko had a look at it and so did Rose. He looked at me and smiled.

"That's easy, Michael. You have half of your coffee left, but what you are really asking is a question about your mug. Truthfully, I see your mug as being half empty although I know that the correct answer is that your mug is half full."

Rose smiled and Janko sat back on the couch.

"I wasn't asking for a correct answer, Janko. I don't think that there is a correct answer to the question. But I do believe that our most honest answer is indicative about our general outlook on life. Thank you, for your honest answer. Calling my mug half empty would suggest that you don't see life as very generous or benevolent. If you called my mug half full it would suggest that you look at things in a positive light and see life as giving and supportive. Now I'm not suggesting that this is a definitive psychological test that can be taken to the bank. But I do think that it gives a glimpse into a person's psyche. It's just something to think about."

Janko looked at his own mug of coffee, took a long sip and said "half full" under his breath, smiling to himself. I smiled too.

"You're getting it," I told him.

Both he and Rose smiled at that one.

Man, it felt good to smile. It seems that I haven't had enough opportunities to smile in my life. At least the doctor had a sense of humor. That was really nice; I needed humor as much as I needed anything right now, I figured.

"But how do you focus on that, Michael? How do you focus on the light when all you've known is darkness and pain?"

He looked at me, still resting his elbows on his thighs, leaning in at me.

"That is the eternal question, Janko. And one that the sages have been asking and offering answers to for eternity. It is also what we are going to try and learn to accomplish in the short time that we might have together. I think it is different for each of us. But I think the crux of it is to live life joyously and in congruence with that which is good and uplifting and compassionate and kind. The golden rule comes to mind."

"What is the golden rule?"

If it was golden and it was valuable then I wanted to know about it. Riches I could definitely see as helping my situation right now.

"Right, the golden rule is to do unto others as you would have done unto you. If you want love then give love freely, if you want compassion and understanding then be compassionate and understanding first. That is very much the basis of the prayer of St. Francis of Assisi. And I think I will bring a copy of that prayer for you when I see you next. I know it is Christian, but its principles are all encompassing. You do not have to be Christian to appreciate it. I have found that all of the religions I have investigated have had elements of the golden rule within them. Nevertheless, I think that with you, Janko, the golden rule might first apply to yourself. I would suggest that you might need to offer yourself kindness and love and forgiveness and compassion. I hope to be able to help you on that path. And please, understand that you will be helping me, too."

Fuck, sounded nice, but how the hell do you get through the shit in your mind.

"It sounds easy, Janko, and it is easy, except that we keep getting in the way of ourselves."

I looked at Rose, she was talking now, trying to get me to understand all of this. Which I clearly wasn't.

"I know I constantly fail, but I think it is through the trying that we come to an acceptance of ourselves and our own humanity. I've come to offer myself the golden rule first. To accept my humanity and frailty and to be kind and gentle to myself. When you can give yourself kindness, Janko, then you can give it to others and you can walk through life with a lightness in your step and a smile on your face. I don't think life is meant to be a chore, a hardship. I mean, sure, it has its difficult moments, but it should be played with and not taken too seriously. After all, none of us escape here alive."

She looked at Michael. I think she was floundering a bit. She was being helpful and unhelpful at the same time.

"Well, then, what is the point," I said, looking at both of them, "I mean, if we are apt to fail, then why even try. I might as well end it now."

I felt dejected to be honest with you.

"I think the point, Janko," said Dr. Malichem "is not to give up, but to continue on as best we can. I think what Rose is alluding to is the fact that life is a journey and shouldn't be taken too seriously; that we shouldn't think of ourselves as winning or losing, but rather learning and enjoying as best we can. I think what might be helpful is to explore some of the wisdom of the sages and see what can be gathered from them. Perhaps we can steal some of their fire and light our own fire with it to illuminate our own path. Key for us, Janko, is forgiveness. You, me, all of us really need to first come to forgive ourselves and by so doing we will come to understand ourselves. From there we will come to know others and the beauty of life, this interconnected web. Loneliness and feelings of being alone are what kill us and destroy our hope and humanity. You haven't had the opportunity to feel community and peace and a sense of place. Much of what ails humanity, Janko, is born from the lonely heart and the abandoned spirit. Love is the light that brightens all souls and illuminates the sanctity and preciousness of our own individuality and abilities, and contributes to the peace and joy that I really think is our birth right. Love is the fulcrum that helps us reach higher and brings us peace through forgiveness, and understanding through the knowledge that we are not alone; that all our hopes and fears, our joys and sorrows are born by us all. We are, all of us, you and I and Rose, a part of God's blanket that he warms himself with. All the many colors are just the expressions of us all. I look at you and I look at Rose and I recognize myself mirrored in your souls. Just as I am for you, just as Rose is for you."

Man, I need to go pee so badly, but Michael really had me mesmerized.

"It sounds great, Michael. It really does. But look at me. I'm a shell of a human being no matter who you compare me to. I'm scratching at the fucking door of the grim reaper. My body begging him to let me in, and I'm scared shitless of what's on the other side and the loneliness that I feel. A loneliness and emptiness that is such a huge pit in my stomach that it weighs me down like a cold, hard stone. I mean, how the hell do I get to the other side of this river when I don't have a boat and there aren't any trees to build one with?"

Michael was almost edging himself off his chair.

"There might not be any boats or trees, Janko, but there's me and there's Rose and the others to carry you across. I think you are getting there. You are starting to open up and allowing yourself to be vulnerable. That is the key. That is the first step to allowing yourself to move forward, to get to the other side. It is a process, Janko. This is so exciting for me, Janko, you have no idea. To see you even considering these questions at this relatively early stage in our relationship is thrilling to me. You are making such huge leaps, that I wish all my other clients were as willing as you. I think you have opened the door, Janko, and you are peering in. I know it is a little dark and a little scary, but you're beginning to trust that I am there with you helping you and guiding you. This is tremendously important and good work that we are doing."

"I really have to go pee, Michael, but thank you for talking to me like this. I can't help but to feel encouraged by your enthusiasm. Even if it only lasts until I get back from the bathroom."

I smiled at him and he smiled back. Then I heaved myself up onto my IV stand and dragged my sorry, sickly ass to the bathroom. But for the first time I kind of felt more comfortable in my skin than I had in a while.

Rose was smiling, her eyes were welling up with tears, though she didn't cry. I nodded at her.

"We are doing good work," I said softly, looking at her, still on the edge of my chair. I felt so alive. To help another human being like this was the greatest gift. And to see that you are slowly making an impact and slowly the hand that is reaching out is being taken, if only cautiously.

There can be nothing better than this feeling of accomplishment. This was why I became a psychiatrist. I wanted to help people, to help them out of the trenches and thus enable them to reach their full potential. My work here with Janko was one of the best opportunities I had, because he was so willing.

Rose got up and grabbed the mugs, taking them into the kitchen. I took my own and followed her in. A galley kitchen it was, but big enough for both of us.

"We really are doing good work, Michael. Already in these few weeks we have made inroads into Janko's care that I haven't seen in the months that I have been with him. Maybe he is ready or maybe it's you, but I can see the life starting to creep back into him. It is so rewarding, to see the light of the soul start to burn behind what were dead eyes. This is why I came into nursing."

I was smiling at her and looking at her as she started to wash the dishes.

"I know exactly what you mean. And I think we all should take the credit for this. I don't think I could have done it alone and I think he is certainly getting to the point where I think he is ready. But most of all, Rose, I think you and the other nurses have helped him gain his confidence back and his trust in us. That is probably the biggest element that is making this so successful."

Rose looked over at me, her hands in yellow gloves with white soapy water clinging to them.

"Thank you, Michael. I'd like to think we are playing a small role in his recovery. If only a small role...Would you like a glass of water?"

I nodded. She handed me a glass of water which is exactly what I needed. I was thirsty from too much coffee.

"Thanks, I think I am going to need the washroom before I get going here soon."

"Tell me, Michael, what you think will be the focus of our future conversations with Janko?"

I leaned against the kitchen counter and placed the glass down.

"Well, I think we need more of the same. I think it's going to take continued effort and patience on our parts. Janko is at a crux here, I think. I believe he is very vulnerable at the moment as he starts to open up to us and let us in.

This is where the hard work begins. He may test us. He may become belligerent and combative to test us for loyalty and fidelity to him and his difficulties. This is where we need to be of consistent focus and purpose in helping maintain balance in what is, no doubt, a very choppy emotional storm for him."

Rose wasn't looking at me but she was nodding and smiling, and humming her agreement.

"Repetition here is probably going to be a focus too. Someone just coming to terms with deep-seated childhood issues is going to need lots of consistent repetition of our help. He is going to need patience and understanding and love and peace from us. All of those things which we were talking about earlier. We have to repeat ourselves with consistency, thereby creating new tracks that will erase and override the old tracks that he has now. Tracks of self-loathing and self-hatred and being too hard on himself and feeling unworthy. All of those sorts of things."

Rose was finished now with the cleaning, having laid all the mugs and plates on the dish rack to rest. I remembered when Margaret and I were just starting out and we lived in an apartment not much bigger than this, without a dishwasher and on very little money. Things seemed simpler then, less complicated and more peaceful, maybe even easier and happier. We certainly didn't have as much clutter as we did now. Far less.

Rose looked at me, leaning against the opposite counter having tossed the gloves across the edge of the sink where they lolled out like tired, yellow dog's tongues.

"How do you do it though, Michael? How do you maintain your sanity against all the stress and chaos in life? Even the sad and difficult times. Because I know I'm not perfect in that regard. I still struggle with these things. With seeing the good out there, with being gentle on myself and practicing the golden rule on myself first and foremost. Sometimes, Michael, it seems that life just beats you down to a point where your resiliency is stretched thin and it is all you can do to get through the day in a state of abject despair."

She crossed her hands over her chest and looked away and down into the corner of the kitchen.

"I'm sorry, Michael, you have enough to deal with, what with Janko and his needs. It's just that it sometimes gets hard. And I've noticed that every time you are here you are positive and happy and pleasant and patient and kind.

Have you managed to inoculate yourself against life's difficulties?"

I shook my head.

"On the contrary, Rose. I struggle probably more than you would think or even more than you can imagine. I have had plenty of my own demons to deal with and I still do. But this is how we do it, this is how we manage the difficult times. We talk to one another and we listen to one another. I may not be able to take your burden from you, but we can set it down for a while and talk about it. We can look at it, look into it and maybe by just sharing it you can come to see it as a more benign burden and maybe if we look at it enough you'll be able to put it down for good and we can leave it. For it is sometimes just comfort that keeps us holding onto what is really weighing us down. And even just listening to one another is therapeutic enough. To connect with each other at deep and emotionally vulnerable places is valuable and cathartic. For example, just listening to Janko today has brought me a huge sense of validation and self-worth and happiness, and I wasn't even talking about any of my own problems. You see Rose, we all are vulnerable and lonely, feel sad and scared, fearful and unworthy at times. I think it is the curse, or blessing of being human. It is in small doses of the carrot that encourages us to improve ourselves and our world and to help those in it. But it is also the stick that beats us back if we are not careful."

Rose was nodding and focused on what I was saying. She had also clasped her hands in front of her. She was more open and receptive. This is the power of words, of acceptance.

"I act as if I am happy and peaceful and confident. Sometimes I truly feel that way, and other times I feel vulnerable and small and scared. But it helps in a small way to believe that if you act you can become, and if you try you can do. As you say, we have to be gentle and kind to ourselves first. That is the key and to take wisdom from those who have come before us. The saying that 'this too shall pass' is one of my favorites and helps me keep things in perspective. You get to savour the good things in your life because they will change and you get to bear the burden of the tough challenges and hurdles in life for they will go away. It is a simple but magical phrase and helped me through some of my hardest times."

"Yes, I suppose you are right. Sometimes though, it seems difficult to even try, to even bother to look for the good in life when there are so many monkeys on your back trying to get you down."

I nodded at her, she had a valid point.

"Yes, I know, Rose. I really do. All I can suggest then is to focus on the transitory nature of life and the world, especially as it relates to our difficult times. Nothing is permanent even though the drudgery seems like it will go on forever. The Chinese or the Japanese have a saying that goes something like this 'fall down six times, get up seven.' I think that sums it up quite nicely."

Janko hobbled back into the lounge and sat back on the couch with a sigh of relief. He lit up a cigarette and started blowing smoke rings towards the balcony.

"Would you like anything else, Janko?" asked Rose.

He shook his head up and down and said "no thanks." He kept looking out towards the balcony. I tilted my head to Rose for her to join me with Janko in the living room. We went back in, me taking my water, and we sat in our same spots.

"So how are you feeling, Janko? Has anything been helpful at all today?"

He looked at me lazily for a little while. Pondering I guess.

"Yes, Michael, you have said many things that have been helpful. But you've said a lot of things, too, and I feel overwhelmed to some degree you know. It seems like such a huge task ahead of me, that I wonder if I will ever be able to climb over it. Like a huge shitty mountain that seems so steep; and me, I seem so tired and weak."

He sighed, inhaled on his cigarette, folded his arms and stared blankly in front of him.

"It will take time, Janko. It really will. Rose and I were just talking about these very things. We all go through difficult times in our lives when we feel insecure and vulnerable. I certainly have, and I bet anybody on this planet if they were honest would admit to having those kinds of feelings and thoughts. Probably fairly often too, and most folk haven't had to deal with the huge struggles that have been your burdens. You really have been heaped with more than your fair share of difficulties. Don't underestimate that, but then also, don't underestimate your power to overcome those very difficulties, too.

I mean you have inordinate strength and power to push yourself over this mountain if that is how it looks to you now. You have all the tools you need, and Rose and Veronica and Salima and I will help you find those tools and teach you to use them.

195

Already I have noticed that you don't seem as combative as you have before, and you certainly aren't cursing as much as you have in the past. These are good and important steps, Janko. Would you agree, Rose?"

We both shifted our gaze to Rose who was looking at Janko and sitting comfortably in her chair with her right leg crossed over her left knee and her arms outstretched magnanimously on the arms of her chair.

"Absolutely, I would agree with you, Michael. And I have to admit that I, too, have suffered insecurity and feelings of lack of self-worth and doubts about who I am and what I am doing here and what the point of all of this is. It is very common, Jay, I think it is probably almost a given condition of being human, to some extent, to doubt and to question and feel inadequate. Would that not be so, Michael?"

Janko had smiled when she called him Jay. He obviously liked it. We were definitely getting somewhere. This was wonderful. Working out better than I could imagine and hope for.

"Yes, I think you are right, Rose. It is probably a condition of being human, but one that we can use to our advantage to strive to be the best we can and ignore its negative voices. It can be done. It has been done by a great many people and they can and will be guides for us on our journey here. I am just so pleased with how well we are doing, Janko. Honestly, I am."

He looked at me with a big smile. A smile that couldn't be helped.

"You really think so, doctor?"

I was smiling too. I was like a puffed up, proud parent. Rose was beaming too. With no corniness, I could feel a lot of love and joyful emotion around us.

"Absolutely I do, Janko. If you knew the number of people that I try to help on a yearly basis, you are definitely in the top ten percent with your eagerness and sensitivity to do the hard work, the sometimes dirty work. But I'll tell you Jay, it is going to get easier and easier. This is just the beginning, the hardest part, and after that it will get easier and easier. Just as you have become accustomed to feeling poorly about yourself, you can and will become more accustomed to thinking positive and joyful thoughts about you and what you are capable of. You will come to love yourself and think highly of yourself, but without false arrogance."

He nodded still smoking his cigarette.

"It is true, Jay," said Rose, "to be able to think of oneself in a positive light. It takes practice but it can be done and I know you will do it. Occasionally I have to keep practicing it, too. As Michael told you, we were just talking about that very thing before you came in. Practice makes perfect, as they say."

Rose got up and went into the kitchen to get a glass of water.

"Would any of you like anything while I'm up?" she asked.

"Not for me, thanks, I should probably get going soon."

"Sure, Rose. I'll take a glass of water, please."

"No problem."

She returned with water for both of them and sat back down.

"So are you doing okay, then, Jay? You'll be okay until I see you next week?"

"Yeah I think so, thanks, Michael. It's hard, but you know that. And sometimes I just wonder what the point is, to go on living, you know. Not that I'm going to end my life right now, that has already been decided for me. But you know if I wasn't dying, I might get to thinking of it as a possibility. I guess I'm just my own worst enemy at the moment or should I say I have been for quite some time, now. It's just hard, that's all."

"Yes, Jay, it is hard, but it is also sometimes easy and sometimes soft. Live for those moments. You are a gentle child of the universe and you deserve to feel good about yourself, healthy, and happy. That is important. It is your birth right and you should fight for it and go after it with dogged determination. Keep those thoughts away. They'll do no one any good. Easy to say, I know, but also easy to do. Keep focused on the positive. Any bad thought that comes your way, slam it away with a positive thought and keep that up. Eventually those negative thoughts will get tired and skulk away as they should. Keep practicing, Jay. As I said to Rose, the Chinese or Japanese have a good saying, 'fall down six times, get up seven'. Simple, honest, beautiful, and also true. Give it a try. That will be your homework for the week, okay?"

I had him smiling again a bit. And that made my heart feel a lot happier.

"Okay, good doctor, I'll do my best. I mean, it can't be all that hard, can it?"

I think it was a question to which he knew the answer.

"No, Jay, it is not that hard at all. Just remind yourself, gently, patiently, to keep trying all the time. Keep trying, keep standing up."

He nodded, "Thanks, Michael, I will. You have been very helpful to me. I think your kindness is overcoming me in a gentle way...Damn you."

I laughed and he smiled. I felt he was going to get well.

"We'll do this, Janko, we sure will. Lots of people have done it before you and we will be able to make it over that bridge, too."

"Yes, we will, Jay, I know we will," said Rose.

"Anyway, I have to go, if you're feeling okay, Jay. I will be taking a look at your file before I see you next time, so I can get a clear picture of some of the issues we might be dealing with. I'll also try to start investigating who your father is and see if we can't get some headway on that. I know some people in Child Welfare that might be able to point me in the right direction. Do you remember your mother's name, at all?"

"No, not really, Michael, but I think her first name was Mary. I can't be certain, I mean I only called her mom and only for a short time, too."

His eyes started to mist up, and he swallowed hard.

"It's okay, Jay," said Rose, "it is hard at first, but you can let it out, the sorrow and sadness."

He smiled and shook his head.

"No, thanks, Rose. I don't think I can handle another round today. I think I'll save this one for another time."

I got up and patted him on the shoulder.

"Everything is going to be all right, Jay. You have life and you have breath. And with those things anything is possible. Things will change, and these things are going to change for the better. Hopefully, I will have some good news for you about your father and maybe your mother, too, if she is still around."

"I don't think she is, Michael, one of my foster parents in a cruel way told me she had died of an overdose of drugs or something. Kind of suggesting I might go the same way. But they might just have been mean. It might not be true."

"Okay, I'll see what I can find out. Here's my card in case you really need to talk to me about anything, okay? Please feel free to use it. I will make myself available to you anytime, okay? But if I don't answer then you must leave a message so that I can get right back to you."

"Thanks, doc, I really do wish you could have been my dad."

He looked away when he said that, embarrassed I think.

"Yes, Jay, I think I would have liked that too. I'll see you soon."

He put my card down on the coffee table after looking at it for a while. I made my way to the door to let myself out. Rose was with me.

"Thanks, Michael, for your kind words to me and to Janko. I feel so much better now for myself and for our patient."

"Me, too Rose. I feel so much better, too, to be honest with you. I was having a crummy day but that's all behind all of us for now. Your help is greatly appreciated; you and the other nurses are fantastic at your work. I'll see you soon and hopefully have some good news for our young man over there about his father…Good bye, Jay."

"Good bye, Michael."

We waved at each other, I said good bye to Rose, too, and then I heard the latch lock behind me as I walked back down the hall. It had been a great day. It had picked me up from some low points with other patients lately and recent disagreements with the psychiatric board at the hospital. That seemed so pointless now to be upset about. In the big picture, helping each other move forward in this big world and to love one another was what counted. In the end it's only love that matters. How much have you managed to love? I think that will be the currency that will be counted when we leave this plane. I couldn't wait to see Margaret tonight. I needed to share this day with her. A wonderful, magical, beautiful day. This day reminded me of my wife, wonderful, magical and beautiful. God, I love that woman.

XX

I drove downtown to pick up Margaret. The roads were dry for this time of year, a little ice on the sides but nothing to worry about. It was around five thirty and traffic was crazy on the main avenues and streets heading out of downtown, and it wasn't even a Friday. Margaret was expecting me for five thirty and at this rate I'd probably be fifteen or more minutes late. I didn't like being late for things generally and especially her. I picked up my cell phone at the red light and dialled her number.

"Hi, honey," I said.

"Hi, darling, where are you?"

"I'm down here stuck in traffic several blocks away. I think it's going to take me at least another fifteen minutes. It's been a hectic day and I guess I'm running a little late."

"Sure, that's okay. I'm still in my office so why don't you give me a call when you're almost here and then I'll come down."

"Will do. You know I had a meeting with Janko again today which went very well."

"I'm glad to hear that, honey. It's about time you guys are able to make some headway."

"Yes, it was very beneficial that way, but there has been something even more interesting come along that I want to talk to you about. I've spent a large part of today going through his file. You wouldn't believe the difficulties he has had as a child. Shipped from foster parent to foster parent. And from bad foster parent to worse it would seem. It is no surprise that he has the problems that he does have."

"Mmm, that sounds interesting Mike. You sound sort of surprised yourself. Anything you want to talk about now."

201

"No, not really, I'd rather wait until I see you. The traffic is nuts and I'm having a hard time driving and talking on the phone, too. But you know what, honey, Janko is schizophrenic too."

"Similar to your illness, darling?"

"Yes, identical. A paranoid schizophrenic."

"Do you find that surprising. I mean a number of your patients are schizophrenic, are they not?"

"Yes, that is true enough. But I didn't catch onto this with him, and he isn't taking any medication for it either. As you know, the only thing he is on are painkillers. He refuses any AIDS treatment drugs and he's also not taking anything for his schizophrenia. You'd think I would have seen that coming."

"Well, I think in all fairness love, you've been focused on helping him overcome his other difficulties. This illness of his could be a manifestation of his childhood difficulties and from what it sounds like, he sure has had enough of those difficulties alone hasn't he?"

"Yes, he has. And perhaps you're right, it could be that I've been so focused on getting him to open up so that we could explore his difficulties that I haven't seen the forest for the trees, if you know what I mean. Anyway, honey, the traffic here is chaotic. Drivers cutting in front of me, people honking. I'll see you soon, okay, and we'll talk about it more then. I love you."

"I love you, too, darling. Bye."

I hung up and tossed my phone on the passenger seat. Was I glad that I didn't have to work downtown. Though I'm often here to pick up Margaret. Very interesting things about Janko I learned through looking at his file. It explains a lot but also begs many other questions too. Margaret would have some good insight into that.

It was getting pretty dark and the sky was beginning to flake snow. Little small down-like feathers of the stuff. Not much, just enough to get the roads slippery, just enough to be melting when it hit the tarmac. I resigned myself to enjoy the drive in the slow traffic and the light snow. The radio was bugging me so I turned it off. Immediately I felt better. I could concentrate on my thoughts which were zooming around my empty head at what seemed like a hundred miles an hour.

That was one of the things I think that I should talk to Janko about. It seems for me anyway, and I bet for most people too, that if my thoughts are all over the place, then that just increases the stress levels and doesn't help me to relax. You ever had that experience? Anyway, I'm sure of it. It's hard to put things in perspective when you can't focus on some of the smallest tasks. That is one of the major hurdles for people overcoming obsessive-compulsive disorders. It takes huge focus and determination to overcome the wandering mind. That is why I choose some of the techniques for helping my patients from eastern religions. Truth be told, it's one of my own favorite tools for helping myself. Now I could use some of that tranquillity. I needed a quiet mind to steady myself on the problems at hand. I was much too splintered with the information I had found out from Janko's file. Lots to think about, and the most important aspect was how best to approach it. Well, that's enough for now; I have to speak to Margaret about it and use her as a sounding board and hear her input. She was great at these kinds of things. She had a lot of objective wisdom. I sure needed that now. And then you'll get a greater sense of what I'm talking about, too. Just focus on getting to Margaret's work.

I was getting there, not far away, when some jerk cut in front of me in his BMW. His license plate read "SLPDR". That could only be one person. My "good" friend Joachim, his inconsiderate usual self. Maybe this time he was the one asleep behind the wheel.

I picked up my phone. Tempted to call him but being so close to Margaret's I called her instead.

"Hi, honey, I'm just a couple of minutes away."

"Okay, I'll be right down."

We said our "I love yous" and hung up. I put my phone down in the storage area below the radio and changed into the far right lane. Just past these next two red lights and I'd be waiting outside her building.

Lights turned green and I pulled up to the curb. Joachim was off somewhere in a hurry it seemed. Weaving through traffic as if he really did own the lanes and we were just his guests on the road. Someone honked at him and I smiled. That'd be the least of it, and he wouldn't care, anyway. But he'd probably just ruined someone else's next few minutes.

There was a knock on the passenger window. I looked over to see Margaret. Drowning in thoughts I had been. I unlocked the doors.

"Sorry, honey, I seem to be in a place far away from here today. My own private neverland."

We kissed each other and hugged. She smelled great. I always enjoyed the smell of her, especially her hair. Soft and fragrant. A little fruity, a little florally, all feminine, and all Margaret.

"How was your day?" I asked.

"Good, got this young kid off for auto theft. He was only fourteen years old and in a pure way, quite naïve. However, you first. I want to hear all about your day first."

I pulled away from the curb as the snow kept falling lightly, the soft sound of the wipers interspersed over the humming of the engine. Soon I was in the midst of the traffic current, just ebbing along with the flow. Slowly, intermittently but still getting towards home.

"Well, darling? Tell me about Janko."

"Sorry, I'm all over the place today. Been that way since I finished up reading his file this late afternoon."

I looked across at her, smiled and then reached over to kiss her as we crept along slowly.

"I just feel grateful for you in my life, Margaret..."

"I know that, but tell me about Janko, or have you changed your mind now and you're trying to deflect?"

She smiled at me.

"No, no, not at all. Just reading about what this poor man has been through, it is no wonder that he is suffering as much as he is. It also makes me appreciate the things I have. Like you, like my family who supported me through my illness. If I hadn't had the healthy childhood that I had enjoyed, who knows if I wouldn't have become a Janko. You know my parents were instrumental in helping me acknowledge and to face my illness and seek the help I needed. By the grace of God I could be in a very different place you know."

"Perhaps darling, but also give yourself credit. You are very courageous, and at the end of the day you had to face your illness. You had to admit that you needed the help and decide to take it, too. I know that you are very compassionate and empathetic about your patient's difficulties, and I think that makes you very effective. But do you think that maybe with Janko you are becoming too close or taking on his difficulties too much?"

"No, honey. I really don't think so. It's just that I see so much potential with him and he has such little time left that I have a huge sense of urgency to do the best work we can. And now, having had a chance to look at his file, I see the huge breadth of difficulties that he has been saddled with, and that makes me wonder how I'll be able to help him to the best of my abilities in the short amount of time we have left."

Margaret smiled at me, reached over to rub my shoulder and kissed me on the cheek.

"Don't beat yourself up darling. I'm sure you will have enough time for what you need to do to help him. You have worked miracles before, my miracle worker. I'm sure you'll do it again, especially considering the way you feel for him."

I put my right hand on Margaret's knee and gave it a gentle squeeze.

"Thank you. You are the reason I'm able to accomplish so much. Just to give you a sense of what his life has been like. Janko was tossed between more than a dozen foster parents before he finally left home at the age of sixteen. That's a little more than one a year. His mother dropped him off at church when he was only six years old. Can you believe it? Just dropped him off and told him she was going to the store. And then you never see your own mother again. She told him something like 'go pray for happy things, Janko. Go prayer for your mommy and for you.' Those are pretty much the exact words, if I remembered them correctly. The policeman wrote it down in his notebook at the time when he was called to the church and he met with the young boy. And that's it, you never see her again. Can you imagine that? So very awful."

"That is awful, it's actually despicable, to be honest with you. Did they ever find his mother?"

"Yes, they did, but that information is missing from the file. That is one of the other things I'm trying to do for Janko. Find the name of his parents for him. Because it came up in discussion today that he wished or even thought that I was his father. Absurd for sure, but I guess understandable. It is a common risk of my profession, that sort of attachment from the patient towards the counsellor."

"I can see that. Does it say in the file who the police officer was who found him at the church?"

I nodded.

"Yes, it does. His name is Robert Peel, if you can believe it, and that's why I was able to remember it. Very ironic I thought. I'd like to read the police report and see what he had to say about the incident. I think it would give me lots of insight into the kind of boy he might have been back then. Before his great struggles and before his illness. I was also thinking that I might like to get in touch with Robert, too, if I can track him down and interview him; that would be of help."

We were getting close to home. Finally. The traffic was easing up now as we were in suburbia. But if I was a rich man like my friend the sleep doctor, who lives in the posh neighborhood of Mount Royal, Margaret and I would be home by now.

"Does Janko know his mother's name?"

"No, though he thinks it was Mary, but he doesn't know her last name. Did I tell you that he and I grew up in the same town of Dundurn?"

She nodded.

"Yes, you had Mike."

"Small world isn't it?"

She nodded again.

"Didn't you date a Mary when you lived in Dundurn?"

"What are you saying, honey?" I asked.

"Nothing. It sure is a small world, isn't it?"

"That's preposterous, Margaret. There is no way in hell that I'm his father. Come on, there must be at least a hundred Marys in Dundurn alone."

"I know. It's just curious that's all. I believe you, Michael, you'd have known if you had fathered any children."

"Yes, I would."

I had no idea where she got that thought from and I found it a little insulting. I'd be a stand up father if I had any children. I wouldn't be a dead beat.

"You know I would have done the right thing if I had fathered any children, Margaret. You know that, I'm a little hurt and insulted."

"I know you would, darling. I just got a little carried away that's all. Your integrity is not being questioned. I'm just having a little fun with the serendipity of life, okay?"

She grasped my hand that was on her thigh and gave it a squeeze. I leaned over and kissed her on the cheek.

"Okay, I'm sorry, this has just taken up a lot more of my day and mental energy than I'm used to."

I pulled into the driveway, waiting for the garage to open, like a big, lazy mouth yawning. A light was on in the living room behind the Venetian blinds.

"Did we leave a light on this morning, honey," I said nodding towards the living room.

"Silly, Michael. Remember we just set up one of those timers on the living room lamp this weekend, darling."

I shook my head and smiled to myself. I was getting either senile or thinking too hard on Janko's file. I'd like to think it was the latter.

"Right, honey. Excuse me while I have a senior's moment to myself."

We both laughed and it felt good. It was starting to clear the fog from my over active mind. I needed clarity if I was to deal most effectively with Janko in the short amount of time we would have. I drove into the garage with the door slowly closing behind us.

"You'll never know who cut me off in traffic tonight as I was coming to pick you up?"

"Dr. Gebs," she said.

I was astonished.

"How do you know?"

"Well, he's probably the only friend we have who would be so rude as to do something so inconsiderate. I mean really, Michael, a Montmarte, and the third one at that, either has a big chip on his shoulder or he's too self-absorbed to care. I think in Joachim's case it is probably a little bit of both."

I smiled at her. A Montmarte indeed.

"Remember though, honey, he isn't a Montmarte anymore. He gave that up a long time ago and doesn't even like people reminding him of it. You can't even jest with him about it. So saying that, I think he probably has a big chip on his shoulder more so than being so self-absorbed, although he is very self-centered, too, isn't he?"

"Yes he is, but at least we can have some light hearted fun with him and his name. He shouldn't take himself so seriously."

"Did I tell you what his license plate was?"

"You might have."

"S-L-P-D-R."

"Well maybe he does have a sense of humor then."

We were heading into the kitchen. I had tossed my briefcase beside the couch and Margaret had put hers on the kitchen counter top. I poured us each a glass of red wine. A Chilean Merlot, our favorite.

"Thanks," Margaret said as I passed her a glass. She started getting busy in the fridge preparing dinner. She asked me if I wanted salad and pasta, something light but nourishing and I agreed. I took a knife and started cutting up the tomato.

"You know, honey, I sometimes think about whether I made the right choice in going into psychiatry. I mean, there are lots of different opportunities in the hospital. And most of those jobs pay a hell of a lot better than what I'm making on my patients, especially those on government disability income. I could be making a killing in plastic surgery or something like that. Hell, even anaesthesia pays a lot more than psychiatry."

Margaret came over to me smiling and kissed me full on the lips and hugged me close.

"I think you are not a plastic person, Mike, and that is why I love you so much. It is because of whom you are that I have fallen, and remained, so in love with you all of these decades. Don't doubt yourself, Mike, you are a wonderfully compassionate and competent psychiatrist and I think you are worth more than a million Joachim's or plastic surgeons. Think of all the people you have helped all these years who are living more productive lives, thanks in no small part to you. Without your special gifts and talent for helping people, this world would be a lot darker than it is."

She had gone back to washing the spinach, having put the pot full of water on the stovetop which was already a glowing orange.

"So you wouldn't prefer me to be making all that huge money in any of the other disciplines and living in Mount Royal and driving around in his and hers Mercedes?"

"Of course not, darling. You are exactly the way I want you to be. And living in Mount Royal or driving a brand new Mercedes, which we could afford anyway if we wanted to, is just not my thing and neither is it your thing. Besides Michael, I could have gone into corporate law to earn that kind of lifestyle if I wanted to. But I've chosen to try and make a bigger or better difference in the world, just like you have…is this about you bumping into Monty?"

She smiled at me, a mischievous one, like the kind that had won my heart so many years and years ago.

"Yeah, I guess it is. And also the amount of work I see that is before Janko and I. I really want to help him, but I'm not sure if we have enough time. He could be worse off than I realize. Perhaps I should phone his doctor and find out exactly what his prognosis is, and of course, the stubborn bugger doesn't want to take any medication that could help him."

"I think you will have enough time for what needs to be done to get him to a place of acceptance and peace before he leaves this world for his next journey. Have faith darling, because I certainly have faith in you."

The pasta was bubbling away in the pot, making me hungry. I drank some more of my wine; it tasted warm and chocolaty in my mouth, and hot in my belly, too. That's what a nice red wine will do for you on an empty stomach. I pinched a slice of tomato and ate that. I needed to get something in my stomach other than wine.

"Thanks, honey, but there are big boulders here in the way of our path together, Janko and I. He seems to have been a loner all his life without many friends at all. There isn't much in his file about him having any friends at all, at least none that were deemed worth mentioning. I mean, don't most people have childhood friends for years?"

"Not necessarily. I don't remember most of my early childhood friends. The friends I've kept have developed mostly in my early adulthood."

"Perhaps, but there are these three friends that he swears he has. I don't remember their names. Two men and one woman. Anyway, I don't think that they are real people. It seems to be a common thread throughout his life that he has had three imaginary friends. Always two boys and one girl."

"Is it really so horrible that he has had to find imaginary friends if he has been forsaken by his real friends? That's sad, Mike, but not horrible. I can't imagine having to go through life without friends, God forbid, and without family. That has to be an unimaginable hardship. If anything, my heart just goes out to him even more so. Just think of what that must have been like on top of his hardships and abuse. Can you imagine the loneliness, Mike? That is awful, if anything it should just give you greater insight into how he must feel and the demons he has to deal with."

"Yes, honey you're right. It is awful, absolutely one of the worst cases I've seen. He is definitely very lonely and sad and scared. You're right, it explains a lot as to why he hasn't been able to trust anyone and why his starting to trust me was such a huge development. It means so much more now that I have a sense of where it was coming from. But if he believes in these people as real beings, it could interfere with our work. That is why schizophrenic patients do so much better when they are on medication. You can deal with the underlying causes about their grief and problems and not have to deal so much with what these fictional characters mean in their lives. Or worse yet, having to deal with these characters first and leaving the important work until later. Perhaps I should ask his physician if we can't cajole Janko into taking his medications."

The pasta was ready. Margaret had tasted it. She dumped it out into the colander and scooped large helpings into our bowls. She topped it with a bolognaise type sauce made with fake meat. I didn't really care; it was one of those things that Margaret and I had agreed to when we first got married. She didn't pester me about eating meat and I let her have a vegetarian kitchen. She grated some fresh Parmesan cheese on top and we headed into the living room. I loved fresh Parmesan, couldn't stomach the prepared stuff. It took us two trips to set everything up. Margaret lit some candles for ambience and I poured us some more wine. The bottle stood upright in the middle of the table, half the bottle it had been, just a while before. I wondered if that was why bottles of red wine were so dark, so that you didn't have a chance to think about how much you were drinking. But in my mind a bottle between two people wasn't too much. And don't get the wrong impression, we don't drink every day, anyway.

I kissed Margaret on the forehead and thanked her for dinner. We both started on our salad.

"You know, Mike, I can't get over the sadness that Janko must be feeling. I can't imagine going through life with hardly any friends, or maybe none at all. That has got to be intolerable. I'm surprised he hasn't committed suicide. I might have. I mean, what else would you have to live for? Life would seem intolerably empty to me."

I got up, turned on the CD player, and put in some Spanish flamenco guitar. No songs, just music. I liked the warmth that the music created in my mind, especially in the middle of winter.

"I agree with you, Margaret. It's a terrible sadness and pain that he must feel. Perhaps he has lasted so well because of his fictitious friends and not in spite of them. It could be that they have served almost as real friends for him, but it is symptomatic of his illness, not a benefit of it."

"How can you be sure, Mike. I know that you are well versed in this field, and I'm not trying to suggest that I know better than you. But could it not be possible, in this particular environment that these hallucinations, vivid hallucinations, are valuable to him and serving an important role in his coming to terms with his childhood. Perhaps these are the same friends he has had all these years. Can you imagine asking him to give them up now, especially if he sees them as real people?"

"Except that most schizophrenics I know realize that their hallucinations are fictitious."

"Okay, fair enough, but suppose that they nonetheless play a pivotal role in his management of his illness. Perhaps they are like lifejackets for him now as he tries to reach out to you. Maybe he sees you handing him a rope but he is not yet ready to let go of his lifejacket. It could be facilitating his courage in reaching out to you rather than hampering it."

Damn it, she had a point. I finished my salad and drank some wine. She could be spot on, actually.

"You could be right, honey. Perhaps I'll talk to him about his friends in a non-threatening way to tease out the relationship he has with them. Then I can take it from there as to what the best approach is. See, this is why I need to talk to you about these things. You have such a great insight into human nature; you'd make a great psychiatrist."

She smiled at me and gave me a wink while chewing on a forkful of pasta.

"I think I have great insight, darling, because I am removed from the situation, I am not as emotionally vested in the relationship as you are and so I can see the forest for the trees. Besides, I like being a lawyer and I think my skills are better suited to defense work rather than counselling. Though arguably, defense work does seem like counselling and babysitting to some degree, too."

"Yeah, I imagine it could."

"Another thing I'm thinking, Mike, is what is the harm in letting him entertain his hallucinations in light of the fact that he has what, maybe weeks or at most a few months left of life? What can really be the worst case scenario for him?"

I was looking outside at the dark, purple, bruised night sky. The snow like little down feathers falling through the orange haze of the street lamps.

"I suppose it wouldn't be the end of the world. Depends if it gets worse and these people start interfering with our sessions together, then that might become a problem. I don't have the time nor would it be valuable to anyone to try and start counselling an additional three fictitious people."

"How did your illness manifest itself in the early days, Mike? Did you have hallucinations too?"

"Not visual hallucinations, but I do remember hearing voices and sounds that couldn't have been in the immediate environment around me. I'd hear horns and sirens and people yelling. Sometimes it would make sense and other times it would be just like a ruckus and I couldn't pick up on any specific words. But it always sounded like it was happening right outside next to me and not inside my head, if you know what I mean. These were not just sounds that were in my head as thoughts. They were definitely projected outside into the real world so that they seemed so real. It was like I was caught up in a school evacuation or fire alarm or something of that sort. It would interfere with me being able to concentrate on the reality around me. It competed for attention and it created a huge liability for me in the real world. Obviously."

We finished up our pasta almost simultaneously. I took the last sip of my wine. I was feeling relaxed, a little more self-assured about myself and my abilities to help Janko. Margaret had certainly helped put some perspective on it for me. She has a great way of helping me become centered and calm. She continually helps me see the big picture.

"That must have been very scary, sweetheart. I can only imagine."

She was looking at me through kind eyes. I'm certain she was an old soul and a deeply compassionate one at that. I'd always seen her eyes as being kind and gentle. Big deep, still pools that mirrored her soul.

"It was very scary. I was coming into my own as an adult. Around nineteen, I think, when I first started noticing these symptoms. Sort of like ringing in my ears that sounded like it was coming from outside of me. By the time I finally got diagnosed and on the medication I was a wreck. I was barely sleeping, I was as thin as a rake and I didn't know how, or if, I could filter all the junk from what was real. I was on a really quick downhill spiral. Thankfully though, I had a great family and parents who were in tune with me and got me the help I needed. I can't imagine having to try and figure it out by myself. So yes, honey, it was very scary, indeed."

"So you never had the same symptoms as Janko, then?"

"No, but then I also haven't had the horrendous childhood that he has likely had to endure either. And admittedly, the side effects of the medications are something that you have to be prepared for, but they've gotten better over the decades since I first started taking the anti-psychotics."

We took our plates into the kitchen to clean up and I poured us a glass of water each. Ice cream was in order and I served us up a big serving of cookie dough. I bet you can taste it. Really, really good. A favorite of both Margaret's and mine.

"Give him a chance Mike. I think maybe that is all he needs. Someone to believe in him and reach out to him as you are doing."

We were talking over our ice cream. Already I was feeling better about the near future with Janko. Amazing what a little sweetness can do for you.

"Well, honey, tell me about how your day was?"

I got up and put the fireplace on. Before it even started giving off its warmth I was feeling toasty inside. Maybe it was the magic of Margaret's insight and wisdom.

"Well, I helped a fourteen year old get off on a car theft charge. A small little boy, probably not much taller than five feet, with a really babyish face. It was his first offence and he just needed a car to drive back and forth from school. His parents wouldn't let him get his learner's permit, either. So he stole this big old American car, an Oldsmobile or something, and kept it down the block from his home. The only reason he got caught was because he saw the police coming the other way when he was on his way to school one day and he decided to duck as he passed them. Needless to say he crashed into them and was caught."

I had to laugh at that.

"Brazen little bugger, wouldn't you say."

"Absolutely, but he doesn't have a malicious bone in him, and I think the judge could see that so she just gave him a conditional discharge with some community service. The sad part to this humorous story is that he can't read. I found that out when I took him to get his learner's permit. He passed because they'll let you take it orally, but it's really going to set him back if he can't get the help he needs. I mean, can you imagine passing a child like this through the different grades so that he doesn't become your problem? A terrible way to deal with him. But anyway, his parents are aware of it now, and they seem very motivated to help him learn to read. I put them in touch with some community resources that will help them get help for their son. They're fairly poor as you might have guessed."

"Yes, I can imagine. It often seems the poor have the greater burden of life's difficulties and the fewer resources to deal with them."

I was finished with my ice cream. It didn't take me long. I put the bowl down on the coffee table and propped my feet up on it as well. I stretched my arm around Margaret's shoulders and leaned over to kiss her on the cheek. I could feel the warmth of the fire emanating towards me like hot, dry breath.

"But you know, darling, even though this young man, Reggie, was guilty, I don't feel too bad about him getting off. He's still young enough to be able to change his ways with the right help, and except for a little minor damage to the front fender of the vehicle, he had taken good care of it. The owners have only been put out for a couple of weeks without a vehicle. In the large scheme of things I don't see the harm. I know that most of my clients are juveniles and most of them are themselves victims of circumstance, rather than hardened criminals. But with Reggie, I really feel that getting him off was the right approach. Some of the others I'm not so sure about. But justice has to be a double edged sword, and if the police or other authorities are dropping the ball, then people are going to get off and that is as it should be."

"It sounds, honey, like you are sometimes frustrated by that?"

"Yes, I am. I have another case right now where this sixteen year old sexually assaulted a female friend of his. Not the worst sexual assault that I've seen, but definitely an assault, nonetheless. I think he needs to be sentenced. Maybe spend time in jail on the weekends or something.

But he is someone whom we need to be watching and punishing early before things get out of hand. But it looks like the police dropped the ball on his charter rights and so he'll likely get off. That's what bugs me. It doesn't teach him anything other than might makes right and that he can get away with this kind of heinous behavior."

"Have you ever thought of throwing this case?"

She turned to me and put her hand on my thigh.

"Yes, I have. You know I've subtly thrown cases before, Mike, but this one just doesn't seem to reach the threshold. Sure, he raped her, but it was more from aggression and omission than forcible, brutal rape. And that's what bugs me the most, being in this grey area of no-man's land filled with these landmines. Should I throw it? Does it measure up the standards? I just don't like being in this kind of position where I have to question my integrity and commitment between my own moral compass and the objectivity of the law. I wish it would be simpler. It should be simpler."

I turned to face her and grasped her hands in mine.

"I know. You get to wonder why we're doing this. What's the point? That's what I feel like sometimes, anyway. I suppose you just have to trust in your intuition and your own inner guide and hope that there is a grander or overarching justice out there that will be meted out."

"Yes, I know Mike. I do question it sometimes. Sometimes I feel like a rat in a cage just spinning around on this big exercise wheel and not really getting anywhere. It seems somewhat pointless then, doesn't it? And very occasionally I start to wonder about what the difference is between spinning my wheels doing what I usually think is important and just work, and becoming a corporate lawyer and spinning my wheels in that arena instead. At least you get paid better and the work is more mundane perhaps and it would keep you busy keeping up with the Joneses and buying stuff and working long hours. God that sounds so pathetic, too, doesn't it? Is there no solution, darling, to the dilemma of finding meaning in life?"

She looked a little tired. She took her bowl of ice cream and started scooping that into her mouth.

"Wouldn't it just be great to be a cat or a dog or something? Laze around all day and get fed and loved and have all your needs taken care of. That has got to be pretty good. Maybe like a child too, just living in the moment and not caring about what will come next.

Your needs taken care of. But then again, children grow up and become adults and have to deal with these same problems. I think the best solution is to become a cat. That's what I want to be if I come back, God forbid. A cat in a good home."

She finished her ice cream and placed the bowl on top of mine on the coffee table. The bowls were stripped with creamy white lines. Little streaks of the ice cream we just couldn't get off the bowl. Camouflaged zebra stripes. Shades of white on white.

"I hear you about being a cat or dog and just sitting around lazing all day long. Getting love and fed and housed. That sure sounds like the life for me. Maybe we should put in a special request when we've finished up this trip, hey?"

I squeezed her hands and kissed them on the backs.

"Well, you can take comfort in the thought that you don't often feel this way, my love. But I do understand how you feel. I often wonder what the point of all of this is. Often I find the answers, too. Like with Janko, I think he is an answer as to why I do what I do. Especially if I can end up helping him as much as I'd like and think that I can. Perhaps for you, Reggie is an answer as to why you do what you do.

I think what we are here to do is to love one another and to find work that helps us to fulfil our destinies and dreams and to become the person that we need to become. I've never felt so alive as when I'm with you, my love. It is love that gives me purpose and drives me to help my clients and to become a better person. The love that I have for you is what inspires me and gives me courage through my difficulties and trials. I think everything is dependent on love. It's like currency. Lack of it creates so many social ills and poverty. Particularly the poverty of the spirit.

And of course lots of love creates abundance and wealth of spirit. You know that babies deprived of love, as made manifest in physical touch, will die even if they are fed sufficiently. That is the power of love and the power that we can harness and use to push us to greater things, to help us contribute to the greater good, and it is love that will help us reach beyond ourselves to become better than we were before.

And as I'm saying this, honey, I'm talking to myself, too. Don't forget that I am not infallible. I need these kinds of words to get me through sometimes, too. And now would be one of those times.

Let's try not to focus on the rat in a cage metaphor; that's an awful one and not helping me for sure. How about we are leisurely big cats strolling in the jungle of love stopping to help others every now and then."

I smiled at her. It was a weak smile, like old tea, and it washed out quickly. This day had taken its toll on me. I was tired mentally and emotionally. Had a great visit with Janko and then I was reviewing his file and started to second-guess myself about my abilities to help him in the amount of time we had left.

"Yes, darling, I'll try and remember that. I'll try to focus on the currency of love. It'll help me, I'm sure, because I love you so very much. I am sometimes amazed at how strong and steady my love for you has been all these years. It has never wavered, never doubted itself. If nothing else, I have found strength and courage and confidence in the love we share and in the love we have together."

My smile brightened now, slapped together with a bit more mortar, though it was fresh and hadn't set very well. Still, it had more staying power than before.

"And besides, Margaret, I don't think you and I could do anything else, anyway. I think we find it, for the most part, to be beneficial and helpful to help others. It gives sense and meaning to our work, as it should. Me going into plastic surgery or you going into corporate law would be to give in and give up everything we believe in. I think it would kill our souls, maybe slowly, maybe quickly, but certainly nonetheless. I believe that you can sell yourself to the devil, and he has a corner office in one of the corporate office towers downtown. Wouldn't you say, Margaret, that you and I work in the trenches, we work in the emergency rooms of society? This society that is so unnatural that our work is built upon its flaws. I think that my patients with their illnesses and perhaps your clients with their delinquencies or criminal behaviors are symptomatic of all that is wrong in our culture."

Her eyes lit up and she nodded her head a few times. I think I was slowly lighting a fire back under her.

"Yes, you're right, Mike. It is symptomatic of our insane social constructs. Maybe I'm just getting tired of working in the trenches, railing against the machine and not being able to see us get any headway. Perhaps we need a breather, a holiday or vacation away from here for a bit. Something to renew our vigor and refresh our spirit and our fight."

"I agree, honey. I think we definitely need to take some time again, just the two of us, and to reconnect somewhere peaceful and romantic. Perhaps somewhere in South America. A place where they are living somewhat authentic lives. I think we have also lost our fighting spirit from a lack of perspective. A trip like that could really renew us. I think we are desperate for finding that truth that makes living bearable. I say we go somewhere where we can see love in action, unencumbered by affluence and the stain of materialism. But it will have to wait until Janko has gone to the light."

"Of course."

"In the meantime, maybe we'd do well to look back at our student days. Days filled with passionate activism and a strong moral compass. And of course poverty in a student way. Uncluttered, unencumbered by the weight of possessions and material and financial gain."

She was rubbing my shoulder now and reached over to kiss me. Light had come back into her eyes.

"It's funny you say that, darling, I was just thinking about our student days, when we were poor and living in that one bedroom basement suite. Do you remember walking to and from university in the middle of winter? It was about a half hour walk, but we didn't seem to mind. We had each other and we had love, and maybe you're right, we had a vision of the world and our place in it. We were passionate about human rights, worker's rights, poverty and equality. It seemed that it gave drive and meaning to our lives back then, hey?"

I got up to turn off the fireplace. It was getting too hot, making me sleepy.

"I think it did give drive and meaning to our existence. And I think it can still do that, honey, if we just try and find the passion that maybe we've lost at the moment, for some reason. Maybe we're just in need of a break. Time to get some distance between us and find that perspective. See the lay of the land again as we once saw it when we were young and our lives were uncluttered by materialism and trying to keep on the treadmill of capitalism. This treadmill which, by the way, seems to be conveying us nowhere, and doing it ever faster.

This whole socially constructed environment that we and everyone else are caught up in is hard on the sensitive and the compassionate and those of us who are independent thinkers.

You go to work five days a week at wage slavery and you barely get enough to get by, or if you do have the money, then you buy stuff to fill in the void that you feel is in your life. But it cannot be filled by stuff because it is a void caused by our poverty of soul that has been socially engineered in some ways. At the end of the day, people just want to get home, plop in front of the couch, watch the tube, and numb out the gnawing pain of their starving spirit, trying to eat itself into the consciousness of their minds. What's happening to us, my love, is that our spirits have gnawed through and we're having to deal with it now. And perhaps we just have to focus on why we chose the work we did. Which was to help make this a better place. Maybe we need to become more patient with ourselves and this world and not expect everything to get fixed right away. It may take time. It might not even come about during our lifetimes. And maybe we just have to make peace with that. Taking a break, going for a holiday might just help us put all of that in perspective."

"Yes, Mike. I think that will be exactly what we need. We haven't taken a holiday in a couple of years. At least not a real one. We've always wanted to go to South America. I think that's the perfect idea. Maybe next fall or winter. Sadly, I imagine that Janko will likely have passed on by then?"

I propped my legs up on the coffee table and sank further into the couch. I was still feeling sleepy. I blamed it on the wine and the residual heat of the fire. I had my arm around Margaret's shoulders.

"Yes, honey. Sadly, I think that Janko will have left us by then. I'm not sure I could give him more than another month quite frankly. But you never know the stubbornness of the human spirit. I have to speak to his physician right away to find out what the prognosis is. To create a plan of attack for our sessions coming up. I hope I can get to the place I want to with him before he leaves. I haven't felt this way about one of my patients for a long time, if ever really. But you're right, the fall would be a great time to go to South America. Perhaps Belize or somewhere like that. We've spoken of Belize before, haven't we?"

Margaret nodded, "Yes, we have. I think that would be a perfect choice. Maybe if we can manage the time we can take a few weeks and try to get to a few countries. Perhaps Brazil and Chile too?"

I turned to her and smiled.

"I like the way you're thinking."

219

We sat in silence for a while, each of us to our own thoughts. Pleasant thoughts I imagined. Our upcoming travels, perhaps. Maybe hopeful thoughts on our clients? I was certainly more optimistic about Janko than I had felt earlier in the day with the overwhelming evidence of his illness and difficulties in life. I turned to Margaret and kissed her on the lips, holding her face in my hands.

"Thanks for your insight, honey. You really know how to steer me back onto the straight and narrow. You know, I love these conversations we have. It reminds me of our student days when we were so passionate about our dreams and goals and how we were going to change the world. I feel fired up again, excited about things with Janko and our place in the world and how we can change things for the better. The fire in my belly has been re-ignited and my vista is full and wide with possibilities."

"I know exactly how you feel, darling. I feel the same way. It is refocusing isn't it? Refocusing on the things we can change and taking a different and more patient approach to change itself. I think we lose track of the changes we have made in people's lives and the change we continue to make in our own little spheres of influence. This kind of chat we had is just what we need to recharge ourselves so that we can go on to be more effective. Plus, I find it helps to support our relationship too."

I nodded, "You are spot on there, my honey. Communication has been the key to our success together, I believe. It is the key to any successful relationship, I think. Me with Janko, you in court and all sorts of human interaction."

Margaret nodded, too, and got up from the couch.

"I'm going to make some tea. Would you like some?"

"I'd love some chamomile tea. What are you going to have?"

"I think I'll join you with that. I'll make a pot."

She picked up our streaky bowls of ice cream. The spoons sticking out of them like thermometers between two lips. She walked off into the kitchen with my eyes following her. I was happy. I was content and all was well again in my world. The love of a good woman can have that effect. Love itself can have that effect. It is the grease that keeps life running smoothly.

XXI

I was tired of not getting enough sleep. I kept waking up at all sorts of odd hours during the night. It was shitty. Tiring and despairing. Mostly I kept waking up to go to the bathroom. Maybe it was time for me to look into getting a catheter to make this part of my life a whole lot easier. Just to pee away freely as I lie in my bed, and not spilling a drop. That sounded so tempting at the moment. Sometimes I would wake for no apparent reason. Maybe I had heard a noise, or maybe I had had a bad dream. Who knew? Tonight, or this morning, whatever God damn time it was, I was awake because my bladder felt like a damn stone melon filled with lead. I didn't want to move in case it made it worse. I didn't want to open my eyes because I knew they would feel like a sandy beach with little gnomes walking up and down them. But I had to. I had to open my eyes, and I had to try and get out of bed or I'd spill my piss all over myself and there was no one here to clean it up or to change my sheets, and I barely had the strength or motivation to be doing that for myself.

I sighed into the room as if releasing a ghost from within me and I opened my eyes. I looked at the ceiling and closed my eyes. And that's when the gnomes started walking all over my sandy eyes. I opened them again and looked at the topographical feature of the ceiling. I liked that word. Kind of reminded me of what its meaning was. Topography sounded like it was a word with peaks and valleys. The ceiling was another world of hills and valleys for people that I couldn't see, just their huge upside down mountains. The room and ceiling were washed in a dirty, dark yellow from the night light in the room. I looked at my alarm clock on the table. The bloody numbers bled out a minute as I watched for just a few seconds. Three eleven it glared and then three twelve. A minute of my life gone in just a few seconds.

I fumbled for the glass of water that was half empty, or as the doctor would have me say, half full, on my bedside table. I nearly spilled its emptiness or fullness, you choose, onto the clock as I tried with difficulty to get up onto my one elbow.

"Jesus," I gasped catching a glimpse of someone out of the corner of my eye.

It was MJ sitting still on the end of my bed her legs crossed and her body turned towards me, her hand propping herself up on the bed close to my legs.

"You scared the shit out of me…"

"Sorry, Jay, we didn't mean to, but we've got some talking to do with you."

I craned my neck forward to see the figure in the chair. I was still propped up on my elbows, the glass now in my hand but resting mostly on the bed. The figure moved closer out of the darkness and into the dirty light. It was Norman. Happy, funny, Norman. And then I looked towards the window and saw Peter staring out. Hands folded in front of him.

"Jesus Christ. Can you guys not leave me alone for just a quiet night's sleep? It's three in the fucking morning. I mean, come on, give me a break."

I was getting tired so I lay back down and sighed or groaned, probably a combination of both. MJ started to rub my shins.

"It's okay, J, we don't want to fight with you. Well, I should say Peter and I don't want to fight with you."

"What? Are you saying I'm just into fighting? Is that it? Because I'm not, okay, but somebody's gotta stand up for what's right sometimes, okay? I also didn't come here to fight, okay? I came here to talk. Isn't that what I just said not a moment ago?"

Norman was getting himself all agitated. He sat back in the chair and started to crack his fingers. Peter turned away from the windows and looked at MJ and then me and then Norm.

"Guys. We came here to talk to Janko together, not to start fighting with each other. We have a lot to talk about and getting upset with one another is not going to help our cause. I know we don't usually get along, and that's why we've usually visited Janko separately. But this is different now. We need to put our differences behind us and come forward as a united team."

"I agree," said MJ to Peter, "and I think that Janko needs us to be united for him, too. How else will we be able to help him or ourselves without a united front? Norman?"

Norman didn't say anything. He could get stuck in sullenness pretty easily and stay there a couple of hours if he wanted to. Just to punish you, or so he thought. I figured he was just punishing himself. I usually liked it when he was quiet. Then he wasn't berating me or bitching at me as he was usually prone to do.

"Well," I said, "while you three try and figure out what the hell you're doing here I'm going to go take a piss, okay? And then when I get back, I'm going to try and get back to sleep. I'm so damn tired. And you people coming to visit me all the time at these God-forsaken hours is taking its toll on me. Just think about that, too. If you are so prone to wanting to help me then just think about that. I need rest and sleep. I mean, look at me. I'm knocking on death's door because I'm too weak to ring the bell and he's just watching me through the peephole, thinking about when it's best to let me in. I don't have time for this shit, okay? Think about that while you bitch away at each other."

I strained myself up to sitting. Grabbed onto my IV stand to hoist myself up. The God damn rubber tube got caught under my thigh and as I reached out to pull myself up, it got caught between it and my wrist. I cursed under my breath and collapsed back onto the bed, my lower legs dangling off the edge.

"Fuck," I said, "you fucking people are killing me."

I wasn't really talking to anyone in particular. I was staring at the ceiling, the dirty yellow ceiling, and getting more pathetic, and feeling miserable about myself. These assholes weren't helping. And I was tired. I had been tired for weeks it seemed and that left me with a crabby disposition, generally. I loved these new words I had been finding in the dictionary. Like disposition or topography. When I had the time that's what I did, read the dictionary and some other stuff. Novels mostly, except that I didn't have the attention span to concentrate on them too much. It was easier to read a word or two from the dictionary.

I could concentrate better that way. Anyway, I'm off on a tangent again. I wanted to rip out my bladder and kick it around the room like a soccer ball. It was aching and pulsing in time with my feeble and weak heart.

I could just see my dick at any moment now squirting piss all over the place with each pulse of my heart. I groaned again and pulled myself up, careful this time to brush the tube aside. I hobbled towards the bathroom. I portrayed a pleasant picture of myself as an invalid and buckled over senior citizen. Invalid summed up nicely how I felt. Not valid. Jesus, these people or my bladder or something was just rubbing me the wrong way.

"Norman, I'm not in the fucking mood."

He had decided to get up off his chair and block my way to the washroom. I was just about ready to piss all over him if he wasn't careful.

"Oh, the great Janko is not in the mood. You're so fucking pathetic. What are you going to do to stop me, huh? Have you looked at yourself in the mirror, lately? You couldn't squash a bug if you sat on it."

He was right in my face. Up close and personal. Inches away and I could see his spit collecting like a blob of pus on the corner of his mouth.

"No, Norman, I'm really not in the mood. And you know what. I'm not scared of you anymore, okay? I'm dying and I just don't give a shit, anymore. And yes, I couldn't beat you up. But what I can do is just start pissing all over you if you don't let me get to the can, okay? I'm serious. I'm desperate and I need to urinate. And as I see it, it's either you or the toilet. You choose."

He didn't like that one very much, so he moved out of the way, but barely.

"You best hurry, okay? We've got lots to talk about when you get back. I'm not happy with you, okay? I'll give you that warning right now."

I brushed past him as I continued into the bathroom. I sat down and it hurt at first but then as my bladder emptied it felt great. As I sat there enjoying a moment by myself I could hear Norman, MJ, and Peter bickering in the background.

"You are an asshole, Norman, you know that," said Peter.

"Come on, Peter. You can't be serious. I mean look at what we're dealing with here. He's being combative with us, and I don't think he likes us or wants us around anymore. You've heard him. He's changed. And not for the better."

"Guys will you just quit it. Janko is still the same he's always been. Give him a chance. He has a fair point, we do usually come and visit him at these odd hours. And he is dying. And that means we will lose him, too, and I think that makes us sad. Let's not waste these moments that we have. They are too few and too precious and God knows how little time we might have left with Janko."

I was finished now, but getting up again was a chore. I stole some courage and got up. I felt faint and sweat pricked my forehead. Cold sweat, so I shivered and bent over as much as I could. I couldn't afford to take a spill in the bathroom. My vision started to darken but I held it back and finally got myself back to normal, and trudged back into the bedroom, and eased myself back into bed. Peter and Norm were crowding around the foot of my bed with MJ still seated on the edge at the bottom. As soon as I was comfortable she patted my shin again.

"You know we care deeply about you, Janko," she said, "Norm too, he just has a hard time showing it. We miss you is all, and we're scared that we're losing you."

I was lying in bed staring at the ceiling. It's amazing what you can find in the ceiling if you look hard enough and long enough. I often wondered if what I saw mirrored my moods. Like, being in a foul mood now, I could easily see three or four dragon faces and devil faces in there. Other times, there were fat little angel faces and smiling baby faces. I spoke to the ceiling, but threw the words out for my friends to hear.

"But you are losing me. I mean, I'm dying and the good doctor knows it, as does my family doctor. He won't say how long but I feel bad. I feel a little worse every day. And you guys picking on me all the time or, should I say, mostly Norm picking on me all the time, is not helping."

Norm coughed, but I didn't look at him.

"I don't know how you guys can say you miss me when I see you so often. I mean, I kind of miss the old times, in a way. But I'm not willing to live in that place anymore. We've spoken about this a lot and you know that I wanted to try and heal and get the help that I need. Dr. Malichem can help me with that. I'm trying to leave this place in a better shape than I've been in for the last twenty years, or whatever it has been. You guys have to accept that and help me move in that direction. And you guys also need to change, too, and to try and get comfortable with it. It isn't easy, and God knows I'm struggling, but I'm finding my way there with the good doctor's help. I need your help too. I'd like your help, too."

I shifted up onto my elbows and twisted myself around to grab the other pillow and put it on top of the other one. I lay back down. It was better. I could at least see them now. Peter was looking at me, and so was MJ. She had kind eyes. She could always melt my heart with her look. Norman however, was staring at the floor, his arms folded across his chest.

"And, Norm," I said looking at him even though he wouldn't look at me, "I know you care for me. You're trying, and I recognize that, but the last time I saw you we spoke about that. Your tough guy attitude and emotional coldness aren't helping me anymore. There was a glimmer from you that I saw that last time. A kindness, a gentleness that really encouraged me, and I'd like to see more of that. I need it. Especially from you. You were my rock when I needed one and you were like a big brother then, protecting me and trying to stand up for me. But I need your strength in a different way now. In a way to keep me true to this new path that I'm on. Norm, your strength now is needed in a kindlier and gentler way. The days of combat for me, and for us, are over. We need to find the peace and love that we haven't found in a long time. Let's start looking behind those layers of armour that have kept me strong before and protected. Let's take that armour off, Norm, it's getting heavy, now, it's weighing me down, now. I need a rest from it. It's time to head out by being vulnerable and unprotected. We are at a safe place now with the nurses and the good doctor. We can do it, but I still need your help to take this armour off of me."

"Yeah, and aren't those nurses good looking you lucky dog," said Peter. He was trying to joke now, lighten the mood. I looked at him and smiled and then looked back at Norm and he looked at me, then. He came up to me and a tear rolled down his cheek. That was followed by another one from the other eye. He came up and hugged me and it felt good. The first time I had ever received physical affection from him. I spoke into the air behind him.

"I do need you, Norm. I need you maybe more than ever. And maybe you just don't see that, but it's true. Your edginess and hardness could be helpful to me now as I embark on this path to peace."

He pulled away from me with his one hand still on my shoulder and he looked at me through wet eyes.

"Thanks, Jay. I'm just not certain that you need me anymore, and that kind of scares me. Maybe it scares us all and we probably handle it differently, but it scares the shit out of me. I don't want to lose you."

He turned around then and walked to the end of the room and looked outside into the black night. He dabbed at his eyes with the sleeves of his sweater. Peter had taken the seat he had been sitting on. I saw a few stars twinkling out in the black night. Maybe Morse code, maybe a signal from God that things just might be okay. I don't know. Who the fuck knew? But I was trying to make sense of it, look for the glimmer of hope in the black sky that mirrored the blackness of my life. Maybe these friends could be my twinkling stars. I don't know. I'm grasping at straws. I'm trying to make sense of it all, okay? Just doing my best.

Peter looked up from his chair. He had his hands clasped in his lap. He looked relaxed but his face was pained.

"Norm's right, Janko. We are all in need of reassurance, and that's what we have come to speak to you about. We are all scared of losing you in many ways, physically, emotionally and mentally. I think I can say I speak for all of us when I say that."

He looked at MJ and she looked back at him and nodded before turning to me.

"It's true, Jay, it really is."

She was rubbing my leg again, looking down at it with sadness on her face and a small frown across her brow. I looked back up at the ceiling. I could see it better now. Still bathed in that dirty yellow light, but it seemed brighter. I thought that maybe I could even see some of those demon faces morphing into something kinder. Fuck, maybe I'm just kidding myself. I don't know, but Jesus, I'm trying, if you'd just let me try. You know it's not easy for me. But let me believe in something. Let me believe that some good will come from this pain, otherwise what is the point. I have to have something to hold onto, right? Something to believe in.

I turned to my bedside table. A trinity of bloody threes on my clock. I fumbled for my pack of cigarettes, took one out, and lit it. I grabbed the ashtray and placed it on my chest. It bobbed like a buoy with my rising breath. I notice that now, my breath. It represents life, and my life can probably be counted now by the number of breaths I have left.

Thousands maybe, who knows. Sounds like a lot, but it maybe only adds up to weeks. And I'm seeing each one as a precious gift now.

Yeah, I know that I was ready to die just a while back, but other times I get scared, okay? Like now. It's inevitable, I know that, but sometimes I just want to hang on a while longer, especially when there seems to be a glimmer of hope. You'd do the same, wouldn't you?

Peter looked at me again. "We are scared of losing you, Janko. And not just to death. What we've really come here to talk about is your developing relationship with Dr. Malichem especially, and also the nurses. We know about your last session, Jay, and we're worried about it. Worried that Dr. Malichem is going to find out about us and not want us around in the picture."

"What do you mean, Peter? The good doctor just wants to help me. I'll tell him you're my friends. He'll understand that, Peter. Come on guys, I need you guys too. The doctor isn't going to take that away from me."

"But, Janko, we're not fucking real, okay? He's not going to just let you continue relationships with people in your fucking head while he's out there in the real world, trying to cure you of your illness and your problems. Think about it."

Norm had turned towards me from the window and walked up to the edge of the bed. There were no more tears in his eyes now.

"But, Norm, you're real to me, okay? I'm not going to let the good doctor interfere with that. And by now if he's read my file he should know that I am not interested in being healed from my illness. I want to make peace with my life and find that peace and love in my soul. It's clear that I do not want any of those fucking antipsychotics administered to me. I'm not going to take them. The only shit they can give me is pain medication. So you guys aren't going to go anywhere, if I don't want you to. You guys have been a big part of my life for over twenty years. I'm not about to give up on that when you're all I've got. When you're the only family and friends I have. I know you aren't really real, but to me you are, and I need you. Especially now. Especially when I'm at my weakest, most vulnerable, and trying to look into my pain. I mean, that is helluva scary, okay? There is no way that I'm going to let anything come between us. Not even the doctor. The work I'm doing with him is so important for my healing. You know how important it is, Peter, MJ."

They both nodded at me.

"I talked to you guys about it and you kind of agreed that it was important for me. You guys know all about the intimate details of my life and how hard it has been and no doubt how it has contributed to the shit that I'm dealing with now. I know you are more scared than I am, because you can't leave but I can push you out. But I'm not going to do that to you, okay? I need you in my life, maybe more now than ever before. Please try to see that and understand it."

My cigarette was off burning all by itself. I tapped the ash into my glass ashtray and I wondered if that was what I'd look like when I was dead and they had burned me up. Just ash, with no phoenix to rise out of it if I didn't get my life in order before I left. Maybe we're all human cigarettes to the man upstairs, and he sucks the life out of us and leaves us empty like this ash when he's done. I'm sorry, okay, I'm getting angry and despondent again. I looked out at the night sky and smiled at the twinkling stars. Maybe they could be old souls winking at me. Lovers that I've never known I've had.

"Why are you smiling, Jay?" asked MJ.

I looked at her and winked.

"Because it's so fucking good to see you all together. I hardly ever get to have you guys visit me all at once. And I was thinking about those twinkling stars out there and what they could be. Maybe they could be the long lost souls of lovers winking at me from the world beyond."

MJ smiled and so did Peter. Norm frowned.

"Jay," Norm said, "we're trying to talk about the doctor, okay? Can you try and remain focused on that."

He wasn't mad just frustrated.

"I understand what you're saying about all of this. But Dr. Malichem might have other ideas for you. He might not want to have us kicking around and he might want you to get rid of us. You wouldn't have to have medication in order to do that, you know. It could work with just his help and counselling. What kind of reassurance can you give us that it won't happen?"

"Norm," said MJ, "I think Janko has been trying to give us reassurance all along here. Haven't you been listening to a word he's been saying?"

"Yes, I have Mary. Yes, I have. I thought we were all on the same team here coming together to talk to Janko as a group. You don't have to get snarky with me, okay?"

I looked at the two of them banter back and forth. Dancing around like sparring partners. I don't think they cared for each other much. And I had to side with MJ on this one. She was my favourite, next would be Peter and lastly Norm. I'm sure you could understand why. I took a puff on my cigarette and blew smoke rings at Norm pretending they were silencing lasers.

"Could you guys stop the bickering please? Norm, I have been trying to tell you and encourage you with reassurance that I am not going to let the good doctor make me forsake you. And this isn't helping okay. I need you to be strong for me and kind and supportive, not heavy handed and belligerent like this. Because I am in a weak and vulnerable place, and I don't know what is going to happen or how I am going to come to terms with my pain, anger, and sadness. You are not helping with your badgering of me. I need your support. I don't know how else to tell you. I think you are going to have to trust me on this. And time will show you that I'm right. You are probably correct that the good doctor knows about you by now. But I trust him like I would a father and I believe that you guys are important to me and I'll need you until the end, probably. I'm sure he will understand that. You are not going to interfere with my healing and I'll argue that you are going to be extremely important in helping me along that path. He will see it, or if he doesn't, I will not be able to work as best as I can with him in getting to the peace and forgiveness I need. I get the sense that he wants that as much as I do. I really think his main focus is in getting me well again. And that can't happen if I don't have you, my friends, to lean on. You are all I have. Sure, I have the good doctor and the nurses, but I haven't known them long enough to be able to trust them. I can trust in you guys because you've been with me so long…"

"And because you've made us up," said Norm.

"Fair enough, Norm, that's true. But you are what I cling to when I dig into the deep, dark, and scary places that I need to unearth in order to heal and to move on. And you are stifling me if you won't support me. I can't cope with that on top of the counselling that I am desperate to finish before I die. I don't think I have a long time left before I die. Weeks, maybe months. You guys know that. So please, help me, be my friends that I need you to be. Be my rock and my shelter and safe harbours in this storm that is my soul's journey to health. Can you do that for me, please?"

"Of course we can, Jay," said MJ. She came up to me and kissed me on the forehead and then went to sit back down on the end of the bed.

"Sure, Jay, I can try and do that for you," said Peter and he came and squeezed my shoulder and then sat back down in the chair. I looked at Norm and raised my eyebrows, he was looking down at the floor.

"I'll try," he said to the floor. And I knew that was about the best I could get out of him for now. But it was a start. His arms were crossed over his chest. He didn't look at anybody. I wondered if he could see faces in the carpet like the faces I could see in the ceiling. I looked up at the ceiling again and yes, I could see the faces, but more of them were becoming gentler and kinder. I wasn't sure Norm was having the same luck as I was.

I smoked my cigarette some more, thinking about our conversations. And I started thinking about what a shit life I'd had. For twenty something years I'd had no real friends, or at least none that I could recall now. I mean sure I'd had acquaintances and people I'd known, but that's not the same as having friends, right? I'm sure you can understand that, or maybe you can't. Doesn't really make a difference to things now, anyway. But fuck, it's been a shitty life, not having any friends except for three imaginary ones who sometimes act like pouting children and not real friends. You'd think that being hallucinations that I'd made up I would have better control over them, but it doesn't work like that and that makes me feel shittier, okay?

Those fucking faces on the ceiling were getting ugly again. I blew smoke up to them to fuzzy them out and make them blurry. And they were getting blurry too, except I realized it was because my eyes were misting up and I was crying. And that fucking pain in my throat, in my heart, was heavy like a cold metal ball. And it hurt. It hurt more than the physical pain of my dying body. Because it was the pain of sorrow, and of life, of destitute dreams, and impending doom. What do you with that at almost four in the morning when the good doctor isn't around to see how I'm doing? Sometimes, the only thing that keeps me alive is the fact that I'm too weak to kill myself and because I'm dying anyway.

Norm walked over to the window, his arms still folded over his chest. I dabbed at my eyes with my comforter. I looked at him and could see his face, dark in this dirty yellow glow of light reflected in the mirror. It looked like he was staring at me, but I think he was just looking outside.

"What's wrong, Jay?" asked MJ.

I looked over at her. She had moved up a bit and was sitting by my side now with her hand on my chest. I smiled as best I could and looked away. Peter was doing something with his hands. Fidgeting, looking at his nails. Who the fuck knew.

MJ rubbed my chest.

"Really, Jay, what's wrong?"

I looked over at her again and held her hand over my heart so she could feel my feeble beats.

"I'm dying, MJ. That's what's wrong, okay? I'm dying and I don't have a fucking soul in the world who knows or cares about me. And the only three people who are real to me are fucking figments of my imagination, they bicker back and forth, and they badger me too. That's what's wrong. I'm dying alone and no one in the whole fucking world gives a shit. No one. Do you know how lonely that makes me feel?"

She looked down at my hand then and frowned.

"No, I guess I don't, seeing as how I'm not real."

She was pouting now, too. Do you see the shit I'm trying to deal with on top of my own problems? I've got to deal with imaginary people who have their own neediness and crap and can't give me an ounce of space to try and get a handle on the shit I need to deal with. It is unbelievable.

"But you know what, Janko. We are also scared that you are dying, too. It is going to affect us too, you know. Because as you said, we are figments of your imagination and so, guess what happens when you die? We die, too. How do you think that makes us feel? It makes us feel shitty because it makes us feel exactly like you do. Because, guess what, Janko? We are you."

She had a point.

"Well, then, why can't you fucking help me in getting a grip on my sadness and let me work with the good doctor to heal myself?"

"Maybe," said Norman speaking to the pane of glass, "because this is how you want to feel. As MJ said, Janko, we are the two kings and one queen of hallucinations made up by you and you give us life. If you like, you could think that you are our God. So really, Janko, it's all up to fucking you. Get over yourself, okay? You pout and point out the shit that we are putting you through. Well guess what, genius? You're doing it to yourself and you're doing it to us, you jerk."

He turned around then and grabbed his hands behind his back. He was looking at the floor just like he was before. I was tempted to ask him if he's lost something there.

"That's enough, Norm," said Peter, "it's not helping."

Peter was still fidgeting with his fingers. Now he was bending them back and forth kind of like he was stretching them or something. I laughed. This shit was so farcical. Norm wasn't making any sense, and Peter was being totally goofy. Only MJ was making any sense or acting like she really cared about me.

"Norm, Peter's right. You're not making any fucking sense to me at all. First you're saying you aren't real so it's all my fault and then next you're saying because it's all my fault I'm making you guys feel all miserable and scared and shit."

"Look," I said to him pretending to pinch his head between my thumb and finger, "I'm squashing your brain."

He looked at me and glared. His right eyebrow was raised in a menacing manner and he came up towards me and meant business except that MJ stopped him with her arm.

"See, asshole," I said, "it's not that easy, okay? I can't just control you as I'd like. Because if I could I'd probably not be in this predicament and neither would you. See, Norman, you're still a fucking asshole wanting to come over here and do what? You gonna try and beat me up. You're the jerk, okay. Not me."

And he is, isn't he? He's a fucking asshole. I sucked on the stub of my cigarette and the smoke was hot in my mouth and thick and acrid. It was my least favourite part of smoking. I blew the smoke up to the ceiling not looking for faces of any sort. Kind or angry, I wasn't interested. I was a volcano letting off steam.

"Norm, Janko, Peter," said MJ, "can we please just get along. It's getting late and Jay probably wants to get some sleep sometime soon. Let's not end it like this. Let's find some common ground so we can all feel good and valued and needed. Is that okay?"

She looked at me first, still holding my hand holding hers on my chest. My heart thumped feebly in its cage. A man knocking eternally on the soul's door. Only no one was home. At least not for now, but I was hoping it'd be coming home soon. With the good doctor's help.

"I'll try, MJ. For you, I will try. For us, I'll try, or should I say for me and me and me and me, I'll try."

233

I smiled at her and she smiled back, life twinkling back in her eyes. She looked at Peter still fidgeting in the chair. Now he had taken to biting at his nails or cuticles or something. He looked up at her, his hand smearing his mouth.

"Yeah, sure," he mumbled.

Norm had gone to stand next to Peter. He was leaning his one hand on the back of the chair and looking over at us.

"Well...?" asked MJ.

Norm nodded and kept staring at us. MJ raised her eyebrows and nodded her head up towards the ceiling looking for something more from him. They stayed like that for ten, twenty seconds. MJ tossed her head up towards the ceiling again.

"Okay, okay, MJ, I'll do my best. Jesus. You're killing me."

He was trying to be funny.

"No, Norm, you've got that wrong. I'm killing us. I'm the one trying to kill us. And I'm doing a good job at it, too," I said.

No one smiled. Fuck, I try and lighten the mood and no one gets it.

"Okay, guys, let's all lighten up, okay? Come on now, why the sour puss faces? We used to be friends once upon a time. And if you aren't going to smarten up and help lighten the mood then I'm going to abandon us and forget the whole lot of you losers."

"You just told us you couldn't, Jay. I'm not buying what you're selling," said Norm.

MJ smiled at him and then back at me. "It's true," she said, "what can you really do, Jay."

I think she was playing with me more than poking fun. But still, my patience wasn't what it could have been.

"Shit, are we gonna go beating this horse again? I'm trying to spread the love here guys. Throw me a bone, okay?"

I noticed my cigarette had burnt itself out so I squashed it into the ash. Now it looked like the phoenix I was talking about earlier. It started to unbend and spread its imaginary wings. I liked that. I was thinking of the hope it represented. Corny I know, but I'm grasping for something small to keep me going. An emblem of hope and if this is it, well then, I think I've earned the right to grab onto it. Maybe not a big thing for you, but this could just keep me focused on my path, okay? Let me take what I can from the smallest things.

That's all I've got at the moment. The smallest things, which for me can mean so much. I looked at my friends. Splintered images of myself. What a sorry bunch, but what a hopeful bunch, too. We could do good things if we came together. Maybe that was my problem, I was so fucking splintered into pieces that I couldn't get a handle on bringing them all together. If I could do that, maybe I'd find myself whole sooner than later. Everyone was so quiet. They came to wake me up and now they had all shut up. I had a good mind to go back to sleep.

"You know what might help, Jay," said Peter resting his hands in his lap now.

"No, I don't. That's what I've been asking you guys all along here, to throw me a fucking bone."

"Well," he continued, "I hope I can speak for all of us here, but I think that you having us around for the next meeting with Dr. Malichem could be very helpful. It would sure show us a commitment to what you are saying about wanting to keep us around and all of that. Then we could get a good sense that the doctor isn't trying to get you to end us and we could get an idea of how you are with him. It would help us build the trust that we don't feel we have. It'd be a huge step, Jay."

Peter looked at me for a bit and then around at Norm and MJ. He was looking for friends and he'd come to the right place.

"That's a great idea, Peter," said MJ, "I love it and it would definitely make me feel more trusted and needed, Janko, if you'd do something like that for us."

They were all looking at me now, and all of a sudden the room seemed a helluva lot brighter and the light was on me.

"But you guys already know what's going on. You don't actually have to be there to get a sense of what is going on between the doctor and me. You are me and I am you, so what's the big deal?"

"The big deal, Janko," said Norm, "is that we don't trust you when you say that you're not going to get rid of us. I mean, come on. We've told you what we feel the doctor is going to do when he catches wind of us. Yeah, you've tried to reassure us otherwise, but you know what, that's not going to help. We need proof. And you inviting us in at your next session would give us that kind of proof and trust that we could start banking on. I mean it's one thing to say you want us to stick around, how badly you need us, and that is all well and good, but you've been hiding us from the doctor.

I want to see you recognize us in front of the doctor, and then I, for one, would definitely feel like you're serious about what you've been saying. Without that, Janko, we've got nothing we can bank on. Without that kind of a commitment you haven't really got our support and you might as well forget about your counselling being as successful as you'd like. It is a win-win for all of us. You get healed in the soul and we get to stick around until the end."

He was still standing by Peter. He shrugged his shoulders and bent his head to the side like he had just won a huge court case or something. I understood what he was trying to say, but I couldn't see how I could get away with it.

"Here, here," said Peter. He was back to chewing his nails.

"Amen, brothers," said MJ smiling and winking at me. "It's true Jay, we could really use such a huge gesture of good will. It would make us all feel better, more cared for, and wanted like you say you want us."

Norm nodded at me. I didn't know what to say. I fidgeted, biting at my own nails. I fumbled for my half empty glass of water and had some of that. I fingered the rubber hose stuck in my arm like it was worry beads. I still didn't have anything to say.

"You see," said Norm to everyone in the room but me, "he's not that interested in us. I told you this was a waste of our fucking time. Look at the loser sitting there looking at his hands. He doesn't have the courage to tell us he can't honor a simple request."

"Shhh," said MJ, "give him time."

They had a point and I couldn't dispute that. It made sense. But I was scared to try and get the good doctor to allow these people into our sessions. It might not help things, it might make things worse. I mean, it was bad enough having to deal with the nurses, and they were helpful. I wasn't sure that my friends here would be helpful. But I was getting tired, and sick of fighting. I needed some rest.

"Okay," I said, "you guys can come and hang out at the next session. But only as observers, okay? I don't want to hear you guys bickering and piping up with rude comments about the nurses, Peter, or ignorant, argumentative remarks, Norm, okay? Just strictly listening in and watching, okay? We can talk about it afterwards. Is that fair?"

It was more than fair. I knew it and they'd better know it, too.

"I think that seems reasonable, Jay. What do you guys think?" asked MJ.

Without looking at her, but looking at me Norm said, "Only if you tell the doctor that we're all there with you."

"Fair enough," I said.

"Then I'm game," said Peter, "and maybe, Jan, it'll be Maria there to help us. You know how much I go for that white uniform, and she is hot."

I shook my head at him.

"Can I get some sleep now, please? Do you mind? I'm so tired and it's not helping to keep me up like this."

"Sure, we'll go into the living room and watch some TV," said Norm.

And they did. I heard them put on the TV, it was an infomercial for a product that helped you lose weight fast. Not what I need. But it wasn't long and I was asleep like a baby or maybe it is better to say like the dead. I was asleep like the dead. Bear with me. I've got to find something funny in my situation. And it helps. You know it helps to laugh about what you fear. Patience, please. Patient be pleased.

XXII

The sky was getting a little blush on it. Maybe it was embarrassed from the night before. Maybe it had been a bad night, a naughty sky and the cold, sober day was starting to make it blush. I had just woken up and I was looking outside. It was a couple of days ago that I had my good friends over to visit. They had left by the time I woke up the next morning. And now it was Thursday, I think. It was a little after six on the clock radio. At six-thirty it would come on to a top forty station. Not that you care, but I'm telling you anyway. I was just thinking how well I had slept. Hadn't slept this well in weeks. I easily got a good six uninterrupted hours and that is becoming rarer and rarer. In my living room I could just hear the TV. It was on the news but I couldn't make it out. Thank God. All you get on the news nowadays is bad shit. And I have enough of my own troubles thank you. I don't need to hear about any of that. It's like the doctor said. If you're thinking of the bad shit, or taking it in, it's going to affect you. I think there could be something to that.

I had to get out of bed and go to the toilet, again. I could be a while. I got up, clinging to my IV stand, and rolled out to the bathroom. I could hear the weather report as I hobbled by my bedroom door. It sounded like it might be a pretty good day. Maybe whoever was in could take me for a stroll in the wheelchair. I haven't been outside in weeks, either, and that was wearing me down, too. I still hadn't figured out the nurses shifts, yet, so I had no idea who it could be.

I came out and shuffled over to my bedside table for my cigarettes. I put them in my dressing gown pocket with the lighter. I picked up my half empty...no make it my half full glass of water and went to see who I had the pleasure of spending the next several hours with. The good doctor would likely be coming around nine.

I had a good session with Rose, but it was still uncomfortable to have to do it again with someone new. But I guess I could nix the deal if I wanted. I figured I'd wait and see who it was and how our morning together made me feel. If they'd take me outside for a stroll then that would definitely earn them brownie points.

"Hi, Janko," said Veronica, turning her knot of hair away from me and smiling her big toothy smile. But you know what, ever since our last chat I've kind of come to like her and see her in a different light. Sort of weird.

"Hi," I said and sat on the couch and then lay down on it. No one came and sat on my couch, I think they knew it was my spot. And I'm glad for it, quite frankly. These small routines, or rhythms, make things easier. Maybe that's why we do things the same way all the time. It's comforting. I reached over for the ashtray which was empty. I loved a fresh ashtray. A small thing, but such a nicety, you have no idea. I fumbled in my pockets for my cigarettes and lighter and lit one. I placed everything on my chest. The ashtray the pack of smokes and the lighter, which decided to roll off of me and onto the floor. I ignored it.

"Would you like some coffee?"

"Sure," I said.

Veronica got up, picked up my lighter and placed it on the coffee table and went into the kitchen.

"Do you want something to eat, too?" she asked.

"Nah, not right now, thanks."

It was six-thirty on the TV now and the news was coming back on with the day's top stories. Violence and mayhem of course. A couple of fatal traffic accidents and the city's eighth homicide, likely gang related, they said. There was also the tragic drowning of a young boy in the partially frozen river. I felt sick, I didn't like listening to catastrophes that you couldn't do anything about. What little appetite I did have, I had now lost.

"V, could you change the channel, please? This news is just ugly and making me ill."

"Sure, Janko, just give me a sec."

She came in and turned it to the country music station. Not my first choice, but better than what I had just been watching. I could hear the coffee pot percolating and slowly the aroma of coffee started drifting into the living room.

I loved that earthy, warm smell of coffee. Veronica came back and sat down in the chair to the right of the TV as I was looking at it. Same chair that Rose had sat in just a couple of days earlier. I looked over at the good doctor's chair with the crocheted blanket on it. I called it my granny blanket, but you already knew that.

"Have you heard of the new program, V?" I said looking at the TV.

"What new program is that, Janko," she said looking at me, "a TV program?"

That caught my attention and I looked at her, smoke trailing up my face from my mouth.

"No, sorry, I meant the new counselling program that Dr. Malichem and I have agreed on where you guys get to sit and chew the fat with us. But you have to be nice and kind, though. That's my request."

She smiled at me.

"Yes, I have heard of that, Janko. It was in the file when I came in this morning, and I reviewed what has happened these last couple of days since I've been here. I think it's a great idea, and I'm very much looking forward to being included in this. I think it is a big and courageous step, Janko. And of course you can count on my kindness. Keep trying to remember that I chose to work with you. We all did, and you know that. And you know why we did too."

I was still looking at her while some cowboy in the background was singing about a broken heart and a woman who done him wrong. I could relate to that.

"Why did you, all of you choose to work with me? I can't seem to see many redeeming qualities in my case. A dying man who's fucked up and running out of time to make himself well enough to leave here with some sense of peace. Jesus, V, you've seen my file. You know the shit I was put through as a boy. Abused and neglected and belittled. Tell me now what you see that's positive or hopeful in my situation. I think I need years to heal and get to a better place. And I probably only have a few weeks, some months at the most."

I sucked on my cigarette. I wasn't sad. Contemplative, yes, but not sad. Maybe it was because I'd had a good night's sleep that I felt okay. Or maybe I was running out of sad. I'd like to hope so but I just don't see that as happening. I was probably storing up a whole pile of sad for later. Especially if the good doctor kept counselling the way he had been.

"That's just it, Janko. I've seen the hope in you. You've reached out and asked for help and that is half the battle. You may not see it now, but you're turning the corner, and around that corner is great peace and serenity. Dr. Malichem is in the top of his field and he wants to work with you. You'll see that the two of you will do such great work. There is going to be plenty of time to heal and to get well and to enjoy it even. I'm certain of that. If you put in the effort, and I know we are, then all manner of great things are going to happen and come into being to bring you the peace that you're looking for and which you deserve. I don't have to tell you that you've been through hell. You have, but you've also made it through. These are not your darkest hours, these are the hours where you can shed light on your life. You've made that commitment to yourself, Janko and the reason I can tell is because you've reached out, you continue to reach out, and you're trying to work through it. You will succeed. I see a lot of potential in you and from what I've seen in your file, you also continue to demonstrate that potential. I am nothing but hopeful for the future and what it holds for all of us in getting you to that good place."

I couldn't hear the coffee brewing anymore. Veronica looked over to the kitchen.

"Let me get us some coffee, okay?"

"Sure, thanks."

She came back with a tray with two mugs filled with black coffee. There was also cream and sugar on it. I helped myself to lots of each. You know that by now. Veronica also took both but she wasn't as generous with herself as I was. We both sipped on our mugs. Sweet, creamy and warm. Just like the womb I suppose. A safe place. I looked outside across the balcony and it looked like the traffic was getting busier. My cigarette was dying so I gave it one more pull and squashed it out in the ashtray. I had seated myself in order to fix my coffee and stayed that way. The ashtray I placed back on the table. It now had aborted twins in grey ash.

"Good coffee, V, thanks. Is it the stuff that the good doctor bought with him the other day?" I asked.

"It sure is. It is pretty good, isn't it?"

She was watching the music channel, intrigued by the artist.

"Do you like this kind of music?" I asked.

"Sure do. It's so uplifting and true. Down to earth. It doesn't have much pretension to it at all."

"I don't know, V, I mean, all of them seem to be singing about being done wrong and people leaving each other and their cars or trucks dying on them. Trying to make a living working dead end jobs. Jesus, I just don't see the uplifting bit about that at all."

"I don't know, Janko. I think you aren't listening to the full song. It's like life I suppose, some of them do sing about pain and heartbreak, although not really about broken down trucks, though. But they also have lots of wonderful love songs and songs about hard work and respect and integrity. It really is good stuff. Listen to this one. He's singing about the love of a woman and how good that is. Looking into her eyes and seeing the love that's there. I know you can relate to that. You had a woman you loved once. Norma Jones was her name, wasn't it?"

I could see her looking at me as I looked at the TV and listened to the words of the song. It was true. It was a beautiful song about love and it was making me think of Norma.

"Yes, V, I have been in love once. And you're right it was wonderful and beautiful. But the death of that was the most painful thing I've ever experienced. I never want to know love again if I have to feel like that when it's over. And it always ends, doesn't it? Either by death or ill will. But I don't think it makes it any easier, however it ends."

"Well, Janko, I'm an incurable romantic and I like to think that it's worth it. And I like to think that death will be the only thing that will bring it to an end."

I nodded. I'd like to think that way, too. But I didn't really have the luxury. I mean, I have to learn to love myself before I can love another and frankly I don't have long enough to do both, I don't think. And if I can learn to love myself before I die then I figure that'll be a triumph.

So we sat in silence for a while. Me thinking about love and how I wished I had known more about it and Veronica probably just enjoying the music. I sipped my coffee and felt better about that. It was good and sweet and warm. I wanted to go out later, I needed to get some fresh air and some sun on my face even if it was the cold, washed out sun of winter.

"Would you mind taking me out for a bit, later, V? I'd like to get some fresh air and I think it's gonna be a nice day today. Should be sunny so the forecast said."

"Sure, we can do that, maybe it will be best after Dr. Malichem has been by to see you. It's just getting light and the traffic is busy, and I don't know about you, but I'd hate to be sucking on all those exhaust fumes from the cars."

"Yeah, that would be all right, I think. Maybe we could go all the way to the corner store for a liquorice or something. I'll even buy you one."

Veronica smiled at me.

"You'd do that for me, you big spender?"

"I sure would," I said, "for you, I sure would."

I was smiling. I was getting to like her. She was growing on me in a good way the more I got to know her. She's going to be all right, I'm pretty sure.

XXIII

"Hi honey," I said into my cell phone.

"What's wrong, Michael, you sound upset?"

I was calling Margaret on my way to pick her up again. I was scheduled to see Janko tomorrow. And I was a wreck.

"I am upset."

"What's wrong, love?"

"I hate to call you now, I know you're getting ready to pack up for the day, but do you have a minute?"

"Of course, Michael, what is it? Has something happened?"

"Yes, honey, things have gone terribly wrong. This whole file is just getting out of hand, I don't know what I'm going to do. I don't think I have time for all of this added responsibility. I think I'm in over my head and I don't know how to handle it."

I was desperate. This was a nightmare come true and how could I ever have been prepared for something like this, I just don't know. They never talk to you about this all through university. I was floundering.

"Michael, hello, Michael?"

I had drifted off.

"Sorry honey, what did you say?" I asked.

"You sound very discombobulated, my love. I was asking you what this is all about. You aren't making any sense. What is wrong? You're making me nervous, now."

"Well, I've been on the phone today with Saskatchewan Vital Statistics and Child Welfare trying to find out who Janko's mother and father were."

"Yes, I know, you told me you'd be doing that."

"Well, I found out. His mother is Mary Amendegal and apparently she is now deceased. Has been for some time. A drug overdose slash suicide it appears, about fifteen years ago."

"That's interesting, Mike, but why are you so upset?"

"It's more than interesting, honey. Mary Amendegal is the same Mary I dated so long ago."

I paused, my mind was racing and I felt sick to my stomach. My mouth was dry and I had lost my appetite. I wasn't thinking straight. I couldn't make sense of it all.

"Wow, Michael. That is very interesting. I guess it's a small world after all and perhaps this just makes it all that more relevant that you are the one to counsel Janko. After all, it appears you knew his mother back then. You may be able to give him some nice memories of what she was like. This isn't that bad, my love, you could look at the good that could come from this…"

"No," I said cutting her off and practically yelling at her, "it is not a small world, it is worse than that. It's a damn nightmare come true for me. Don't you get it? I'm his fucking father."

I stopped, letting the words tumble through the air towards Margaret. I couldn't believe it, I couldn't really believe it, but it seemed more than likely. It had to be true, I had spent the whole day trying to deny it but it couldn't be done. And in my own defence I had never known about it.

Margaret was silent for some time.

"Margaret? Did you hear what I said? It appears that I am Janko's father."

"Yes, I did Michael. But how can it be?"

"Well, my name had been put down on the birth certificate by the mother. By Mary."

"But that doesn't prove anything. She could have put it down in spite. Do you really think it's possible?"

"Yes, I do, honey. I wish it wasn't so, and I never knew. I never knew that I had a son. Shit, what have I done? I've traced back the time. He was born almost thirty-four years ago and that puts me in the picture. Easily within the picture. I mean our relationship only lasted less than six months and she would have become pregnant at least a month before we broke up. At least."

"Well, Mike, maybe she wasn't the most faithful woman. I hate to say it, but maybe she was going around behind your back."

"I know, honey, I thought about that, too. But she just wasn't like that. She was faithful I know that. We were together pretty much all the time. We were inseparable. The reason we broke up was because she started getting into drugs with some girlfriends of hers. You see, Margaret, I was her first and she was devastated when we broke up. She begged and pleaded with me for months afterwards. She told me she would change and that she would stop doing drugs and all of that stuff. But one thing I cannot imagine her doing is being unfaithful to me. And the strange thing about it was that she never once told me she was pregnant."

I felt sick. I felt horrible and guilty for not having known and for not giving her another chance. Jesus the things we do, the choices we make that have such a huge fallout. I felt utterly alone with this. Could Margaret understand and support me.

Margaret had gone very quiet again. I was nervous.

"Are you okay, Margaret? Is everything okay?"

"Wow, Michael. I just don't know what to say. How long are you going to be?"

"Maybe about twenty or thirty minutes."

"Okay. Let me go and think about it. Maybe we can go for a coffee once you pick me up and we can talk about it some more."

"Okay...Honey?"

"Yes," she said.

"I love you...You know that, don't you?"

"I love you, too. I know you do."

And then we hung up and I was eager to see her and have some sense made of what seemed like the rubble that my life had become. It had taken just a few phone calls to demolish this life of mine. A whole construction crew couldn't demolish my life as easily and quickly as these few phone calls had done.

All along the drive to pick up Margaret I was thinking and scheming and trying to deny it. But there wasn't any denying it. And if I couldn't deny it, then what? How would I have to handle my relationship with Janko? These are things I needed some distance from in order to get a better understanding of them. I just didn't know what to think. Janko had no family left in the whole world.

At least not a mother, maybe he had siblings but I doubted that. I was the only family left to him now, and he didn't even know about me. I was racing to get to Margaret, weaving and ducking in and out of traffic. I was desperate to see her. I wasn't certain about anything anymore, my whole world had been turned upside down and I didn't know what to do. I couldn't trust anything now. My sense of self was shattered. I felt like I was in dire need of some counselling and the only place to turn was Margaret. But I wasn't sure if this had damaged our relationship. She had never wanted children and now by virtue of me she sort of had one. Granted, he wouldn't be around for very long but that was beside the point. I felt vulnerable about the relationship and her feelings for me. I had never felt like that before. Margaret had always been my rock, but now here I was feeling stranded and uncertain of the one thing that had been consistent for me. The undying commitment of how I felt our relationship was for each other. I needed to get to her quickly, to see her and touch her and feel our love once more. I needed some reassurance from the woman who had been with me for almost half of my life. I felt like a ball of string unravelling. And unravelling hell of a fast, too. Can you understand that? The feeling of vulnerability and of one's world just crashing in? I think at least I would have a better understanding of how my clients have felt, or how they have tried to explain their feelings. Janko no doubt amongst them.

I ordered a camomile tea. I needed something to help relax my frazzled nerves. Margaret ordered a peppermint tea. A Moroccan peppermint tea that smelled fresh and slightly sweet. The coffee shop wasn't very busy and I was happy with that. I needed to feel like I could talk freely with her without prying ears. We grabbed a couple of comfy high backed chairs in the corner, but before we sat down I took Margaret in my arms and hugged her close for a long time. I didn't say anything. I couldn't, my throat was clogged and my eyes were streaming tears.

"I love you," I finally said still holding her in my embrace.

"I love you, too, darling. Are you okay?"

She was squeezing me tight. After some time when I hadn't said anything else she pulled back from me keeping her hands around my waist but looking into my eyes.

"Michael, my love, what's wrong? Talk to me."

I nodded and went over to the napkin dispenser and took a few napkins. I blew into one of them and dabbed my eyes with the others. I came back to the table and Margaret put her hand on my waist as she gestured me gently to the chair. There was deep concern in her eyes as she looked at me.

"It's okay, Mike. Everything is going to be okay."

I had to steal myself. I reached in deep for some courage so I could stop spilling tears all over my face. It was hard. I felt like an empty shell. I didn't know anything. I didn't feel I could trust in anything or anyone. Alone and barren, being buffeted around by the fickle winds of misfortune.

"Are you sure, honey? Are you sure? I don't know. I just feel lost right now. I don't know if I'm in denial or what. I just never thought I'd feel the way I do about this. It has completely destroyed any sense of security about who I am and what I'm doing with my life."

I paused to sip on my tea. I was feeling better just getting it off my chest. I looked outside watching the traffic going by as the day was turning in towards dusk. People going home or out and about with a sense of purpose. I felt like a total outsider. Margaret squeezed my hand in hers and sipped her tea.

"Is everything okay with us, Margaret? Does this change how you feel about me? I mean, you know that I had no idea I was a father. I would have stepped up to the responsibility. You know I would have, don't you?"

"Yes, darling," she said holding my one hand in both of hers, "I know the kind of man that you are. This is big news for sure, but not insurmountable. We can get through it together. I think you're being too hard on yourself. Maybe that is more of the problem than what this actually means. I love you, Mike. I love you for your compassionate and kind self. Your quiet strength of character and love for humanity. You've demonstrated that for the last twenty years. This must be hitting you quite hard. I can only imagine. But it doesn't make one bit of difference in how I feel about you. About us."

I looked at her, searching her face for any crack in credibility. She wasn't lying to me. I could tell she meant every word. I leaned over and hugged her again. I needed this.

"Thank you, honey. Thank you for your kind words. I need to feel your love and the stability of our relationship. This has hit me so hard and I'm not sure why.

It's made me come to second guess everything. Like the choices I've made in my career. It's making me second guess that and think about Joachim and the choices he's made. Maybe I should have done something like that. Gone into psychiatric research of pharmaceuticals and made a fortune on discovering the next miracle drug…"

Margaret was shaking her head with a smile on her face.

"What?" I asked.

"You wouldn't have wanted that, darling. You're kidding yourself about that. There is no way I can see you as being happy with that kind of life. It would be eating up your soul. I think we should stay focused on how this is making you feel and how we can manage it. Let's try not to bring up tertiary issues, darling, that will just confuse us and muddy the waters."

She let her one hand go from mine but squeezed my hand with the remaining one. She reached for her tea winking at me and mouthing, "I love you."

"Don't you sometimes wish or think about a different life we could have had. We could be rich or at least a lot richer than we are now and have all the fancy toys instead of our domestic car that is a couple of years old. We could have a brand new Mercedes or something every couple of years and live in a fancy neighborhood. Don't you sometimes think that we should have gone that route?"

I knew what kind of answer I was looking for. I was fishing and Margaret probably knew it, but I was certain she'd give me the truth anyway.

"No, Michael, I don't, actually. My feelings on this are the same as they were last time we spoke about it. I'd be happy to live in a one-bedroom apartment with you. As long as we had a loaf of bread, a bottle of wine and thou, to bastardise the Rubaiyat of Omar Khan, I would be in paradise. That is the honest truth, my love. I do not want for material possessions. As it is we have a hard enough time cleaning them, storing them. We have enough. I know how you feel, though. You are looking for something that might take your mind off this shock that you've come upon. Everyone seems prone to it, Michael, but it doesn't help. It's like trying to fill a bag that has a hole in it. You might get momentary satisfaction from it but then you need to find something else to replace it.

It's a vicious circle. As you've said to me before, darling, and I love how you said this, we as society are suffering from a poverty of the soul and we keep trying to fill it with stuff when the only things that can enrich our souls are our relationships with one another and how we treat each other. Kindness, compassion, tenderness, integrity and ethics are the ways to do that. We have that in our relationship and that is why I don't want for anything more. Our love is enough for me."

It's the milk of human kindness that gets me every time. Margaret is right about that. It's how we treat one another that counts. At the end of the day all that matters is love. And I felt a lot of that now and it was making me feel much better. Her kindness and the kindness of strangers is what greases the social cogs, makes this living easier. I smiled at her.

"I was hoping you'd say that." I said.

"I know you were, darling. But I mean it, too, and I think that deep down inside, you feel the same way that I do. We are soul mates, you and I, if I can use that clichéd term. But it's true, the soul mate thing. I believe in it. And I believe that you are my soul mate. And I think you feel the same way I do about this. Don't you?"

I nodded.

"Yes, I do. If I have to be really honest, then yes I do. I just wanted to hear it from you, honey. This day has been so hard on me. I'm just now trying to come to terms with it. I need your help. You've always been so good at understanding me and human behaviour that I sometimes wonder why you never went into Psychiatry."

"Because I'd find it too hard to take on people's burdens all the time."

She smiled at me and I reached for my paper cup of hot tea and took a few short sips. I looked outside again at the people going by. I sighed. I still felt detached from the greater world.

"What am I going to do about this, though? I don't know how this will help us, Janko and me. I don't know if I should tell him or if it is better not said. I just don't know, Margaret. What do you think?"

"Well, I think that is really something that you need to decide. How do you feel about him? What are your thoughts, Mike?"

I looked at her. She had placed both her hands back on mine. I shuffled my chair over to hers to be closer. So she didn't have to lean in so much to hold my hand.

251

"I'd like to tell him. I think it's the right thing to do. The honest thing to do. But I just think it'll open up a whole new can of worms that we are going to have to deal with, and I don't know if I have enough time to deal with his other issues, let alone deal with the fallout of him finding out I am his father."

"Perhaps you should offer to have paternity tests done so you both can be certain that you are in fact his father."

"Yes. That goes without saying, although I am certain about it. I've tried to convince myself otherwise, but the more I look at it the more certain I am. So, we have to deal with this then, somehow. And I'm just fearful that it will bog us down. This is very life altering news, honey."

I looked at her and leaned over to kiss her.

"Yes it is, my love. But it can be life affirming and uplifting. It doesn't have to be despairing if you don't want it to be. And I refer to 'you' in the plural. Perhaps Janko has been searching his whole life for his father. This could be very beneficial if you look at it that way. You only have a short time left with him, and this could aid in your counselling. To develop some sort of familial bond could give him the hope and courage and trust he needs to move on from his hurtful past, his painful past."

"Do you really think so?"

"I do. And I think that because you only have a short time left with him you could plunge in without inhibitions. You could give him your best attempt. It is unlikely that you will develop the bond that comes from raising a son all his life. But this could be even better. You have no excuse, darling. He is not going to be in your life to hijack a long term relationship with you. And that's not to say that you wouldn't be up for that, either. But this is a short term opportunity to offer him a glimpse at the kind of father you could have been to him. To offer him an example of healthy human relationships that he is obviously in desperate need of. This, Michael, I'm sure will give him the security to allow him to confront his demons quickly and courageously. And in the meantime you have an opportunity to find out what kind of a son you had, and what kind of a father you might have been. Let's focus on the large number of positives that this could create. I know you have always wondered what it would have been like to be a father. And I know that in some ways you would have wanted to be a father except that I didn't. Well, Michael, grab this opportunity to find out what it might have been like."

She sipped her tea and I sipped mine, too. I was always grateful, especially in times like this, for her. She had an amazing way of making me fell valued and respected and worthy. She continually taught me how to be a better person, a better psychiatrist. I used a lot of what she taught me with my own patients. It worked with them just as it was working with me.

"Margaret, you have the most amazing ability to pull me out of the deepest and darkest slumps. You always make me want to be a better man. How do you it?"

I reached over and kissed her. I hugged her for a long time.

"It's the power of love, my darling. It is my love for you that does it. Isn't it love that heals all things? The omniscient salve for all life's ailments."

She was speaking over my shoulder. Tenderly, as I held her in my arms, feeling the love that she was talking about. Feeling her love for me.

"Thank you, my angel. Thank you for your love. You are my soul mate, but you already knew that."

I ended the hug eventually, but with difficulty and we both sat back in our chairs. We held hands over the arms of our chairs and I was again at peace and content and even happily looking forward to this challenge that had earlier ruined my day. I would make the best of it. Janko would need me to be an example of courage and hope and integrity. I would step up to the plate. It was time to take my own medicine, to be both patient and doctor for both of us. This was, if I could make the most of it, the opportunity of my career. It could be, God willing, my finest hour.

I squeezed Margaret's hand as we both stared outside the window. Night was falling. Quietly, as it always does. Unpretentious and with dignity she covered the sky with her blue blanket and the world was hushed as if to a lullaby.

"I love you, Margaret," I said to the outside world. And I was in love with the world too, and night and her sister day. Love was all around me and I aimed to make it stay.

"I love you, too, darling," Margaret said squeezing my hand and speaking to the world as well.

XXIV

The conversation with Margaret had really done me wonders the night before. I'd dare say there was a spring in my step as I walked from my car towards Janko's apartment complex. I was looking forward to talking with him today. I wasn't sure who would be there but it would likely be someone other than Rose, from what I knew of their schedules.

I'd stopped off at the corner store to pick up some liquorice. I hadn't had any in a long time and it reminded me of fun times when I was a student at the university and Margaret and I would go for walks in the summer to the corner store and get red liquorice, the thick pieces, and slurpees too. Times when life seemed simpler and in many ways, I suppose, it was. I had picked up three pieces of thick liquorice for the three of us. I wasn't sure if Janko liked it, but I didn't know many people who didn't enjoy the odd piece now and then. And oh well, if he didn't that'd be an extra piece for me. I think I could live with that.

I hadn't picked up slurpees. It was too cold for that. Not that it was going to be a bad day for this time of year. I think we were expecting a high of around thirty-two or something. Not bad, but too cold for slurpees.

V and I had been hanging out on the couch watching television. Well, mostly watching music videos. Country music videos. But to be honest with you I was actually starting to enjoy it. With Veronica's help, of course. But these songs which seemed so sad before, started to have an uplifting beat to them. They might have been talking about loss but these guys were also talking about hope and courage and finding your way again after you've become lost. And in many cases, after you've lost just about everything. It was speaking to me. And it was starting to make sense and give me just an inkling of hope. And of course there were the love songs about fidelity and loyalty and being in love with your partner for decades.

And even after having loved them for so long, still appreciating them for what had drawn you to them in the first place. I was listening to "Amazed" by Lonestar, and I was buying it. I caught myself thinking that I would've liked that. To be in love with a woman for the rest of my life. To have that sense of loyalty and commitment to someone and have it returned. Seemed to me it'd be one of life's most precious gifts to be able to experience something so special and unique. You might pooh pooh me, I mean, after all I've been through I can see how you might not be buying my thoughts on this. But I was, I was just going with my thoughts, and my heart felt soft and tender when I was listening to the words. Like this was something good and true. I wanted to believe it was possible. I'd like to think I could've had something like that if I had been given a chance.

"So you think this is possible, V? What these guys are singing about. Loving forever and being committed to one person. Do you think that can be done?"

Veronica looked at me while singing the chorus to "Amazed".

"It sure is, Janko. It sure is possible and I see it everywhere."

"Really." She was getting my hopes up and I was trying not to show it.

"Sure. My parents are great examples of that. They've been married for about forty years, or thereabouts, and they still hold hands and kiss. I can tell they still love each other very much."

"Hmmm."

I didn't know what to say. It was encouraging. It was hopeful, but I just couldn't really understand that myself. I mean I hadn't even had parents, forget about parents that stayed together for forty years or so.

"Well, what about you, V? You're not married are you?"

I was hoping to chip away at her theory. I figured she hadn't had a long term committed relationship so how would she feel with me cracking open her theory of love ever after. It was kind of mean, I suppose, but I wasn't meaning it to be. I was just reverting to my old self, I guess. Disillusioned and doubting that there could be such happiness or goodness in the world. Let alone love. Maybe I'd be proved wrong. In some way I was hoping I'd be proved wrong. But we'd see.

"I'm onto you, Janko. You're trying to hog tie me. But it's not going to work, because belief is a powerful ally even if you've never experienced it yourself, you can still learn from those around you.

No, I've never been married. I have had a few relationships and one long term one in particular that ended less than well."

I looked at her, searching for more.

"How did it not end well?"

"Well, he was cheating on me. And this was after a couple of years of great times, or so I thought."

"That must have been tough. How did you cope? How did you deal with that and still hold onto this idea of faithful, loyal love like your parents have? I don't think I'd be able to handle that very well. I'd lose my faith, I think."

And I would too, it'd be awful. After everything I've lost already, I'd lose any hope or faith in humanity. Gone. It'd be fucking gone for good.

"Well, you just bounce back, I guess. You have to dig deep and find that resiliency that is in all of us. You have it. You have a lot of it, Janko. To be here where you are now and trying to improve yourself with the little amount of time you have left and especially after everything you've been through. That shows a large well of resiliency that you must have to be at this place of moving forward…"

I nodded at her and I was smiling a little too. Couldn't help myself, she was making me feel good.

"I cried a lot, that's for certain. But over time, with the support of friends, and reflection upon the pain and life in general you begin to heal. It helps to reach out to others, that's for sure, because you realize you're not alone and that so many other people have been through such equally horrible situations. A lot of people have been through worse. I'd say that a lot of people have been through a lot worse situations than even you have. You have to become hopeful again. For me, I needed to believe that there was good in people and that there are men out there who are loyal and faithful and ethical. And slowly I started to see examples of that.

And I had some smaller successes and they built upon one another, now I am in a great relationship with a man who is ethical and loyal and faithful. Hope is crucial. I think if you take away someone's hope then you might as well take away their life, really. It is hopeless people who do the worst things to society. So if you can find hope and something to look forward to and something to believe in, then you are halfway to healing.

And you have found that, Janko. You have that hope and something to look forward to. Even if it is only to feel a little better every day. I guess hope is about options and choices. Feeling that all is not lost and that you do have choices and freedom. Hopelessness is probably the feeling of being trapped, a total lack of choice or freedom."

I nodded at her. She was making a lot of sense. A lot of people were making a lot of sense, lately. Or maybe I was just learning to listen better. Maybe, hopefully, if I could be so damn bold, I was easing out of my negativity. I'd like to think so. I really would.

"Hope," I said, "that's an interesting idea. Maybe I am beginning to feel an inkling of hope with the way things are going. I've noticed that you and the good doctor are beginning to make sense to me. And I don't think it's anything that you've done, but maybe I've just become more receptive."

I smiled and fidgeted with my fingers. I was pulling and picking at my cuticles. I took a bite at one and tore it too far down. It fucking hurt like a bastard and started bleeding. I needed a cigarette, but I was trying to slow down on how much I was smoking. I don't know why. Maybe I was beginning to respect myself more. I don't know, okay, I'm just trying to do the best I can. I'm sure you can understand.

"Yes, Janko, I think you are. I think you've taken that first step towards healing. You've decided to trust and that has come about because of hope. You are hopeful that you can heal, that you can move from the anger and pain and resentment to forgiveness and some peace. And I believe you will get there. That is the hope that has driven you to this point. And by moving forward like you have, despite your negative feelings and self-doubt, you build upon your strengths and your self-doubt relinquishes its power and grip on you. It's perhaps only now like a distant whining child. An annoyance that you're paying less and less attention to. This allows you to hear us better and to listen, I suppose, with less clutter and mental noise interfering with your growth."

"You guys are good. You guys are definitely worth your money. I know I've probably been difficult to deal with in the past, but I thank you for putting up with me, I guess. I am trying my hardest, V, that is for sure. It's just so damn hard sometimes, but you're right, it is getting easier."

"Well, don't worry about it, Janko. It's not been difficult to deal with your anger. It's to be expected. We are all only humans and as such we are fallible. Don't go beating yourself up, now, about it. We all knew that this wouldn't be the easiest path, but we chose it, seeing the potential. And you're proving us right. You're showing us the potential and I'm just really happy and excited for you and for us. This is definitely one of the highlights of my career."

"Really?"

"Yes. Absolutely, it is. The kind of strides you have made these past months have been incredible. It makes my career seem all that more worthwhile. Janko, you have to be in the top one percent of patients that I've had who have handled their difficulties so maturely and evolved and grown so quickly and successfully. It is amazing and I take great pride in being part of your healing."

I was grinning now from ear to ear. I was looking forward to seeing the good doctor soon. Things were falling into place. Slowly, but surely. Just as well, too. My body wasn't feeling very good. It seemed to be getting more tired and weaker every fucking day. I was running out of time. The funny thing is, though, if I died today I'd almost be okay with that. I mean, not that I want to die. Not like wishing I would die, but just that things are beginning to wrap up and I'm beginning to feel better, like I'm making headway. Can you understand that? That if I had to die, and I'm going to have to within a short time, then I'd almost be okay with going now. But I'd prefer just a few more sessions with the good doctor. Just a few more.

"Thanks, V. I think you're right. I think things are coming along and I'm getting to that place where I'd like to be before I die. A peaceful place. A place of acceptance."

"You sure are. I can tell. Can I get you something to eat, Janko, or something to drink? You should try and eat something before Dr. Malichem comes. And he could be here any minute."

"Sure. I'll have a piece of toast with just margarine and maybe a glass of water please."

Veronica acknowledged me and got up to get my water and toast from the kitchen. There was a buzz on the intercom and Veronica answered it. A short while later there was a knock on the door. From the corner of my eye I caught some movement coming from my bedroom.

I cursed under my breath as I looked in that direction. It was Norm, Peter and MJ coming to join us. They said they would but I was hoping they wouldn't have. I was doing well, and I didn't want them coming here to fuck things up. Peter looked at me and smiled.

"It's okay, Jan," he said, "we're just here to observe. Don't even think about us. We've all talked and we just want to support you, that's all. Norm here is on the same page, too."

I frowned at them, hearing Veronica open the door to the good doctor.

"Hi, Veronica," I said as she opened the door for me.

"Hi, Michael. It's good to see you. I think we're going to be in for a good session today."

I offered her a piece of liquorice which she accepted taking a bite out of it.

"I was just making Janko some toast and getting him a glass of water. Can I get you anything to eat or drink?"

"Nothing to eat thanks, but I'll take some coffee if you have."

"Sure, I'll make a fresh pot."

"Thanks," I said as I moved inside, looking at Janko on the couch. He was looking away from me but then turned his head around. His furrowed brow transforming into a smile. An honest smile, too. Something I don't get to see a lot of from him lately.

"Hi, Michael," he said.

"Hello, Janko. It's good to see you again."

I took a seat in my usual chair, pulled out my piece of liquorice and put the last piece which was still in the packet on the table. I slid it towards him.

"I got this for you, Janko, if you'd like?"

"Thanks, doctor," he said reaching for it. "I was talking to Veronica earlier today and asking her if she wouldn't mind going for a walk outside later and taking me to the corner store for a liquorice. Red is my favorite kind."

He was smiling still, and I was smiling, too.

"Well, that is something else we have in common, then. You know, it looks like it's going to be a fine day for a short stroll outside. The three of us could go, if you'd like that?"

"Yes, I would like that."

He looked off to his right again, in the opposite direction to where I was. I couldn't see anything there. Veronica came back in with water and toast for Janko.

"The coffee will be just a few minutes, Michael. It'll be nice and fresh."

"Perfect, thanks. Have you had a chance to hear or read about how Janko and I are conducting his counselling now?"

"I sure have. Janko and I were talking about it earlier and I feel very honored and excited about being included in the dialogue. I'm proud of Janko, Michael, and I think that this in itself is a huge step in healing. Trust is such a big issue with him. We've spoken about that and he agrees. I'm very happy to be part of that expanding circle of trust, Janko."

Janko smiled at her, leaning back on the couch he was on.

"You're right, Veronica. This is a huge step and I'm excited about how quickly things should start going now. Trust is fundamental to the kind of work and healing that we have ahead of us. This step in trust that you've made, Janko, is a huge move towards healing. You'll see. Things will be flying along now as you learn that this trust you've offered will be honored and respected. With that you'll easily be able to come to terms with your very difficult and painful life experiences and more than that, find a peace and acceptance of yourself as you move on towards something that I am sure will bring you eternal peace."

Janko was smiling all over himself. He was looking at me and Veronica and couldn't wipe the grin off his face. I was looking at him for the first time through different eyes. I was looking at him as his father. It was odd but not scary, though.

"Sorry, guys, I just can't seem to wipe this damn smile off my face."

"Don't let it worry you, Janko. Enjoy it, life is meant to bring us happiness. It is one of its gifts. Don't deny yourself the joy that you deserve. And you do deserve it. Try thinking of this moment as the beginning of the joy that you so deservedly have earned. With all your pain, you should be hungry for this happiness and determined to find more."

He was only smiling more and I was proud of him. As his psychiatrist and in a paternal way too.

"Yes, you most certainly deserve this, Janko. You of all people should be entitled to nothing but happiness from here on out," said Veronica.

Veronica looked at me. The coffee had stopped percolating.

"Can I get you some coffee now, Michael?"

"Yes," I said nodding my head. "I think that's a great idea before we get started."

She went off into the kitchen. Janko was starting to eat his toast. He took a large bite, chewed it for a bit and then took a big sip of water. I thought he was looking like a cement mixer. Now it was my turn to be smiling. I felt good. I felt that these next few weeks or however long we have will be useful and hopeful times. Even in this closing chapter of Janko's life I felt that the knowledge I was about to share with him and the optimism I was feeling would only be beneficial as we moved forward.

Veronica came back with a tray of coffee. She had a jug of cream and sugar. At least it looked thick like cream. Most likely was, because I know that Janko was enjoying some of the small things like that as his life waned. His cream and sugar and cigarettes. And I didn't really blame him. With such little time left, why not give in a bit to the vices.

"I didn't remember how you liked your coffee so I got you a bit of both so you can do it yourself," said Veronica.

"Just black thanks," I said.

"That's pretty good, doctor," said Janko watching me taste test the coffee, "I usually take a couple of tries before I get it to my liking."

"What can I say, Janko, it's a gift. Black is black." I smiled at him.

"You know, V, I might actually like another cup of coffee if you don't mind. Sorry to be a pain. But I figure I might as well join both of you."

Veronica got up smiling at Janko, asking if I wanted anything else which I didn't. We both waited for her to return in silence. I was looking outside. Watching a few birds fly by and thinking how uncomplicated their lives must be, except for the cold of winter. But today was going to be a good day for this time of year and I figured that we could all learn something from them.

The way they just go about their lives, living in the moment. I was getting sentimental and I knew I had to come out of the gates strong and quick.

As soon as Veronica came to sit back down I was going to start off with the news that I was Janko's father. That had to happen first. Veronica was coming back to the living room with a mug of coffee for Janko. I watched him splash cream and sugar in it. Then he tested it and he liked it.

"There you go, Janko. First time's a charm, hey?"

He smiled at me nodding his head as he sipped his coffee.

"Yeah, I did get it that time, Michael, didn't I?"

I waited. Nothing. I waited some more. Still nothing. I was being a chicken, I admit it.

"I have some interesting and very important news to tell you, Janko. Something that I'm hoping will allow us to dig deeper into the benefits of what our relationship and counselling can achieve for you."

"I'm glad to hear it. I'm glad that I'm not the first one having to spill my guts this morning."

He was smiling at me, cradling his mug of coffee in both his hands. I reached for mine to sip on but more importantly to give idle hands something to do. I was stealing courage as you've probably guessed. Veronica was looking intently at me.

"Well, I have managed in this very short time since I last saw you to determine who your father is. I had to find out who your mother was first, though. Her name, and I don't know if this will ring a bell for you was Ms. Mary Amendegal. Does that ring a bell?"

I was trying to buy time. Thinking of how best to approach this. My mind was all of a sudden a whirlwind.

"No, doctor, I can't say that I remember that. But at least I remembered her first name. You say her name 'was' Mary Amendegal. Is she now married or dead?"

He said it without emotion but I thought I caught a shadow of worry pass across his face. There was no time for pussy footing or lying.

"Yes, Janko. I'm afraid your mother has been dead for about twenty years or so. I'm afraid I don't remember the exact date. But she was found in Vancouver."

He looked into his mug for a while and then he looked outside. He didn't say anything and I couldn't read anything. Then he looked back at me.

"How did she die?"

He sipped on his coffee and looked away. Maybe hoping to create some distance from the news I was about to give him. I looked at Veronica. She was no help and I didn't blame her. She didn't have a clue as to how Janko's mother died, so I looked outside. The birds were gone. Nobody was sticking around to help me out.

"Doctor?"

It was Janko, he'd caught me drifting off. My attention was outside.

"Sorry, Janko."

I steadied myself and looked at him intently. He looked at me and held my gaze for a moment to be sure he'd get an answer from me this time. Then he looked off outside again. Maybe the birds were flying around for him.

"Are you sure you're ready, Janko?"

He nodded still looking outside. I looked at Veronica. She nodded, too, and raised her eyebrows in encouragement.

"It appeared that your mother committed suicide. She jumped from the Lion's Gate Bridge and landed on the train tracks below. The autopsy also found lots of drugs in her. Crack cocaine, marijuana and a lot of alcohol."

I stopped for a moment to gather my thoughts. There was no way that you could talk about these things softly, compassionately. They fell out of my mouth hard and sharp as shards of glass. They were cutting us both, and I was still being a chicken.

"On her belly was written in black crayon 'I'm sorry, very sorry'."

Janko looked at me again then, still holding his coffee.

"She was sorry, Michael? What could she have been sorry about?"

All three of us turned for comfort to our mugs. We each sipped them and then held the warm mugs in our hands. Insulating us from the frosty words I was exhaling.

"Well, Janko, I don't know if you ever knew that your mother was a single child and that her parents had died. It appears she didn't have many friends either."

He looked at me again, his eyes wet glassy orbs.

"Okay, doctor, you're fucking around, will you just please tell me the truth without bullshitting all over the place for God's sake."

He wasn't angry as much as he was sad.

"I think she was sorry for abandoning you. I don't know if you knew, but you were born by caesarean and her words were scribbled above and just below the scar. But those are just my thoughts. Neither the police nor the Medical Examiner drew that conclusion. Just my thoughts, but I think I'm right."

Veronica looked at me quite bewildered. Janko's eyes welled up with tears but they didn't spill. I gave him a moment. I gave us all a moment, I suppose. I also didn't know how to go on from here. Where do you go from that bombshell. Oh, and by the way, I'm your pa. I don't think so. There had to be a better way. A kinder, gentler way.

"Are you okay, Janko? Do you want to talk about how you feel?"

He looked at me through those sad eyes I'd come to know quite well. He had lost his edge though. He was gentler in his sadness and anger, although the anger seemed to have become greatly reduced lately.

"I don't know, Michael. I mean I'm sad in a way, but I'm also angry and also indifferent."

"Tell me about why you feel each of those things. I can understand it for sure, but tell me why you think you have those mix of feelings."

"Well, I'm sad for me and what that means. I mean, Jesus Christ, Michael, I could have been her son and lived with her and maybe had a better life. I wouldn't have minded being poor. Kids just need to be loved and feel secure. It wouldn't have mattered if we'd been poor. Shit I wouldn't have been beaten or neglected as much as I have. I might have enjoyed love in my life. The only time I've felt loved unconditionally if at all is when I was with the Antolinis. And that didn't last all that long. I mean I do remember my mother trying, okay. She tried to make me feel loved and in her way I can still feel it. Was she perfect? No fucking way but I'll tell you, good doctor, she was a helluva lot better than any other parents, if you can call them that, were. Except for the Antolinis, like I've said. So I'm sad she ditched me, okay? It didn't have to be that way. I mean, Jesus, Michael, I had no idea when I was left at the church that I was then on my own in this horrible, shitty world. I'm sad because it would have been better with her. She never beat me except for spanking my ass a few times. It should have been better. It could've been a lot better but it's not. Is that okay? I mean, come on, who wouldn't be sad at that."

"Yes, it's okay, Janko. It is more than okay, it's to be expected. I know I'd feel the same way, too."

He looked off to his right again and shook his head and waved his hand out towards the wall. I thought he was trying to wave away some dust or something.

"Tell me about your anger, Janko."

He looked back at me and then took a sip of coffee.

"Well, I'm angry because of the way my life turned out. I'm angry for the same reasons that I'm sad, okay? She was my mother and she shouldn't have done that to me. She shouldn't have ditched me when I was a boy. That makes me angry. I'm also angry at the world and the government for letting me down, for not protecting me. All the people that should have known or could have known and they did nothing. That pisses me off too. And why shouldn't it? I'm angry at my mother for killing herself, too. I was hoping I might have been able to talk to her and ask her why she did this to me. I wanted to maybe try and talk to her and forgive her and now I can't do that. I'm angry that I was never told by anyone until now that she died. I'm angry that she was alone and she died alone and she never had any help or anyone to turn to. The whole fucking world, Michael, our whole society should have been there to protect her, to protect me. This kind of shit shouldn't be allowed to happen. People deserve better, doctor. But no one fucking cares, it seems. I'm angry at that, especially."

He turned away from me again and waved his hand in the air towards the wall. He did it a few times. Now I started to think maybe his hallucinations were starting to bug him, to impede our work here. But I was going to soldier on. I had to. We were running out of time. Not just for today, but for the rest of his life.

"That anger can be used for good, Janko. We can push that to help you heal. You have a right to feel angry and I agree with you about how society lets the vulnerable down. That's one of the reasons why I chose my profession. To help those that society had neglected, sometimes even discarded. I know how you feel about that. It makes me sad and angry too."

He said something to the wall that I didn't hear.

"I feel the same way as both of you," said Veronica, "I think all of us in these kinds of professions are interested in helping the underdog, if I can call it that."

Veronica was sipping her coffee and Janko went to light up a cigarette.

"Tell me about your indifference, Janko. Do you have a sense as to why you feel indifferent to this information about your mother?"

"Well, Michael," he said exhaling smoke between us, "because it's not like I ever really knew her, now did I? I mean, she gave me up when I was just a little boy and never looked back. Maybe that makes me angry but it also makes me indifferent to her plight because I never fucking knew her. She might as well be a stranger that I've heard about jumping off a building. I mean you can't expect me to have a huge investment in her. Especially considering that she was the one that cancelled our relationship. Jesus, Michael, what is a little boy supposed to do? How the hell was I supposed to find her? It's not the responsibility of children to be parenting their parents. I mean seriously."

He was continuing to blow smoke between us. Gray clouds thickening between us.

"It's okay, Janko I'm only asking you to explore your feelings. They are legitimate and I'm not judging you. You must try to understand that. I'm here to help you, okay? Not to make this more difficult or confusing to you."

"Yeah, I suppose. I'm sorry. It's just that I'm so fucking confused, and mixed up with all of this that you're telling me. I mean, is it normal for me to have such a mix of feelings? I wonder if I'm not just splintering and becoming some sort of mentally deranged person."

I looked at Veronica. This was an easy question, and I knew she'd know the answer. Janko followed my gaze to her. She sipped her coffee and then put the mug down on the table.

"I think it is very natural, Janko. That is why it is helpful to gain perspective and insight from people like us who are in the helping profession. Dealing with emotional events in life and the feelings they create is very unsettling. And a large part of why it is so unsettling is because it creates such a turbulent and tumultuous mix of feelings. It helps to gain perspective by using Dr. Malichem and myself and the others as sounding boards. So yes, it is very much normal and to be expected. We are emotional beings and the emotions are deep and varied and life's events cause them to bubble up in a unique mix dependent upon the event."

I nodded my head when Janko looked at me.

"Very well said, Veronica. And very true, Janko. Life is a deep well of unexplored mysteries. The water may seem murky, but once you plunge in you get to see the depths and beauty hidden beneath."

"I don't know, Michael, all I seem to see is dark scary places. I mean, when am I going to be able to start working towards something better? Towards improving my predicament. All that has been happening lately, as I plunge into these dark scary places, is that I find more hidden dark corners. Like this bomb about my mother that you've told me about, now. I want to get to a place where I feel I'm moving forward towards healing, not finding more issues to deal with."

He wasn't helping me with this. I had more to tell him that wasn't going to help.

"I understand, Janko, but I think that even though you feel like you are finding darker corners as you search your soul, you're still searching with light and you're shedding light on all these areas and that is a good thing. You're bringing light to the dark; and soon all the dark will be run out of those corners by the light that you're carrying. That we're helping you to carry."

"I agree with the doctor, Janko. You're shedding light on all these things and there a lot of them. But look how you're handling it. Weeks ago you would have been combative and angry with us for mentioning these things. But now you can talk about your anger and your sadness and your indifference. Those are big steps, Janko. Huge strides that you've taken in a relatively short time. Hold onto that as you continue forward. You're doing fantastically well."

Veronica was smiling at him and then at me.

"Do you really think so?" he asked her.

"Absolutely. I mean, look at me. I'm beaming at you like a puffed up and proud parent. I'm tremendously excited about the future for you and us with the work we can do."

He smiled at her and then at me. Smoke leaking upwards from the corners of his smile.

"Do you think so too, Michael?"

"Absolutely," I said to him, "but there is something else I need to tell you, that weighs heavily on my chest. And after this I think we would've explored all of those dark places and the light will be shining brightly in."

I was going around in circles and I knew it. But I wasn't prepared for all of his doubts about these dark places. I should have come out strong, right from the get go.

"What is it, doctor? We might as well finish up. I'm not sure I could take any more surprises after today."

I had been looking outside. Still no help or support. The birds had gone. I was hanging out on this limb by myself.

"I found out, Janko, who your father is. It is me."

I stopped to see what kind of response my words would have on him. He didn't say anything. Veronica didn't say anything, they both just looked at me and their jaws went a little slack.

"There is only one way to prove it definitively and that is through genetic testing which I'd be happy to do if you want. However, Janko, I am pretty certain that I am your father. But I never knew that Mary was pregnant. She never told me and I never knew. I had no way of knowing or even thinking that it might be a possibility. I'm sorry, Janko. I just don't know what else to say."

I felt I was listening to myself from another room somewhere. I waited. Then I waited more and the silence was a big brass band banging and clanging around in this empty room. There were miles between all of us. Great spaces of time and distance and silence, and I didn't know what to do. So I waited and the more I waited the worse I felt. Not that I could have done anything in my youth to change things, but yet I still felt bad. Impotent and alone. That has never happened to me as a counsellor before.

Janko was leaning on his elbows. His cigarette had now grown a long grey nose between his fingers. He looked off to his right, craning his neck. He wasn't looking at Veronica and Veronica wasn't looking at me. She was staring at something on the floor.

"Wow, Michael, dad. What do I say?"

He broke the ice. He had Veronica and me smiling now.

"That doesn't sound so bad hearing it. And I had thought as much, hadn't I? I thought I would have liked to have had you as a father. And I'm kinda glad that you are. Not that I know you as my father, but still. Something about what you've just told me validates my life in some small way. It's helpful, Michael, it really is. I think it will continue to bring me the courage and hope to work on my problems. I guess, maybe I feel that I can trust you more now, for some reason."

He remembered his cigarette and tapped the ash into the ashtray before inhaling on it again.

I looked at the good doctor. I thought he had gone pale. Maybe not, maybe it was the smoke I was looking through. In a small way, and I don't know if you can understand this, I felt good about what he had just shared with me. I mean I could get a lot of information on my mother as he would have known her back then. And I think I could trust him better now, because I believed he didn't know. Because if he had, he would have kept this from me, because I'd never have found out and it's riskier telling me than hiding it. Yeah, I think this was a good thing.

"Yeah, Michael, I think I feel pretty good about this."

MJ had come around from behind me and was now standing in front of me on the other side of the coffee table.

"This is so incredible, Jay. But a good incredible," she said.

"Hardly. Fucking guy, where was he when Janko was getting beat up and neglected," said Norm.

"I disagree, Norm. I think I'm with MJ, it is a great thing, a courageous thing to be talking about this now, for him to come clean about it," said Peter.

"Yeah, you would say that. Always agreeing with MJ, aren't you?" said Norm.

I just wished they'd all shut the fuck up. This was a big deal and I wanted to talk to the good doctor about this more. I wanted to explore what kind of a guy he is and what kind of a father he might have been or could still be. I gave them all my fiercest look.

"I'm glad you feel that way, Janko. I was hoping you might be able to see the positive in it. It's been worrying me since I found out, and I feel awful and sad that I never knew. That by my lack of knowledge you had to suffer so much. But I'm here now and I'm going to be here until the end. You can trust in me, Janko, and we can work through this and find you that peace and happiness until you have to leave this world. I believe it can be done, and I think we have lots of time for it, too."

"Do you really, Michael? I mean some days I wake up and think that I'm leaning in on death's door. I don't think I have many weeks left at all. My doctor has given me four to six weeks but I think he just doesn't want to hurt my feelings. I'd be surprised if I've got another four weeks, actually."

"I think we could do it within that time period, Janko. The key is going to be learning to be present in different emotions, and exploring different feelings. If we can get you to explore love and tenderness, perhaps forgiveness for me and for others, then I think those feelings will act as salves for your wounds and we won't have to necessarily dissect and analyze the ways you've been mistreated. I think that exploring new and positive feelings will be of great benefit in soothing and healing your wounds without us having to over analyze them. Does that make sense? Can you sort of understand what I mean?"

I nodded my head. I did understand. Norm had gone off to sulk by the balcony window. I was happy about that. I didn't want him around with his crappy attitude. MJ and Peter were sitting next to me. Peter to my right, MJ on my left. MJ had her hand on my knee. I put my cigarette out.

"What was she like, Michael? My mother. What was she like? How were the two of you as a couple?"

I don't know why I wanted to know. I guess I was looking for hope that I'm not inherently bad. That maybe I come from good people. That maybe there is hope for me if there had been, or is, hope with my parents. My father, sitting in front of me now, my sole surviving relative.

"Well, Janko, I loved her, that was for sure. She was the first woman I ever loved, even though we were only together for a handful of months. She was kind to me, Janko, but she was being taken down the wrong path with her friends and the people she was hanging out with. I think she probably got caught up in a difficult lifestyle that she couldn't quite extricate herself from. But I know she would have loved you very much. To the best extent that she could have. She had a good heart, Janko, but I think she had been led astray; I couldn't pull her out, I couldn't save her, and I couldn't allow myself to get sucked in either. I had to leave and it was so hard. I was saddened about it for months. But I never knew about you, Janko. I would have done my best to be there for you if I'd have known. But I didn't, and I feel bad about that."

I believed him and I felt good about this news in a way. If you can understand that. It might sound weird, but it helps explain a lot of things and it places me in history. I now know where I've come from, and that gives me a better sense of myself.

"Why would she have given me up, though? I just don't understand that."

"Well, Janko, it seems like she was losing the battle to her demons and I think in her way she wanted to try and protect you from that. I don't believe she knew what else to do. I think she was trying to protect you. It might sound bizarre to us now, but with the skills she had and the mental and emotional difficulties she was experiencing I really believe she was doing the best for you that she knew how. At that time. You might not ever understand it, but I hope you will come to a place where you can forgive her. That will help you heal. And I hope you can come to a place to forgive me, too. Though I never knew."

"I know you can, Jay. I know you can forgive them both, but I don't think the doctor needs forgiveness. He probably just wants that for himself because he feels terrible. You could do a good thing here, Jay, by forgiving. And you know what. I think it is a choice. Just choose."

MJ was talking to me and she was making sense.

"Did she have any mental illness that you know of?"

"Not that I knew of. But she'd most likely be depressed and becoming addicted to drugs doesn't help, but so many people with depression or other mental difficulties do try to self-medicate with illegal drugs, and of course it makes things worse. But no, I don't think she had a mental illness in the way that you and I do."

"So you've read my file? And what do you mean by you and me?"

"Yes, Janko, I have read your file, like I said I would. And I also suffer from schizophrenia so I have some insight into what that is like. To be honest though, I think you'd do better to be on medication for it."

MJ and Peter looked at me. Norm turned away from the balcony and looked at me with raised eyebrows.

"So you know about my illness? Why haven't you said anything before?"

"Well, I've only read your file in the last couple of days and I wanted to get this more important information out. But I think you are hallucinating at the moment am I right?"

"No, I'm not fucking hallucinating, okay. My friends are here if that's what you mean? And I'm not going to take any fucking medication for it, okay? I've relied on my friends for a long time. Way before you came into the picture and I told them I wasn't going to let them down. So if you have a problem with that we might as well end this right now."

I was angry. I looked at Veronica. She remained silent.

"You tell him, Janko," said Norm.

"Getting this angry is not going to be helpful, Jay," said MJ. Peter sat in silence staring at his lap.

"It's okay, Janko. I'm not threatening you with anything. We can call them your friends and you don't have to take any medication or let them go. But you do understand don't you that they are not real, right?"

"Yes."

I looked at my friends and they seemed more relaxed now. They all got up and went off to stand by the wall where they first were when the good doctor came.

"They won't interfere with us, Michael. But I need them, okay. I'm only getting to know you and to trust you. They've been with me for most of my life, through all the tough shit that you were never there for. I've come to rely on them and they've been of comfort to me like an old teddy that I've carried around since childhood, okay? I need them if I'm going to get through this."

I leaned in resting my forearms on my knees. We almost lost it there but Janko got himself back. The mugs stood empty on the table as I looked at it. Ash piled in the ashtray with a couple of butts. And at this moment I knew we would make it through. I looked at him and I loved him as I imagined a father would his child. I saw the courage and vulnerability, the trust and hope that was burrowing out from his dark places. He was a beautiful person and I loved him.

"I love you, son. You are going to be fine. We are all going to be just fine."

I was smiling. He looked at me and he smiled back in spite of himself, and then his eyes welled up with tears and he started to cry.

"Nobody's ever said that to me, that I can remember," he said.

Veronica and I got up at the same time and went to sit next to him on opposite sides. I took him into my arms and hugged him and he cried into my shoulder and my eyes got wet too and I looked at Veronica and she was also crying softly, quietly. Her hand on his knee, squeezing it.

"You're a beautiful human being, Janko, and I love you," I said.

"I love you, too, Janko. There is so much that is lovable about you. Your hope and courage and your spirit which has never been destroyed despite the hardships you've had. You've always been worthy of love and you need to know that and embrace it now. Accept it. Let it in and let it heal you," said Veronica.

I held him for a long time and he wept freely. My shirt was damp by the time he withdrew from my embrace. Veronica had gone to get some tissues and he took a few and blew his nose and dabbed at his eyes. Veronica did the same. I felt warm and peaceful and content inside. I was healing too. I was forgiving myself for not knowing, and for not being able to be there for him.

He looked at me and his eyes were bloodshot and his bald head was glistening a little from sweat. He looked away and outside as he spoke.

"Thank you, Michael. Thank you, Veronica. I haven't felt this good since I can't remember when, despite the way I look."

He looked at us with a smile and we both smiled back at him.

"I would have liked to have come to know you when I was much younger, Michael. I think you would've been a great dad. And frankly, I wouldn't have been through all this crap that I've had to deal with. The abuse and neglect. I could've used way less of that."

He looked down into his lap and fiddled with the blanket he had dragged off the back of the couch.

"I know, Janko. I know. In many ways I wish I could have been there for you, too. That's what eats me up so much about this. I feel guilty in a way that I wasn't there for you. Even though I never knew, I still feel guilty. But as a psychiatrist I know that for both you and me, thinking about what could have been or what should have been is not helpful. I know it's hard but it will just spiral us down into despair and self-pity. I know I'm struggling with my guilt, which is not helpful or useful to you or me. Nothing can be done about it. Just like we can't do anything about not having known each other as family before now. But what we can do is make the most of the time we have left. You can get to know me now as your father and I can get to know you, now, as my son. We can build on that the best we can in the short amount of time we have left."

Veronica and I were still sitting next to him. Veronica still had her hand on his knee which was now under the blanket. My hands were keeping to themselves. Janko looked up at me through his still glassy eyes.

"I do forgive you, Michael, for not being there. You couldn't have known and I believe that. And I guess you're right. There can't be anything gained by thinking of what could have been and all the what ifs. I just don't know how to get there. Maybe it is my way of continually beating myself up or looking for more problems. I just don't know."

I thought I'd wait to see if Veronica wanted to try this one out. I looked at her smiling.

"It could be, Janko, that you dwell on things that can never happen because it can feed a never ending battle against the self. It could also be that you are just exploring your sadness and this is part of the grieving process."

Veronica was sitting on the edge of the couch sitting towards him and looking at him. He kept looking up at her but then down at his hands again.

"What do you think it is, V?" he asked her.

"Well, Janko, I think it is probably your way of dealing with the sadness and grieving a loss. The loss of your fatherless childhood I'd say. But at the same time you'll have to monitor yourself carefully to make sure that it doesn't become a means to do battle with yourself."

He looked at me and asked me the same question.

"I agree with Veronica. I think it is a method for you to grieve and I think you should allow yourself that luxury. It is something earned but more than that it will allow you to heal from the pain, and that is what we are all very interested in, Janko. Helping you to heal from the pain. And Veronica and I and the rest of us will help to keep you true to the grief and help you steal away from the internal battling that won't get you anywhere.

Veronica nodded her head which I'm sure he saw out of the periphery of his vision.

"Thank you also for your forgiveness, Janko. That takes courage and strength, you are helping me to heal in a small way, too. I encourage you to continue to pursue forgiveness in other areas and towards other people. I'd suggest that maybe you try next to start with your mother."

I put my hand on his shoulder and gave it a squeeze. I was a little nervous about pushing him too hard too fast. I wasn't sure he would be up to it and might quickly return to his sulky, angry and combative ways. But I was wrong. I was learning more and more about this young man who was my son. And the more I learned about him the better I liked him and the more respect I had for him. He was smiling a little into his lap.

"You're welcome, Michael. And I'm sad about my mother and angry and all those other things we spoke about and I'd like to forgive her. Maybe you can help me with that so I can see how to forgive her. Maybe you can tell me more of what she was like.

I mean, I was only six years old when my memories of her end, so I don't know how accurate they'd be of her. And I don't suppose you'd have a picture of her would you?"

He looked at me and I shook my head.

"Yeah, I didn't think so. Maybe you can tell me what she looked like and what you did together. I remember her being tall, but then again everyone seems tall to a six year old. I remember her having long brown hair, which she usually let hang down naturally. I remember her being slim and attractive but I don't remember her smiling much. I do remember a lot of anger and her being short tempered though she didn't beat me too much. Not like the rest of the pseudo parents I had."

I smiled at him in encouragement.

"I'm glad to hear that she didn't beat you. It pains me to hear that you've been mistreated so much by so many people who should have known better and were in positions of trust."

"Yeah I know, doc, but you've just told me that the shoulds and the coulds aren't helpful anymore."

He looked at me with his big bright eyes filled with mirth this time and I had to laugh. Through all of this he had tried to maintain a sense of humor.

"Touché," said Veronica.

"Yes, you're right, Janko. It is no help but my pain is still sincere. Back to your mother, though. She was an attractive woman with long brown hair as you've described her. It fell down to her shoulder blades and when I knew her she liked to keep it naturally cascading down around her face. It had a slight natural curl to it and I remember it smelled of apples mostly from the shampoo she used to use. She was slim and if I remember correctly about five feet seven inches tall which I guess is on the taller side for women. The one thing that I remember as being different from your recollection is her sense of humor. She was very fun and always laughing at my silly jokes. She was always a good sport if she was teased and she loved to laugh and I loved to make her laugh, too. I think she went through a difficult and terrible transition when she got involved with the wrong crowd. But she was naturally a fun and vivacious woman as I remembered her."

Veronica and I got up and went to sit back in our chairs.

"Is it okay if we sit back here, Janko?" I asked. "We don't want to crowd you."

He nodded his head and fidgeted with the blanket still in his lap. He shifted then and lay down on the couch covering himself with the blanket. It didn't seem cold to me inside his apartment but he had a chill.

"This is how they do it in the movies right, Michael. The patient lying on the couch the doctor going 'tell me your problems'?"

I smiled and Veronica laughed. He had tried to put on a deep, serious voice when he was speaking as the doctor. It wasn't very convincing, but that added to its charm.

"Yes, Janko, that is exactly how it goes. Now we will be able to make great strides with you lying on the couch. Unless of course you fall asleep on me. But I'll be testing you to make sure you don't. I'll be asking you questions that are going to require great thought and careful answers."

He pulled the blanket up closer around his chin and shivered.

"Would you like me to turn up the heat for you, Janko?" asked Veronica.

"No, thanks. I think I'll be alright in a bit with the blanket. Besides you guys will probably cook if I do that."

He wasn't looking at any of us but he was right. Already the apartment was pretty toasty. I'd say it had to be seventy-seven or higher, but neither of us had the heart to agree with him.

"Well?" he asked.

"Well what, Janko?" asked Veronica.

"Well, isn't it warm in here for you?"

"Yes, I suppose it is a little warm," she said.

I took off my cardigan and lay it across the arm of the chair I was in.

"You too, hey doc?" he said.

"Yes, Janko, me too. It is pretty warm in here but manageable. I'd rather be too warm than too cold."

"I know. I just can't seem to get very warm lately. It seems like I'm always cold. Like I'm always getting tickled by the icy fingers of death and it's getting worse. I don't want to die before we've had a chance to finish our work, Michael. It makes me scared."

He was looking up at the ceiling. Talking to the space between us.

"I know, Janko. But in these short weeks we've been together you've made tremendous strides. Ask Veronica. Ask any of us. I know I speak for all of us when I say that we are very impressed with how well you've done. Just consider the small things.

Like your swearing. You used to swear like a sailor, to use an expression that your great grandmother used. But now you very seldom swear and when you do you are aware of it. That shows great improvement and it is in no way a small thing. As I told you a while back your swearing is indicative of your state of mind. A clean and healthy mind is not sullied and dirtied by the curses. You paint your mind with the strokes of your tongue, Janko."

"Very true, Janko, what Dr. Malichem is saying. I know that all of us nurses have spoken about the great strides you are making and have made. It's terrific. Just hold tight and keep the courage to soldier on," said Veronica.

"Tell me about my great grandmother and my mother, Michael. What were you and she like?"

He was still talking into the spaces between us. But the spaces didn't seem so filled with distance and time anymore.

"We used to go ice skating a lot in the winter. She had done a lot of ice skating when she was younger and she loved it, but by the time I knew her she was living with her mother and they weren't very rich. It had been rumored that she had been sexually abused by her father. Not that you want to know that, but it might help you understand her and the demons she maybe had to face herself. I never met her father and I wouldn't have cared to either.

But what I was saying is that she never could afford to go back for ice skating lessons as she and her mother were pretty poor when I knew her. But she loved to go ice skating in the winter. Around this time of the year actually, and she could skate circles around me. We'd spend just about our whole Saturday on the ice if it wasn't too frigid. She loved it. We'd pack a thermos of hot soup and another thermos of hot chocolate. It was wonderful. I can still see her now, sipping the hot chocolate with the steam swirling up around her and her mittens gripping around the thermos lid. Her cheeks were so rosy and her eyes sparkled and she just kept on smiling. She was always smiling in those days, as I remember. She was happy then. We were happy then, and young.

Life was a treat and we didn't need much except each other and our love. It makes me sad now thinking about it. That it had to end. But when I think back now on those days by the ice rink, I'm happy and I see us smiling at each other. I see us kissing and hugging and holding hands as we sailed around the ice, oblivious to everyone else.

It was on one of those days that your mother first told me that she loved me. And I told her the same. Those are the memories I'd like to remember her by. When we were having fun and the kind things we did to help each other, to care for each other. Those are good memories, Janko. Those are the kind of memories that maybe you can imagine and hopefully get a fuller picture of your mother. The kind of woman that she once was. And the kind of woman I'm sure she wanted to be for you as best she could. She made some bad decisions and couldn't honor her true self. She couldn't overcome her demons, but she wasn't an evil or malicious woman. I know she cared for you the best she knew how. She did her best and I know it wasn't anywhere near good enough, but maybe you can learn to forgive her knowing that she had been better than she was once. That she wasn't always a bad mother or a monster, and that you are not what your mother was when she abandoned you, but rather you are what I am now and what she was then. When I knew her. I see the goodness in you now, Janko, as I saw it in her, then."

I saw him smile just a bit even though he wasn't looking up at me. His grip on the blanket had lessened. I think he was getting warmer. I looked at Veronica. She was smiling at me sitting back in her chair with her hands folded in her lap.

"That is so true, Janko. We are not who we come from, what we do for a living or our difficult situations. These are not the things that define us, or should I say these are not the things that we should allow ourselves to be defined by. Unfortunately a lot of people do define themselves by these very things and this is I think, a large contributing factor as to why we feel so alone and disconnected from one another and the world in general," said Veronica.

Janko craned his head to look at her.

"So then what do you think we are?"

"Well, we are who we want to be and who we think we can become. I think this is the great gift of being human. We can reinvent ourselves as we wish, and this carries with it huge potential. We don't have to be victim to our circumstances and we don't have to be tossed around by the winds of fate. Each day, each moment we can decide how to react and what to think and by so doing we can become more than we are.

If we only try to reach farther there are plenty of examples out there to show us the courage and determination of the human spirit. You and I and Dr. Malichem can choose which path we want to travel down. We can choose to be good or bad, to live with love in our hearts rather than hate."

Veronica stopped then and looked at me. I nodded my head and mouthed 'good words' to her. Janko had closed his eyes and was breathing deeply and slowly.

"I like that, V," he said, "I think I could come to see that point of view. Right now I'm just thinking about when I was six years old and after that when I was bounced around from orphanages and foster parents and how shitty I was treated. That doesn't make me happy to think about those things. It actually pisses me off to tell the truth and I can't find my way to a better place. Especially with my mother, when she should have been the one person to help me. The one person who should've been there to protect me and to love me."

He sighed and squeezed his eyes tighter. I wanted to try something.

"Uh,oh, Janko, you're entertaining the shoulds. You reminded me about them so I've got to remind you about it, too. Fair's fair."

He didn't smile but he didn't say anything either. I figured that was a victory.

"Sometimes it's best to try and not think about those things that we have no control over, and to instead focus on the things we can change or the thoughts that build us up. Everything you say is valid, Janko, that's for sure. But it isn't necessarily helpful. Speaking from personal experience, you can't focus on things you have no control over. It won't do you any good. Your mother should have been there for you, there is no disputing that. But she wasn't and there isn't anything that can be done about that," said Veronica.

I liked the tough love approach Veronica was trying but I wasn't sure it was going to work.

"And when you get caught up in that kind of thinking it isn't going to help. It'll make things worse as you're now experiencing. Perhaps you could train your focus onto more positive things. Like the fact that through Dr. Malichem you're getting to know a different side of your mother.

A side that paints a nicer picture. Not necessarily truer, but nicer and now you have a fuller flavour of what she was like. It doesn't negate the fact that she handled her role as your mother poorly, but it could help you move on and heal if you allowed yourself to see her as a human being rather than as a monster. What you have control over is what you can do now. You can focus on getting to know your father. Getting to know more about your mother and getting to know more about yourself. And along this journey you can start to take control over how you feel and how those feelings are driven by your thoughts. Thinking of forgiveness and love will allow you to heal as Michael said earlier on. You need to get to that place and you yourself said that you don't have much time. It is never too late, Janko, but why not start trying to focus on more positive and constructive thoughts and feelings."

I felt like I needed something to do. I thought a mug of water would help. I felt thirsty and my hands were lonely, fidgeting and animated on the arm rests of my chair. Janko got himself up to sitting with great effort. He fumbled with his cigarettes, finally pulling one out and setting fire to it. He inhaled deeply and spoke through grey clouds again.

"I like what you're saying, Veronica. And you too, Michael, but I'm just so damn tired. Mentally tired and probably emotionally, too. I mean this is so much to take in all at once and my brain feels like fuzzy wool. I'd like to get out and go for a walk. I think I could do with some head clearing."

He wasn't looking at either of us. He was staring at the table with his hands clasped in front of him. The cigarette pointing outside in agreement. The smoke was trailing up, curling and gyrating like a belly dancer and there was smoke leaking out of the corners of his mouth. He was breathing heavily like he had been in the ring for a few rounds. And he probably felt like he had been in the ring, at least mentally and emotionally.

"I think that is a good idea, Janko, if you think you'll be up for it. Do you think you'll be warm enough?" I asked him.

He nodded.

"I'll need some help getting dressed, V, if you don't mind."

Veronica nodded and got up and went into his room to get some clothes ready, I assumed. Janko looked at me.

"How am I doing, Michael? I mean I feel better for the news you've shared with me. It makes me feel like I can trust you more easily now that I know you're blood to me. It might sound stupid, but that's how I feel, anyway. I'm really trying doctor, Jesus, I'm really trying and yet I'm not sure how far I'm getting. I feel better, or at least I think I feel better from weeks ago. Shit I feel better even from just a day ago. But I'm scared, too, that it won't last. I mean should it be this easy to start feeling better when my whole life has been a catastrophe. And I'm trying not to think about it like that, but it has been. The shit I've had to deal with. Well, you probably know about most of it. It's probably in my file."

I nodded. It was and I had become familiar with it. Horrible, horrendous abuse and neglect. One of the worst cases I had ever come across. He looked at me and tried to smile, but it fell off his face.

"Am I, Michael...dad, am I doing okay?"

"You sure are, son. You sure are. I'd be proud of you if I was just your psychiatrist, but I'm doubly proud of you because you're my son and I see that Malichem courage in you. My life hasn't been the easiest either. But yours is one of the worst cases I've come across and here you are talking to me and exploring these very difficult issues and emotionally challenging thoughts. Your strength of spirit is phenomenal and you have come leaps and bounds already. I am especially pleased with how well you're doing with finding out that you are my son. I thought it would be a stumbling block and not something positive and uplifting and hopeful.

This is really great news. And in light of all of the tumultuous emotions and knowledge we've been dealing with in such a short time I believe that your improvements are well deserved and earned and not at all unusual. As Veronica said, if you can start focusing your thoughts on more positive patterns that is often all it takes. Not to say that you might not slip back, but if you keep trying and keep reminding yourself to be kind, gentle, positive, and uplifting about yourself, then you will exponentially increase your mental health and well-being. We don't have to focus on the pain and sadness of your past.

We can focus on getting to know one another as family, and I think that maybe that is what is most needed more than coming to terms with your past. Nothing can be done about the horrible things that have happened to you when you were younger.

But we can develop positive memories of the two of us and we can explore some of the positive memories of your mother and what she was like. And I'm hoping that through all of that we can help you come to forgive the misguided people in your past, or at least help you to come to a calm acceptance of things as they were then. And hopefully you'll realize that things are not like that anymore. Your life can now be an experience of love and contentment and peace in these last days of yours. This, I believe, is definitely within our abilities and time frame. And it is what I think is needed to help you, rather than a deep exploration of your painful childhood. I don't think that would be helpful or desired. Would you agree?"

"Uh, huh," he nodded.

I went over to help him up as he struggled to his feet.

"I'll wait out here for you."

I sat back down and watched him. Watched my son shuffle into his bedroom. I had a mix of emotions, the predominant one being optimism. He didn't need to try and understand why things were the way they were. I don't think any of us need that or find it helpful. What he needs and what we all need is the gift of hope and more pleasant experiences and the security of feeling that we are safe, that our past can no longer morph into our present. He needed, and I'd argue that all of us who hurt need, the present to be filled with forgiveness and love and hope. Kindness is the salve by which we can help heal each other from the scrapes and scratches that we invariably collect on this thorny path of life.

I stood up and went to the balcony window. It looked like a nice day out there. Blue skies with just wisps of high altitude white clouds. I saw the birds out there again, flying around from balcony to barren tree branches and back. They hadn't let me down, they were just waiting for me to figure it out myself. And I had. In a way, I suppose I had. But I kept getting that gnawing feeling in my mind that I was becoming the patient as much as Janko was. And what that was all about I wasn't sure. Maybe time would answer this question as it healed Janko's pain. Then all would be good in the world and I would have succeeded to some degree.

I needed something to do with my hands instead of stuffing them in my pockets like I was trying to keep them warm. This apartment was hot and they were just getting clammy in there.

I went to the kitchen and poured myself a glass of water. I'd done enough thinking for now. I could use some fresh air myself. Maybe it would clear my head too. If nothing else it might just help me focus on something other than the walls of this apartment, which reminded me a lot of my own place way back when I was a struggling student.

XXV

They came out and I wasn't that impressed with how Janko was dressed. I raised my eyebrows at Veronica but she just shrugged her shoulders at me.

"He said he wanted to be comfortable," said Veronica.

"Sounds good," I fibbed.

He was wearing grey sweat pants, a white long sleeved t-shirt with both the arms and the waist hanging out from under the hooded sweatshirt he was wearing on top of it all. It was black with a splashes of red and green and yellow blotches on it, and looked like he might have taken some paint to it himself. I couldn't quite tell and I didn't have the courage to ask.

"The wheelchair should be just inside the jacket closet in the front."

Veronica pointed to it and I slid open the doors and took it out. It was collapsed so I opened it up thinking it would be easier to get down the stairs that way. Veronica was holding Janko's IV. They had left the stand for it behind. There was a little hook for it on the wheelchair that would come in handy once Janko was in it and either I or Veronica were pushing him around.

The good doctor led us out. I had to wait with Veronica while she locked up after us. She was holding onto my IV and I was trapped to her. Like an umbilical cord or something. Apron strings and neither of us had the guts to cut me loose. In good time though, I'd be loose and free, into the wild blue yonder as they say.

It was incredibly hard work standing and then walking down the hallway. I was panting and wheezing. I hadn't remembered my cigarettes and that kind of pissed me off.

Not that I could smoke now, the way I was huffing and puffing. But it sure would be good to have a cigarette once I was seated in the wheelchair.

I walked slowly down the hallway with Veronica. I had to have my left arm over her shoulder. I was dizzy, weak and dying. Well, literally I was dying but I also felt like I was dying from the fire in my lungs. Breathing was just so damn hard lately. Veronica had her right arm around my neck and her left hand held the IV. She also had a blanket tossed over her left shoulder. It felt good under my hand.

"Would you like to swap rolls, Veronica? Maybe I should take Janko and you can wheel the chair down the stairs?"

He wasn't meaning to be funny, but he was. I couldn't help but smile to myself. But I shook my head at him. I just wanted to get down the damn stairs and be seated in the wheel chair. I didn't want to be wasting any time pissing around with different possibilities of how I might be best helped along.

"No, thanks, I think we'll manage. Might just be best to get him down as soon as possible and get him into that chair."

Now, at least someone was thinking clearly. Thank God for woman. Or Veronica. Jesus, I just wanted to curse the doctor, my old man, but for the life of me I could barely breath let alone speak. I hissed a 'yes' or something and he carried on.

We finally made it but not before I had to sit on the stairs on the second floor and rest for a couple of minutes. Veronica was standing over me holding my IV like a frigging noose over my head. But it felt good just to have that short respite.

The good doctor and Veronica helped me into the chair and I sat heavily in it. All my one hundred and maybe ten pounds. Veronica placed the blanket over my lap and around my waist. I was warm for a change. The walk and those stairs had made me warmer than I had felt in what seemed like months. My gang had followed me down, which I hadn't noticed until they were all huddled around me, except for Norm who was leaning against the tree just outside the entrance to my apartment complex. Sullen fucker, always so sullen. He had his one leg kicked up behind him with his heel on the tree trunk and his hands crossed over his chest. So cool, just like a fool. I pretended to ignore him. It was easy to do as MJ was fussing over me tucking in the blanket here and there and asking me if I was okay.

"I'm not sure we're going to be able to do this too many more times, hey Janko?"

I looked at the good doctor. He was full of optimism and enthusiasm. I liked it, it was kind of contagious in a way.

"No, I don't think we'll have another chance to do this at all actually. But I like your optimism, dad."

It didn't feel all that weird to be calling him dad. As a matter of fact I couldn't care what he thought. I was a dying man and that gave me a sort of 'couldn't care less' attitude which was probably the only thing that was going to help me over the next couple of weeks, if that. Besides, it actually felt good to call him my dad. He was, after all, and God knows I've spent my whole life looking for a father, if not my own real father.

Veronica started pushing me from behind. I turned around behind me and saw Peter and MJ walking arm in arm with Norm, sullen Norm trailing behind them staring intently at the ground, his arms still folded in front of him. To my left was the good doctor. I smiled up at him as he looked ahead staring off into the distance, the future, as if there was one. Maybe for him. He looked over to me and smiled back.

"It sure is good to get out for a stroll, my son. This was a great idea of yours, I think I probably needed it as much as you."

He patted my shoulder and I kept on smiling.

"It sure is nice, Michael," said Veronica, "not too cold for a stroll but cold enough to keep it quiet out here. I say we make our way to the corner store and see if we can't get some hot chocolates for the return trip."

"Yeah, I'd like that."

"Sounds good to me," said my old man. He looked at me again.

"Are your friends with us, Janko?"

I nodded, not sure what he was trying to get at. I looked behind me and saw Norm staring a hole into the back of Michael's head. MJ shrugged her shoulder half assed and Peter was kinda smirking all the while.

"Tell me about them, son, I'd like to hear what they're like and how they might have helped you through your trials."

As he spoke, steam escaped from his mouth and looked like cigarette smoke. He could have been a smoker and that damn image of him exhaling into the chilly air just made me madder at myself for not remembering my smokes.

I'm sorry if this is bugging you, all this talk about me smoking, but it's the closest friend I've had besides the figments of my imagination trailing around behind me like wedding cans on the back of a car. Besides, cigarettes have always been there for me, okay? I know they're bad for me, I've said as much before, but come on, you know I'm dying and it doesn't make a difference anymore now, does it? How about if I tell you I would have stopped if I wasn't going to die? Would that make it better? Would you feel all right with it, then? Well, then that's what I'll say. If I wasn't going to die, I'd quit smoking, okay? Besides, I'm gonna quit sometime soon, anyway. It's just going to happen when I die.

"Hey, Janko…Are you listening?"

I turned to look at the doctor and forgot what he had asked me earlier. I saw the fog from his mouth trail back around his ears like a scarf as we continued on.

"Sorry, dad, I can't remember what you said."

He looked down at me frowning and then smiled.

"I asked you if you'd tell me about your friends. Their names and such."

"Oh, right, okay. I just got lost in thought thinking about smoking. I could sure use a cigarette and seeing you talk and the clouds come out of your mouth like smoke just made me want a cigarette even more, but I left them back in the apartment. Did you ever smoke, Michael?"

I was still looking up at him, and he was still staring off into the future.

"No, I never smoked. It's no good for you. But I'll tell you what, we can buy you a pack of cigarettes at the store when we get there if you'll stop stalling and tell me about your friends."

He was smiling as he looked at me and took a playful swipe at my head, brushing the hoodie.

"Okay, you've got a deal. If you look behind us," and he did, "you'll see a woman and a man walking arm in arm. Their arms are through each other at the elbow like debonair couples walk sometimes. They're about the same height and they've got the same color hair. It's brunette. Hers is short and cropped around her face. She doesn't wear much make up but she sure is cute. I wished she could have been my girlfriend.

Her name is MJ which is short for Mary Jane. Anyway, that's what she told me her name was. She's really nice, kind of like I'd imagine my sister would be. She was fussing with me earlier making sure I was all tucked into the blanket, nice and snug. I've known her probably the longest but probably only by a few months or so, I guess. They both came to me when I was around eight years old, I guess. But I met her when I was a sad and lonely eight year old and I was hanging under the bridge down by Bowness Park. I was sitting there with my hands wrapped around my knees and my head between them and I was crying because I was so sad and I had no one. I had no friends. The kids at school were teasing me and bullying me, and I'd already been through a few foster parents who were all so fucking mean, you have no idea."

I looked around me again and I had to squeeze my damn eyes closed hard first, because they were filling up with tears, again. I wanted that shit to stop. MJ winked at me and that made me smile. I looked back at the good doctor and he placed his hand down on my shoulder and squeezed it gently.

"It's okay, son. This is a safe place for you to explore your sadness."

That's all he said but it was the way he said it, you know. The kindness in his eyes and the warmth in his touch that gave me courage to carry on.

"I'm sorry, doctor. There's just been so much pain and sadness back in those days, it's hard for me to go there sometimes."

I was trying to steal courage from somewhere but I couldn't find it. I blinked my eyes hard again. Then I started searching deep inside for something to hold onto, something from which to tell the rest of the story.

"Well, that's how I met MJ. And to be honest with you she was so kind and gentle and soft. One of the few who has been kind to me. Do you have any idea how far a little bit of kindness will go? It'll take a man half way around the world if it's genuine kindness. Well, she gave that to me.

And she's kept on giving it to me, and I've kept on loving her and I've wished so often that she was real so that we might have been able to have a real relationship, maybe even have started a family. I think, Michael, that these are some of the kinds of thoughts that have kept me going during my darkest hours.

Call them hallucinations or whatever you want, but they've literally kept me alive, okay? The hope, even if it wasn't real, and the dreams that these people have helped me carry. I've needed that, dad, I really have. Without it I would have been dead a long time ago."

He looked down at me, breathing like a dragon. Smoke snaking out of his nose and his mouth as he spoke. But he was like a friendly dragon.

"I do understand, son. I really do, I just wish that the milk of human kindness could have been real for you and not manufactured like it has been. That just makes me sad. But don't worry, Janko. I don't have concerns with your friends. They've offered you something you've desperately needed and you've held onto that. I could call it loyalty, and that's admirable. Just keep the dialogue open and we can work within the parameters you're setting."

I liked that. I liked it a lot that he was letting me drive the process. It gave me some sense of control. Veronica wasn't saying much. She kept pushing me along towards the store, but every so often I could hear her breathing heavily as we went. Not too heavily, but sort of deeply through her mouth. I looked up and craned my head behind me to see her and she smiled down at me like a gargoyle or something. It was weird and it also made me dizzy so I flipped my head back to see in front of me again. We were making good time towards the store. I was looking forward to a hot chocolate but especially my cigarettes.

"She's always been there, Michael. And I know she's not real but to me, she and the rest of them are as real as they get, okay? And they've been loyal and faithful. And MJ has been the pillow that I've fallen on during hard times. I love her if I've ever loved a person before. She's just wonderful. I know you'd like her if she was real. You really would."

"Yeah, Janko, she sure does sound wonderful and warm and compassionate. Seems to me she would be a wonderful female role model. You know that these kinds of hallucinations are manifestations of your psyche and are to help you to try and make sense of the world. She would make perfect sense when you think of how you were abandoned by your mother and the void that that would have left. You'd be looking for someone to fill that and I think that MJ would be the perfect hallucination to fulfil your search for the female ideal. I'm encouraged by that, son; she is arguably a good influence if these manifestations of schizophrenia can ever be considered good."

He was looking straight ahead still. His hand still on my shoulder, the other one in his pocket. His breath still wrapped around his neck like a scarf. A bus rumbled by and I couldn't hear what the last thing was that he said. That and also Norm ranting behind me.

"See, I knew it. I fucking knew it. Here he goes, Janko trying to find ways of dismissing us. Sure, he likes MJ, but wait until he gets to hear about Peter and especially me. You better say some nice shit about me, okay? I'm not going anywhere and I'll make your life miserable if you give him anything on which to hang me, you hear?"

He was walking to my right now and I was looking at him turned sideways to talk to me. His arms were flapping around like loose birds and he was stepping sideways over himself and over shrubs and flowerbeds trying to get his point across. I stuck my tongue out at him.

"Tell me about that one, Janko," said Michael.

"Which one?" I asked turning to look at him.

"The one you stuck your tongue out at."

Veronica chuckled behind me and I smiled at the good doctor as he gave me a wink.

"He's my least favorite. His name's Norm and he was just threatening me if I told you the truth about him. He was telling me how he would make my life hell if I gave you anything that you could use against him and to make me get rid of him. But he's always been pretty ignorant and angry."

We all stopped then. The good doctor had turned around to face me and Veronica had stopped the wheelchair and stood behind me. Michael got down on his haunches and looked at me. He was all seriousness now.

"You know that he can't really affect you in anyway, right?"

He was holding my shoulders in his hands and his tone was sombre. He was looking me straight in the eye and his breath was clouding the space between us. Did he really think I was an idiot? I mean, sure Norm had made me scared before, but I was onto him now. I knew he couldn't affect me in anyway. Not with my dad here in front of me. Not with the courage I had knowing that I wasn't alone anymore that I had family and I had blood to rely on. Of course he couldn't affect me, anymore. He was a lonely, pathetic child. Just like I had been all those years ago.

"Right, son? You know he can't get to you anymore, right? It's okay if he stays, but you have to remember that you're in the driver's seat now. You can determine who is going to affect you in whatever way. And I bet you're more interested in having people around who are going to lift you up rather than bring you down."

I nodded my head. I turned around to look at Norm who was fuming and I stuck my tongue out at him again. Funny thing is, his breath wasn't condensing. And that was good, because it just gave me a real feeling then that I knew he wasn't real. I really knew it then as I hadn't before.

"Yeah, dad. I know he can't hurt me anymore. But you know what? He did have a place once upon a time. A long time ago when I was a small and scared boy being abused and neglected by just about everyone I knew, he was there for me like an older brother. He gave me courage to be strong and to stand up to some people. Especially the bullies at school and that worked well. It didn't work too well when I was standing up to the foster parents. I'd get beat even worse then. But he was the one who gave me the courage to leave when I was only sixteen and get the hell out of those situations. I've got lots to thank him for and I'm loyal for his help and support. I know he probably isn't that helpful now, but he was a long time ago and I'm going to keep him around for a while. He's lonely, now. Peter and MJ don't support him anymore and he just kind of hangs out by himself and sulks. But he's been an important part of my life if you can understand that."

Dad got up and looked around. I didn't know if he was trying to find Norm or he was just thinking. But then he looked back down at me.

"Okay, son," he said, "I understand."

We all started moving along then and we were getting closer to my cigarettes. That and the hot chocolate. I could almost smell it, I swear.

"Don't take it so personally, Norm," said Peter, "that's your problem. No wonder none of us want to hang around you much, anymore. Janko's right, you're too arrogant and angry, you should learn to relax a little and just go with it. Am I right, MJ?"

"You sure are," said MJ.

I turned around and saw Norm was back behind Peter and MJ. He was trailing them with his hands crossed over his chest again and his eyes fixed on the ground.

It was like, if he didn't watch where he was going he was going to fall down or something. I sort of felt sorry for him then. I mean he had been an important part of my life for a long time but now he was no longer really needed. That's gotta hurt, right? You'd be sad and sulky too, wouldn't you?

"We're all still your friends, Norm," continued Peter, "it's just that you make it hard to be around and that's why we don't talk to you too much. I mean, just think about it for a moment. If Janko wanted you gone, or any of us for that matter he could make it happen. He could ask the doctor for the drugs and voila we'd be so outta here. But he hasn't, has he? No, he's keeping us around because he still needs us and is showing us loyalty. And I'm afraid, Norm, that you're being the antithesis of loyalty at the moment. Or rather should I say for the last several weeks? Buck up old boy, or I'm going to start asking Janko to bump you off."

"You're pretty quiet now, son. Everything okay with Norm? I'll be happy to have a talk with him."

Michael was looking at me and then scanning off behind me and to my sides. He wouldn't find Norm, because he couldn't see him. Ha.

"Yeah, dad, everything's fine with Norm. I'm just listening to him get a lecture from Peter. I haven't told you about Peter, but I think you'd like him. Norm's all the way behind us by himself, doing his classic sulking and pouting game."

"Okay, okay, I get it, Peter," said Norm, "but it isn't all that easy, okay? I mean for fuck's sake, it isn't like you've lost anything. You've actually gained esteem in Janko's eyes and you used to be a pussy before, okay. Listen to Janko extol the fucking virtues of you and MJ to the doctor. So give me a break, okay? He tore a strip off of me to the good doctor. So how do you expect me to feel?"

"All I'm saying, Norm," continued Peter, "is that you are going to catch more bees with honey. You going on and on like this, feeling so sorry for yourself, isn't going to endear anyone to you. And even though my esteem has risen lately in Janko's eyes, I have always remained consistent. I've been the same since before Janko liked me as much as he does now, as I am now. So just think about that, Norm. I'm not the enemy here. The enemy is yourself."

"Very true, Norm," said MJ.

"They're trying to give him good advice," I said to Michael.

"What kind of advice is that, Janko?"

"Well, they're, or should I say Peter is mostly, telling him that he'll catch more bees with honey and not to be such a sour puss."

"Sounds like good advice to me."

We were waiting at the traffic lights to cross the road. We'd be at the strip mall then and close to hot chocolate and cigarettes. The little white man seemed to be taking forever to change to the red flashing hand. I could see little crusts of icy snow tucked into the creases where the road met the sidewalk. There wasn't much of it around. It had been a pretty dry winter and we'd had some pretty good Chinooks lately to melt most of the snow.

"I'm feeling a little bit crowded knowing there are so many of us on this walk," said Veronica.

"What do you mean?" I asked.

"I'm just teasing. But there are twice as many of us now that we've been introduced to your friends, right? Six of us now instead of the three."

"Yes, I suppose you are right. I hadn't thought about it, though. Mind you, I can see them all and I don't imagine you can. So really, I'm the only one who should be feeling crowded."

I was smiling at her.

"Hey, Janko," said Norm.

I turned around to look at him. He had moved up just off to my right, slightly behind me. The light changed and we started moving again across the road.

"Is it true what Peter was saying? That you're loyal and that you want us, me, to stick around?"

I nodded at him. All of a sudden I felt pretty self-conscious about talking to imaginary people, even if the good doctor and Veronica knew about them.

"Okay, then, I'll try and be a little more cordial. But can you understand how I've felt, feeling like I'm being left out and marginalized? It isn't easy when I've been the go to guy for most of your life you know."

"Yes,I do understand, Norm. It wouldn't be easy, but your attitude lately hasn't been helping."

"What's that, son?" asked Michael.

"I was just talking to, Norm. He's looking for reassurance that I'm going to let him stick around and I said I would if his attitude changes."

"Good. I think the more positive thoughts you can have, the easier this whole process will be."

"Okay, Jay," said Norm, "I'll give you your space. Maybe we can talk later?"

I nodded at him again and he disappeared off behind me somewhere, but he didn't seem all that sulky. That was a really nice change.

"Tell us about Peter, Janko. We haven't heard anything about him yet," said Veronica.

My hands were getting cold so I put them under the blanket. I looked like an old fucking cripple or something, but God knew I couldn't walk this distance. It was all I could do to walk down the hallway and stairs. I looked behind me and saw Peter preening himself. He tossed his head back and winked at me.

"Say something nice. Tell him what a stud I am," said Peter.

I laughed at him, and then realized that Michael and Veronica were looking at me.

"Sorry, it was Peter, he's just playing the goof."

We were crossing the parking lot now, a quarterback's throw from the store. I was salivating, but not for hot chocolate, mostly for cigarettes. Word to the rest of you, if you don't smoke, don't start, the shit will kill you and you won't be able to quit. But I suppose I'm preaching to the choir aren't I, gentle reader. You've been bearing with me and my nic-fits for a while now. Thanks for that. It won't be long now and I'll be dead I'm sure, and then you won't have to worry about it anymore.

There were a couple of young juveniles hanging around the outside of the store. They were just kicking back and enjoying a smoke. They were probably playing hooky from school. They watched us as we approached and none of them bothered to open the door for us, the fuckers. The good doctor got the door for me and V. Norm stared them down as he entered, but it didn't do any good. They never even saw him. Inside I got the good doctor to pick me up a chocolate bar, a bag of chips and a large hot chocolate. While I was having a good inning I got him to get me a pack of American cigarettes, too. That was a treat for me. I liked the flavor better, or maybe it was the fiberglass in the filter. Or so I had been told once.

"You're asking for a hell of a lot, Janko, and you aren't sharing anything with us about your last friend. You gotta pony up, okay?"

He said this as we came up to the cashier to pay for the stuff. He was pretty good, he wasn't staring me down like most folks do when I'm out and about. A thin, gaunt Auschwitz victim, wheeled around as if on display. And I'm not even Jewish.

"As soon as we get out, Michael. I'm not trying to hide anything."

Michael paid for everything but forget about matches. Non-smokers usually do. I had to ask the clerk myself.

The juvies had left once we got out into the parking lot and started making our way back home.

"You know what we should get, son, while we are here, is a nice freshly baked loaf of bread. They have a pretty good bakery here if I recall."

"Yeah, it's just up on the right there."

We slowly made our way there. I fired up a cigarette, enjoying that first waft of tobacco before it became acrid. I inhaled deeply and then coughed it out. I still wasn't used to the strong American cigarettes.

"Peter's a nice guy," I started off, just out of nowhere.

"I'm listening," said Michael not missing a beat. He was always cool and even tempered. I liked that about him, gave me hope in his abilities. He looked down at me then and patted my shoulder.

"No, I mean he's really a nice guy. Whereas Norm has been arrogant and angry most of my life, Peter has been more like you, dad. He's been nice and even tempered. I've very seldom seen him angry or upset. But then again he isn't very outgoing or boisterous either. I'd say he is more shy and reserved. He'd probably sit on a couch with maybe one or two people at a social gathering rather than mingle with the whole crowd.

He's always been supportive but in a more laid back way, encouraging me not to rock the boat but to sit tight and try and fight from within. Wasn't always the most helpful advice especially back in the day. I preferred then to follow Norm's advice, but now I'm beginning to see the wisdom in what he is saying and his approach. MJ thinks he's very cute and the way she looks at him sometimes, well I wish she'd look at me more like that.

I think if he was real he'd be a hit with the ladies, unlike Norm who would rather just be fighting with people. As a matter of fact the one real girlfriend I ever had, Norma Jean, I was able to date because I listened to Peter's ideas about what to say and how to behave. I don't think she would have gone out with me if I hadn't had Peter's help back then.

But then I also fucked it up, thanks to Norm and by not listening to Peter. I started looking for shit and started arguing with her all the time. Peter told me to watch it and to relax and settle down but I just wouldn't listen to him. Norm started feeding my insecurities about how she was behaving and that maybe she wasn't that interested in me and that she was just dating me because she felt sorry for me. And I believed the bastard and she finally couldn't put up with it anymore, me badgering her. I still feel shitty about it."

Michael looked down at me.

"I can understand, son, you still sound quite upset about it."

"I am," I said, sucking on my cigarette. Clouds of smoke and condensed breath fogging up around me. Fogging me up like my own emotions.

"I still feel lousy about it. I loved that woman. I really did, dad, I don't know if you can understand that."

"I can," he said.

"It didn't have to be like that. But you get into a place where you just can't let go of these jealous thoughts and they start to eat you up. And thanks to Norm feeding them and my insecurities, I started seeing things that weren't there. Not hallucinations and such, but you start to misinterpret things. I don't know. Like, if I called her and she wasn't home I'd start wondering where she was and I'd start thinking that she was out with some other guy or something like that. By the time she calls me back I've got this whole scenario in my mind and I start off talking to her in a combative tone. And things just get shittier from there."

I stopped talking. I'd said enough and I was getting myself choked about something that nothing could be done about. I stuck my cigarette in my mouth and squinted my eye closed so the smoke wouldn't burn it. I rubbed my hands together under the blanket to get them warm again.

"You know, Janko, that your jealousy over Norma Jean is not that uncommon. I think the problem for you was that you had Norm feeding it and you couldn't manage it appropriately. I think most of us feel a little insecure in our relationships from time to time, but we just learn to manage it appropriately and see it for the irrational fear that it is. It would be extremely difficult for you to do that, I imagine, when trying to combat your own illness as manifested by Norm."

"You really think so?" I asked him.

"I do. Ask Veronica, I bet she can vouch for me too."

"Yup," she said, "it is true, Janko, and I can attest to having felt that way myself at times. We all do. We all want to be the center of someone's universe and anything that shakes that makes us feel insecure. But you can't make people love you. That's the kicker. You can only be loved for who you are, not for what you want. So a woman, in your case, wouldn't love you because you want her to or you try and make her. She can and will only love you for who you are, those qualities that she sees inside of you that resonate within her. And then you will be the center of her universe and she yours. But it's a natural thing, a subtle thing that just happens by allowing it to. By being yourself and being present in the relationship, but without attachment."

Michael went into the bakery and Veronica and I pulled up just outside. It wasn't too cold, but too cold not to have gloves. But the damn smoke from my cigarette was bugging me so I had to take my hand out to hold it. But I cupped it under my palm so the smoke would curl up and around my hand and give it a little warmth.

"I'm still learning about that now with the guy I'm currently dating," continued Veronica, "I really like him but sometimes I get scared that it won't last or he'll find someone else that he prefers and then he'll leave me. So if he doesn't call when he says he will or he is late picking me up or he says something in jest that makes me feel vulnerable, I start to misinterpret things. And it drives me crazy, because he hasn't done anything to make me think he will be unfaithful or that he isn't totally happy with me. I know it's irrational but you know, Janko, you just can't help yourself sometimes. So don't beat yourself up about it. It's difficult enough for most of us to learn to trust in a relationship without messing it up before we get to that comfortable place. And with your illness, it would only be that much harder. So don't get too down about it. I bet you did the best you could at the time with the skills you had."

I looked up at her with the cigarette still stuck in my mouth and a big frown on my face trying to shut out the smoke from my eyes.

"Thanks, Veronica. And you're right. There is just so much of my life that I wish had been different than it was. But I guess you can't cry over spilled milk, right?"

"No, and it doesn't help things, either. But what one should do is figure out how the milk was spilled in the first place so that you don't spill it again.

Or at least so you don't spill it again the same way. Learning from our mistakes so we don't repeat them is the most we can ask of ourselves. And if we can do that then we're doing pretty good I think."

I threw my cigarette butt on the ground and Veronica stepped on it. Squashing out its light.

"Yeah, I suppose. But what could I learn from it, I mean, it's not like I'm going to have another chance here in the next few weeks or whatever to start dating."

I looked down at my lap and pulled the blanket over me some more. I always liked the light of this time of year. It was rich and yellow but not strong. For some reason it reminded me of old people napping in chairs with shafts of light spilling over them. Probably because that was a fond memory of mine from when I was with the Antolinis, who were just about the only good foster parents I had. I must have spent this time of the year with them and he'd take a nap on Sunday afternoons in his armchair with the light from the sun all over him. It was a good memory.

"I think, Janko, that your lessons might be nothing more than learning to forgive yourself for how you reacted back then and realize that you did the best you could. And maybe as you are doing now, you can practice with us in becoming more present in your relationships and more amiable and not so quick to anger or sadness. Already you're doing great with that."

MJ and Peter were standing against the storefront of the bakery looking out into the horizon. They looked fairly relaxed. MJ had her eyes closed. Norm was off by himself a little way in the parking lot. He was kicking at something with his shoe, nothing that I could see, but he was intently interested in it nonetheless.

The bells on the door rang and the good doctor came out with a brown paper bag with a loaf of French bread sticking out of it. It was steaming in the cool air.

"That was great timing," said Michael, "they had just finished baking a batch of baguettes. Look how fresh this is. Give it a sniff, Janko, I bet it'll make you hungry."

He stuck it under my nose and it did smell doughy. Warm and yeasty, for a change it made me hungry and my mouth salivated. He stuck it under Veronica's nose, too, and she oohed and aahed.

"We should get back and have a couple of slices of this with butter and jam, maybe a pot of tea."

He looked at me as if he had asked a question.

"But don't you have to leave soon, Michael. I mean our sessions are only an hour long, aren't they?"

"Yes, true, but I've decide to clear my mornings now on Tuesdays and Thursdays to be with you. If you'd like me to stick around for a bit?"

That was a stupid question but I thought I'd humor him anyway.

"Yeah, I'd like you to stick around."

"Excellent, because I think, like I've said before, that our best approach is just to get to know one another and by doing that, help you to get to know yourself better so that you can forgive your past and find some enjoyment in the present and in our relationship and your relationship with Veronica and the others. That's my hope anyway."

With that we all started back towards home. Veronica gave me my own hot chocolate to drink as she finished hers, throwing the cup away.

"That would be my hope, too, dad," I said sipping on the sweet, warm beverage and just feeling good and warm and light inside. Something that I hadn't felt in quite a while. Michael shook my head, because I didn't have any hair and also because I was wearing my hoodie. But it felt good and he was teaching me things about what it was to appreciate the warmth of a human touch and not the pain. He was a good man, and if he was and because he was my dad, maybe I could be a good man too. I'm only saying maybe. I glanced around and saw MJ and Peter walking silently behind me. Norm was on MJ's right. The three musketeers walking together. My three friends, and they are my friends, even if they're not real. The only thing that makes friends real is our perceptions of them anyway, okay. So, they're real to me and they've helped me like real friends would've if I'd had any.

I smiled at them and winked at them and then turned around to rest my neck. It was too fatiguing on my muscles to turn around for long like that. MJ patted my head.

"You're a good guy," she said.

"Sure are," said Peter.

"Yeah, I guess you're all right," said Norm trying his best to be funny.

We got back to the apartment with some difficulty. I felt like I was going to pass out. I was tired, weak, panting like a dog, and I had a splitting headache.

I had to ask Veronica to up my medicine to take the edge off the pain and discomfort. My lungs were on fire, too. She basically had to carry me to the couch. She and Michael. He left the wheelchair down on the second floor when he saw how much we were struggling. Me mostly, and making V struggle with my weight and bodily apathy. I lay down on the couch and closed my eyes as V fumbled with my IV and attached it to its stand. The morphine came seeping into my body like a warm spilled wave. It felt great. The headache started to clear up like fog burning up in the sun. I was still panting like a dog, though. I couldn't find enough air in the room to breathe. I heard the good doctor come back into the apartment and close the door.

"Okay. How are you doing, son? Shall I get us all some fresh French bread?"

I nodded.

"Yes, please," said Veronica. "Let me come and help you with that."

"How many pieces do you want, Janko?" she asked.

I held up two fingers in a peace sign. Two peace is what I thought and smiled to myself.

"Two peaces," I said to them. "Do you get it? Two peaces."

I had to laugh, I thought it was pretty funny.

"Very good, son. Nice to see you keeping your humor. To peace and love it is, then."

He wasn't half bad himself.

"You guys are terrible. You should be on the comedy tour. How about some tea Janko?" asked Veronica.

"Sounds good."

I heard them off in the kitchen, clinking and clanking things and the sawing of bread and crust. I loved that crunchy, crackly sound that fresh crusty bread made. MJ and Peter and Norm went off to my bedroom. I figured I'd have to join them soon. I was so tired and fatigued. My body felt like lead and each breath was like sucking through a straw. I didn't like the feeling. I was feeling worse and worse as time went on.

Although, mentally and emotionally I was feeling better and better. The funny thing is, as I started to feel better and better in my head, my heart started feeling sadder and sadder in a way.

In a way because I didn't want to die now. Now that I tasted the sweet fruits of life I wanted to live longer to enjoy them more. To make up for all that lost time. But I couldn't, I knew I was dying, and quickly at that. But I felt like I was between a rock and a hard place. I'm not sure if you can appreciate that. When I was angry, sad, and depressed, I couldn't wait to die. Now that I was beginning to feel the start of happiness and peace, I wanted nothing more than to live and to be given a second chance. But I guess that just isn't in the cards for me. Maybe some people are given a second chance. But not this mutt. I'm a pound dog on death row. Ain't no respite for me. And as I start to feel sorry for myself, like now, I start to feel better about dying. It's a shitty vicious circle, isn't it? Feel shitty about yourself and you can feel good about dying. Feel good about yourself and you can feel shitty about dying. I guess like the good doctor says, I'm going to have to make a choice, eventually. Choose to be happy or choose to be sad. And I'll be honest with you, I've been both happy and sad and I'd rather be happy. I just don't want to die is all. Can you understand that? I mean, it's been hard having to live a shitty life, I'm sure you can get that. And just this sweet syrup of life at the bottom of my bitter bowl, is just a tease and nothing more. I don't know if it's cruel or if it's kind. But I sure do love the taste and I wish there was more.

Dad and V came back with a tray of tea and French bread glistening with gobs of jam. It sure did look good. I had been able to calm my breathing down a bit by now and I could smell the fresh floral bouquet of the tea and the sweetness of the jam. It was raspberry, I figured. A dark purple like a fresh bruise. I hoisted myself up to sitting as best as I could. Veronica poured me some tea and some for the good doctor, too. He took it black and I splashed cream and sugar in mine. I didn't have to add any more, I got it right for the second time in a row. I was on fire. Funny how the small things can make you feel so good.

"Two times a charm, hey, Janko?" asked Michael.

"Yeah, I guess so. Hopefully I'll make it a hat trick. I'd like that. It's the small things that make sense of life sometimes."

"Absolutely. It has to be, because there aren't enough big things to keep us happy all the time. It's the small things that keep us going from day to day and smooth out the bumps along life's hilly road. Like this bread, for example. A small thing, but so damn tasty it makes the day all that more worthwhile."

We ate together in silence. Something about eating with other people was so much more appealing than eating alone. Crumbs were being dropped all over the place. Mostly on the plates but quite a bit on the floor, too. I didn't care much because I didn't have to worry about cleaning it. They had a lady who came in once a week or so to do some of the cleaning. The nurses were too busy for that.

The bread tasted pretty good but I couldn't stomach much. I couldn't even eat the one piece so I put it down.

"Not too hungry, Janko?" asked Veronica.

"No, not really. But it's not that, I just can't stomach much food nowadays. It's tasty, but I feel sick. Actually, I don't feel well at all. I'm going to have to go and lie down soon, I think. I'm so damn tired lately."

"That's okay, son. Do you want some help right away?"

"No, thanks. I'll just hang out here a bit. I just need to rest and relax a bit. I think I'll just lie down here on the couch for a bit

I was lying down by now. It felt much better, but I was so tired and weary. My body felt like a thick lump of wet concrete. I closed my eyes, but sleep wouldn't come and snuff me out. The backs of my eyelids were still scratchy and sandy, but it felt much better to be resting them across my eyes than keeping them open. Sleep was such a sweet respite that I just couldn't get enough of. Sure, I could rest for hours on end but it's not the same. There is nothing like the thick, warm blanket of sleep to bring peace and an inkling of health to the weary body. Not that I'm getting my health back.

"I just want to tell you again, son, that you're dealing remarkably well with everything that is on your plate. I'm proud of you and I'll be speaking to my patients about your amazing strength of character in the years to come. I think you are going to become an example for many people on how to overcome life's obstacles that invariably are thrown in the way of all of us. I know that you are encouraging me to become a better psychiatrist, but more than that, you're encouraging me, by your example, to become a better man and a better human being."

I looked over at the good doctor and smiled at him as he stuffed the last big piece of bread into his mouth. But then my lids got heavy and I had to close them again. Not that I could sleep but it felt a lot better. Sometimes, and I don't know if this has ever happened to you, but my lids feel like they're made of lead plates and they're just too damn heavy for my little muscles to keep them up.

"Thanks doc, at least I'm encouraging someone to be a better person. But I'm the one here who needs encouragement to be better. Shit, I'm running out of time. My body is weary, dad, but more than that, my soul is ready, I think. But I'm scared to leave, if you know what I mean. For the first time in my life, I'm scared to die. And that's weird because I've never felt like this before. Even just a couple of weeks ago I was more interested in dying and having that sweet respite from my life, which has been a blob of pain, than in living. But now, it's like I'm trying to cling to life and my body is trying to die. It's scary, it's unfair, and it makes me angry, too."

"But you are encouraging yourself, Janko," said Veronica. "You are, by your very act of courage and being present in this healing process, encouraging yourself to wellness."

There were splotches of yellow with blue halos against the orange of my lids. It was like a kaleidoscope I saw once as a kid. Funny how you could still see when you were trying to sleep and your eyes were closed shut. Looking at the back of my lids and contemplating the mysteries of the universe, and still trying to focus on the conversation at hand.

"I guess I am in a way. But I keep getting scared that I'm going to run out of time. That I'll die before I come to that peace I'm searching for. I don't know, I mean yeah, from a certain perspective I look like I've done well and I feel a lot more steady about things and more trusting with you guys. But I'll be honest, I'm just scratching the surface here. I want to be able to close my eyes at the end of this life and think, yeah, it's okay to move on now and die. It's so fucking bizarre to me that the more I'm coming to terms with the shit that my life has been, the more desperate I am to live longer and enjoy the good times, the love and the small bits of peace I'm enjoying."

My lids were still heavy lead plates with orange insides, and the more I moved my eyeballs underneath them the more my eyes got scratched. Maybe that's what it was, lead plates sitting on my eyes with orange sandpaper insides. I wasn't feeling a lot of peace at the moment. I really wanted to try for the respite of peace, which of course wouldn't come for me.

"But, Janko, my son," said Michael, "that is a great start. The fact that you want to live longer now means that you are starting to enjoy life more than you ever have. Or at least a lot more than I remember you enjoying it.

I remember not even a few weeks ago and you were telling me how keen you were to die but that you couldn't muster the strength to kill yourself. And yet, here you sit now, afraid to die and looking forward to the little bit of life you have left and the work that we can still do. I can't promise you that when the time comes you'll die with that peace and acceptance that you talk about. I think only the great saints have been able to accomplish that. But if you can die with some peace in your heart, and more importantly, peace that you've made with yourself and the demons of your past, then I think you would have done very well. I would have considered my job a huge success. We all want to die when we're ready, but I don't know how many of us actually get to do that. Maybe some people die when they think they're ready, maybe they're just kidding themselves. Maybe they're just so full of anger and hatred for themselves that they don't want to live anymore. Well, son, that ain't being ready to die, that's giving up and doing the cowardly thing. I think we should all rage into that dying light as a great poet once said. They should have to take us kicking and screaming into Valhalla. This life is a gift, Janko, and it should be treasured and guarded safely. We should live to our fullest, sucking the very marrow out of life. That is the purpose. Maybe the mystics and the saints can go to the other side peacefully, but that's for them. They live on a different plane I'm sure. We who fight with our demons and live life in the trenches need to take all the good and peaceful and loving moments in our lives and multiply them right up until the end. As you've encountered, there is plenty in this life to fill our cups with bitter dregs, but there is also the sweet nectar of human kindness, of love, hope, and courage. If we can find it within ourselves to empty our cups of the bitter dregs we can fill them up with that sweet nectar. Isn't that what you are only now exploring and experiencing? Why shouldn't you want to carry that cup longer, sipping from its lip the sweetness that life has to offer? I say carry on, my son, carry that cup as long as you can. Don't worry that you are scared now to die. I'd say that is only to be expected. Let us focus on enjoying this new journey of compassion, forgiveness, love, and hope. When the time comes, I am sure there will be a certain comfort and peace in your heart, but that's not to say that you won't want to hang on a bit longer. That's courage my son, to carry on to the other side while you still carry the hope of a longer life in your breast."

My dad spoke well. That I knew for a fact. Because every time I felt down and depressed or even just scared or angry, his words would always buoy my spirits and encourage me to do better. I was glad he was my father. I just wish I could have known him when I was much younger and in need of good direction in my life. See, that's my problem, I get bogged down with all this shit of wishes and unfairness and poor me. And that's fucking hard to break out of when your life has been shit and it should've been better and you did have a bum rap compared to others. Can you understand that?

"That sounds good, dad, but I've gotta be honest with you. I just get so down on myself sometimes about the shitty life I've had and how hard it has been. And God damn it, it's been hard. It has been unfair and shitty and now I'm going to die with just having had a taste of the possibilities that my life could've been. And that is so unfair. I should've had it better, I deserved it."

I stopped, mostly because I was too damn tired to carry on with my tirade. Each breath was a sigh, a heavy sigh with the weight of a stone on my chest. A big stone, like the size you'd look for to sit on if you were out on a hike and needed a rest.

"Everything you say is true, son. You are deserving, and God knows I would've wanted you to have had an easier life if I could've done anything about it. And you're right, it is unfair and it is horrible how your cards have been dealt compared to others. But all of that isn't going to change a thing that has happened.

And I'd bet that it will make the present that much harder to live in. We're all susceptible to it to some degree. But dwelling on the past, a terrible past, and harping on how badly life has treated us is just going to keep us down. There is nothing uplifting that can come from that. Nothing that can be gained and improved upon.

You and I are blood, son, and yet look at how different our lives have been. Yet even my life can seem awful if I compare myself to others. For example, I have this friend who has lived a great life. He's had everything given to him on a silver platter. He's a doctor like me, but he makes oodles of money. He always has a beautiful woman on his arm; he has all the newest and nicest toys. He's like a poster boy for the good life.

Except the thing is, I don't think he's happy, and I'd never change my life for his. So what I'm trying to say, son, is that not only is living in the past and feeling sorry for oneself a hindrance, comparing yourself to others is never legitimate because you never know what their life has really been like. I know it's probably hard to hear this right now, because life is sometimes unfair and callous. But life is also beautiful and wonderful and awe inspiring. Life gives us the tools to overcome all the obstacles that might befall us. We are never challenged more than what we can overcome, and you have overcome mountains of difficulties, son. Just don't let yourself spiral into the despair of victimization, because all that does is keep you helpless and unable to work towards something better. It is more courageous, Janko, to take your past and let it ignite your determination to doggedly pursue a better present and future for yourself that you can, perhaps only now, imagine. But what can be imagined and envisioned will become your reality, your life, if you commit to it with unwavering determination and focus. Yes, my son, your life has been horrendous, but it no longer has to be like that. It can be better, happier, and more successful if you only take the reins and start building a life out of what you can imagine. Your life can be anything you hope for and are willing to work towards with determination, enthusiasm and focus. Never give up, never give in and never let go, son, and your life will be the dreams that you now cherish. Just like you, Janko, life is beautiful, courageous, hopeful and abundant in possibilities."

I opened my eyes. My spirit was a little more invigorated by the good doctor's, my dad's, words. He had a way of motivating me. He should've been a motivational speaker. He probably could have made more money at it, too. Veronica was looking over at him and nodding her head, fidgeting with folded fingers in her lap. Her eyes were wet, kind of oily.

"That was beautiful, Dr. Malichem. Absolutely beautiful and so true. My God, never before in my life have I felt so optimistic and astounded by the possibilities that I see between us. You, Janko, as Dr. Malichem has said, are in a great position to continue enjoying the grand inroads that you've made already. I feel the same way that you do. I don't want to die, either. I see life as the beautiful, hopeful and wonderful journey that Dr. Malichem talks about.

Arguably, I have longer to live, but you never know. I could be hit by a bus as I leave today. And yet I don't have the same sense of urgency to enjoy and explore this sweet nectar of life that was spoken about.

Harness that, Janko, harness that urgency and use it to propel yourself forward into positive and uplifting directions. Use it to burn up the hatred and anger and self-pity. I already see you doing such a fantastic job of that, just keep up the courage and keep fighting back those demons with this fuel of urgency that you have. Maybe as you say, we do only have weeks or less left. But from where I sit, and compared to just a couple of weeks ago, you are like a new man. You have become the phoenix and have, as far as I'm concerned, reborn yourself from ashes. Keep soaring higher and farther towards the light. The brightness will direct you and its warmth will protect you from the chill of the darker and colder emotions."

My eyelids had closed again. Huge leaden plates. I kept the eyeballs steady, that way they didn't hurt so much. Opening them again, Veronica's eyes looked a little dryer, too.

"Thanks for those kind words. You guys are full of love and optimism and hope for me. And I mean that sincerely. It does make me feel so much better."

I was talking to the back of my eyelids. Talking to orange, the color of nicotine and not of oranges. That made me want to have a cigarette.

"I'm just so tired right now that I've got to try and get to bed. Seems I can't focus on much now except trying to steal some sleep. Not that I'm sad or angry or happy for that matter. Just tired, and that's all I can seem to focus on."

"Yes, you do look kind of tired," said Veronica. "Would you like me to help you to your bed?"

I nodded as I heaved up into a seated position.

"I'll help him with that, Veronica," said Michael. "You relax for a bit, okay?"

Veronica nodded her head and got up anyway to make sure my bedroom door was open. It was, my friends had gone in there already. The stone had dropped off my chest as I sat up right, but someone had turned my ribs into concrete. I couldn't open up my chest to breath. I was sucking air in through a straw again.

"Okay, son, I can see you're struggling. Let's try and make it quick so that we don't make it any worse."

With that he pretty much picked me up and carried me into the bedroom. Now Veronica had to come in wheeling the IV stand in behind us.

I felt like a baby in my father's arms. He was pretty strong for a slim guy I thought. Though I don't weight much more than a pre-teen probably. Dad laid me down on the bed. I felt myself melt into the bed like heavy mercury. My ribs were bone again but some fucker had placed the stone back on my chest. And the straw was still in my mouth. Now there seemed to be a shallow little pool of liquid phlegm at the bottom of my lungs. I felt myself purring but I wasn't a happy kitty.

"I need more," I said to Veronica flapping my hand at the IV. She fiddled with it and I felt the warmth swim through my body. It made me more comfortable, too.

"Is that better?" she asked.

"A whole lot."

"Could you give us a minute," said Michael looking at Veronica.

She left us, and my dad sat on the edge of my bed. He held my right hand in both of his. I could feel the warm softness of his palms around my hands like putty.

"Does it feel pretty bad, son?"

I nodded. I'm pretty sure there was some little leprechaun sitting on the stone, no, jumping on the stone that seemed to be on my chest. I opened my eyes and smiled at my father. There wasn't much pain, but I was scared. Scared because I thought I was suffocating.

"We might not have much time left, son. But even if we don't, you've made me more proud in these weeks I've known you than I think I ever could have been if I'd known you all your life. You have shown so much courage and hope and optimism in spite of desperate circumstances. You have shown me how to overcome obstacles with dignity and strength that will carry me for the rest of my life."

His eyes got all fogged up and then the tears spilled out and down his cheeks. He didn't bother dabbing them with his sleeves. He wasn't embarrassed. I shook my head at him and smiled.

"No, dad, now's not the time. It isn't time, yet. I know. We'll have time, soon probably, but not yet. I'm still here for a while longer."

Norm and MJ and Peter were all crowding the bed looking at Michael. They were quiet. No one was talking. It was like I was in that church a long time ago when my mother left me. Church quiet I'd used to call it. And I never liked things that quiet, church quiet, it scared me. Until now. But I wasn't alone, now. I had my family with me. All four of them and for the first time in my life one of them was real.

"The breathing's hard, dad. And it's scary, but it doesn't feel like time, yet."

He smiled at me and then dabbed the tracks of his tears.

"I'd like to bring my wife next time, if you wouldn't mind. She's a wonderful woman. Margaret is her name and we've been married over twenty-five years. You'll like her, I'm sure."

"Yeah. That'd be nice. I'd like that."

And that's all I remember because then I was asleep.

I returned to the living room and Veronica got up to greet me.

"Shall we have some tea, doctor?" she asked.

"Yeah, I think that would be really nice."

We both walked into the kitchen to get some tea ready. We chose some jasmine green tea. Probably because we both felt mortal having seen Janko take a turn for the worse. And we were older than him. Me by a fair bit for sure. Veronica poured the hot water into the mugs and watched the liquid turn a light yellow before hinting at green. We went back into the living room to sit down. There was a lot of silence between us. We were both looking outside at the clear sky. My cheeks felt warm now as I remembered the cool air from outside. I rubbed my right cheek and my hand was hot on it after having cradled the tea.

"He didn't look so good did he, doctor?" asked Veronica.

She had barely whispered those words to me, but they clanged about the room like giant cymbals.

"No, he didn't. And please, Veronica, call me Michael."

"But we're making good progress, Michael. I think we're making good progress."

Veronica was looking into her mug. Maybe trying to read the tea leaves. Maybe giving me a tea leaf reading of the future. Her hands were cupped around the mug and the steam hovered above like a cloud. I sipped my tea and it was hot.

"Yes, I think we are making good progress."

There was silence again. I didn't know what to say and what Veronica wanted to say she couldn't quite manage. The tea was endlessly fascinating to both of us.

"Would you like any snacks, Michael?"

I shook my head and told her I had to be leaving soon. I don't think she liked the silence and I can't blame her. It was an awkward silence. Not peaceful and meditative.

"You know, I'm just getting quite attached to him. To Janko, and now the reality of his mortality is beginning to hit me, I guess. It seems so unfair for such a young man to have been burdened with this. And now as he starts to come to terms with his difficulties he will be dying. It's hard for me to keep upbeat and positive about it for him. It's very unfair. He should at least be given a few years to enjoy his new found peace and dare I say happiness."

"I know, Veronica, and here I am trying to help him come to terms with his own history and horrendous problems and at the same time I've just now come to learn that he is kin to me. I'd like to be able to get to know him as my son. But that won't happen. The best I can do is to help him become the man that he is underneath all the ugliness of his past. And you're right, it doesn't seem fair that he should have to struggle for so long with his hardships only to realize the freedom and sweetness of peace and happiness, and then have it torn away from him in short order. It doesn't seem right and by our standards it isn't right. But maybe he wouldn't be so motivated to change if he had a few years left to live. Unfortunately, Veronica, sometimes urgency is the taskmaster it takes to create change. And not to sound callous, but he has been HIV positive for some years now so he could have sought our help or someone's help sooner."

She nodded at me and sipped her tea. I looked at my watch. I don't know why, my day was free. I had taken it to spend with Janko as I would all my Tuesdays and Thursdays from now on. I was looking to leave. My heart was heavy and weary. I drank some more of my tea. It was still hot but getting cooler. I'd probably be here for a little while longer if the heat of the tea was any indication.

"How long do you think he has?"

She asked the question to her mug, maybe fearing the answer.

"I don't know, Veronica. But if I had to hazard a guess I'd say we have less than three weeks, maybe a month at the most. But then I haven't been around dying people for a long time. Sometimes death can come much quicker. I remember my grandmother taking a turn for the worse after breaking her hip, and after surgery she was dead within a month I think.

I think it also depends on the stubbornness of the person. I guess I get the feeling from Janko that as much as he wants to live on, I think his spirit is ready. Not weak but ready for its next journey."

"Yeah, I was thinking not more than two to four weeks. Do you think that is enough time for us, for him?"

"Yes, it's enough time for him. I think his soul is ready to move on even now. I think he has found that peace, or as much peace as is needed, to wipe the tainted past from his spirit. It has been quite easy, really. All he needed was a sense of family and understanding and empathy more than anything I think. That's all we really need, I think, at the end of the day in order to heal. A sense of place and belonging. Being understood and sympathized with. The rest we take care of for ourselves. But I don't think, the way Janko has affected us all, that there would ever be enough time for us to prepare. He will leave an indelible mark on my heart for sure."

"Yes, that's true for me too, Michael. He has affected me more so than any of the other patients I've had before. Maybe it's the personal setting, taking care of him in his own home. Or maybe it's because I've spent so much time nursing him generally. Or maybe it is just as you say, his strength of spirit and character that has affected me. Who knows, but I do know that he will be with me in my heart for a long time to come."

She sipped her tea and blew away the steam.

"I think I'll get some cookies," she said and she got up to do that.

I found myself grieving for Janko already, even though I didn't have a clue about how long he'd still be with us. But I was weary, and it was the weariness of a heavy heart. I knew that from before. From when my grandmother died and my parents too. It wasn't so much a premonition as an understanding that soon there will be that void in your heart which nothing can fill except for the slow trickle of the sands of time. There was nothing to do but ride it out. It felt like a long journey through a desert without much water. The weariness stretching on like the unending terrain. But somehow I had to manage it appropriately for Janko's sake. I had to be strong for him. The last thing he needed to deal with now was my weariness. That wouldn't help him, and it wouldn't really help me either. I'd have to roll this weariness up into a tight and heavy little ball and pack it away somewhere out of sight. Margaret could help me with that. I'm sure she could.

Veronica came back with some chocolate digestive cookies. I liked them. They were some of my favorites.

"I guess I'm going to have to stick around now and help you finish these cookies with my tea." I smiled at her.

"I was hoping I might tempt you with them. You had said that you had cleared your morning to be with Janko, if need be."

"Yes, though today he doesn't need me. But you're right, I don't have anything else to really rush off to. These are great cookies, some of my favorites."

I took a cookie and dunked it quickly into my tea. I didn't want the chocolate to melt but I wanted the cookie itself to get a little soggy. I loved that. Reminded me of my youth and of simpler times and quiet, peaceful times. I looked up and saw Veronica smiling at me. She had dunked her cookie too.

"Isn't that the best?" she asked.

"It sure is. I see you like doing it, too. I've been dunking cookies into my tea since I was probably at least eight years old. My favorite to dunk is a simple oatmeal cookie."

"Yes, oatmeal is good, but a ginger snap is even better."

We enjoyed our cookies and tea in silence. It was a peaceful, quiet time and I felt better already. The weariness was not so heavy and the company was pleasant. There was nothing like warm tea and soggy cookies on a cool spring day.

"What do you think about Janko's imaginary friends? Is that a concern for you?"

I looked at her and then I looked off towards Janko's room. The door was closed, and for just a brief moment I wondered if Norm or Peter or MJ could hear us talking. But of course that's ridiculous.

"I was at first, but not anymore. At this stage of things, Veronica, no good can come from trying to rid him of his hallucinations. Besides, he'd require pharmaceutical intervention for that, too, and you know as well as I that he isn't interested in that and we can't force him to take anti-psychotics; I don't want to either. They seem pretty harmless. All three of these characters. They seem to have served a purpose in his life and probably continue to do so as some sort of Linus blanket or something. They're also part of his makeup, of who he is as a personality.

So, if they help him to move forward and to heal from the pain of his past then I think there is no harm in that. In actual fact it might even be beneficial and helpful. With these types of hallucinations or psychotic episodes, there is often mistrust of authority, like you and me.

313

I think that with us showing acceptance of them, or his psychosis if you will, then these hallucination or friends of his will likely come to see us as benign if not helpful to him. With such little time left, Veronica, I think we need to encourage anything that might help us. What are your thoughts on that?"

She took a sip of tea and a bite of crumbly cookie. She looked outside at the sky before returning her gaze to me.

"Well, as you know, I've known about Janko's hallucinations since I started caring for him. His schizophrenia is well documented in his file and he's admitted that he has these imaginary friends to previous doctors. But I'll be honest with you; I was somewhat sceptical about him not being medicated for it, because as you know, these psychoses can end up getting worse. But having cared for him all these months I've come to view them the same way you have. If he was to live for some years to come, then I think we'd have to address it. But as it is, and with the limited amount of time we have left I agree that we need all the help we can get. And if that means bringing his hallucinations on board then so be it. And I think I speak for all of us when I say that."

"Yes, I agree. I think it will work in our favor, and we don't need to create stumbling blocks for ourselves that don't really exist."

I drank most of the rest of my tea except for the quarter inch at the bottom. Soggy cookie was one thing, but chunky tea just wasn't nice. All those cookie crumbs soppy at the bottom of the mug like curdled milk. I couldn't stomach it. I guess not everything with cookies and tea was peaceful and comforting.

"I'm going to get going, Veronica. My heart is a little heavy and I need to think of our next approach and how best to make the rest of our time with Janko. I think fresh air and quiet will be the order for the rest of the day."

I got up to leave, taking my plate and mug to the kitchen first. As I lay the mug down I noticed the cartoon on it. It was of a guy climbing out of a manhole cover in the middle of a road thick with traffic. The caption read 'some days you're always getting run down.' I thought it was very apropos for the way I felt. I smiled at it in acknowledgement. Seeing myself in the emerging manhole man. Veronica led me to the door.

"Thanks for staying a little longer to enjoy some tea with me. And thanks for your kind words earlier."

"You're welcome. And I will also be available to all of you when the time comes and Janko leaves us. I'm sure it will be tough for us all."

She nodded and I patted her on the upper arm. We said our goodbyes and I wearily trudged down the hallway as the door closed behind me and latched locked. The memories of us struggling down this hallway not hours before with a weakened Janko brought a tear to my eye. I let it roll down my cheek freely. I kept wondering how much longer I would have to embrace this patient who was now also so much more. He was my son. The son I had always wanted, but also the son that I had never been there for. Soon, all I'd have left of him would be ghostly memories rattling in my pockets like the loose change I was fiddling with now. I stepped outside and the wind kissed me coolly. The sun was bright but he wasn't warm. It was a cold, dead day and the lump in my throat burned hotly.

XXVI

Days drifted by wearily. I watched them go by the dimming dusk and the yawning dawn. Life seemed now to be a thick fog and only now and then would patches clear and I'd be able to think clearly. I felt like I was drifting in a swampy sea. The nurses would come by like ghosts or wisps of clouds carried on the water. The only companions that I kept seeing when I awoke from my deep haze were my companions of old. MJ and Peter and Norm were always there when the fog would lift. They'd shift and move positions each time I'd wake, but they'd always be there. I was dying.

Yeah, I know I've told you that before, but I was really dying this time. I mean, I could tell the time was imminent. It was soon and I'd be kissing this pillow goodnight one last time. And I wasn't getting scared anymore, like I used to be. I was tired and resigned. I mean, I didn't want to die, but I wasn't any use to anyone the way I was now. I was getting ready. The time spent with the good doctor, my father, had become more and more helpful. I don't really know what he had done, but somehow I was experiencing more peace. I was moving away from my past and that was interesting.

It was helpful and it was soothing in a deep way that I had never experienced. Maybe it was just the way I was able to trust him and talk to him without feeling judged or belittled. Or maybe it was the fact that I had come to know him as my father in a small way. Maybe it was all of these things, and the hope that he inspired in me to be more than I had ever thought I was capable of. Whatever it was, and probably it was all of these things, he had helped me come to an acceptance of my life and a peace with my past in these short months we had known one another.

Yeah, I was dying, weren't we all. But at least I can say as I exit this door, I was really living now, really living like I hadn't before, and I hope that you can say the same when your time is up and they come looking for you and cash your cheque. I've lived a short life and I've lived a shit life, but these days as I lie dying have almost made it worthwhile. I hope that this journey I've been on might in some small way give you the clarity to leave with the same peace, if not more. And if it doesn't, well hell, you've stayed with me this long that's gotta count for something in the end. I'll put in a good word.

I rolled onto my back. My body ached from lying in bed too much. I had been able to get up out of bed a couple of times a day, but I was starting to get bedsores. I opened my eyes and it was day. I turned my head to the clock radio and it was three-thirteen. Red of course, probably like the whites of my eyes. I got myself up to sitting, hunched over myself like a large 'C'. I noticed a red, blotchy sore spot on my right elbow. My breathing was heavy and labored and I concentrated on the sheets which were all crumpled up over my groin, giving me a package like nothing I'd ever dreamed of. If only I was healthy enough to do something with it, if I had it, of course. I smiled at that, at the lump, the hump between my legs. That was the one thing I missed the most I guess, ever since I had been sick. The ability to masturbate. I hadn't had a girlfriend in forever, but at least I used to be able to take care of my own stirrings. A small pleasure in some ways, but not all, but a pleasure nonetheless. One of very few pleasures I'd had and I could have used a lot more. But then again, you knew that.

I struggled with the blankets to throw them off my legs, the rubbery serpent of the IV slapping against my forearm. I looked up and noticed that they'd attached another bag to my IV stand and I hadn't authorized that. It pissed me off and I aimed to talk to someone about it. It had better not be any of those anti-psychotics. But I was too weak at the moment, having fought with the sheets, to yell out to whoever was there. I swung my legs over the edge of the bed and waited awhile for the fatigue and the nausea to wane.

"How you feeling?" asked MJ.

I looked at her for a moment and nodded and mouthed 'okay' to her. I focused on the bathroom, stood up, and took a moment to steady myself before I weaved and bobbed my way there. I sat heavily on the toilet and started squirting out bits of piss in short, sad dribbles. I'd been doing this for days it seemed, living my life from bed to bathroom and back again. Denying myself food and waving off the nurse, when I was lucid, with the flapping of my hand like a wounded bird. They must have snuck the IV bag on when I was drifting in and out of my fog. I squeezed my stomach muscles and they felt like pudding. A little more piss dribbled out and yet my bladder was fucking bursting. This took some time. If I was healthier I would have grabbed at a magazine, healthier and richer. I couldn't afford magazines or books, not for a while now. I squeezed my penis and it felt as rubbery as the IV tube only not half as leaky. I reached over to the tap and turned it on and tried to concentrate on listening to the water spilling out and gurgling down the drain. That helped, and my piss burned out of me like a trail of yellow acid. Just so you know, I've given up washing my hands now. I don't have the strength anymore and besides, the nurses keep coming round and given me sponge baths. It's amazing how they can clean someone who lies around in a bed all day. I suppose it's the miracle of modern medicine.

MJ saw me winding my way towards the bed and asked me if I needed a hand.

"Jesus, MJ, be real, how the hell are you going to help me. It's impossible."

I didn't say it quite so easily but you get the idea. It was more in little pants of breath.

"No need to get so crabby," she said.

"I'm not getting crabby, but you people know that you aren't real. We established that a long time ago with the good doctor, okay. We don't have to pretend anymore, okay?"

"Oh, okay, so what? You're gonna kick us to the curb now. Now that you're finished with us, is that it?"

Now it was Norm's turn. The ever-present asshole. And really, he was getting a lot better.

"Don't be silly Normal. I wouldn't do that. Although, if you keep ranting I might try my best when the good doctor comes in."

I liked teasing him about his name. I had found a new boldness now, since I had started to find my peace and acceptance. He sulked off to look out the window, again. Peter was sitting on the chair with the blanket over his lap. He was grinning at me.

"What?" I asked him.

"Nah, it's nothing, I'm just enjoying you more now that you've found your cojones. Brass cojones, too. I never thought I'd see the day, but I'm happy and I'm proud of you, my friend. Although it makes me a little sad too, because I figure you'll be leaving us soon, won't you?"

I stood there for a while, swaying like a flag in a breeze, attached to my IV stand. I was just too tired to let myself flop into bed and too sore. My body ached from lying around in bed all the time. The pains of slothfulness. I bet if I counted really hard I could be living the seven deadly sins right here in this room. Yeah, I was definitely slothful. Let's go through the rest of them. Maybe I'm kidding myself.

Yeah, maybe I'm suffering from pride, that's one of the ugly seven isn't it. But I don't really have the arrogance for pride so we'll strike that one off the list. Okay, how about lust. Yes, I've lusted as recently as a few weeks ago, hell, even just earlier I was thinking of my groin and the sheets enhancing my package. Yes, I'll give myself lust. Wrath. I think, gentle reader, that you'll give me wrath, too. I'm getting better, I mean I don't fucking curse as much as I used to do, but I still feel the dragon bubbling up like hot lead, sometimes. Hey, how about envy, for sure I'm envious. I'm envious of everyone who gets to live.

Well okay, maybe I'm not quite envious right now, but I was up until a couple of days, maybe a couple of weeks, ago. So I'm on the down swing of envy but let me have half a sin on that one. Okay, coming into the home stretch now with the final two I'm losing steam. Gluttony. I definitely do not suffer the outrageous fortunes of gluttony. If only I could eat more than I do, maybe it would prolong my life. Mind you, I've never really suffered gluttony, but it's a nice idea in a way. Maybe if you're some huge fat bastard you'd think it was a burden. Well, take it from me, dying is a sure way to lose weight and I'm not just talking about the twenty-one grams of the soul.

I've heard cancer is a good one for losing weight, too. I'm sorry, okay, maybe my humor is fucked up, but you might try to squeeze just a drop of mirth out of your death, if you could. Especially if it's the only little bit of joy you might have.

Jesus, I am getting cynical, sorry about that, I am trying to get better, really I am. And you'd agree, I am, aren't I? Anyway, we're down the to the last one; greed. I don't think I can say I'm greedy. I have nothing to want except a little bit of a longer healthier life with the tastes of happiness and peace I've been experiencing, but I don't think I'd call that greed. Seems like greed is the incestuous kissing cousin to envy, from how I see it. And maybe lust, too.

So looking at it from where I stand, I think I've got three and a half. That's half marks isn't it? Maybe that's what the doctor is trying to do for me. Maybe he's like a religious teacher trying to rid me of the deadly sins. Funny thing is, though, I figure as soon as he does I'll be dead not long after. Killing myself to be rid of the deadly sins. I love the irony in that. But it could be true. I mean, I'm getting rid of envy and wrath and I'm feeling a helluva lot better. I'm gaining in ways that I couldn't have imagined as I start giving up sinning. I've got to mention that to the good doctor, to my father. I'm sure he'll like it. I've never been religious, but everybody knows about the seven sins.

"Janko, how come you aren't talking to me?" asked Peter.

I looked at him for a moment and realized I'd been ranting all to myself while wobbling like a spinning top.

"Sorry, Peter, I forgot what you asked me."

"I was asking you about how great it was to see you with your cojones, but that it makes me sad because I figure you'll be leaving soon. That you'll be dying soon, right?"

I was standing like a statue, a flimsy weaving statue, but I felt light; as if I wasn't really in my body, anymore. Like I was just air around myself and tucked into myself. Like I was a hollow man filled with cotton or clouds. That's how I felt and it felt great. I was looking outside at the sky, the blue sky. That was one of the things I liked about this place. The blueness of the sky. It was so often sunny during the days and the skies were blue.

Stretched like balloon skin from horizon to horizon. You could tell the weather was getting warmer by the way the light of the sun made things look. It made it look hotter, whiter. I don't know, it's hard to describe. Sure the weather is warmer and the air starts to feel warmer or should I say less cold.

But there is something about the light of the day that is clearer, cleaner, and sharper that teases you of spring and summer on their way. I don't know, maybe you think I'm crazy or something, or maybe, just maybe, you can understand what I'm trying to say. Anyway, hope was springing eternal in my heart, and my soul was feeling light and airy. I thought of myself then kind of like a fairy, like Tinkerbell.

"Janko, will you just listen to me, please," said Peter.

I turned to him and saw him sitting in the chair like a granny might. Like my granny might have if I'd ever known her.

"Sorry, Peter, I'm just not myself lately. You're right, I'm going to be dying soon. I can feel it."

Norm turned around then and he looked sad and frail. They all looked that way then. Even MJ. Beautiful MJ looked sad and beaten down and despondent.

"Nice, Janko. Nice. Just as we're getting comfortable with that doctor coming in here to ruin our fucking lives you are going to go and die on us. And you don't give a shit about what will happen to us, do you?"

He was trying to look tough and fierce but he wasn't doing such a good job. He looked thin and tired and weak. And I knew why. So do you. It was because we were all dying.

"I don't give a shit Norm about what'll happen to you, because I know what will happen to you. The same damn thing that is gonna happen to me. When I go, my friend, you go with me."

MJ laughed at that. She kind of snorted a laugh out like it just happened upon her quick and she couldn't stop it. Then Peter laughed and it infected me and I kind of chuckled the best I could, with my ribs on fire. And Norm couldn't help himself, either, he smirked, smiled, and then laughed a little in spite of himself.

"You fucking guys," he said.

And then I started looking through binoculars and the sun set pretty quickly and my lights went out. I woke up and I was lying face down on my bed with my hands right out to my sides. My right forearm was on fire as the needle was poking into my brittle vein with a vengeance. My feet were sort of dragging on the floor and my knees not quite touching the ground.

I hadn't meant to kneel to say my prayers, so soon. I opened my eyes and the world was still dark, because I was looking at my sheets and my nose was squashed into the bed like a piece of wet clay. I hauled myself back up with difficulty and then put myself into bed the proper way. Ass first.

"You should probably lie down and rest Jay. We'll be here for you when you wake up, again," said MJ.

I nodded at her. These fucking people, so helpful. Mind you, I was being unkind. They had been helpful plenty of times before, when I really needed them to be. I should be more patient and understanding with them. Patience and understanding, those things are virtues right? From sins to virtue. I was doing better, I was definitely doing better. I think the good doctor, my father, would be proud. It's kind of weird to call him my father though, even if he is. It still is kind of weird to call him that. Maybe because I've never had that kind of relationship with him, and the one that did develop first was as his patient.

MJ came up and stroked my brow. It felt good, if something that wasn't really real could feel good. It was harder now to see these people, these friends of mine as just manifestations of my illness. I mean, I knew that they've always been hallucinations, but they always seemed so real to me, before. Maybe it was some kind of side effect that I was dealing with from my time with the good doctor, that these imaginings were becoming less authentic. Or maybe I just didn't need them as much anymore, now that I was getting to rely and trust in my father and the nurses more. I felt sad about that in a way. It was like all of sudden they seemed lost and insignificant, and I found that sad. They had been such a big part of my life and such a pivotal part of my life before. Shit, I was getting sentimental over people that didn't even exist. But you'd understand. I mean, you do understand, right? These people have been as real to me as the good doctor is. They've been the only consistent people in my life; I'm sure you can understand that. And now they seemed hollow and unreal, like they had always been, but I'd never seen it before. And that was sad, okay. It made me sad to see this change come over me. I'd like to hope they'd be with me to the end, but maybe their usefulness is coming to an end. And that just doesn't seem like the right way to treat people who've been so important in your life, even if they aren't real.

"Don't give up on us, Janko. Not now, okay. Not when we need you like you've needed us before."

It was Norm again. He'd come to sit on the edge of my bed and he'd taken my hand in his. I looked at him and his eyes were sad and he looked scared. His eyes were wet in the corners and a little bloodshot.

"I'm not going to do that. I'm just a little sad because, like Peter says, I am going to die soon. I don't know how soon but probably sooner than I'd want."

MJ was still standing by the head of my bed but she had stopped caressing my brow. Her hands were on her hips and she was biting her lip. Peter was on the other side of Norm. He had the blanket with him still, which he had draped over his legs as he sat on the edge of the bed across form Norm.

"That's not what Norman meant, Jay. And you know it. You told us you wouldn't give up on us and now it sounds exactly like that is what you are going to do," said MJ.

They were right. Of course, they were. They knew what the hell was going on in my mind as well as I did. But I was trying to be gentle, you get it, don't you?

"I'm not going to lie to you guys, okay. Yes, I'm dying and that makes me sad, but I'm also sad because you guys aren't as important to me as you used to be, and yet I still hope that you will be with me until the end. I'm just not sure if you will be, that's all."

Peter shifted and patted me on the shoulder. I looked over at him.

"Bullshit, Janko. I say bullshit on that. We aren't about to leave you in your last hours. And the doctor also said he didn't have a problem with us hanging around as long as we didn't interfere with anything. And we've been really good with that, haven't we? Even Norm. And it's not only up to you, okay? We've stuck around lots of times before when you have tried to get rid of us. And we're stubborn, we are. Norm will vouch for that, won't you?"

Norm nodded and so did MJ. I felt like they were ganging up on me and it brought a smile to my face, because I didn't want to lose them. Not yet, anyway, not yet.

"I'm glad to hear it," I said, "because I don't want to lose you guys, yet. You're still important to me. You're still a huge part of my life and my history, and that's what all of this is really all about. The exploration of my past.

I'm clearing out that closet of all the bad stuff and making room for new stuff, but also for the good stuff that had been weighed down by all the bad stuff. And you guys, and you know this, are the good stuff from my past. At least as far as I'm concerned."

I looked up at the ceiling again and saw pustules of white paint. I hadn't smoked in several days and I missed it, but I couldn't afford it. My breathing was continually shallow and just getting up to go to the bathroom was like going a few rounds with a heavyweight. I looked over and just beside MJ was my packet of cigarettes. I reached for them, just brushing lightly against MJ's leg. I brought the packet to my chest and fumbled feebly with it to get a cigarette out. Now, just relax, I'm not going to be smoking it, I just want to hold it and caress it and smell it. I brought it to my nose and inhaled as deeply as I could, which was probably just a sniff. It wasn't lit but the sweet burnt smell of wood and cherry was intoxicating. Now you know better than to be killing yourself smoking, but you're dealing with an addict here and cigarettes have been like Norm and MJ and Peter to me. Cigarettes have been a friend. I know that sounds crazy, but it's true. My friends have been bad for me in some ways and unreal too, but in my fucked up world they've been really important. So indulge me a moment, okay? I inhaled a few more times and then stuck the cigarette in my mouth. That was good enough. The way I was feeling, I wasn't having to deal with any withdrawal issues from cigarettes. I was like death warmed over, anyway. Nicotine withdrawal ain't nothing compared to what I'm dealing with.

"Do you want me to light that cigarette for you?" asked MJ.

I shook my head. And she couldn't anyway, not really. I mean I could pretend she could but I was tired of pretending that way. I looked at each of them steadily for a moment.

"I'm glad and I'm grateful that you've been in my life. All of you, for your different gifts to me. And I'm glad I'm going to be able to keep you until the end. That's what I want and that's what I think we should all want. As they said in that movie I saw a long time ago. One for all and all for one. I'm glad to hear that you guys are going to go down with this ship. It's not going to be that bad for me, then. It'll help knowing that we've been through it all together and we've seen it all to the end. Thanks, you guys for your loyalty and stubbornness. Especially you, Norm. My rock, in so many ways."

Norm smiled at that and bent down and kissed me on the forehead.

"You're welcome," he said.

"Yes," said Peter.

"Me, too," said MJ.

"Who put the other IV bag in me?" I asked them.

"It was the nurse Maria, when you were sleeping," said Norm, "but I checked it and it is only an electrolyte solution. That's why we're still here. No anti-psychotics yet."

"And there won't ever be. I've told them and they'd better honor that," I said.

"Don't be too hard on her, Jan," said MJ, "she's just looking out for your best welfare, and you've hardly been eating or drinking for quite a while now. It's for your own good."

Yeah, I suppose. Nothing wrong with easing the pain of my departure. That would be all right with me. I just don't need these damn surprises at this time in my life though. I took the cigarette out of my mouth again to sniff its sweet aroma. I figured I might be able to eat a little something today. I had a craving for a banana. I think I could eat mashed banana all right. I looked over at my side table and hit the bell. It shrieked in my ears like I had scared it or something. It was one of those squat domed bells like you see at hotels. I waited for a bit and Maria came in.

"Hey, Janko. I was just about to come and check on you. Do you need something?"

She had come and stood where only moments ago MJ had been. MJ was now at the foot of the bed.

"How come you put this new bag in my IV?"

"Well, we have to take care of you, Janko. It's only electrolytes to keep you hydrated. No medications. But without it you could die pretty quickly and we have to make sure that we don't let that happen."

She was caressing my forehead, or at least that's what it seemed to me. She took my temperature too with her ear thermometer.

"You're doing really well."

"Are you sure that's all that is in the bag?"

"Absolutely, Janko. Until we have authorization from your doctor to change anything we can't and we won't. Also, your doctor is not to go against your wishes unless he feels that you are no longer mentally capable to make those decisions yourself.

For that he would need Dr. Malichem's opinion and you're a long way away from being deemed mentally unfit, as far as Dr. Malichem is concerned. So don't worry about anything. We're all here to help you and to protect you. We're not here to harm you or to go against your own wishes okay? And you know that, anyway."

I smiled at her and my eyes welled up with tears and they spilled out.

"Thanks, Maria."

She took a tissue from my side table and dabbed away my tears. Her touch was soft and gentle and only made me feel worse, so I cried some more.

"Hey, there, Janko, what's wrong?"

"I don't know. It's just that I feel like I don't have much time and your kindness is making me feel sad and bad for the way I've been all my life. But especially for how I've been rude to you, the rest, and the good doctor. Who, I don't know if you know, is actually my father. Did you know that?"

In a way, I was actually proud of that. My father was a real man. A man of character and someone who was very successful, from all accounts at the top of his game. And he cared for people. And I was proud that that's where I came from.

"Yes, I did know. It's in your file now and we always check that at the start of our shifts. It's our way to communicate with one another because we don't always have the chance to talk about everything as our shifts cross. I speak for all of us when I say that we are all so happy to have heard this good news. We all love your father. He is a very intelligent, likeable man and a very accomplished psychiatrist. You should be rightly proud to have had the chance to come to know him. Even if you only have a short time left in which to do that. I just think that it is such a neat coincidence that it turned out this way."

"I am proud. I just wish that I could have known him a lot longer. I just wish that I would have been able to have been raised by him. I know my life would have been so much better then."

She sat next to Norm on the edge of my bed and put her hand on my knee.

"I truly believe that your father never knew he had you. Dr. Malichem is just not the kind of man to shirk his responsibilities or to turn his back on his friends or family.

And you're right, Janko. Your life would have been different if you had been raised by him. But dwelling on that is a waste of your precious time, these precious last days or weeks that you have. Try and focus on what you can do with the time you have left to enjoy your relationships with us and Dr. Malichem. And in the same vein, don't beat yourself up with how badly you think you might have treated us before. You weren't that bad. We have thick skin, and we've always seen the goodness in you from the beginning. Remember that we all chose to care for you after having read your file. That's got to count for something."

She smiled at me and winked.

"Thanks, Maria. You guys are really great and I appreciate all the help you've given me. I just wish there was more time to show my appreciation for you and to enjoy your company."

I wasn't crying anymore. It was just a sudden wave that had come over me. Soft emotion. Maria wiped away the rest of my tears and held the tissue to my nose so I could blow it. I felt bad for her. That had to be one of the shittiest jobs. But I suppose that considering they hadn't had to start wiping my ass, it wasn't all that bad.

"Can I get you anything, Janko? Are you up for trying to eat something and drink something?"

"Yes. That's actually why I called you. It wasn't to cry all over you. I'd love some mashed banana; I just have a craving for that. And maybe a nice camomile tea would be great, too."

"Would you like it brought in here or do you want to come out to the living room? Only if you have enough energy. I'm just worried about bedsores, and I know that you've been in bed for quite some time the last several days."

"Yeah, I think I'll try and come out to the living room, if you'd help me. My body aches all over. I feel like my muscles have been squashed flat and I'm numb and achy. I think getting vertical will help a bit, even if it's only to stagger into the living room."

I held my arms out to her and she helped pull me up to sitting. Little beads of sweat pricked at my brow. I was wheezing and breathing hard, already.

"How do you know if you're gonna die?" I asked her.

She looked at me and patted my thighs. She squatted down in front of me so she could look into my eyes.

"I don't know if you can know, Janko. I've heard that some people get a sense of impending death, but others don't seem to have any idea at all. What do you think? I certainly don't have any idea of my own death, other than it is the only certainty in this world. For all I know I could get run over by a bus tomorrow, to use that cliché. And God forbid that happens. Knock on wood."

She knocked her knuckles on my bedside table. It wasn't wood. Some fake plastic shit, probably with a wooden veneer. I wondered if that counted. Maybe it'd be best if we knocked our fingers against our heads or something. I tapped my fingers against my bony knee. The way I figure it, we're carbon-based life forms, the same as trees. Maybe our bones our closer to trees than plastic. Just a quick thought, but I digress.

"I feel like I could die any minute. Just getting up to sitting like this is killing me. My lungs burn brightly and I feel like I'm sucking air through a wet cement facemask. But then again, I've known that I'm gonna die for some time now. Probably a few years. But how soon, I couldn't say. I wouldn't give myself more than a couple or three weeks."

Maria looked away then. Looked over at my bedside table and rearranged some stuff that didn't need rearranging.

"Do you want to try and stand up now and get moving into the living room?"

"Sure," I said.

I put out my arms again, and she took them, grabbing onto my forearms. Her small hands wrapped almost completely around my forearms. I was thin as you know, and I was dying to be thin, but it wasn't on purpose. Maria leaned back to leverage herself and started to pull me up. I got to standing and found my knees wobbly and weak. I started looking through those binoculars again so I took a few deep breaths as best as I could and the light started coming back into my field of vision. Cold sweat was still pricking at my forehead like little fire ants biting at me.

"Shall we rest for a bit? Just steady yourself, Janko."

I clutched at her shoulders and wobbled back and forth. I was staring down at my feet. Bony knobs of flesh that looked prehistoric.

"You know we're all going to die, Maria. Only, I'm going to do it first before the rest of you."

I was talking to the floor still draped over her like a defeated prize fighter.

"I know. But we don't have to talk about that right now."

"Okay, I think I'm ready to get going. Would you mind bringing my cigarettes?"

She took them from the table and we staggered out of the room. MJ, Peter, and Norm hot on my heels. My arm was around her shoulder and she had the IV stand. It was easier this way than when I had made the journey myself to the washroom not half an hour before. Maria eased me to the couch.

"I think I'd like take a moment to stand over by the balcony."

She helped me over there and waited a moment as I took over control of the IV and steadied myself. I knew I was swaying, but I felt stable.

"I'll be okay," I said.

"All right. I'll go get some tea and banana for you. Holler if you feel dizzy, okay?"

I nodded at her as she went to the kitchen. I was looking outside at the blue sky, just one swipe of blue paint. One tone. No different hues. It was deep and beautiful. MJ and Peter and Norm were crowding me. They were looking at me as I was looking out into the deep blue yonder.

"Guys, will you give me some space, please."

They moved off a little and we were like a line of toy soldiers all staring out at the day. There were a few children getting off the bus, likely on their way home from school. I watched them jostle and laugh and push each other as they walked along the sidewalk towards home. They made me melancholic as I thought of their ages, probably around twelve or so. So carefree, young, and happy.

How I wish my childhood had been like that. How quickly things can change. Like, my childhood was happy and relatively carefree until I was about six. You know that. And look what happened after that. It all went to shit. It could easily happen to any one of those carefree kids. And the joy or curse of it all was that they didn't have a clue. They could be visited by some catastrophe and then it'd be all different. Makes you think that we don't have any great degree of control over our lives. I mean, half the stuff that's happened to me no one ever thought to consult me on before it happened. How do you reconcile that? How do you keep going when some of the worst crap to happen to you had none of your input into it? Maybe that's the key.

To make the best choices we can with what we've been handed. So maybe it's a little bit of both. We have free will over how we handle the crap that we've been dealt. Maybe life is just like a card game. We get cards, we make choices over what to do with them, we hand them in and get other cards and make choices over those. Eventually we win or fold and play the next round. I'd like to think that I'm in the final round here, and maybe if I look at my cards carefully I've got a winning hand. I mean, what's the choice? To fold this late in the game? I don't think I could do that. That's not what the good doctor would want or expect. Nah, I'm on a winning streak. Maybe I've only got a pair of twos but they're enough to win this final round. I'll bet my life on it that they're enough to win this round. Are you with me? Are you betting for me or against? Doesn't matter, anyway. It's my game. I'm the one in it. I'm the one who has to see it through. Anyway, at this late stage if you've been with me this long, I'd like to hope you've thrown a Benjamin down on my side, even if the odds are against it. I could use a little support right now. You know that.

I was getting tired so I wobbled myself over to the couch with the IV. I fell onto it and leaned back into the cushions. I melted into it. MJ and Peter and Norm turned around and looked at me. They looked lost. They didn't have anything to say and I didn't have anything to say to them either. I reached down to the coffee table and grabbed my packet of cigarettes. I was going to try and smoke one. I put it into my mouth, but only after fumbling with it and dropping it into my lap first. It took me a few tries to get a flame out of my lighter. I was too weak to flick the wheel hard enough. I inhaled feebly on the cigarette filter and the end of the smoke burned angry red. The smoke leaked out of my mouth. I didn't bother trying to inhale it. That wasn't going to do me any good.

"Here's your banana and tea, Janko. Hope you enjoy it."

She set a bowl of dirty yellow banana in front of me. There was a spoon leaning against the side of the bowl and the top of the mashed banana looked wet. I reached down and took a spoonful into my mouth. It tasted like heaven, having not eaten anything for a while. The cup of camomile smelled like flowers. Maybe because it was.

"I'm not sure that smoking is the best idea for you at the moment, Janko," said Maria.

"Yeah, I know, but I'm hardly smoking. Look," I took a puff on the cigarette and then exhaled the smoke out of my mouth without inhaling. For me that was as good as the real thing.

"Okay, I see. But doesn't it interfere with the taste of your food?"

"Not really, Maria. At this stage in the game, smell and taste come and go. But I will say that this banana does taste great. Maybe it's because I haven't eaten anything for a while."

I took another spoonful of the mushy stuff. Dirty yellow-brown. Didn't look appetizing, but it was exactly what I needed.

"Why are you ignoring us, Jay?" asked Peter.

I looked up at him and frowned.

"I'm not ignoring you guys. I've just got nothing to say to you."

"I'm sorry, Janko, what was that?" asked Maria.

"Nothing, I was talking to Peter…one of my imaginary friends."

Maria nodded at me. Peter stepped closer, across the coffee table from me.

"That's rude, Jay. After all the four of us have been through, you're going to ignore us while we stand here."

"I'm not ignoring you as I said before. I've just got nothing to say to you. Why don't you guys sit down and talk to me if you want, and I'll tell Maria what you're saying, then she won't feel excluded from the conversation either. Do you see how retarded this all seems?"

Maria was looking at me and then towards the balcony. She was following an invisible tennis ball that was the conversation between me and my inconsiderate friends. Peter went and sat on the chair opposite to Maria. MJ came and sat next to me on my left side and Norm budged himself in on the right. Now I couldn't lie down. Not that I wanted to, but it would've been nice to have the choice.

"And another thing, Peter," I said, "how do you think this is going to sound to Maria, with me spouting off to imaginary people. You know she's going to put this in the file and exactly how is that going to look. They'll force me on those anti-psychotics in no time."

"No, we wouldn't," said Maria.

I shot her a glance and winked.

"Well, not immediately, anyway," she continued.

"Or maybe," I said, "I'll just ask the good doctor to get them for me next time I see him."

"Oh, no, you won't, you bastard," said Norm.

He was reaching out trying to strangle me with his bare hands. I started laughing the best I could. It was pathetic. These hands that looked so real but which I couldn't feel and which had no real substance to do any harm.

"Don't be ridiculous," I said to Norm, "he's trying to strangle me, Maria. That is Norm is trying to strangle me."

I smiled at her.

"Are you okay, Janko? Really. Is it okay having your friends bait you like this? I'm a little worried, to be honest with you."

"See. Look what you guys have started," I said to them.

MJ looked like she was about to cry. Norm was wringing his hands and biting his lip and muttering something. Peter was staring at me as if he wanted to come out of his chair and clobber me. Only he couldn't because he saw how useful that was to poor old Norman.

"You wouldn't dare, Janko. You wouldn't dare. I don't believe it for a minute," said Peter.

MJ looked up at me with wet eyes.

"Would you do that? Would you really do that to us, Jay?" she pleaded more than asked.

I looked at them for a while. I looked at Maria and her forehead was creased. I really think she was a little nervous. So I took a sip of hot tea to buy myself some time in trying to figure out what to really do with this. I mean I didn't want to go on the anti-psychotics. Or should I say I wouldn't go on them but at the same time I wanted my friends to give me a frigging break. But maybe this could also be used as an opportunity to show Maria that my relationship with MJ and Peter and Norm was not harmful to me. Then she could put that into the file. The hot tea made me think of fields of flowers. Spring time in Saskatchewan and all the wild flowers by the mountain. And streams too, with clear water that I drank from and never got sick off. I looked outside and saw that it was still the tail end of winter and probably cool like it had been the last time I was outside with my father and my friends. I looked at them then. Peter now staring off into space somewhere towards the far wall. Norm with his hands collapsed in his lap and MJ with her eyes still wet. The only one still looking at me.

"Don't worry about them Maria, they're okay. I've been dealing with them for well over twenty years, and to be honest with you, they're a lot easier to deal with now than they have been."

I took another drink of flowers and saw the fields and streams of my youth again. I should've been drinking a lot more tea, especially camomile tea during my adult years. A small thing to help mitigate the pain, the loneliness and the sorrow.

"I just don't want them making you upset. You don't need anything to make you upset right now as you move towards healing and peace. You especially don't need to be made upset by imaginings, if you'll forgive me for saying that."

I looked at MJ and patted her knee. Or at least did my best to try and do that with someone unreal.

"Thanks, Maria. They're not upsetting me and they won't. I'm in a very different place at the moment. I really feel like I've made some great inroads in coming to terms with my sadness and anger and self-loathing, if that is what it is. My friends don't have any hold on me like that anymore. And really, it was only Norm who had that kind of an effect on me. MJ and Peter were much nicer. Norm sits next to me here and wrings his hands because he couldn't affect me by pretending to strangle me. Before, he would have been able to intimidate me with that. Now, he can't. None of them can, Maria, and they'll never be able to do that again. And as I said, it was really only Norm who tried it, anyway."

I figured I was doing a great job at convincing her, primarily because it was the truth. I'm sure you can see it. Norm doesn't have anything on me anymore. He sat like a sullen child next to me and I went to shoulder him, but I got no response. Maria sipped her tea.

"Okay, Janko," she said, "I believe you. But if you are having any problems with them you let us know, okay? At the very least we can help you through it by talking about it and working through it that way."

"Sure," I said nodding, "but honestly, I really don't think there'll be any more problems with them."

MJ was still sitting with wet eyes and Peter was still staring off into space with his hands folded in front of him.

"I'll be honest with you, Maria," I said, "what makes me feel the worst is seeing them in pain. Because that is my pain really, isn't it? MJ is sitting on the other side of me and she's almost in tears because she doesn't want to be done away with. Peter over there," I said pointing at him, "is sulking and staring off into space, and even Norm in his way is looking like a sad and pathetic character at the moment with his hands folded quietly in his lap.

I mean shit, these are pieces of me, Maria, and I don't want to see them hurting. I don't want to see me hurting. And that's what's happening at the moment, in a way, when you look at them all. Sure I seem all content and that, but deep down inside, maybe these people are part of my character, reflections of my soul. And I don't want to spend the rest of my days in sorrow in whatever form it shows itself. I want, and I need these people to be with me until the end. I don't think that is asking a lot. Sure they're rebelling at the moment but that's only because the hierarchy has changed and they're unsure of their places and insecure in their staying power. Once they get over it, they'll be a lot happier and more at peace with the way things are."

I looked at my friends and they were all looking at me. MJ had a small smile on her face and both Peter and Norm weren't looking as uptight as they just recently were.

"We all need those people around us who help us. Especially as I'm on the final corner now, I need all those who want to be there to be cheering me on at the finish line. And Maria, that finish line is coming up pretty quickly as you well know."

"Well, said," said Peter.

I smiled at him and he winked at me and came up to me and patted me on the shoulder. MJ kissed me on the cheek. It felt warm and moist and nice. Even though I knew it wasn't real, I chose to feel it okay and it felt good. Nothing wrong with that if you don't mind. I'm choosing love; I'm choosing to feel the goodness again. Norm smiled a little in spite of himself, he patted me on the knee, and I felt that too. Then he looked over at Maria who was sipping her tea.

"Good, Janko," said Maria, "you have me convinced. But always remember that we are here for you. You don't have to do this alone. And as a matter of fact it will be much better if you let us help you with it. With all of us working together we can expedite the process of your healing so that you are ready for whenever the end comes and in whatever form. I'm also talking of your friends or those splintered facets of your personality that you mustn't let undermine you."

She was looking at me over the edge of her mug. Sipping it now and then. I picked my mug up from the table and took a couple of swigs. It was warm now, not too hot and just about perfect for enjoying.

That short window of opportunity when a hot drink is warm enough to enjoy but not hot enough to burn. Before it gets too cool to enhance the flavors. If you had days and days with which to kill time you'd understand what I'm trying to say. You get reflective and you start unravelling all the small mysteries of life like those small windows of time when tea is at the perfect temperature to be enjoyed. You'd also start thinking about why we drink flowers. Like this tea here, which is basically flower buds of the camomile plant, as I understand it. You'd try and figure out why someone would think about drying flowers and brewing them with hot water. And how many different flowers would've been tried to find the right ones? And the bigger question. How many idiots died trying to figure out which were the safe ones and which ones killed or poisoned or gave you fevers and cramps and stuff like that? All I can say is that I'm glad it wasn't me trying to figure it out. I wouldn't know where to begin. I mean drinking this tea and thinking about all those wildflowers from my youth and those green fields. Shit, they all looked good enough to eat. I would've tried them all and probably be dead before I figured out which ones were safe and which weren't. So, you see how easy it is to digress when you've got nothing but time on your hands. And solitude too. You definitely need solitude. Without all this emptiness in my spirit and in my life, my mind takes to rattling around in its little cage and looking for stuff to do. This is the stuff it does when it doesn't have my friends to entertain it. What's the alternative with all this free time? Get miserable about yourself and think of ending it all and feeling all sorry for yourself and having a pity party? I don't think so. You've seen me there and it ain't pretty, is it? No. It's ugly and shameful and I'm trying to make the best of the time I have left. I hope you'll give me leeway. I'm sure you will. Thanks for that.

"Are you with me, Janko?" asked Maria.

I looked over at her. Jesus, I'd got all caught up in my reminiscing. I'm getting soft and contemplative and melancholic in my dusky days. I took another swig of my tea. It was amazing. Sip of tea, flash card of fields full of flowers. So I had another sip. And then another flash card of streams and green grass. It was brilliant, so much better than the bad acid trips I'd had before.

"Yeah, I'm with you."

"Okay. So?"

"So I agree with you, okay."

I turned to Peter and squinted my eyes at him. He laughed and so did Norm.

"No, I think you've just forgotten what I said."

"Yes, I did. Sorry, Maria, I was off daydreaming again."

"What about?"

"Well," I said, "it seems that every time I take a sip of my tea it reminds me of the fields of wildflowers that I played in when I was a child in Dundurn."

"Where's that?"

"Sorry, that's in Saskatchewan. I spent some time at Blackstrap Mountain. Or Mount Blackstrap which was manmade not long before I was born. Can you believe that, naming a mountain, a small mountain, after molasses. Maybe they didn't name it after molasses, but it seems weird, anyway. It was also one of the things that made molasses easier for me to have on my porridge. The fact that the park where I played was named after molasses. Anyway, I never minded that as much when I was told that they'd named the mountain after the molasses on my oatmeal. That's one of the few kind memories that I can remember of my mother. I don't have many memories of her at all, but that is one, and it's a good one too."

I stopped talking then and my eyes drifted off into the blue yonder. I was thinking about those times. Those times when I still had my mother. My eyes misted up and my throat was stuck with a wad of wet bread.

"What is it, Janko?' asked Maria.

I turned back to look at her and dabbed at my eyes with the top of my pyjama shirt.

"I was just thinking about my mother. I can still remember vividly the day she told me that the mountain was named after the molasses on my oatmeal. I was sitting in our tiny little apartment and there was this huge bowl of oatmeal in front of me. At least it seemed huge to me then. And I was asking my mother for some sugar but we didn't have any. We were really poor. It was only the two of us and she was working some dead end job. So she looked around in the cupboards and found some old blackstrap molasses which was thick and she had to take a spoon to scoop it out. I didn't like the look of it and so I asked her what it was and she told me it was like sugar but was so special that they named the mountain after it. I fell for it and it didn't taste too bad either."

I wiped at my eyes again. Lumpy bread was stuck in my throat again so I coughed trying to clear the lump in my throat. Maria came over and sat next to me and gave me a hug. I had put my mug down first. It didn't help, I started crying then, but it was good. Maybe I was mourning my mother. Maybe I was mourning my own innocence lost. The loss of my childhood. Probably it was both. But it felt good to cry into Maria's shoulder and to be held by her. Her warm embrace and her hair smelling like sweet flowers. Not camomile. Something nicer and sweeter. I'd say roses but it wasn't roses, but along those lines if you know what I mean. I couldn't see Norm. I figured that Maria had squashed him when she sat in his lap. And at that moment I didn't care where he was. I was feeling lonely and sad and I needed the warm embrace that Maria was offering. Besides, Norm would never embrace me. You know that.

"That's a beautiful story, Janko. Your mother seemed like she was really quite cute back then," said Maria.

The tears came more freely then. I wasn't sobbing, I didn't have the strength left in my body but the tears fell nonetheless and it felt cleansing. It felt like I was wiping away some of the stains on my soul. These hot tears washing away my sins. They felt hot, but maybe it was just the blood in my face. You know how you get worked up when you're crying. I had my arms around Maria as best as I could, but they felt like wet noodles. I had barely the strength to rest against her, let alone hug her back. After a while she held me out in front of her. Her hands on my shoulders like she was inspecting me.

"You're doing really good, Janko. It's good that you can cry about these kinds of memories. It's important and part of the healing process for you. And you're starting to think about positive memories which is a very good sign. Feel free to let it out at any time you need to. It's cathartic, I find that myself. I always feel better after a good cry."

She leaned over to the coffee table and pulled a couple of tissues out of the box. She handed them to me as I sat awkwardly turned towards her, smiling at her last comment. I thanked her and blew my nose and wiped at my face and my tears.

Crying did feel good, if I'm going to be honest with you, and that's hard for me to admit to, okay. I've never been allowed to cry before. Not openly at least.

It was shameful and not something that big strong boys do. I mean, for fuck's sake. You can beat and whip a little boy, like they did to me, but he can't cry out in pain. Emotional or physical. You won't let him. That's cruel and disgusting, okay. The way they did that to me, not wanting me to cry out. To cry to the heavens for retribution and justice. But I did, anyway. Secretly, and my prayers and my cries fell on deaf ears. I'm going to talk to him about that when I see him, that's for sure. Why he let me down like he did. Why he let my mother abandon me in his own fucking house. What kind of a God does that? Suffer the little children. That just isn't right. It's not right, at all. You agree, right? Yeah, I thought so. But crying does help. Maybe that's why they didn't want me to do it. Double the punishment. Well, I hope they all rot in hell to unbearable punishment. Yes, I'm healing, but don't expect forgiveness from me. I don't have it in me. It's all I can do to forgive myself.

Maria got up and asked if I'd like a top up of tea.

"Okay," I said, knowing full well that I wouldn't be able to drink another cup. I picked up my bowl of banana and finished up the last few spoonfuls. It was all I could do. I was stuffed and tired and eating had lost all joy for me. I slumped back down into the couch. MJ was still sitting next to me and she put her hand on my thigh and reached over and kissed me on the cheek. I smiled at her. All this tenderness was killing me. Turning my insides into mush.

"I love you, Jay," she said.

I looked at her for a while and believed her. But then again, I'd always had a soft spot for her. I'd been in love with her for years and had always wished we could have been boyfriend girlfriend. But you knew that didn't you? I think I'm repeating myself, but I don't care. Might as well get it all off my chest as long as it takes.

"I love you, too," I said turning away from her, kinda embarrassed about having said what I did.

She squeezed my thigh and Maria came back in with my mug and hers. The steam drifted up in wormy wisps. She placed it on the coffee table and picked up my empty bowl and took it into the kitchen. I turned around and slid myself lengthwise down the couch. I was tired; it was getting time for sleep. Norm who had returned out of thin air to the seat he had had on the couch got up, as did MJ.

"Thanks for kicking us off, buddy," he said.

I smiled at him.

"Where are we supposed to go now?"

"Sit on Peter's lap," I said.

"No fucking way," said Peter, "MJ for sure, but not Norm."

"What's that?" asked Maria.

"Nothing, I was just talking to my friends. They're all sad now that I've kicked them off the couch so I could lie down on it."

MJ did go and sit on Peter's lap. Norm walked back over to the balcony doors.

"I was only kidding," he said staring outside at the sky.

"I know," I said. "It's okay Norm, I know. It was nice to hear you use some humor for a change."

I looked over at Peter and gave him a look and thrust my head out towards Norm.

"Janko's right, Peter, you should apologize to Norm," said MJ.

Peter looked over at him. Norm was still staring outside at the sky, his hands thrust into empty pockets.

"I'm sorry," said Peter, "it's just that you're way too heavy Norm. You know that. A big strapping lad like you. You'd break my legs."

Norm turned around and I saw a tear roll down his cheek. He was sad and fragile. He was getting more fragile all the time.

"It's okay," he said to Peter.

"What's wrong, Norm?" I asked him.

He looked at me with those sad eyes and another tear rolled down the other cheek. He dabbed at them with the sleeves of his sweater.

"I'm a human being, too, you know," he said, "and it isn't easy being me, okay. Always having to be strong and angry and unemotional. It isn't easy. It isn't easy being the only one alone in this room. I also want to belong and be friends with all of you. But it's like you've never wanted me around or you've always been embarrassed by me or something. And that's hard, okay. I have feelings and I need help and care, too, okay? And you guys have just treated me, especially lately, like I don't have any feelings. It's like don't worry about that Norm, he's just angry and distant and a loner. Ignore him and pretend like he isn't there. But that's hurtful, okay. You used to need me, Jan, you used to turn to me to help you be strong, and it hasn't always been easy for me to be that strength that you've required."

He turned around again and looked outside. He crossed his hands over his chest. I couldn't see his face and I wanted to get up and go and hug him. But I couldn't, I didn't have enough energy.

"It's okay Norm. You know we've all been friends over the years. It's just lately that your anger hasn't been appropriate, and it seems like it's been taking you a while to understand that and to get to a place where you are less combative. That's why we aren't warming to you as much as you'd like. You're just too hard for what's required at the moment."

My eyes were tired and closed. I could go to sleep anytime now. I didn't have the energy to debate back and forth with Norm.

"What's going on, Janko?" asked Maria.

"Nothing really. Norm is just unhappy that we seem to be ignoring him and he thinks we've been mean to him. But really Maria, he is just too angry and belligerent lately for what is helpful. He needs to become kinder and gentler. You know that, we all know that except, it seems, Norm. And I'm tired, and I'm not about to be spending the rest of my days trying to baby-sit Norm's feelings. I'm sorry Norm, that's just the way it is."

"Sounds fair enough to me," said Maria. "Where is he?"

I opened my eyes to check that he was still by the balcony and he was. I told her.

"It's true, Norm," said MJ, "we need to focus on helping Janko right now and not be too worried about our own difficulties. Your humor earlier was good. That's what we need now. That, and some understanding for Janko. This is not about us anymore, okay? This is about helping Janko heal in these last few weeks that he has left. Like we've helped him in the past, we need to help him now. Not in protecting him from the abuse he suffered back then, but being easy on him and encouraging him to continue to progress and to find that peace and joy he is searching for. If we keep squabbling like we are, we're going to prevent that from happening for him. And that wouldn't be the thing that friends do for each other, right? And besides which, Janko said he might just go back on those drugs to try and get rid of us if we don't smarten up. And even if he was sort of joking, it still is something to be aware of."

MJ looked over at me. I smiled weakly at her and watched Norm for a while before my eyes got too heavy and I had to close them. He kept looking outside and didn't say anything.

"Come on, Norm. Get a handle on yourself big fella. We need your toughness even now, but in a gentler way. As MJ says, we are all friends but you've just been hard on us with your sullen and angry ways lately. Lighten up my friend and we can all enjoy the last few days that we have left together," said Peter.

Still no response from Norm and I was drifting into a nice relaxed state. Soon I'd be asleep. Hopefully, if it all went well. Lately sleep was such a frail experience for me. Sometimes I could get snatches of it and at other times good stretches of it. But that was getting rarer. Just as I was thinking of this I jerked awake. Fuck, I hated that sensation. Just as I was thinking I was going out for the count. I opened my eyes and saw Maria taking my ashtray away with the half burnt cigarette in it. So much for enjoying my smoke.

"Look Norm, I'm sorry if I've been hard or mean to you. I didn't mean to. I just thought that you could handle a little teasing. I mean, you've always been the tough one amongst us and you've always handled yourself well under stressful situations. I thought you could take it. Besides, I was kind of getting sick of your grumpy moods all the time."

Norm turned around then and there were no more traces of his tears.

"It's okay. I guess I have been kind of grumpy, lately. But that's only because I've felt unvalued and at a loss about what to do. I've also felt like I was about to be kicked to the curb and that's scary, okay. I used to be needed a lot by Janko when he was younger and even lately, the way he was angry a lot of the time, helped fuel me. But he's been changing and becoming gentler and more relaxed and accepting of things and that's scared me. Because I've never fitted into any idea of him being like that. I've always been around because I was the tough one. Now what do I do when he's changing and beginning to behave and respond more like you guys? I want to feel valued and needed and important even in these last days that we have. Especially in these last days that we have. But I haven't, okay, and then with all the talk about the doctor finding out about us, I was getting scared that I might not be around for much longer. And I want to be. I want to be around until the end. Until we all bow out, but I felt like all of you guys were ganging up on me and trying to get me to leave. I didn't know how to respond other than the way I've always been. Angry, aggressive, and if that didn't work, then sullen."

He sighed and sat down against the glass doors that led out to the balcony. His legs stuck out in front of him like two dead tree trunks. He didn't move them. They just stuck straight out. His hands he tossed casually in his lap and they lay there like dead birds. He seemed to have aged right in front of my eyes. He looked tired and weary and old. He looked off towards Maria, towards my bedroom. I wondered if he wanted to go and lie down and get some rest, too. I closed my eyes again. It was a nice speech he gave, but I was too tired to comfort him and give him the reassurance he was looking for. Maybe MJ and Peter could pick up that torch for now.

"You're not really going to go on those drugs are you, Jay?" asked Norm.

"No," I said keeping my eyes shut and trying to find a small dark corner in the world where I could just get some fucking peace and quiet to sleep. See what happens to me when I get tired. I get grumpy too, and that's not helping.

"But he could always change his mind," said MJ, "and that isn't something I want to risk. Because, if he goes on those drugs, Norm, then none of us are safe. So we all have to pull together and take care of him and each other, or else we'll all be gone sooner rather than later. I'm sorry you've felt the way you have, but we're all working on the same team here and you have to try and come to terms with that. And we need to work together and to do that you have to become kinder and gentler for all of us. Don't you realize that you isolate yourself from people when you're hot headed and angry and antagonistic all the time. People aren't going to want to be around you."

"That's true, Norm. And I like you, I really do, but not when you're uptight, angry and combative. Come and get a hug from us all. Come and feel the love."

There was some sound and some rustling of clothes or something. Maybe it was just in my mind or maybe it was Norm and MJ and Peter having a big love in. I just couldn't be bothered to open my eyes to find out. I was so close to sweet sleep. I could almost feel myself wrapping up into its warm soft arms.

"That's nice guys," I said, "I'm glad we're all becoming friends. I still need you like I've always needed you, Norm. Just be nice, that's all we're asking."

"Okay," Norm said, "I think I can do that. But I'll need your help to keep me focused and on the gentle path. The kind-natured path. I mean it's not what I'm used to, okay?"

"I'll keep you on a short leash, my friend," said Peter.

"And I'll keep Peter on a short leash," said MJ.

"And I'll keep all of you alive in my mind," I said yawning shallowly into lungs that felt like thick rubber.

"Are you tired, Janko?" asked Maria.

I grumbled my response to her.

"Would you like me to help you to bed?" she asked.

"No," I said, "I just want peace and quiet so I can get some sleep and I want to sleep here, please. Just let me drift away."

And in my mind's eye I could see Maria frowning at me for my impatience. But you know what? I'm not perfect but I'm trying and I think I'm doing a great job. I've come pretty far, I'm sure you'll agree, in the short time that I've had. So I didn't open my eyes to see if she was frowning, because I didn't really care. Norm, MJ, and Peter were quiet and had made up and I was happy about that. The last thing I heard was Maria heading into the kitchen, running water, and the sound of mugs and dishes clinking in the sink. It made me feel safe and secure, it was my Ativan. The lights dimmed and then went out.

XXVII

Margaret and I had had a wonderful evening together. We'd gone out for a meal and shared a bottle of wine. I'm embarrassed to admit that I drove us home when I probably shouldn't, but the pub was just down the road from us. A few minutes' drive from us. It was called The Crow's Feet and all night it made me maudlin. Either that or the wine, but probably both. I could see Margaret's crow's feet and it got me thinking about the long time we had been together. Twenty-odd years and they had all been wonderful. But it got me thinking about Janko's thirty-odd year life and how difficult it had been. The thought of that stung me when I compared it to the blissful life I'd had with Margaret, the blissful life I'd had all my life, really. My childhood was a charm and I'd had such warm and loving parents. Lots of friends and all the opportunity in the world. Well, you probably don't want to hear about that. But the point I was trying to make was how glaringly different our lives had been. And what does that mean? Was it just fate, or happenstance, or did we choose our lives before we were born. That idea just seems ludicrous to me when you have no inkling of it in this life. Especially because I was this man's father. That hit hard. That made it all the more difficult to deal with. I felt like I should have been able to help him somehow. I should have somehow known.

These crow's feet that mapped our lives, our laughter got me thinking about this. I loved Margaret's lines around her eyes, because I was there, it showed the places we had been together. Our lives intertwining merrily all these years. We were writing all over each other's bodies as time went by and what a wonderful, magical story we were writing. I liked to think that we were merging into one, that we were melding our souls and the body was the physical representation of that.

"Would you like something to drink, my love?" asked Margaret.

"Water please. I think a tall glass of water is exactly what I need."

I went over and turned on the fireplace. The tongues of flame licked at the back wall and drooled all over the fake logs. The days were getting warmer but the night was still clutched by winter's icy grip. Spring was coming slowly, like a small child peeking into dark corners, but old man winter never died quickly or quietly in these parts. I stood by the fireplace holding the flames at bay with my palms. I wasn't cold, just contemplative. The wine had smoothed out my wrinkles of the day and I felt newly minted. But still, my mind throbbed with a little doubt, a little existential angst and a little remorse for something that logically wasn't my doing.

"Here you go, honey. Come and sit by me on the couch so I can also enjoy the warmth of the fire."

She winked at me and went to sit down, tucking her legs up under herself like she usually did. She leaned her head against her hand and in the other she held a glass full of water. I sat next to her and leaned over to her and kissed her on the lips.

"Thanks for a lovely evening. We should do that more often," she said.

"Yes, I know, we should. I had a wonderful time with you too, and the meal was good. For me, anyway. I always feel bad for you though, there doesn't ever seem to be enough of a choice for you whenever we go out."

"That's because we hardly ever go out to vegetarian restaurants. But seriously, Mike, they still made a good effort and I enjoyed the stir-fry. The wine certainly smoothed it on its way down though, didn't it?"

"It did," I said. "And next time we will go to a vegetarian restaurant of your choice. You know I enjoy vegetarian food."

"I know. I was just giving you a hard time."

I took my glass of water from the table and took a couple of big sips from it. It was half full when I put it down again. I had to think of that though. I was originally going to say it was half empty, but I couldn't do that seeing as how I've been berating Janko lately about half full versus half empty mugs and jugs and such. I looked at the fire and its mesmerizing dance. It was alive, like some wild beast. A dangerous beast but one safely caged for now.

"What's on your mind my love? You've seemed quite distant or thoughtful most of the evening."

I looked over at her and she smiled at me and then sipped from her glass.

"I'm sorry honey. It's just my patient, Janko. I'm worried about him a lot lately. And this evening when we were at The Crow's Feet, I started admiring your beauty and how when you laugh I see the creases at the corner of your eyes and it got me thinking of our lives together. I started thinking of all these wonderful years I've spent with you and how blessed I am to have had that. I started thinking of how our lives get written in our faces and on our bodies as we age gracefully. How our lives are being written together on each other. How wonderful that is, but how sad it made me feel when I compared that against Janko's life. My son's life. I guess I feel like I should have somehow been able to help him. To have been able to give him a chance at a different life. Somehow, I should have been able to help afford him greater opportunities. I mean, how is it that my life has been so charmed in contrast to his? I just can't reconcile myself with the reasons why that could be."

I reached for some more water and sipped deeply from my glass.

"Or maybe it's just the wine speaking. But whatever it is, I've been thinking a lot about that lately."

"I can only imagine. Are you worried, too, that you are running out of time to help him now?" she asked.

"Absolutely. I don't think we have more than a week or so left together and there seems to be so much that remains unsaid. So much that remains unexplored. So much that will likely remain unexplored."

"I can only imagine your sense of urgency, Mike. But you've made great headway, already. From what you've told me, you should be proud of yourself. There is no need to second guess yourself, my love. I'm sure Janko is happy just to have this time with you now. That is all you have anyway. No good will come of exploring the past and how it might have been different. Certainly we need to learn from it, and isn't that what your practice is based upon? To help people learn from their past mistakes and move forward in a more positive direction?"

"Yes, it's true. I suppose that is true enough. But sometimes the medicine is easier to pour than to swallow. I'm having a hard time taking my own medicine now, I guess. Maybe it's because Janko is my son and that is probably making it harder than if he was solely a patient."

"No doubt, my love. But try and think about all the positive inroads you've made with him. You should really try and find that peace in yourself that I know is there. That peace that is your own contentment in knowing that you've done the best you can. You never knew you had a son, Mike. You can't change the past now. But by dwelling on it, you're diluting the present moments that are left. You and I both know that you would have taken him under your wing if you had known about him as your son before. I'm sure Janko knows that, too. I'm wondering if you're also unsure about your feelings of having a son. Are you really happy about it? Or maybe, in a way, you are not disappointed that you've found out about him now when he is soon to pass on. Have you given that any thought, my love?"

Dammit, I hated the way she was so perceptive and often times so spot on. That's probably what made her such a good lawyer. Being intuitive to other people's motives and feelings. I looked over at the fire for a while. It wouldn't give me any answers. It kept on dancing seductively like a belly dancer. I drank the rest of my water and got up to get some more. I brought the jug back into the living room and gave Margaret a fill up, too. I returned the jug to the fridge and then stood by the fire. I looked at a picture of Margaret and me that was on the mantle. It had been taken many years ago. We were at Lake Louise, in front of the actual lake. It must have been late spring, for the mountains were heaped with snow but there was still the brown strata of rock showing through in places. Like a huge chocolate cake with icing. Margaret was behind me on a rock with her arms around my neck and her smiling face over my right shoulder. My hands were holding her forearms and I noticed I was wearing a beard then. God knows what I was thinking. Our pose cut the lake in two and on either side of us was the turquoise blue of the water. It was beautiful, and interestingly enough there were hardly any other people in the picture beside us. I couldn't remember who took the photo. Probably some other tourist we had asked, but I admired its composition. I picked it up, brought it back to the couch, and handed it to Margaret. It was in a simple silvery steel frame.

"Do you remember this picture?" I asked her.

She looked at me with a frown on her forehead.

"Of course I do. So young and so much in love."

"I know. We were happy, then. I mean, we are happy now, too, but that would have been taken in our youthful prime when and if things had been different we could have been parents."

"It was taken in nineteen-ninety."

"It always amazes me how you remember our dates so well."

I smiled at her, sat back on the couch next to her, and looked at the photo with her for a while. I put my arm around her neck and kissed her head. I still felt the same way about her now as I did then. Probably more so.

"I'm not sure where this is going, Mike. Do you want to tell me?"

"Well, I'm just thinking back to that time when I wanted children and you didn't. You never did and it was something that I came to respect and upon which we eventually agreed. And yet, back then, even though I wanted children I was still happy. And now that I've found out that I have a child I'm not any happier. In fact if I'm honest…"

I stopped for a moment, not sure if I could speak the truth. The cold hearted truth. Margaret looked at me silently.

"Well, if I'm honest, then I'd have to say that I think you are probably right. There is probably a part of me, let's be honest, a big part of me that is happy or at least content that Janko is going to die and I won't have to explore that relationship with him. Maybe that makes me callous or cold hearted, and I'm not happy that he's going to die, it's just that I won't have to explore a familial relationship with him."

I looked over at the photo of us again that Margaret had put on the coffee table. Next to it was my glass of water, sweating. I picked it up and took a sip. It nearly slipped out of my hand. I ran my fingers around it and dried my hand on my trousers. It was only water. Margaret didn't say anything but she was still looking at me.

"Almost dropped my glass," I said.

She still didn't say anything except smile at me. I felt like I was walking the plank so I figured I might as well finish up what I was saying. Fill this room with the vacant air of my lungs, my thoughts.

"I don't know Janko that well, honey. In the sense that I don't know him as well as I would if we had been kin from the beginning. My relationship with him has been founded in the patient/psychiatrist motif and how do you overcome that when you've found out lately that you are family to each other.

I just don't think it is that easy. And I doubt if you can ever recreate the bond between a father and his son that forms in infancy and is cemented during childhood. I don't know for certain as we've never had children, but I honestly can't see how we could overlook that. I'm not trying to be cruel Margaret, but I wouldn't know where to begin in forming a relationship with Janko that is familial rather than purely platonic. We don't have any shared experience for one thing and how could I ever see him from a purely patriarchal vantage point when I've known him mostly as my patient. Surely this doesn't make me a bad person does it?"

My glass continued to sweat and I felt suddenly hot, as well. Though no one was judging me I felt like I was being interrogated. I looked over at the picture of Margaret and me at Lake Louise. It made me feel better. The man in the picture, the earlier version of me was oblivious to the knowledge I now held. Knowledge may certainly be power but it can be a power that is self-destructive. And at the moment, the power I was wielding was too hot in my own hand to do me any good.

"You're definitely not a bad person, my love. I've always been attracted to your compassionate and caring nature. It is a gift that you have to be able to step into other people's shoes and empathize with them. That is what makes you such a great psychiatrist. I definitely understand how you feel. And I agree with you. I think it would be exceptionally difficult to develop a relationship with Janko that would be, in essence, if I dare say, fraudulent. You can't force something that isn't there. I think what you need to do is to manage the relationship that you do have with him. You have been a great psychiatrist and counsellor to him and you've been a great mentor to him and an example, too. Focus on those aspects of your relationship, Mike; that will be of the best use to both him and you at the moment. He needs you to focus on the task at hand, I'm sure. To help him continue his transition towards that dark door that is death. Just keep being what you are to him. And I know that you feel more for him than you have for your other patients. He has already become so much more to you than just another patient. I've noticed that you have more care and concern about him than you have for any of your other patients. Enjoy that, my love, but don't try to force any more than is there already. He'll pick up on that and you'll feel horrible for not being able to be authentic in your feelings."

Margaret leaned over and kissed me on the cheek. She got up and put the photograph back on the mantle.

"It's hot over here by the fireplace."

I noticed the picture of our wedding next to the one of us in Lake Louise. Margaret was beautiful in her white dress and tiara. It was a black and white photo of us and I didn't have a beard, thank God.

"You're right, Marge, I just get caught up in my own expectations sometimes, I guess."

She turned around then and looked at me with mock sternness.

"No, you're just too hard on yourself sometimes. Your compassion and empathy is a double edged sword that sometimes cuts you as you try to cut through your patients' difficulties."

"You're right," I said. And she was.

"But listen," I continued, "I'd really like it if you would come and meet him the next time I go over."

She came back to sit with me.

"Do you think that is wise Mike?"

"Absolutely. I want to give him a sense of what our family is like. I really think he'd like to see that. I asked him about it and it was something that he wanted. Only if you'd be interested, of course."

She looked down at the coffee table, at my sweating glass of water. Hers was also sweating. She held onto her one foot, her legs tucked under her.

"You won't be alone," I said, "I've also decided to invite the cop who picked him up from the church those twenty-odd years ago, and also the Antolinis, the foster parents whom he really liked. One of the very few that he did. I just get the sense that time is coming to an end, and I think this would be a way of helping him come full circle. I think this would be a wonderful way for him to exit this life and move forward to the next one. To be surrounded by the people he loved, or at the very least liked. The Antolinis are on board and I'm trying to track down the cop, Officer Peel but the police service is making it a little hard for me at the moment. He's been retired for a few years and I guess they don't want to hand out his contact info to just anyone. So I think you're the only holdout."

I smiled at her.

"I'm not holding out, Mike, you only just now told me. And besides you haven't gotten hold of the police officer yet, either. Maybe he won't be interested, and that's if he actually remembers the child."

I shook my head at her.

"Nah, I don't think so. I can be pretty persuasive if I want to be, you know. You're the harder nut to crack."

I was joking, smiling at her, but she didn't seem to be much in the mood. She frowned at me.

"So you're calling me crazy, hey, Mike?"

"No, it's not that, I'm just trying to lighten the mood here a bit. I really think it would do a world of good for him. And it would mean a lot to me, too."

"I don't know, Mike. I don't know him and he's on death's bed. Frail and sick and how am I supposed to behave towards him. I can't feign love or empathy for someone that I haven't met or someone that isn't even related to me."

That hurt a bit, but I wasn't going to let it dampen my enthusiasm. I reached out and held Margaret's free hand. Her other hand still cupped her foot.

"I know and I'm not asking you to be fraudulent or to pretend. Just be yourself. I'm sure he'll make it easy enough for you to be around him. He's really come a long way. He's not belligerent anymore and he's found some peace and tranquillity. Besides Margaret, he is my son, after all, even if he's nothing to you."

She looked away towards the fireplace.

"That's not what I meant."

"I know, but it still hurt."

She pulled her hand away from mine and got up and walked towards the fireplace. I looked down at the coffee table and found my glass of water. Now it was definitely less than half empty. I drank the last of it and tried to place it back directly on the wet ring it had just left behind, but I missed and I was now on my way to making goggles. Margaret was standing in front of the fireplace with her hands folded in front of her. I admired her curves, and as much as I was hurt I wasn't angry, but she was beginning to get upset.

"I don't know, Mike. I just don't know," she said to the mantle.

"Why, honey? What is really the difficulty with coming with me to see him? I'll be there; the Antolinis will be there; probably the cop, and also the nurses. I'm going to try and get all of them there, too. This might be the last chance we have to all get together before he passes."

Passes…I loved that. Not even I could say "die" with Janko, if only because he was my son. Sometimes I think we don't speak directly enough and I'm just as guilty of that as the next person. I think I was getting grumpy now, too. Margaret turned back around and walked to the other side of the coffee table. She was now directly across from me. Looking at me intently.

"Okay, Mike. I'll do it, but don't expect me to be unnaturally happy."

"I won't. But what is it that you have such great difficulty with? I don't really see how this is such a big deal for you."

She came around the coffee table and plopped herself heavily on the couch. She couldn't have put herself further away from me if she had tried. Her arms were still in the imaginary straight jacket. I put my hand over into the gap between us with the palm up. I flopped it up and down a few times but got no response so I reeled it back in. She definitely was grumpy now.

"Well, Mike, frankly I just don't like to be around death. I've never been around someone that was about to die or dies right in front of me. I don't even like funerals. I remember both of my grandmother's funerals and my mother's father's funeral and they were horrible. That's why I could never be a doctor. I would never want to deal with death. I don't know why, maybe it reminds me of my own mortality. It just seems so vile and so useless. All the living and striving for naught, because we are all going to die. It seems to make life pointless, really. And I don't want to be reminded of that. I mean, what is the use of this life if it all ends up for nothing because we all end up dead in the end. And death is so lifeless, so sullen and sad like a spoiled child. I hate it. It is the total antithesis of life and living and dreaming and scheming and striving. I just don't want him to die in front of me, okay."

She looked over at the fire again. It wasn't alive but it sure looked like it. I moved myself closer towards her and put my hand on her thigh. I gave it a gentle squeeze and then reached over and kissed her on the cheek.

"I never knew that about you," I said with a cautious smile on my face.

She kept looking at the fire, her arms folded defiantly.

"It's okay, honey. I don't think he will move on…" Jesus, why couldn't I say it, "Die while you are there. And I really appreciate you coming to do this for me. I know he'll be very happy to meet you. It's just to make him comfortable and feel included in my life to a small degree. He's a good boy and I want him to feel like I've cared for him as a son as well as a patient; I think by doing this it will help to reassure him of that. And I do care for him, despite my comfort with him dying, honey, I can't help but to feel a certain paternal instinct towards him. Just knowing that he is my son changes things, if only in my mind."

I leaned over and kissed her again, this time she met me and we kissed on the lips. I hugged her then, too.

"I'm sorry, my love. I don't mean to be hard on you, it's just that I struggle with the death motif so much. I want nothing to do with it. It seems to lay waste to life for me and yet, it is such an unavoidable aspect of it. It seems to make fun of everything we strive for while living. That's why I became vegetarian, as you know. I want no part of death and suffering."

"But maybe death is the end of suffering, Marge. Maybe in Janko's case it will be the beginning of a lasting peace that he has never known."

She looked off at the fire and I picked up my glass and set it down again, making a trifecta. One more and it'd be a car and one more after that and I'd have the Olympics. Three of us and I already knew the winner in this macabre race. So did Marge and maybe that is what was making this all so difficult.

"Yes, Mike, maybe in Janko's case this is true, but that still doesn't help me any with having to view the suffering ahead of time."

"But he is heavily medicated with pain killers. I think his suffering is minimal at best."

"Still, I'm sure he will look like hell, Mike."

"Yes, he does. He is gaunt and frail and with a waxen, yellowish sheen to his skin. But I think you'll get over that quickly once you've had a chance to meet with him."

She nodded; I think she was trying to steal herself to the reality of what this might mean. I never knew this would be such a big deal for her. But perhaps my mind has been clouded because of the relationship I have with Janko.

"I'm not that upset by death, honey. I see it as the opening of another door to arguably a better place. And even if you don't believe in the after-life, then surely it's imperative for us to do the best work we can while we are here. Otherwise as you say, what's the point? And if you do believe in the afterlife, there is even more reason to do good works and to strive to fulfil one's talents, because then surely you will be judged for what you've done. I certainly don't want to die, but that shouldn't stop us from doing the most with what life we've been given. You could see it as a way of having the last digs at death by doing the best we can while alive."

She put her hand on my thigh.

"Yes, I suppose you're right, Mike. I can't argue against the logic in your argument. I guess I'm just feeling a little fragile and mortal lately."

"Do you know why, honey?"

She shook her head.

"No, it's just a general malaise, maybe all this talk of Janko and his dying. And then there's Michelle at work whose father just died of heart disease and also Brock's wife who got breast cancer recently. It seems wherever I look death is slapping my face. It's just too much. Why can't it be hidden off to the side somewhere? Snatching people quickly and discreetly. But no, death has to come on in and make a big scene while killing people. I guess that's what I hate most about it."

I took her hand from my thigh and kissed the back of it.

"I understand, Marge. That would be very difficult to deal with when you've had so many blaring examples of horrible death and disease recently. Why didn't you tell me about it?"

"Well, Mike, you've had your hands full with your patients and especially with Janko. And I thought I was handling it pretty well. I guess not."

"I always have time for you, honey. I need you to talk to me about what's going on in your life and I'm sorry if I've kept on hogging the conversation. I haven't meant to."

"I know, Mike, and as I said I thought that I had been handling things well, but I guess I haven't really."

I moved the glass on the coffee table again. It was running out of condensation and I wasn't sure I'd be able to make the Olympics, but I had the car. I was getting somewhere, finally.

"I like to sometimes think that life is just a journey or a mansion. This experience we have right now is only one room within this mansion that we are experiencing. Maybe death is the butler coming to get us and bring us into the dining room where we'll feast with other enlightened souls and so on. There's so much for the soul to explore in its journey, we haven't even been outside in the yard. Hell, maybe we're only walking up the path to the front door. Maybe death is that front door opening up the extravagance inside for the next step in this soul's journey. Maybe this life is like hell. Perhaps we've been wandering a desert and only now come upon an oasis as this corporeal existence nods off to sleep."

I didn't have all the answers but I was trying to give Margaret a better perspective. None of us knew what was on the other side of that dark curtain. But we could choose to imagine a hell or a heaven and I figure there's no point in depressing yourself about a hell. Rather, I'd choose to focus on a magnanimous and generous spirit of giving in the afterlife. Either way it made this journey so desperately important in easing the burdens of our fellow travellers, many of whom were bowed down with unnecessary and unjustly heavy baggage.

Margaret turned to me and smiled. She kissed me on the lips.

"I love the way you think, Mike. You have always been so optimistic and enthusiastic. I've always loved that about you. I don't know how you do it."

"It isn't always easy, honey. But at the end of the day it's a choice. Why not try to enjoy this moment, this only reality that exists for us right now. I know I'm far from perfect or even good at it. But it's catchy. Enthusiasm and optimism that is. I think that already you are becoming more optimistic and content with meeting Janko. It's just a way of seeing the world. A world of love and peace or a world of pain and hatred. Call it self-preservation, but I couldn't live in a world that I saw as hateful and painful."

"Yes you're right. So when would you like me to meet him?"

"Tuesday or perhaps Thursday, depending on when and if I can get Officer Peel to join us."

"This Tuesday or Thursday, coming up?"

"I think so, honey. At the very latest a week from this one. I don't think we have that much time at all. I really don't. Maybe Thursday would be best, that way I can give Janko a chance to get accustomed to the idea, and give him a chance to ready himself for all these visitors. I don't think he's had any visitors since I've known him. Other than his own imaginary friends and the nurses and I. But I don't think you can really count us. I think it will do him a world of good to have some visitors. Some people who have felt kindly towards him. It'll take him out of his comfort zone and help him embrace empathy and compassion and warmth. It will be so invigorating for him I'm sure. For all of us really I think."

I looked at my glass and it was mostly dry. I picked up Margaret's and set it down on my rings. Then I returned it to its original place on the coffee table. We had gold. Margaret and I had managed to make the Olympics.

"Okay," she said. She was looking at the fire and biting her bottom lip like she did sometimes when she was deep in thought.

"Are you sure you're okay with it?"

She turned to me smiling and nodded.

"Yes, I think so, my love. I can see how important it is for you to have me there. I'll steal myself and I'm sure it'll be fine. You did say we'd go on a vacation when you're finished up with Janko. That's still the plan right?"

I smiled to myself. I guess I wasn't the only one who had trouble with calling death by his proper name.

"Absolutely. I don't know who will need it more you or I, but I'd wager you a cold margarita that it might be me."

"Deal. It sure will make it easier for me too, Mike, to have a trip to look forward to. We haven't had a vacation for a few years now. We're way overdue."

"I agree. And maybe we could renew our vows, too."

Why not. I was feeling the love. I was feeling comfortable with what little time was left for Janko and me. I was doing my best and I was confident in that. I would help him through to the end, making it as peaceful and compassionate as I could. I was feeling at ease with the reality and the role I was playing. Questions of why I couldn't afford to dwell on, and neither did I want to. I was happy just to let things be. Sometimes you had to let the stream of life take you where it must.

LIVID BLUE

XXVIII

Things were blurring for me now. I was living in a fog or a bog. A big misty, warm bog. My life was becoming cloudy as if I was looking through cataracts. I couldn't be certain when I had last seen the good doctor, my father. It seemed like just hours ago, but it could easily have been years ago. The nurses were being really good at managing my pain. I guess they've had lots of experience with people dying. They knew just how to put me at ease. I was dying. I knew it with a certainty now that I hadn't grasped before. And you know what? I was at peace with it. I'd almost say I was happy about it. I hope that doesn't sound too weird to you. But I felt like I was cocooned by something warm, peaceful, and safe. I didn't think I'd ever get to this place. Shit, you probably know that, having been with me for the ride. I didn't think I'd ever find contentment in dying, in leaving this, okay I'll say it, shitty world. And it has been mean to me, and it wasn't like I didn't want to die. Before, I was angry and pissed off and just wanting to die to get it done with. Be finished with this journey through hell. But now, it's like I'm coming home. It's like I'm a weary traveller who's looking forward to a warm bed and a home cooked meal. Hell, maybe I sound like a crazy man to you now, but I'm not. I still know my friends aren't real, and they still hang around. Only they're quieter now, more subdued. They look on like angels rather than vultures. I'm just peaceful, all right? I'm feeling the love and care from everyone. The good doctor, my father, and the nurses, too. Maybe it's just me, but it seems like I'm seeing all of them lately at different times and sometimes together, but I wouldn't trust my senses, if I was you. Salima's been around, as have Maria and Rose and Veronica. It's like a big love-in and I like it.

To be honest with you, though, I was sure hoping that I wouldn't die alone. That's the only request I'll ask for. I'd like it if at least my father was around. Throw in the nurses, too, and I'd be happy as a pig in shit. If they really are happy in shit, but I wonder about that. Anyway, I'm digressing. If there's a God out there, and I'm beginning to think that there might be, well, I'd like him to hear this plea from his forgotten son. I've never asked for anything, shit, that's a lie. But I've never before received anything from him that I've asked for. He never gave me my mother back. He never gave me any good foster parents since the Antolinis. So if I can just ask for one last thing, I ask for my father to watch over me as I transfer to the other side. That's not too much, is it? Surely it isn't. I mean, after everything I've been through, that surely isn't too much to ask for. Considering how he wasn't there for me in his own damn house. At the church where I was dropped off. He owes it to me now to give me just one last wish for a dying man. And I'm not asking for a special meal or anything. I was barely eating anyway. You're on my side, right. He owes me big time, but I'm big-hearted, I'll forgive him not being present in his own house when a small boy needed a helping hand. I'll forgive him that if he'll just give me the good doctor to watch over me as he covers me with his veil. You'll put in a good word, too, right? I know you will, I mean, you've stuck by me this far, haven't you? You're good people. It comforts me to know someone's been there for me, through this. Besides the doctor, my father, and the nurses. Shit, that's hard, you know, referring to the good doctor as my father. I mean, I know he is, right, but at the same time it's not like he's been my father at all. It's awkward, that's all. I'll just call him whatever feels more natural at the time. Maybe before I was looking for too much from him. Trying to force those feelings of family which I've never really known, anyway. But you can't blame me for wanting it. You can't blame me for trying, but it feels awkward. Unnatural. And maybe now as the lights are dimming it's just too much to pretend that we're family. I mean, in the sense that we're a tight, warm, loving family. Don't get me wrong, I'm comforted to know that I have a father and he's a good man and he's been helpful, exceptionally helpful, to me. And I need him here, more so as a counsellor than my father, but it gives me extra trust and comfort to know that he's my father, anyway.

Shit, you're probably bored. Hell, I don't even know if I'm making any sense any more. Do dying people really ramble on like this, incoherently? Who knows, I feel like I'm making sense to myself, anyway. Could be my mental vomit here is just confusing you. Well, thanks for your kindness and patience. It'll all be over soon and then you'll get to go back to important stuff.

When I do wake up and find myself pretty lucid I keep seeing blue sky. It's always blue here. Like paint, if you know what I mean. It seems thick and wet and new like it's just been freshly painted. Sometimes I see wisps of clouds and then they move on and when I wake up again there's a different cloud or most often blue sky. I can't tell you how long it's been since I've seen rain or snow. And it could still snow here in these parts even if it is May. Just.

I've propped myself up now against my pillows. Jesus, the effort just about killed me. And I'm looking out, now, at the sky which is stabbed with a couple of telephone poles and telephone wires like it's been stitched back together. There's some wisps of clouds way high in the sky and they remind me of white strands from Santa's beard. I remember once my mother taking me to see Santa at the mall and having me sit on his lap. It wasn't a happy experience, I was shit scared to tell the truth, but I did it anyway and he was a kind Santa. Anyway, those clouds up there remind me of some loose strands from his beard. This rectangle of sky, with white clouds and telephone poles stuck up like toothpicks, looks like it could be a modern painting. And I wonder if you get to keep some memories with you when you die. I'd sure like to be able to take this one with me. Just something to hang onto, you know. Make the transition to the other side easier. Postcards from the other side of the curtain. It'd give you something to talk about with the other folks. Ice breakers, you know. Here, have a look at this memory of mine, this frozen memory, my postcard from back there, as I jerk my head behind me. This one's of the good doctor, and see, here he's standing with the nurses who helped me transfer to this place. And another thing, he was my father.

Do you get what I'm saying? It'd make it so much easier. Less scary and less lonely too. I'd like that, but I suppose it's unrealistic, isn't it? But this sure would be a memory I'd want to take with me. This blueness is so thick it's like I could taste it. So comforting I want to wrap it all around me.

I'm probably making no sense, but I don't care. I'm just enjoying my last moments here the best way I can. My friends are sitting in the chair in the corner there, just off to the side of the window. They're a huge human tower of flesh. It's weird, because they're naked, but not sexual or anything. Norm's on the bottom with his one hand around Peter and his other hand around MJ. Because Peter is sitting on top of him with his legs off to my right and MJ's on top of Peter with her legs off to my left. Her hands are in her lap and Peter's arms are around her. They're all looking at me vacantly. The funny thing is, even though they're naked, I can't see their private parts. I mean they're just not there, just flat skin like they're dolls that aren't physically accurate. Not even nipples, none of them have nipples and they don't have any hair either. No hair on the legs or arms or chest of Norm and Peter and no hair on any of their heads or eyebrows. Nothing. I shake my head and rub my eyes. I look at my side table and the clock is showing nine thirty-three. Red, and the two little dots after the nine are blinking at me. I look back at those three and they're still the same. Naked, hairless, vacant stares. It's way too weird.

"Why are you all naked?" I ask them.

"Same as you," they all say together.

I look down at myself and I'm not naked. I've still got my pyjama pants on and my white vest.

"Am not," I say.

"Are not," they reply.

This is fucking me up, if you'll excuse me. They're acting all strange and it's freaking me out.

"Hello," I say, trying to get the nurses attention. Not knowing who's out there.

Rose pops her head into the room.

"Everything okay, Janko?"

"No, thank God you're here."

She moves into the room and comes up to the bed and takes my hand in hers. She fiddles with my IV and touches my forehead with the back of her hand.

"What's wrong?"

"Would you sit with me, please, for a while? My friends are freaking me out. They're all naked and sitting on top of each other and they don't have any hair. They look like dolls or mannequins and they're talking to me funny."

"I sure will, Janko."

Rose moves over to sit in the chair where my friends are and I'm
thinking this should be interesting. As she sits down into their laps they
melt away into the air. Disappearing, and nothing like that has ever
happened before. I look around the room for clues, for anything that
suggests they're still here. But they're not. They're gone. Like morning
frost that just evaporates in front of you as the sun comes up. Weird. I rub
my eyes some more to make sure that they're gone. And they are. Not a
trace. I stare at Rose pretty hard but she's all by herself on that chair.

"What's wrong with your friends, Janko?" she asks me.

I peek into the bathroom, the sliver of it that I can see. Nothing
there. I take a look into the cupboard, the rectangle that's in my sight.
Nothing there, either. Maybe they're cowering in the corner of the
cupboard under some of my dirty laundry.

"I don't know, Rose. Just some weird shit. I was looking out at the
sky and just enjoying the view, when I went to look at them and I saw they
were all sitting on top of each other. That's never happened before.
They've never really been able to merge that much of themselves together.
I mean they can hold hands and stuff, and I've even seen them hug, but
nothing like this. Norm was sitting on the bottom. Peter was on top of him
and MJ was on top of Peter. And they were all naked too. Completely
naked and completely hairless. They looked like mannequins or dolls,
because they had no private parts. And when I say they were hairless I
mean they were completely hairless. No eyebrows, no eyelashes, nothing.
And when I asked them why they were naked they freaked out and said it
was because I was, and then when I looked at myself and realized that I
wasn't naked I told them so and then they said that they weren't naked
then, either. But, Jesus, Rose, honest to God they were…I mean, I'm not
naked, right?"

I looked down at myself again and saw my pyjama pants and my
white vest which wasn't white like it was new, but white like it had been
washed in dishwater a few times.

"Yes, Janko, you are clothed. You're wearing your pyjama
bottoms and your white vest."

"Jesus, thank God, Rose. I thought for a minute I was losing my
mind there. And I don't want to do that you know. Shit, it's the only thing
I'm holding onto before I die, my sanity. I need it. I'm not quite done with
the good doctor, Rose.

I need this clarity before I die. I need to die with clear mental vision if you know what I mean. Just to help me transfer and see myself through to the other side."

I was scared as hell. My heart was pounding like I had raced for miles. Cold sweat was pricking my forehead and I felt cold as a shiver ran down my spine. I held my hands out in front of me and they were shaking slightly and not from lack of nicotine. I needed my sanity. I wish you could tell me if I was making sense or not. I just can't seem to rely on myself, lately.

"You're okay, Janko. You seem perfectly coherent to me. If I could offer some thoughts on this recent development to help you feel better?"

She waited for me to answer. I was looking around. Looking outside, looking for any visual clues as to my sanity or lack thereof. Like, if I saw a cow jumping over the moon or a man eating with a silver spoon. But I didn't, so I felt that maybe I was okay. It helped a little to make me feel better.

"Would you be interested in my thoughts, Janko?"

Rose was looking at me earnestly. She caught my eye, so I steadied my gaze on her and stopped looking around. I hadn't found anything, anyway.

"Sorry, Rose. Yes, I'd be very interested in anything you have to say."

She was leaning forward on her elbows now, still looking intently at me. I was feeling tired again and my eyelids were lead plates. They kept shutting on me.

"I think that what is happening could be explained as the general death of these characters that you've developed over the years. I think, Janko, that as you come closer to the end these hallucinations start to dim and fade. To die out, if you will. So, I'd tell you to try and look at it in a positive light. This could be seen as very good news. Maybe you aren't in need of them as you once were and you're able now to focus on your true self without the need of these crutches, if you'll let me call them that."

Eyes closed and then open. Closed. Open. I wasn't winning the fight. It was like someone kept putting the lid on a simmering pot. So hard to keep those eyes open.

"I'm listening," I said to Rose before she had a chance to think otherwise.

"But if it continues to worry you, you could always ask the doctor for some anti-anxiety medication or if it becomes that scary for you, you could go on the anti-psychotics."

Okay, so that's where they were. My eyes were wide open now, and I was staring right at Norm. He was kneeling on the foot of my bed, trying to reach out his hairless, stringy arms towards Rose, like he wanted to strangle her.

"Maybe I might need that, Rose. It is pretty scary, and Norm has now reappeared and is trying to strangle you...now me."

He had turned around and was now reaching out towards me like a zombie. But with Rose's explanation I wasn't feeling nearly as scared as I had just felt. I kept looking at Norm and it was like he was receding from me as he kept trying to grab at me. He looked useless and pathetic in his unsexed waxy body.

"But I think that if you can get used to this disintegration of your hallucinations without the use of drugs, then you'll probably fair a lot better. Dr. Malichem might have a difference of opinion and you'll definitely want to ask him, but I think that managing this transition without chemical help will keep your rudder steady. It will allow you to grow and develop more holistically towards your exit. Do you know what I'm trying to say?"

Norm had now relaxed. I think he was getting himself all wound up about Rose talking about me taking drugs. He had now flopped down on the end of the bed. Lying there like a corpse. His hands were outstretched and his palms facing up. I kept looking at him, at his groin, because there was nothing there and that seemed so freaking odd to me. I saw him breathing though, so I knew he wasn't dead. Not that he could really die, but you know what I mean. His breath was shallow and his chest was the only thing that moved up and down like a sail slowly catching wind. And the other weird thing was that he didn't have any definition. Like, he was thin enough that I should be able to see his ribs, but I couldn't. Just smooth, waxy skin. It looked plastic. I wanted to touch it and see, but I couldn't reach that far and it would have been too much of an effort.

"Janko?'

"Yes, Rose."

"Do you understand what I'm saying? You seem very disinterested."

"Sorry, Rose. Yes, I do understand what you're saying. I'm just very interested in how weird these people have become. It is so unusual. I'm looking at Norm who has just flopped himself on the end of the bed with his knees over the edge. He's given up trying to strangle us ever since you suggested I don't take the drugs if I can help it. And I agree with you, I'm not gonna take them unless these friends of mine become unbearable. I think it's important for me to keep my mental clarity, to keep my wits about me, and I don't think that drugs will help that much. I won't be me then, you know? I won't have full and clear vision. It'd be like I was looking through a veil and I want to see clearly now. Especially now at the end I want…I need clarity at the end here. And also, I had made a promise to these figments, these friends of mine, that I wouldn't let them down and I wouldn't get rid of them through drugs."

There was a human sandwich happening now. MJ was on top of Norm face to face. Her body straight out and her arms straight out and her legs straight out too. She was lying on him for sure, but it was more like she was suspended on top of him and nearly weightless. Peter was on top of her. His back lying along her back. He was the mirror of Norm, also taking the corpse pose. And he also looked somewhat suspended on top of MJ. I figured it should have been too heavy for Norm, but he seemed to barely notice them, and they weren't sinking into the bed like you'd expect if they had been appropriate weights.

"Good," said Rose, "but I think you should take this up with Dr. Malichem. He'll be here in a little while and I think he needs to know about this. He might have different advice for you. Those are just my thoughts."

I looked at the clock. Those two little vertical, beady, bloody red eyes were still blinking at me. I got to thinking it might be the grim reaper's rat trying to gnaw his way out of my clock at me. But I wasn't scared. Come and get me, I'm ready. Yes, I am.

"I will, Rose. Thanks for your help and concern."

"Janko?"

"Yes," I said looking at Rose. She was still leaning on her elbows and looking at me steadily. Her hands were knitted together in a tight ball.

"You know that Dr. Malichem was trying to get some people to come and see you. That hasn't happened yet, has it?"

"No."

"Do you know who he might have been trying to get?"

"Yeah. He was going to bring his wife by. I'd like to meet her, I think she'll be a cool lady. And I'd like to get a sense of what his family life has been like. I guess, to be honest, maybe I'd like to have a peek at what my life might have been like. I mean, she could have ended up being my stepmother, if my father had found me or taken me in back then."

"Yes, I can only imagine. I'm sure she is a neat woman. But please don't put too much emotional weight into it. We can't change the past now, we can only try for a better future and live an authentic present."

"I know. These are just things that I think about, and which actually brings me comfort more than sorrow. Because, Rose, it's all possible, in my dreams anyway. I'm dying and it could have been possible that I'd have been a different boy, enjoying my seventh birthday just like a normal boy, rather than in a state institution. It makes me happy to think about how things could have been, actually. And maybe it'll make all the difference on the other side. Maybe then I'll get my fair share, a better chance at enjoying what was denied me here. No, what was stolen from me on this fucking journey, if you'll excuse me."

Rose nodded and looked at the floor. Her hands still knitted, her nails going white as she clung to herself harder than I think she realized.

"It does help me, Rose. I hope you believe that. It really does, because I've got nothing else to believe in now, other than my dreams of what might have been. And it helps. It helps to come to know the doctor as he is and you guys as you have been. I'm bathing in the milk of human kindness now, Rose. Don't sour my milk. Please. Don't sour my milk."

She looked up at me and unknotted her fingers.

"Sorry, Janko, I'm not meaning to rain on your parade. I just don't want you to cry over spilled milk, if you'll indulge me with the dairy analogy. We've all come so far with you. You've come so far by yourself and I just don't want us to lose any ground. Sometimes I think we're on a slippery slope here and I just want us to keep our footing sure."

Peter was now standing up and looking out at the window. MJ was standing next to Rose and trying to stroke her hair. Norm was sitting on the edge of the bed smiling at me and leaning on his one hand.

"But don't you see, Rose, that I trust in all of you now. That's what's going to keep me strong and true. I've come to trust in the realness of our relationships and the benefit that you've all offered me and the hope, too.

I've seen how you've all been behind me all the way and that has given me the confidence to continue on this path, which has been scary and lonely at times. You've all been there and that's what keeps me focused or my rudder steady, as you say. We're on solid ground because all of you guys are holding me up and supporting me. I'm strong now because you've all been strong for me. I'm at peace now because you've all been patient with me. I'm calm and content now because you've all believed in me."

I stopped there thinking I had done a pretty good job. I was pleased with how I'd just communicated my thoughts. Not bad for a guy on his deathbed, hey?

"Well said," said Peter as he turned around to face me, smiling, "but you forgot to mention how we've believed in you, too."

"It's inferred," I said.

"What's that, Janko?" asked Rose.

"Nothing, sorry, I was talking to Peter. He liked how I had put my thoughts but told me how I had forgotten to mention them, too, as being supportive. And I suppose they have, really. So there you are, Peter, I'm acknowledging you guys, too. Jesus, they're like insecure little children."

"What?" asked Norm.

"Who not what," responded MJ.

They were becoming idiotic again as they had earlier. Talking nonsense. Peter was scratching his crotch, the smooth skin, leaving straight red lines like prison bars. MJ was still trying to stroke Rose's hair.

"Looks alike, but it's not me, see?"

That was MJ talking to who knows, but she was looking at Rose.

"What am I going to do with these idiots, Rose? And I say that seriously, they're becoming like blabbering fools, making no sense at all."

Rose leaned back into the chair and rested her arms on the armrests. She crossed her legs over one another at the knee.

"I'd probably ignore them if you can, unless they're talking coherently to you. Otherwise you might just start encouraging them."

Norm was now lying on the floor next to my side of the bed and Peter was lying on top of him facing. It was all so bizarre. Again, it was like they were unaware of each other or made of a thin shell of plastic and hollow on the inside. They seemed so light, barely touching each other. And I noticed now that they weren't breathing either.

I looked at them each for several seconds, and not one of them was breathing. Their chests didn't move. Not even by a hair. I think that Rose was right. Maybe the sun was setting on my schizophrenic hallucination's empire.

"So, Janko, do you know who else Dr. Malichem is trying to get invited to your party?"

She smiled saying that.

"Yeah. He told me he was hoping to get that cop who found me at the church to come. He made a big impression on me, but I don't remember his name. He was one of the few people who were nice to me since my mother abandoned me. Other than social workers and people like that. I'm looking forward to seeing him, if he is still alive. I guess I need to thank him. He helped take care of me. I remember he bought me a chocolate milk and a bag of chips while we were waiting for social services to come and get me. And he would always keep in touch with me every so often and he actually got me out of a couple of the worst foster care situations. And then, once I was with the Antolinis and he found out that they were good people, I guess he figured I was fine, and I lost contact with him then. But it was always comforting when he checked in on me from time to time. You have no idea how much it meant to me, just to know that there was someone out there who cared about my welfare. Especially when I was in some of those really shitty homes that you guys probably already know about."

"I can only imagine that he must have been very important and helpful at that time. It makes me happier that you had at least a few people, if only a scarce few, that were helpful and kind to you. I wonder what might have happened if you hadn't even had that."

"I'm sure I'd be dead or in jail, Rose."

I fiddled with my hands in my lap. It was true. I most likely would have ended up dead or in jail. Probably in jail, I figure. I had a lot of anger, as you can probably tell, and I was ready to spray that all over society, but then the Antolinis came by and after that I was just too tired and getting too sick in the head to become criminal. And maybe they had a greater effect on me than I realize.

"Anyone else he's trying to get?"

Rose was settled nicely into the chair, her arms still resting on the armrests. MJ had left her alone by now and was sitting on the edge of the bed where Norm had been. She was looking at me with a stupid smile on her face like she was mentally retarded or something.

"Yeah, I think the good doctor is trying to get the Antolinis to come by, too, but I'd be surprised if they were even alive. When I was with them they seemed old. I'd guess around fifty or something like that and that has to be around twenty years ago or more by now. But I'd love to see them, too. I think they gave me a real opportunity at a life that seemed stable if only for a little while. I just wish it could have lasted longer. That stupid bitch who was also an orphan and living with them told her social worker that they had sexually molested her. It was total bullshit. They were never like that, she was just upset because they had rules and she was doing drugs with this asshole of a boyfriend and staying out all night and being a bad influence on us other three foster kids. She was the oldest then, too, probably fourteen or something. Such a whore. I'm sorry, Rose, but she was, okay? And then they were investigated, but by the time that had ended we'd all been shipped off elsewhere. Me to fucking hell. Lily was her name. They used to call her Lily of the valley as a nickname when she was still a good girl. Lily. Fucking bitch was named after a flower and she was so damn poisoned. Go figure. I just don't get it. Sorry, Rose, I'm trying to watch my tongue, but I hadn't thought of that girl, woman by now, until now. And she just gets my blood boiling. She robbed me of a decent life too. Two women, Rose, can you imagine? Two women who have robbed me of the best life I could have had. My mother and a roommate. No wonder I've had a bad attitude towards women for so long. Anyway where were we?"

MJ was still giving me that idiot grin. I glared at her. I liked her better when she was young and pretty and real. As real as she could have been. I haven't forgotten they're all figments of my imagination, okay.

"I think you've done pretty good, Janko, considering you've had four female nurses. Speaking for myself, I can't say that I've ever felt you being personally vitriolic towards me or any of us. You've had your anger for sure, but that has always seemed to spring from your personal hell and has often been directed towards those that maybe deserved that anger. So, don't beat yourself up about it. I was just thinking of the irony when you were talking about Lily. I'm named after a flower too. Maybe I'll be able to change your mind about women named after flowers."

"You already have, Rose. You already have, and I never even considered the comparison when I was talking about Lily. You guys are just so totally different. Not even in the same game, let alone different leagues."

I looked at my hands. The palms and then the back of my hands. I had noticed that my nails seemed to be growing way slower lately than they used to. Maybe it was my imagination but they always seemed short and I never chewed them, either.

"We were talking about who's coming to your going away party. You had mentioned that Dr. Malichem was going to try and get the Antolinis to come."

I looked up at her. I was finding it hard to concentrate. All sorts of things kept pulling at my attention. The blue square of my window. My hands, for Christ's sake.

"Yeah, the Antolinis. I'll be happy to see them if they're still alive. They were really good people. Maybe they gave me just enough hope to keep on the straight and narrow. I've always been a little surprised that I never turned into some sort of criminal. Maybe it's thanks to them, and maybe also, thanks to my mental illness. It's hard you know, to keep up with society when your mind is playing tricks on your reality. I don't know how I would have had the mental capacity to be doing crimes and not getting caught right off the bat."

"Yes, I think you're right. It's probably aspects of both. But then, don't underestimate the power of kindness. It might have done more for you than you realize. Is it not our kindness now that is enabling you to make these tremendous gains in such a short time? I would never have thought it would be possible to heal so quickly and come to terms so hopefully with your past and pain as you have managed to do. That, in my mind, Janko, is the power of kindness. You spoke of it yourself not too long ago when you mentioned the milk of human kindness."

"Mmmm...milk of human kindness. Can I have some chocolate kind, if it please your kindness?" said MJ.

She was lying on top of me now looking up at the ceiling. I couldn't feel her at all, she was weightless. Her head was resting in my lap. I hadn't had a woman's head in my lap in years and I remembered it fondly, too, if you'll indulge me a little sexual memory.

I looked at the rest of her body as it stretched out over my legs. She was naked and how I wished that she was a fine specimen of woman. But she wasn't. No breasts. No pubic hair. No slit between her legs. Not that I could do anything about it and I know she's just a hallucination, but still, can't a dying man have some final visual enjoyment if nothing else? All I had were memories. Memories of sex that was so far distant I didn't trust their authenticity. When most of your memories have been shit, you start to doubt you've ever had good ones.

"I've got some vanilla milk for you, MJ. Come have a sample, hey?" said Norm as he grabbed at his crotch, which was nothing but smoothness. MJ looked over at him.

"No way, Norm, I want some chocolate milk. The kind that's thick and warm, Norm. Not a dribble, but a shower, now that's power. Kindness flower into a tower."

"Stop it…you morons, just stop it," I said.

Rose got up and came over to me.

"What's wrong, Janko?"

I watched MJ roll over and off the bed landing on top of Peter, she was still looking up at the ceiling.

"It's my friends, Rose. They're talking nonsense with sexual overtones and it's driving me nuts. I don't see how this is going to be helpful to me."

"Maybe you should be thinking of some medication for it?"

Rose was touching my forehead again. Checking my temperature or something.

"No, Joe, not the pills, Bills." That was Peter now, the one who had been the most unaffected by everyone else's babble.

"Shhh…quiet as a mouse in this house. No noise little toys."

Norm speaking to Peter. Looked more like they were kissing each other. MJ had her finger over her lips. I was getting tired, my breathing was hard and heavy and rattling in my throat. Was this how I was gonna die? A mad man trapped inside the decaying filth of my own mind. God I hoped not.

"Help me, Rose. I don't want to go out like this. Not with the lights flickering and dimming in my own mind."

I clutched at her hand. I didn't even recognize my own limb. It looked skeletal and the skin on it was old and scaly. Dry and wilted. Dead. My eyes were getting wet and acid poured out of them.

"It's okay, Janko. Just try to ignore them. The doctor will be here soon and you can talk about the anti-psychotics with him. It might be a valid option now. I'll sit with you on the edge of the bed for a while if you'd like."

I nodded my head. Still looking at my hallucinations. I couldn't call them friends because that was the last thing they were to me now. Rose sat on the edge of the bed and took a tissue from my side table and dabbed at the tears slinking down my cheeks. She held my hand in both of hers. The white tissue like a flag of defeat between her fingers. I was done. I gave up. I was ready to be called home. Those three friends of mine who had once been helpful to me. Had once kept me sane and alive through the madness that had been my daily bread. Now they were the insanity killing me. How could I just ignore them when it was my own mind which had created this crap in the first place? I just didn't see how. How do you ignore your own thoughts? Especially the mad ones that just rattle around like ping pong balls with no stopping. Maybe if you were a Zen monk you could do it. But a sick man like me, I don't see how. Especially a mentally sick man like me. I just couldn't see it happen.

Rose still held my hand. She dabbed at my cheeks again. The tissue was getting soggy and it folded over her hand as she brought it back down to hold mine. The defeat seemed imminent, the white flag was impotent, and so was I.

"Sad is bad. J, why do you cry today?" said MJ.

"Shhh. No sound from this fleshy mound," said Peter.

"Sad is mad and mad is bad and dad the doctor is bad and Bill's pills are sad. So don't cry me a river, I'll dry that sliver and make you quiver. Straight as an arrow decay down to bone marrow. The morning sparrow catches the worm turns in the grave and we all end up a slave to this life is strife."

That last one was Norm. I kept looking at them and wondering why the fuck everything had to rhyme. They weren't making any sense, but with Rose comforting me I didn't feel like I had to dissolve into their madness. No one could hear them except for me and as long as I didn't start babbling on like them, then I figured maybe I could retain a drop of my sanity and salvage a dignified death.

"Just try to ignore them, Janko," said Rose, "I think that the more capable you are of managing that, the easier it will be for you to bring back control over them. Just keep trying. Focus on me, think about other things. Look around and focus on your surroundings. Whatever it takes to make it easier to ignore them. Here, let's turn on the radio."

She pushed the sleep button and fiddled with the dial and tuned in some easy listening station. It was quite nice, actually. No song. Just melody of some brass or wind instruments. It helped me focus on the music and not on my hallucinations although I noticed MJ's mouth moving but I couldn't hear what she was saying.

I closed my eyes and tried to snatch sleep but I couldn't get much. I was too scared that if I fell asleep then Rose would leave and that was the last thing I wanted. I couldn't stand to be left alone at the moment. Not now. Not when I was on the verge of a premature mental death occurring before my physical demise.

Rose was looking off at the door as if waiting for someone to pop by. She patted my hands every so often. I'd close my eyes and get scared so I opened them again. Then I'd look outside again at the blue sky and the pokey telephone poles. The wires looked like weary smiles on a ventriloquist's dummy. This blue rectangle that had come to seem so important in my life. This postcard that I wanted to take with me to the other side. What did it all mean? Life was lived like a slide show, wasn't it? Memories captured as photographs and pictures, only the present seemed to have a fluid, movie like quality to it. The rest were pictures and we sat like old men rifling through them so focused on the past, not even watching the present slip by. These old pictures that were stained and dog-eared and faded. They didn't matter and yet we held them so close to our heart, so dear to our soul. There's me smiling when I was six years old, there's me having my first kiss. Meanwhile, Rose holding my hand now becomes numbed out and all that matters is this frigging slide show in my head of my dismal past. And yet, I bet we all do it. Don't you? I suppose it can't be helped. It seems that it's only the pleasant postcards of our past that we keep and we especially refer to them in times of trouble. The problem with me is that I never had much of a chance to develop many positive memories. And as I rifle through them with my mind's hand, I bet you, there are only about a dozen or so. And they're so old it's like I hardly believe they're real. Could be someone else's memories I've collected.

"Do you ever think about your past, Rose?"

She looked at me then and stopped patting my hands. Her gaze was steady.

"Sure, I think we all do. Don't you?"

"Absolutely, but it's like I'm looking at postcards and small little snaps of time that seemed pleasant. And I get to wondering if we're just wasting our time looking at the rear-view mirror rather than our surroundings or the road ahead of us. Like, are we wasting our time with the past when the present is just slipping by?"

She kept looking at me, still holding my hands. My tears had dried up, but I couldn't look at her. I was embarrassed. Not so much at my crying, but more at the fragile state of mind that my friends had put me in.

"I guess, Janko, it depends on how and why you spend time reflecting on the past. Sometimes we need to view the past in the soberness of the present in order to appreciate the mistakes we've made and to learn from them. But on the other hand, if we're dwelling on the past because we're unhappy with the present, then that is a very different issue and I would say not likely to be beneficial. Sometimes we look at the past through rose colored glasses, and that's problematic. If you're doing that then you're obviously attempting to escape or minimize problems in the present. And that will only make things worse. I don't think that's something that you're doing though, Janko. It seems to me that you are proactively taking an interest in the present and your mental health in the here and now. That's important and good too."

I looked at her and then outside and then at my hands. My fingers looked like skeletal twigs covered by thin cloth. They were the hands and fingers of a dead man. And I couldn't figure out how death wasn't somehow a violent painful end. I mean, sure I'd be in pain without my morphine, but not the excruciating acute pain of a violent end. It didn't seem right. Maybe we made death out to be a macabre, ugly thing because we were so damn scared of it. We figure something that snuffs out life has to be a horrible monster.

And it caught me by surprise, I'll tell you that for free. Looking at myself wasting away here, I'm thinking how come death can be so easy, so quiet, so unobtrusive. I moved my fingers, watching the twigs bend and not break. I wasn't brittle yet. This death, this masked man, he seemed to be more friend than foe.

At least for me. At least the way I saw it. If I could just gently drift off to sleep, die like that, cradled and carried off in his arms without much fuss. That'd be okay. I wouldn't complain. I mean, how bad can the other side be if death is a gentle friend? I'm ready to be carried away. I'm ready for those distant shores. This view in my rear-view mirror isn't so pretty anyway. It looks nice over yonder on that other side.

"Janko? Did you hear me?"

I looked at her then, bending my fingers back and forth. The twigs bending, not breaking. I was greatly amused by that. They didn't seem like my hands, my fingers. Rose wasn't smiling.

"Yes, thank you, Rose. I did hear you. I just got to thinking about the fact that I'm dying and how pleasant that is in a way. The lack of pain. The way the body just slowly evaporates into nothingness. I mean, as we speak, I feel my life slipping away like sands in an hourglass. It's weird. Soon I'll be dead and all of this will be memory for you, and nothing for me. Just this cloth that once held my life."

"That's a little macabre, Janko. I was talking about how well you're doing focusing on healing and the present."

Now I patted her hands with mine. Hers were so thick and meaty like clay sculpted by an artist. Nice hands. Just so fat next to mine.

"I know, Rose. And can't you see I am focusing on the present. And the present has me dying. Yes, you could say it's macabre. But I'm ready now in a different way than I was before. So that's good, isn't it? To be in the present rather than the past like I was talking about before."

"Well, yes, but sometimes, as I said, you need to look into the past and learn from it."

She was making as much sense as the three musketeers on the floor over there.

"I understand, Rose. But seriously, what am I going to learn from the past that is going to help me with dying, when I do. Which could be any minute, actually. I mean, what I've got to focus on, which the good doctor my dad says, is to forgive my past and myself and come to a place of peace and kindness in the here and now. That's what I've managed to do. Going back and dredging up all that ugly shit is only going to make me feel worse, to be honest with you."

She looked over at MJ and Peter and Norm. They were now all lying side by side. They were holding hands. Actually, that's a little wrong. They were melted together at the hands like those paper cut outs you used to do as a kid. Little stumps where they're arms joined together. I don't think Rose could actually see them. She was probably looking at the carpet.

"You can't see them, can you?"

"No," she said, "I was just thinking that Dr. Malichem is going to be here soon. And I was also thinking that Salima and Maria and Veronica should be here soon, too."

"I thought they were here already?"

"No, not today, Janko. Yesterday we had all of us here to see how you were doing and intermittently for a few days before that. But I've called them over, because you don't look well and you've said as much."

Now she was being the macabre one.

"Are you okay, Janko?" she said.

"Yes, I am. I just didn't expect you to point out the fact to me that I was on death's door."

"Come on, Janko. You said as much just moments ago."

"Yeah, I suppose. It's just odd how you said I was being macabre when you're being just as forthright as I was back then."

"I think I just misunderstood you. Let's not get upset over it. I'm glad and very encouraged by how well you've done with your progress, Janko. I guess I just didn't want the inevitable to come so soon if at all."

"The inevitable?"

"Yes. You dying. I guess I'm not fully prepared for that, at the moment."

There was silence then for a while. I watched my idiot friends for a while mouthing silent words at the ceiling. It was working just ignoring them.

"No, it's not," said Peter, "we've just been pretending, letting you think you were mending."

Fucking clowns. I didn't care. They weren't that important to me, anymore. Just pathetic losers.

"If you guys don't watch it, I'm gonna have you murdered with the anti-psychotic drugs. And don't think I'm not kidding, okay?"

"Ooohh…Such a mean man, with such a mean plan. Maybe we should give him the can first?" Norm was speaking to the other two.

"Just try me," I said.

"Just ignore them," said Rose, and she was right.

There was a knock on the door. The good doctor's triple rap. He must have been let in by someone exiting the building.

"I'll just go and get the door, Janko, it's probably Dr. Malichem, I think. Now do me a favor and just ignore your hallucinations. Try not to pay them any attention."

I nodded and closed my eyes. Not that I'd sleep, my father was here, but I might just rest a bit. See no evil and hopefully evil would be gone.

I'd done this lots of times. The climb up the stairs and the walk down the long hallway to Janko's apartment. I'd come to enjoy the place. It had come to have a familiarity about it and a warmth. A place where I'd felt almost at home. I stared at the door now. It's wooden veneer smooth with just the tell-tale signs of nicks and scrapes from people moving their lives in and out of it. I looked down the hallway and noticed how the carpet was duller in the middle where people trudged and trekked their lives up and down and all around town. I looked at the door again and at the peephole. I saw a darkness move towards it and heard the bolt unlock. I had brought some donuts thinking that it might be something Janko would eat. And for the guests too. I had a dozen of them, more than enough I figured. Rose's head peeked around behind the door as she opened it. We said our hellos.

"Are the other's here, yet?" I asked.

"No, but you could've been them. I'm sure they'll be here momentarily."

I walked into the entranceway and took my shoes off, handing Rose the box of donuts and the three coffees that I had bought for the three of us. I thought I'd be the first one to arrive. And it was just as well. I couldn't have managed ten or so coffees.

"How's he doing?" I asked her as we walked into the kitchen and Rose pulled out a couple of large plates to put the donuts on.

"Not well frankly. I can't imagine him lasting more than a few days if you ask me. And he's struggling with his hallucinations. They're acting up in inappropriate ways."

"What did you tell him to do? Did you give him any advice?"

"Yes. I told him to try and ignore them as best as possible and to talk to you about drug options. Not that he has the time for that, but I thought it might help him cope knowing that there were options available. And it seems that the part of him that manifests the hallucinations is upset by that, so I thought it might help to alleviate some of the symptoms."

She looked at me seeking approval. Or so I thought.

"Good. That's good. I think that's about the only thing you could have done."

I looked down at the linoleum floor. The blotched and patterned face of it belied its cleanliness. I was not surprised by Janko's state. The last time I'd seen him, only last week, I didn't think he had very long to go. I just hope I was able to have the next few hours with him. That's all I wanted. I hoped that he would last through the day to meet everyone who was coming. If we had at least that much time then I'd be content. Happy no, but content, yes.

"So who else have you been able to get to come for our visit?"

I looked up at her and she was creating pyramids out of the donuts. It looked nice, but wouldn't take long to be messed up.

"Robert Peel is coming this morning around eleven. My wife will be here soon, and I've been able to get Alfredo and Gabriella Antolini to come, too. They should be here soon. They were very excited to hear from me and about Janko. Though they didn't seem so surprised that Janko's life had turned out as horribly as it had. They also asked if they could bring anything for him, but I told them that it would likely be pointless."

We picked up the coffees and took them to the living room. I went in to see Janko.

"How are you doing, Janko?"

Rose was right. He didn't look too good. I checked his IV, not sure why, maybe I was getting paternal on him. He was ashen with a waxy, yellow sheen and his skin seemed fragile and brittle. It wouldn't be long now at all. And I was sad. His death now was becoming apparent to me in a very real way. I had to stop a lump in my throat from burning too hotly in my chest. I turned away from him and walked towards the door.

"I'm okay, Michael, dad."

I liked it when he called me "dad", though I understood the difficulty in it for him. But at this end stage in the game, why not create some familiarity, some familial bonds even if they were a little forced. I turned back to face him and smiled as bravely as I could. I was carrying his coffee in my hand. I looked at it and it felt hot. I looked at his hand and it wasn't mine. There was nothing familiar about our hands. I wanted to reach out with my hands and hold him. But I felt awkward and frozen.

"I've got you a coffee here. Would you like it here or should I take it back into the living room? Rose and I will be out there having our coffees. I need to talk to her alone for a moment. Is that okay?"

"Yeah that's okay. I want to rest for a few minutes anyway. I'm so tired, dad. I think I'm dying," he smiled at that, "I mean, like, I think I'm dying soon. I think I'm already on my way out."

"I know son," I said with my eyes brimming.

"Take the coffee into the living room. I'll try and join you there soon if I can."

He was talking to me through the back of his eyes which was a good thing. I wasn't handling this reality very well. I looked at his bedside table. The clock was a red ten oh one. The colon blinking between the two sets of numbers. It was a palindrome, maybe. A numerical palindrome. We were living life forward or backwards. Didn't matter it all ended the same way. That gave me some hope in an odd way. Maybe Janko's life was meant to be like this, to have ended up this way. For him, for me and maybe for all of us. I don't know much about mathematics, but it seems to answer a lot of questions. The way things add up seems too rhythmical to be coincidental all the time. Perhaps there are guiding hands involved in the lives we live. But I didn't want to go down that road. It could make you end up depressed. And I was sad enough as it was.

"You're getting a lot of visitors today son. I've been able to firm up everyone I was trying to get to come and visit you. Officer Robert Peel said he'll be here. My wife will be here soon and I know the Antolinis are very excited to see you, too."

"Thanks, Michael, for arranging that. I'm happy with it. It'll be nice to see familiar and kind faces that I haven't seen in a while."

It was ten oh two, now. We're living in forward time. There was no stopping the inevitable now. We were on a path that was no longer stalled. Ten oh one had paused time for a moment. But now we were gaining steam on a forward motion. The grim reaper was pulling the carpet of life towards him. We couldn't get off now. Janko was tired. His breath was shallow and quick. I tried to pull back on the carpet, but I had no grip. I felt hopeless. My throat burned and my vision blurred. The coffee was hot in my hand, and the carpet was hard under my feet.

"I'll take your coffee out to the living room and wait for you there son. Or I'll be back in soon if I don't see you in five minutes or so. Okay?"

He nodded weakly and mumbled his agreement.

"I love you," I said as I walked out feeling soft. But I didn't care. It was good, it was necessary, and it was never a sign of weakness. You could never be a tough guy if you didn't have a soft spot for the weak. And my soft spot was a pulpy, mushy piece of meat at the moment. I dabbed at my eyes and sat down in the armchair I had come to call my own. I almost took a sip of Janko's coffee before realizing. I put it down and picked up my own one.

"How are you doctor?"

"Geez, Rose, to be honest with you I'm sad, actually. For the first time I've really come to see the end of this part of my journey as being very close. I don't even know if I'll get a chance to have another session with Janko. Not that he needs it. He's been doing so well. But I sure could use more time with him."

"I know how you feel. We're all sad, too. I've come to grow fond of him, even from his early grumpy days. And especially now with how well he's come to an acceptance and peace with himself. We're all sad. He's left an indelible mark on all of us."

"Yes, he has, Rose. And it's the goodbyes that are so hard. I don't think it ever gets easier. Not that I've had a lot of practice thank God. But I don't think it gets easier. I keep wondering if I've done everything that I could've. Was there anything that I might have done differently? Was I kind enough and supportive enough? So many questions, you know. So many doubts."

Rose got up from the other armchair. She picked up the plate of donuts and offered me one.

"I think we could both use a little sweet indulgence," she said.

I took a blueberry fritter and bit down on it, almost spilling jam down my chin. Rose had chosen a maple glazed.

"He's told me, Michael, that he is so happy to have found you and had you counsel him. He believes, and I'd agree, that you have been instrumental in helping him heal the best way he can in such a short time. The only thing to doubt, if you'll let me be so bold, is God's compassion and love for us that he lets this happen to such a gentle soul. And I do think Janko, underneath it all, is a very sensitive and gentle soul."

I nodded. He was, and I guess that's one of the most attractive things about him, that sensitivity that we all saw beneath the frosty and belligerent layers of his protective self. I sipped my coffee and chewed on my donut. It was an infrequent indulgence and Rose was right. It did make me feel better.

"I feel like we're in the waiting room at a funeral parlor or a dentist's office. It would be great if some of the others would arrive soon," I said.

"I know. It's such a great day to be having visitors for Janko, and for getting all of us together. The sun is shining. The sky is baby blue. If I had to die, Michael, I'd choose a day like today."

"Yes, you're right, Rose. It isn't the worse thing that can happen to us. It's only part of the on-going journey of life and of the soul. Sometimes though, the theoretical aspects of death are easier to stomach than the harsh reality of it. The way I've become more at peace with the idea of a loving God allowing horrendous suffering, is with the idea of karma. Maybe, in a way that we don't understand, Janko, or his spirit, chose this life before he was born to learn from past mistakes or maybe even to gain greater enlightenment. Honestly, Rose, I'm not sure I would have turned out half as well as he has if I'd been given even a small percentage of the hardships he's been under."

"Yes, I suppose you're right. I generally try and stay away from thinking about the suffering inherent in the human experience. My mind seems so confined and constrained in understanding the complexities. I like your idea of karma, but if I think too hard on that, then I just get myself eaten up inside about the lack of current knowledge of past errors. How would one be able to make appropriate compensation for incidents that you can't even recollect? But I have to agree with you, it does seem a more satisfying way of coping or explaining this inherent difficulty with being alive."

"I know. And I think of how well Janko has done in this relatively short time. He's had these months with us in learning or paying for any karmic debts he might have had. I'm really encouraged by his progress and the ability he has shown in moving beyond the pain that he has suffered for so long. I'd like to focus on that aspect of his life. The growth he has been able to achieve with, I'd like to think, our help."

Rose smiled at me and took a bite of her donut. I shoved the rest of mine in my mouth and she still had half of hers left. I was tempted to take another one, but none of them did I enjoy as much as the fritter. I should have saved that one for my second one. I hadn't eaten breakfast. I looked at the plate of donuts longingly, but none of them were sexy enough. I sipped on my coffee, which was great, except it got rid of the lingering taste of donut in my mouth. The paper cup was still hot in my hand but not uncomfortable, like Janko's had been. I put the coffee down and looked at my hands. I pushed back the cuticles and ran my fingers over the vertical ridges on my thumbnail. I looked at the back of my hands. Coarse hair stuck out like antennae or a field of stiff grass. My hands were dry, dusted white on the outside.

"Do you have any hand cream?" I asked Rose.

She fished around in her bag for some and gave it to me. It felt wet and greasy as it dried. My hands felt softer and smoother. I thanked Rose and gave it back to her. I was looking at myself in a new light. There seemed to be no resemblance between Janko and me. Not in our hands, he was almost hairless, and not in our faces. Yet there was some invisible thread that tied us together, and it wasn't the knowledge that we had come to know each other as biologically entwined. It was more than that; I had felt a special connection to him since I had first met him. There was something remarkable about him that I saw buried deep within. And there was this thread between us, as if we had squashed our thumbprints on the thick, moist putty of each other's souls. If you'll allow me some leniency, I'd say that we had been kin to each other long before we had come to know one another as such. If you'll buy into my theory of the soul's journey being a continuum and not a linear path from birth to death, then it should be probable that we had come to know each other in a spiritual sense before this mortal journey. Perhaps we had made a pact with one another to meet up towards the end. But what that pact stipulated I don't think I'd ever know. And was I doing everything possible to honor that contract? Maybe you'd be the judge and a kindly one at that.

I got up out of my chair clutching my coffee. I looked at the molasses color of it and swirled it around in my hand. These tangible things, these material objects cemented me, however loosely, to the present reality while my mind drifted and danced frantically with theoretical arguments designed to, hopefully, make me feel better with the current predicament. It worked only to a degree. Intellectualization was such a poor salve for the emotional pain that we endure. And this life, this soul's journey on earth, was an emotional one. And the only way to enlighten one's soul, as I saw it, was to survive the emotional Treblinka that goaded us through this life. And no amount of thought or intelligence or intellectualizing could overcome that lesson. Life was a boiling, choppy emotional sea. The best we could do was to keep the rudder steady and get to the other shore and hopefully enjoy the ride.

I looked over at Rose as she sat watching me and sipping her coffee. I smiled at her. It was a cagey smile, she knew it and I knew it, but she smiled back. We were veterans already in the war of life. Compadres that had fought together long enough to allow each other the discretion needed in times of turmoil. In times of battle. This battle with the self, primarily, and I knew that the aftermath would be littered with corpses that would take time to bury. We both knew that. When Janko passed, the real pain would just begin for us who had been touched by his life. His lust for life, which had lately become so apparent.

I walked over to the balcony doors. I stared out at the skeletal twigs and rangy branches of the trees. They were like ghouls frozen in their outrage at heaven. Their arms outstretched and stuck in pointing accusations beyond the shroud of our sky. There was no snow on them and no bulging little buds. We were in the throes of winter. The wasteland of death. How apropos. The chimneys of the houses across the street vented their frustrations in steady streams of steam. Waving beards or perhaps white flags. I was getting maudlin as you could tell. But I was struggling with impending loneliness and thick sadness that cloaked me in its prickly, cold blanket. At least the sky was blue, as Rose had said. But blue had a mixed meaning anyway.

I heard the buzzer. Rose got up to answer it.

"Hello," she said.

"Hi. It's Margaret. Dr. Malichem's wife."

The voice crackled and hissed through the intercom. Not at all how Margaret sounded in person.

"How nice of you to come. Please come up," said Rose as she buzzed Margaret in. And her voice was sincere.

"That was your wife, Michael," she said.

"Thanks, Rose."

I turned around and looked into the kitchen. Rose had made her way there. I sipped on my coffee. I was making quick work of it.

"Would you mind making a pot of coffee, Rose? Looks like our guests are beginning to arrive."

"I was just thinking the same thing."

I was looking forward to Margaret coming. I was going to lean on her for support. She could keep my mind off the macabre and help me focus on my professional duties. She had the objectivity of not having met Janko before. And that was needed now more than ever. Especially amongst a roomful of emotionally attached people.

I fidgeted. I drank the rest of my coffee and walked towards the door to wait for Margaret. On my way I picked up a donut without thinking much. What the hell, it was a chocolate glaze. It would do, and I was fairly certain that Margaret wouldn't have any. Besides, there were more than enough.

I heard the buzzer and wondered who it could be. I heard Rose tell my dad it was his wife. The party was beginning. I lay in bed. I was now too tired to get up. I was the man of the hour and people were coming to visit me, so visit me they must. I looked around for my friends, if that's what they were. MJ saw me looking at her.

"We're okay, now," she said.

"How can I be certain?" I asked.

"'Cause we haven't called you Fred and you ain't dead." That was Peter.

"Funny, you guys are fucking hilarious. I'm not going to listen to you as long as you're wasting my time with your insanity."

I looked up at the ceiling. It's pimpled, yellow face, and I wanted a cigarette. Something to do.

"Listen shmisen. You've never heard us because you're a turd, yes," said Norm.

I was ignoring them. Like Rose said, and I'm sure like the good doctor would tell me, too. No use in encouraging them.

"We the undersigned, will not be maligned," said Peter.

"Yes 'tis true Drew. And how sad sits the dying man, now mad," said Norm.

They were a tag team of poor humor and childishness. Still I looked on at the ceiling, imagining myself a small bacterium slipping across its face. My ceiling would be a whole world and my apartment the universe. I wondered if bacteria think about the bigger questions of eternity and infinity. Only because I was trying to ignore the ignorant losers that had splintered from my mind. I was surely a universe to the bacterium, and yet they could hop to Rose, let's say, a whole other universe. I wondered if we had the same choice. Maybe death was just a wormhole to another dimension, another earth where we get to do things over again. Maybe the same way, maybe under different circumstances, but in any event without the gift of hindsight. That had to be God's ultimate irony if it was the case. Watch us like little Atlases shrugging worlds up mountains and each time we slip down and start anew we have no frigging clue that we've just hopelessly tried the very same thing before.

"Do you think he's deaf, Jeff? Or is he just dumb, chum?" asked Peter.

"Could be he's just a little odd, Rod. You know he's dying and not even crying," said Norm.

I was starting to wonder if it was worse thinking of the miserably infinite possibilities of death and dimension or of listening to those morons. I wanted a coffee now, and a cigarette. At least with a cigarette I could blow smoke up their asses like they were trying to do to me. I looked outside and pretended to use the telephone poles to pick at my teeth. MJ appeared in my periphery and I looked at her, mostly because she was naked and I wanted to see if she was a woman or a mannequin. She was a mannequin.

"Sorry, Janko. I'm not going to play those silly games with you," she said.

I patted at the edge of the bed, close to where I was lying. She sat down on it. It would have been a whole lot more enjoyable for me if she was a naked woman rather than this sexless doll. But I was dying and I knew my mind was slowly failing me. It wouldn't even give the pretend thrill of seeing my hallucination as a naked fully endowed woman.

"You can stay with me then, MJ. But I'm not going to listen to Peter or Norm as long as they're being stupid."

She took my hand and patted it and held it in both of hers.

"Will you listen to that tool? How cruel, Norm," said Peter.

"I hear you, good buddy, that's bloody rubbish and snobbish," said Norm.

MJ looked at them sternly. I didn't bother; I was getting better at it. Ignoring them, that is. I couldn't stop hearing them, but I could ignore it and not let it affect me.

"Don't worry, MJ. They're just not going to be able to enjoy these last moments with me. And you."

She smiled at me and looked at me for a long time.

"I wish you were real so you could go and get the doctor. I'm thirsty for some coffee, and I thought I heard him say he brought something good to eat, too. I wouldn't mind a bite of something you know. My last supper. But you can't help me, can you?"

She shook her head at me. At least she was being sincere. Better than the other losers who still lay on the floor like dirty, discarded socks.

There was a knock at the door. I had seen Margaret come up to it, as I had had my eye glued to it, like a kid on Christmas morning. She came up to it distorted and rounded by the peephole. She gave it a tentative knock and looked back down the hallway the way she had come. I was wondering if she was thinking of escaping back that way. I was glad she had come, though. I needed her now, more than ever. I opened the door and let her in. She gave me a peck on the cheek.

"Thanks for coming, honey," I said.

"I told you I would."

We walked into the living room and Rose said hello.

"We've got some donuts if you'd like and I think Rose is just making some coffee. But you could have tea or water or something, if you'd like."

I was a nervous host; or a nervous boy on his first date. But there was so much riding on these next few hours. Hours that could well be within the last double digits of hours that Janko might have left. I wanted things to go well. No glitches for him, but especially for me. I needed this to be perfect if only for my own closure.

"No donut, thanks, love, and I'd love some coffee when it's ready."

We sat down on the couch together. We both sat upright. Stoically. I was leaning a little forward and twisted towards her. I had her hands in mine and mine were rested on her knee.

"How are you doing, love?" she asked.

"Nervous, scared and for some reason I'm overwhelmingly sad now, too."

Rose busied herself in the kitchen. Not that she needed too, she was being kind, giving us our space. Margaret hugged me.

"I know, Mike. I know. But I'm really proud of you and all the help you've offered him. Given him and all your other patients. You've been down this road before and you'll manage just fine. Don't put any undue pressure on yourself. You've done everything that you can to ensure his transition to the other side. You've helped him immensely to cope with the way his life was, and you've given him the opportunity to find peace and closure with that. I know all this because of how you've talked to me about him."

"Thanks, honey. I know you're right. It's just so much easier when you're not as emotionally entangled in their lives as I have become with Janko, even if it is only at the intellectual level. I don't know, maybe I'm just judging myself to harshly for this because I'm his father and I'm kin to him. But I shouldn't really. If anything it should be easier because I've never really had that familial or paternal bond with him that I imagine would really create a catastrophic emotional loss for me. I think that is how I will try and look at it for now. See the positive aspect of the knowledge of a family connection and the benefit of wanting so much more for him because of that, but without the emotional turmoil, that if I'm honest, I really don't feel."

"Exactly, my love. And I'm here and the other guests will be here soon. You've managed a real coup in getting everyone together for this young man. Focus on your achievements. This is really, Mike, your hour of excellence. This is where you shine. This is what your life's work has been all about. There can be nothing more satisfying than supporting and nurturing a soul onto their next journey."

"Yes, it is rewarding in a way. Especially if I can come to acknowledge, as you say, my work in this. That I can get to that point and sit back and say to myself

'Yes, I've done the best I can for him and it hasn't been that bad at all.' Then I will be able to say that this is one of the most rewarding times of my life. But nonetheless, the parting always seems bitter sweet."

Margaret smiled sadly, knowingly.

"I know," she said, "I always feel melancholy when I think of all the people in my life that I have lost. My grandparents, especially my grandfather Eric, my mother's father. And of course when my mother was taken too. It's always hard my love. I've lost more people than you have, and I can tell you that it never gets easier. That's why I don't like funerals and these sorts of things."

She gestured around her with her arms, embracing the apartment in a swoop, a dive of arms.

"You're right, Mike. It is bitter sweet. The celebration of the life and the achievements and the sadness of the actual passing. But time makes it so that you can come around to enjoy the sweet more often, again, than the bitter."

"I know," I said, "I know. Thanks for your insight and encouragement, honey."

"You're welcome. I think the key now is to focus on the living. This is a celebration of Janko's life right? Not his funeral. There will be time later for the tears. The many tears, I'm sure."

I embraced her and kissed her. She had a way. You know what I mean.

"Coffee, anyone?" asked Rose.

We both asked for some and I picked up Janko's mug. It was still quite warm. I waited for my own mug and decided I'd go and check on him.

"I'm just going to go and pop in on Janko quickly, if you don't mind. I'll be right back."

"Would you like me to join you, Mike?" asked Rose.

"No. I want just a few moments to myself and to see when he might be ready to start entertaining guests."

I took my mug from the table and grabbed a donut with hundreds and thousands on it. I placed it precariously on the top of Janko's paper cup and carefully made my way to his room.

"Mike, dad, you're a God send. I was so desperately looking for something to drink. Coffee, particularly. And a donut, too. You must have read my mind."

He placed the coffee with the donut on top of it on my side table.

"It's still quite warm, but probably just about right to drink."

"How about a taste? Not a drop to waste. Be a good lad to your dad," said Norm.

My father's feet were plunged deeply into Norm's chest but he was oblivious. They both were. MJ looked on at me and smiled, not saying a word, just shaking her head. Probably at Norm and Peter, if I had to guess. I reached for my coffee, leaving the donut shaking its bits onto the table.

"How are you doing, son? How's the coffee?"

He looked forlorn, lost and out of touch. Probably because he was. Perhaps he was bridging the gap between the two worlds. That of the living and that of the dead.

"I'm okay, dad. The coffee's great. Thanks. I don't know if Rose told you, but I've been having problems lately with Norm and Peter. And you're standing in Norm's chest by the way."

I didn't move. I wasn't about to. Now wasn't the time to be playing into his hallucinations.

"What kind of problems have you been having, son?"

"Well, it's Norm and Peter. They keep talking in nonsensical rhymes and making absolutely no sense. And I sometimes think they keep trying to make fun of me, too."

He looked like he was on the verge of tears.

"Like right now, Peter is going 'Tears because it's us he fears. Let's give him a leer a jeer but hell no not a cheer.' That's just one example."

I came up to him and sat on the edge of his bed. I squeezed his shoulder and took a napkin from his side table and dabbed at his eyes. He was scared.

"It's okay, son. They can't harm you. It's the fear of dying which is creating this transference onto your hallucinations. I'm here and there are a lot of people here who want to help you. You know that Norm and Peter are not real.

They can't harm you. I know that their nattering is very disconcerting, but try your best to ignore it. It's just your own mind which is coming to an understanding of your impending death. With your illness, it is hard for you to comprehend that, so your mind is slipping nonsensical musings into your schizophrenic hallucinations."

"Rose had said that I might be able to get you to give me some anti-psychotics that could make them go away?"

"We could do that, son. But I don't think that it's the best idea. I don't think you have enough time for them to work and I think it is important for you to try and work through this with your own strength of character and the peace that you've worked so hard these months to attain. These are your secret and potent weapons."

I rubbed his shoulder and squeezed at it.

"I know you can overcome this, too, my son. I have been so proud of your achievements up until this point. This is next to nothing for you now."

He was making feel a lot better. I felt less fearful and more in control.

"You can't do it. You can't put your sissy ass into it," said Peter.

"I hear you my brother, and he ain't got no mother. He's dangling loose on that neck tied noose."

"Tell me what he's got that stupid twat."

And so they went back and forth, but I was looking at my father. I was focusing on getting myself out of here in as healthy a mind as I could.

"You guys cut it out before you make me shout," said MJ, "oops," she said again realizing that she was starting to rhyme now, too.

"I'm not like them," she said.

"I know," I said, " thanks, dad. I'm feeling better already."

MJ was the good doctor and the good doctor was MJ. They were one and the same in some ways. Most likely because my father sat right where she was. This wasn't supposed to happen. The real merging with the unreal. It had never happened before that they could mingle.

It was like I was drunk and seeing double images, my vision blurred, not by two of a kind but by two of a different kind. If Dr. Malichem was speaking I could focus on him. If MJ started to speak, I could focus on her, otherwise it was like they flowed in and out of one another.

It was so strange, but I was not scared, because both of them cared for me, unlike Norm and Peter, you fucking losers.

"Loser, chooser, you're the one that's gonna be gone," said Norm.

I shouldn't have done that. Paid any attention to them, like my dad said. I looked away from them and at the good doctor again. Or MJ, it was both of them I suppose.

"This air is heavy like lead, the impending doom of he who will soon be dead. The groom of death, the bride sucking his last breath," said Peter.

"Nicely done, this is fun," chimed Norm.

I was looking at the good doctor when Norm and Peter got up, hands still melted into one when they started dancing with one another kicking their legs out. I saw them in my periphery.

"We can, I can, can you Can Can?" they both sang.

I drank my coffee and eyed Janko's colorful donut. The little bits of hundreds and thousands could have been punk sprayed ants. I still had my hand on his shoulder and I noticed that his eyes kept looking all about me.

"Are your eyes tired?" I asked.

"No. It's just that you are sitting in or on MJ and I keep seeing you then her. It's very strange."

I moved further down the bed, towards his knee.

"How's that?"

"Good, but you didn't have to move. I can keep the two of you straight."

He smiled, but I could tell it was effort. I turned my head around towards the window looking outside at the blue sky to see if the sun was about. I was hoping he could dry the mist in my eyes. I sipped on my coffee and the condensation drifted up wetting them further. I tried my best to keep the wetness at bay. I didn't want to dab at them. That'd be too obvious. My ducts held out draining them before I had to resort to my sleeves. I got up and walked towards the window. It would be a good day to die. The sky so blue and the day almost picture perfect.

This was the sort of image I'd like to take with me to the beyond. Something bright and sunny I suppose. I steeled myself.

This was Janko's party, a celebration of people who had cared for him and for whom he had cared in return. This was not a funeral. Margaret was right. There'd be plenty of time left for maudlin tears.

I turned back to face him. Quietness had stolen into the room and muffled it. I wondered if that was helping him or hindering him.

"How are your friends, Janko?"

"All right, but I'm finding it easier to ignore them. MJ helps, to have a friend amongst the assassins."

"Good, keep a close tether on her as best you can. Use her to focus on as much as you can if you must focus on your hallucinations."

He nodded at me and smiled at something else. MJ I guess.

"Listen. How about getting ready for your guests. Margaret is here and I'm sure she'd love to meet you, and I think the other nurses will be here soon, too."

I nodded.

"I'd love to meet your wife, dad."

And I would, too. But I was losing enthusiasm in holding court for all these people. The body was weak and the mind was failing. What was the use now of trying to create false bonds between people of history. The awkwardness. Did I really need that now as I lay my head on my bed ready for everlasting rest? But perhaps I should rather be grateful that considering the life I've lived I wasn't dying alone. At least I would be amongst people who cared about me. Or who had once cared and had enough pleasant memories to be with me at the end. I don't know. Questions were getting difficult to answer now. There were too many unknowns and not enough time to know a fraction of them. Perhaps peaceful and quiet company would suffice. Perhaps they would be content with that. I'll see, I guess. I was in no mood to try, anyway.

My father, the good doctor, left the room encouraging me to eat some of my donut. I asked him to help straighten me up on the bed. Prop me more upright so I could chew and not choke on my food. For a man in my condition, that would be embarrassing. He did and as he disappeared through the door I reached out for my donut with a feeble hand.

These skeletal twigs, this arm covered in loose cloth. My own body was becoming a foreign thing to me. The distancing, the closing of the doors to the rooms of the house.

The looking back and the nodding of acquaintances and the shuffling through dim hallways towards the exit of this life, this body that held the dying embers of a once passionate life. Now cool to the touch. Now smoking, blunting my senses.

I came out smiling to my wife. Things were going well. I was managing better now that I wasn't alone. Such a terrible place to be. Was it better to die alone or to be the only witness to a death? I didn't know the answer and I didn't want to find out. I just knew it was better to be amongst others with the specter of death in the room. Comfort in company.

"He says he's ready for guests. He'd like to meet you, my love. Are you okay? Are you ready?"

I went over to her and kissed her on the forehead and took her hand. The buzzer screeched again and Rose got up to answer it. Margaret and I made our way to Janko's room. We both carried with us mugs of coffee like alms bowls, gifts to the spirit world.

"Janko, this is my wife, Margaret. We've been together over twenty years."

Margaret put out her hand and held Janko's for a long moment. She was good at this.

"Nice to meet you, Janko," she said.

"Me, too. I've heard a lot about you from the doctor…my father. I feel honored, he's told me how wonderfully talented you are in the law. I could have used some lawyers on my behalf a long time ago. When things were different and I was young…and vulnerable."

"I'll go and get a couple of chairs quickly," I interjected.

When I got back they were in the middle of a conversation that was thankfully, easy to follow. I nudged the chair just behind Margaret's knee and she sat down. I did the same.

"I've often thought about that, Janko. Going into child welfare law. I've always been interested in helping the underdog or the vulnerable in our society. But I'm not sure I could bear the pain and suffering that I would come across when working with children. I think it would break my heart and cause me to burn out. I'm not sure I have the stomach for it."

Janko didn't say anything for a while. He put his donut back on the side table and some hundreds and thousands jumped to their death. He had barely nibbled at a bit of the icing on top of the donut. It looked like white paint had flaked off an old browned wall.

He sipped on his coffee, looking outside. And for the first time in a long time I saw how blue his eyes were. They mirrored the sky, and I wasn't sure if he was melting into the great big yonder or if his eyes had always been that blue. Probably it was the latter, but I found myself not trusting my own sense and senses at the moment.

"Yeah, it would be tough, but not as tough as having to live the pain and suffering. And advocates are so needed. Well, especially when I was growing up. Hardly ever saw my social worker and of course when they do come by they always give a head's up to the foster parents, never taking advantage of their ability for unannounced visits. So what you get is foster parents making themselves and you look presentable. Plus, don't forget the threats of atrocious violence if we were to say anything about it. Anyway, doesn't make a difference to me, anymore."

He stopped then and sighed. If a man dying with tightened lungs could sigh. It was almost a whisper like maybe a slight breeze had come through the room.

"It breaks my heart just to hear you talk of these things. But I do know, Janko, that things have improved in the last twenty to twenty-five years as far as children's rights and welfare has come. Of course this doesn't mean that children aren't still being abused. But I think, as a society we've become more aware of the problem."

We all sipped on our coffee, looking at inanimate things. Janko took in the blue sky to melt his eyes into. Margaret took in his packet of cigarettes on the side table and I took in a piece of the faded, washed out comforter that draped lightly over his small frame. In the background I heard a knock at the door and Rose answering it. From the mumbled voices I could hear, it seemed that Salima, Veronica, and Maria had arrived. I was itching to go and see them but I thought it'd be rude for me to leave Margaret in this hole of silence. I'm sure Rose would come and interrupt us.

"She seems very nice, hey, Janko?" asked MJ. She was still sitting on the edge of the bed. Very close to the good doctor now. She kept her hand on my thigh and she had no nails. I noticed that now. Yet I could still feel her hand, or thought I could feel it on my thigh. It's light warm touch like a bird landing on a tree.

"Yeah, MJ, they're all nice. That's why they've come to visit me and that's why I've wanted them to."

Margaret tried to keep a poker face, but a brief questioning look shadowed across her face before she composed herself.

"I'm schizophrenic," I said to her, "and I have hallucinatory friends that seem pretty real, to me anyway. I was speaking to MJ, Mary Jane, and she was saying how nice you seem. There are two other so-called friends. Norm and Peter, but they're not playing nice at the moment."

"Nice, what are you talking about, we're quiet as mice," said Norm.

"That Margaret, though, she sure is hot. I'd like to give her some of what I've got."

If you guessed that was Peter the pervert you're right. They had stopped dancing like morons and were standing next to me on the other side of my bed. Their hands were still melted together. They looked like lovers.

"I understand," said Margaret, "I bet she's nice, too."

I looked at her. She held her mug of coffee close around the front of her chest. She was trying her best, I suppose.

"Yeah, MJ is really nice. She's been the only consistently nice one. Peter used to be a good guy too, but Norm has always been difficult. I used to wish that MJ was real, because I really liked her a lot and would've have wanted to be her boyfriend. That kept me hoping. We used to pretend, I guess, and sometimes it just helped me get through the days of hell."

"Hell, well isn't that swell. Ring the bell I think he's heard his death knell," said Norm.

"You're on fire, sire. Let's kill him now. Throw him over the bow," said Peter.

"I bet she kept you good company during many hard times," said Margaret.

I nodded, looking at MJ. I sipped on my coffee. There was only a swill of it left. I had a good mind to throw it at Norm and Peter but I knew it'd just end up on the floor. But God, was that tempting. Salima, Rose, Maria and Veronica came into the room. It was filling up now. They all came and settled around the end of my bed like angels to protect me. That's how I'd come to see them. Rose was next to my father and Salima was next to Peter. Veronica and Maria were in between Rose and Salima. Everyone said their hellos to each other and to me. Mike introduced his wife to the other three nurses. They hadn't met before.

"You look well, Janko," said Maria always the eternal optimist.

I smiled at her. I couldn't help it.

"I feel like hell," I said.

Salima grabbed at my foot gently and gave it a good-natured gentle shake.

"You look great to me," she said.

Outside, a flock of what looked like seagulls flew away from the building on some sort of bombing mission. You know, seeing how many cars they could splatter with bird shit.

"I'm glad you've come. All of you," I said looking around at everyone except for Norm and Peter.

"Over here my dear," said Peter.

"I'm really touched and moved that so many people have come to visit me during my last hours. And I'm getting a premonition that it is during my last hours. I never thought I had any friends except for MJ and Peter and Norm…"

"Aww, isn't that nice," said Norm.

"And now I have real friends and I even have family."

I looked at my father and his wife. She was a warm and caring person even if she did seem a little awkward in meeting me.

"Yes, you do, son. You have family and you have friends and many people who care about you. More to come, too."

"If I don't get a chance later, I want to thank all of you for your support. Salima, Maria, Veronica, Rose. I know that I was a handful at first. Maybe I still am, but thanks for putting up with me like you did. Like you do. I hope to be able to carry you with me in my heart or soul on my next journey wherever that may take me."

I looked at them all. They were getting blurry. My eyes were wet and welling with tears. I was sad now, looking around at all these people who had shown me such kindness and who I would not be able to be with for much longer. Maybe it was the fear of the unknown that was causing me concern. Or maybe it was my guilt for how I treated them and other people who had tried only to be helpful to me in my life. I didn't quite feel deserving, I guess. Was it enough, what I had done to make up for my indiscretions? I don't know. When I'm gone, maybe you can decide and maybe you won't judge me too harshly. Not to rehash the past or to make excuses, but you know, I was dealt a shitty hand when I came into this world.

"We know old pally ol' pal," said Peter.

"I wasn't talking to you," I whispered to him.

I looked back at the nurses and dad and Margaret.

"Sorry, damn hallucinations interfering with me again."

"We know son," said my father.

"Anyway, I hope that maybe I've tried to make amends in the last weeks to be a better person. To try and take your advice and help and to improve. I did do my best I, can say that honestly. And I hope that you will take me with you when I'm gone. Maybe you'll pause once in a while and think fondly of me when you've moved on. I'd like to hope that that wouldn't be too much to ask?"

"Of course, Janko," said Salima, "I have really enjoyed working with you and taking care of you. You've inspired me with your courage and ability to look your future squarely in the face. You've done exceedingly well. I'll be very sad to see you go."

My dad had passed me a tissue which I was using to dab at my eyes. He passed the box on to Salima who had wet eyes now, too. All of them had. The box went around to all of them like the tithing basket at church.

"You're wonderful, Janko. I'm so proud of you," that's all that Veronica could get out before blowing into her tissue.

"You have come a very long way, Janko. Remember we all decided to take you on after we had read your file. We knew it wouldn't be easy. And it wasn't at first, but we've all worked together to help you. And you've helped yourself immensely. You've done extremely well and I will always carry you in a special place in my heart. You have encouraged me with your courage and determination. I am sad to see this journey ending. I've enjoyed spending these many months with you. But I know that you are ready for this new path. You are ready. You've prepared yourself well," said Rose.

Norm and Peter sat down now and were looking at the four nurses. Their hands had become unglued but they had their arms around each other's shoulders. Maria had her arms folded in front of her.

"I agree with everything that Rose has said. You are a special and courageous man, Janko. I knew that when I read your file and that was the main reason that I wanted to work with you. Admittedly, it took a while for us to get to that place. For you to work through your anger and such, but I've thoroughly enjoyed it too.

I have learned a lot about courage and patience in the midst of great difficulty from you and I'm thankful for that. I, too, will carry you in my heart for as long as I live. And who knows, perhaps in the hereafter we will find each other again as friends," said Maria smiling.

My father had left the room to collect the last two kitchen chairs which he placed just off to the other side of my bed, at the end, across from where the armchair was. He stood up and offered them his chair and the other chairs. He stood behind Margaret, his one hand on her shoulder. Rose took the comfortable armchair.

"Thanks, guys, for your support. I mean that. I don't know how else to thank you. I would have bought you all flowers if I had the money and the stamina, and chocolates, too. I'm sorry I couldn't. Words seem so useless now, like the moulted skin of snakes. There's nothing there but hollowness."

I sighed, picked up my donut and nibbled at the icing. The hundreds and thousands cascaded down my chest like shaved beard.

"You don't have to say anything, son. We all understand. It is the feeling, your presence, that we appreciate and which is more tangible."

I looked at all of them and smiled. I put my donut down. There was nothing left to do. Death was scraping at my door like tree branches on windows. I was okay with it now. It was peaceful if I didn't freak myself out about the unknown. I couldn't do that anyway, I was too tired. It was all I could do to watch them and talk to them.

"I'm really tired. I hope you don't mind if I just lie here a bit and rest. Close my eyes. I'm not meaning to be rude. I'm basking in the warm glow of all the love in this room. Thank you all for coming. I didn't realize how important it was to me. I never knew I couldn't stand to die alone."

"Don't you worry about trying to entertain us. This is all about you. Rest and let us just visit and enjoy each other's company," said Maria as she reached for a tissue to dab at her eyes.

I had just closed my eyes and was easing into a deep restful state when there was another buzz on the intercom. I could tell there wouldn't be a moment's peace before I died. But I'm not complaining. If certain people are right, I'll be resting for the rest of eternity.

Dad got up to answer the buzzer but I couldn't make out what he said or who was there. It would be a surprise. If I had to guess I'd say it would be the Antolinis, but then again I have a fifty-fifty chance, anyway.

It was only them and the cop left to visit, and I think they cared for me more than the cop. If only because I lived with them for a while.

I started feeling quite nice and warm. Probably because there were extra bodies in the room. Six extra bodies, or five with the doctor just having left. Surely that would make a difference to the ambient temperature. I figured as much, anyway.

I heard a knock at the door. More a feeling than actually hearing it. I was slipping away into a deep restful state or the beginning of death's smothering smooch. I felt anaesthetized and tried to swim thickly out of it. My dad opened the door and I heard two voices. A female one and a male one. I was craning now, quite alert or trying as best as I could. They were older voices. I was right, it was the Antolinis. They took some time in getting into the room. But when they were here, I could see why. They both had coffees and donuts. They were short, stout Italians. He was bald and reminded me of a picture I'd seen once of Picasso. She was close to his height and thicker than he was, but she had a full head of hair which was obviously dyed a brunette but not very well because in the light it glinted maroon at times. It was curly like a wig. The same length all around like most of the old ladies have it now. She put down her coffee and donut and came up to me with her arms outstretched. There was delight on her face.

"Il mio figlio bello, ahhh," she said.

I didn't have a clue, but it sounded nice the way she said. She hugged me around the neck, kissing me on both sides of the face. They were wet and warm, I could feel that much. But as they dried they cooled and I didn't like that as much. Her hands were thick with short fingers and her nails were brightly painted. She was loud and she had barely said anything, if you know what I mean. He came up to me and looked me carefully in the eye trying to see if he recognized me. I didn't blame him, I wouldn't have recognized myself. He put his hand on my chin and then gently patted it.

"Ciao, Janko, ciao," he said and then stepped backwards a bit.

These people. Was he leaving already? I thought I understood ciao to mean goodbye. This is too hard. Here I am dying and these guys are speaking in tongues. Jesus, would English be too hard.

"You look the same, Janko, as you did all those years ago," said Mrs. Antolini.

They were being kind. Of course. That's how they had always been. I'd never known them to say a mean word. Not even to that bitch when she screwed everything up for all of us. I never heard them say anything bad about her or any of us. They were just sad. Mrs. Antolini dug her stubby fingers into her overcoat pocket and pulled out a beaded chain. It had a cross on it at the end and then went up with some beads before opening up into a loop. I'd seen one of these things before. You say prayers with them or something. She put it around my neck.

"This is a rosary for you. It will help take you across to heaven," she said.

Everyone was smiling. It had baby blue beads on it. Plastic I was certain. And the metal was cold around my neck.

"Thank you Mrs. Antolini," I said.

"That's beautiful, Janko," said Veronica.

"Indeed," said my father, although I didn't get the sense that he was a religious man. I looked around and saw her coffee mug on my side table. Her lip had left a thick smudge on the rim like a fat red worm. I remembered that from when I was with them. I smiled at it. Another good memory. I was on fire.

"We're sorry we were never able to get you back. We really wanted to," she said.

"I know. It wasn't your fault. Do you know what happened to any of the other kids?" I asked her.

She shook her head and her eyes got all misty.

"They took you all away and never told us anything else. We made some inquiries because we wanted to get you all back if we could. Especially you. But they wouldn't tell us anything," said Mr. Antolini.

Margaret and Salima got up and offered their chairs for Mr. and Mrs. Antolini. They took them and inched them closer to me.

"How do you feel, Janko?" asked Mrs. Antolini.

"I feel like I'm ready to go on. I'm not scared anymore. Too tired by now to be scared about anything. And how can you be scared when you have so many friends surrounding you on your last days? I'm not scared, just tired and ready."

She took my hand in hers. They were wrinkly and thick with puffy pads under the fingers. Mr. Antolini took his mug and sipped on it. I fingered Jesus, feeling his emaciated form in relief.

He was too small and hopeless to save me now. Though I figured I could get in on the sympathy vote. Don't you?

"This is comforting to me. A wonderful gift," I said still fondling it in my free hand. MJ and Peter and Norm had moved out by the bathroom. MJ between the two of them. All three the same height as each other, as me I guess.

Sleep or rest or death or whatever you wanted to call it was clawing at me like I was a rodent hiding in a hole from a bear. Or maybe a beaver would be a better example. Everything seemed muted and thick and warm.

"I'm glad Dr. Malichem was able to find us so we can see you one last time. You always had a special place in our hearts and in our lives, Janko. Even when you were gone we thought about you and we talked about you a lot. I know your life hasn't been easy, and I wish it could have been easier. But the suffering is over now and soon you will be with Jesus and the saints."

She was sincere. A true believer. They used to take us to church with them on Sundays, but I could never buy into it fully. Not with how my first experience being in his house was. I just couldn't get over that. I couldn't forgive him, who should have helped me. Just a little boy, scared and frightened in his big house. And it is a big house to a small boy. Those ceilings that arch upwards towards heaven. You've seen it, I'm sure. Well, I didn't find it comforting, okay. I couldn't get around my first experience. It still makes me shudder when I think about it.

"I hope you're right. I'd like to believe that there is someone who is kind and compassionate waiting for me over there. A Jesus like I saw on those little prayer cards stuffed in your bible. He looked peaceful and happy, even if his chest was open exposing his bleeding heart. It'd be okay if I was going to meet someone like that, I think."

I looked away out through the window. I couldn't see anything happy or alive or peaceful. Things were quiet, but that's not the same as peaceful. And the telephone poles like concrete soldiers, weren't alive. They might have been trees once, but they were just wood now.

"You will, Janko. You will meet Jesus and he will take you into his arms and you will never know the pain that you once knew. Which you should never have known. But your rewards are in heaven. You have a front row seat, I know."

She still held my hand in both of hers. She smiled at me and her eyes were bright. She was certain, if not misguided, but it was kinda contagious and a small part of me wanted to believe. Wanted to think that it could be that easy and that simple. But now wasn't the time for me to repent to get into heaven. That wasn't the kind of God I believed in. My God didn't gamble with people and play favorites. My God didn't let you out of jail just for saying sorry. You had to make amends. Surely you had to be accountable for your mistakes. Otherwise why the hell had my life been such shit? But nevertheless I smiled at her, and at him too. They were good people and they had come to wish me farewell. More than most. A helluva lot more than most. And if anything I had earned a front row seat. Shit, I'd earned the right hand chair if God was decent and fair.

I looked over at my friends. They stared at me blankly from the doorway of the bathroom. No words, just staring. Wallflowers, like I'd been most of my life.

"Anyone want any more coffee or tea?" I asked.

Janko was propped up in bed against pillows. He looked just like a heavy rag doll. His limbs so thin and spindly. The mask of death wasn't beautiful, but his soul, his being shone beautifully through his sack of skin nonetheless. He was looking past me at something behind. His hallucinations most likely. I hoped they weren't giving him grief. I wanted his last hours to be peaceful and quiet and compassionate. And I could see that these were his last hours if he had that much. No one wanted any more coffee or tea. I stood next to Margaret with my hand around her waist. I looked at her and my life seemed complete. I was so blessed with her in my life. With being able to be with my dying son. To offer, hopefully, some solace and comfort during his last moments. I felt like the luckiest man alive. It was good how everything had come into place as I had hoped, as I had tried. There was deep sadness in my heart but it was a forgivable sadness, a sadness that was needed and necessary. I kissed Margaret on the cheek and she looked up at me and smiled. Mrs. Antolini held onto Janko's hand. It was trapped in its soft grip. These were good people. If only he had been able to stay in their care, things might have been different.

"I'm so happy to have all of you here for myself and for Janko. Thank you all for coming. It means a lot to me and I'm sure it does to Janko, as well."

I looked at him. He smiled at me, at the room, at all of us.

"I am happy and thankful. This makes it all worthwhile, to have you all here. It makes my hard life okay. I wouldn't want to repeat it, but it's okay now. This ending to my story makes the other chapters regrettable but forgivable."

His eyes were closing every so often. He was tired. Tired of this life and who could blame him. His whole body seemed to sag and sink with each passing minute, into the quicksand of death, a transition. At least that's how I'd like to think of it. A transition rather than an ending. I didn't buy Mrs. Antolini's ideas. Too simplistic, but some people needed something black and white to believe in. Me, I'd like to think that there were more weaves and threads and color in the fabric of life. More at stake than forgive and forget. Either way, Janko was going to a better place, whatever that might be.

"What do you want done with yourself when you're finished here?" asked Mr. Antolini.

Everyone looked up at him. There was just a brief shade of shock across their faces. It was a bold question to be asked, perhaps impolite but I didn't think so. These were real issues of importance so why not talk about them. Politeness just gets in the way of living and dying authentically and with dignity. Can't not look at the pink elephant when it's propped up right in front of you and talking away, now can you?

Janko opened his eyes and looked around.

"I want my father to scatter my ashes by Blackstrap Mountain in Saskatchewan. That's where I was born. You will do that for me won't you dad?"

I nodded at him. "Of course," I said. We'd spoken about this before. It was a wonderful idea, and would probably give me more closure than him. Margaret would be coming with me, too. Mr. and Mrs. Antolini nodded in agreement. Which I found odd. I'd thought the church was against cremation. Maybe they were just being kind.

"Good idea. I remember when we took you there once when we had you and we all lived in Saskatoon. You loved that place. I've never seen you so happy as that day we spent playing around in that park and lake they had there, too. We have a picture of you at home playing with some twigs at the base of that mountain. We keep it in a drawer and have pulled it out every so often when we think of you being happy.

We don't keep it out, because it was too painful to think about how we lost you and what had come of you. Gabriella feared the worst. I always liked to think that you were with some other good family. Terribly, Gabriella was right. But it is good that you are going back to the place you were from. A full circle completes the journey," he said.

Alfredo put his mug back on the table by his wife's. There was a thin band of coffee stained around the inside, about three-quarters of the way up. A bangle of sorts. The buzzer went off again. All I wanted was some tranquillity and peace for Janko and the rest of us. The buzzer was a horrible sound, like an annoying intrusion or brief infestation of buzzing bees flying around the room. It was no doubt Robert Peel. This should be the last of it. Everything was coming full circle now. I went to answer the buzzer.

That got my attention. I always hated that buzzer's sound. It was surprising I had lived so long in this place with that damn annoying sound. But then again I didn't get many visitors, usually. It was the cop, the bobby, the officer. I smiled at that. I thought it was pretty funny. His name being Robert and all. I heard dad talk into the buzzer and let someone up.

"That'll be Robert Peel, I think," said Veronica.

Everyone agreed.

"I've never met him," said Salima.

"I don't think any of us have," said Maria.

They all looked at me then.

"Do you remember him?" asked Margaret.

"No, not really. I mean, I remember the idea of him I think, more than the actual man. I can't say I remember what he looks like though."

"It's quite interesting that he has the same name as the first police officer. Or bobby as they call them in the UK, after his first name of Robert," said Margaret.

"That's interesting. I just thought it was coincidental that he was named Robert and they call the coppers bobbies in Britain. So Robert was the name of the first cop in Britain?" I asked.

"Yes. His actual name was Robert Peel. Just like your imminent guest," she said.

"Did anyone else know that?" I asked, "or am I the only ignorant one."

I was smiling, I was trying to joke around. There was mostly shaking of the head which made me feel better. But apparently Rose knew that, but had kept coy all this time. Wasn't really important anyway.

The good doctor, my father came in followed by a large middle-aged man. I was expecting someone much older. Someone probably closer in age to the Antolinis but instead I figured that Robert was probably not much older than my father. But he was tall and thick with curly brown hair and a red fat nose on the end of his face. He smiled at me and seemed quite jolly.

"Janko, young man, you don't look a day older than the last time I saw you."

Everyone smiled and my father laughed. He just seemed like a good-natured man. I liked him immediately. The last time I saw him I was probably no older than ten or so.

"Can't say the same about you," I said.

He looked at me raising an eyebrow and then laughed. It filled the room like a big ping-pong ball bouncing around.

"Yes, life has been hard these few years since I retired. The belly gets bigger when you're not off chasing the bad guys and you're still eating donuts."

He moved in closer to the bed. Ms. Antolini gave up my hand and he grabbed it giving it a good shake.

"That's my boy. Still got that iron grip eh?"

He was a generous man. I barely had the strength to hold his hand if it were a cooked noodle.

"I brought you something with me," he said reaching into his pants pocket. "These here could fetch a pretty high premium if you wanted to sell them to your other friends here," he said looking around.

He took two Saskatoon Police shoulder flashes from his pocket and pressed them onto my shoulders.

"Yup, I should think you'd make a pretty good copper. Bad guys would be running from you in fear."

He placed the flashes in my lap and I picked them up in my hands.

"Thanks a lot," I said.

"It's nothing. I just wish I could have seen you sooner. Better late than never though, eh?"

We all sat then or stood around in silence. I was looking at the flashes in my hand and thinking about what could have been. I might have liked being a cop. And I got wet eyes again thinking about that. No use is it. What's done is done and I'm dying. There are no more what ifs for me, now. I dabbed my eyes into my shoulders.

"It's okay, my boy," said Robert but it was plain to see that he didn't really know what to do. None of them did. And what was there to do. Nothing. My father came up and held my hand. He caressed my head, sat on the edge of the bed and pulled me into him. The tears came easily but the crying didn't. I was too tired or weak to cry.

"I'm sad, too," my father said and I could hear his voice break, and the sound of it echoed around the room and then came back and rested softly on my ears.

"I'm going to miss you, son. It's been an honor and a privilege to know you. I love you so much."

I could hear his tears flow freely then, and I felt one warm, land on my head. He rubbed it off and it evaporated into nothingness. Much like I was about to do, I guess. These tears of mine dried up and I felt hollow. There was not enough life left in me to experience prolonged human emotion. My body was folding in on itself and getting ready to pack me into that eternal closet, right at the back on the top, where people didn't dare to look, to be reminded of the dead and departed.

XXIX

We had been sitting around visiting while people kept coming and going to the living room for snacks and drinks and then returning. I thought I was at my own wake, only I wasn't dead, yet. My father had been pretty much a constant companion since he had arrived. He'd only left me once to get a sandwich and a glass of water and once he had gone to the washroom. The washroom was seeing a lot of visitors today. Coffee was all around and tea and juice and people were liquefying their bladders at the rate it was going. It was getting dark now and I could see a few stars twinkling weakly in the night sky. My father was sitting in the comfy chair by the window. Rose was fiddling with my IV and checking my temperature. She turned to him and gestured something.

"I'm getting close, aren't I?" I asked him.

He looked at me, resting his forearms on his knees. His hands were interlaced as if he were in prayer and then he looked at the corner of my bed.

"Yes," he said, "yes my son. I'm afraid it is getting close. But you know that don't you?"

His eyes even from this distance were watery, and he was choking on his voice as he spoke. I nodded my head. I did know. This close in, I knew that my time was up. Before the witching hour I was sure.

"I'd like to say goodbye to everyone if I could."

He got up and went out into the living room.

"I'll miss you, Janko," said Rose.

She bent down and gave me a big hug. It was firm and warm and I tried as best as I could to reciprocate. She heaved, catching a sob in her throat. She let me go and got up and looked me in the eyes while hers brimmed with tears.

"I love you. You know that, don't you?"

"Yes I do. Thank you for everything, Rose. I've loved you, too."

She turned and walked away clutching at her mouth with her hand. This was a sad time for them all. I knew that. But for me it was a tiring time. I was ready and waiting to go. And thanks to all of these people I felt a warm glow emanating from my heart or soul I think. Anyway, it was calling me home. I was packaged in the warm soft cradle of love and I was going home. Salima came in next and gave me a short stiff hug. The best she knew how, I guess.

"Take care, Janko," she said, "I've enjoyed working with you."

That was it.

"Thanks for everything, Salima. You've always had a special place in my heart where the love is. I love you."

I was reckless but I was dying and that gave me a courage I hadn't known. Besides my father had taught me the expansiveness of love, and how to give it freely.

"I love you, too," she mumbled as she left.

They were beating down my door. In a way I felt like a pope and they were coming to kiss my ring. Or maybe a Buddha and they'd come to rub my belly. Only I'm not rotund and I'm keeping all my wishes to myself. One of them has to be the key to unlock the other door. Veronica was next up.

"Hi, Janko," she said coming up to the bed and sitting on the edge.

"You've always been my best and favourite patient," she said.

"Seriously?" I asked.

"Yes, seriously," she said into my ear as she hugged me warmly, "I hope to see you when it's my turn. Will you meet me when I go over?"

"I'll be waiting, V," I said.

I could smell her perfume. It was warm and gentle like fallen flowers. I thought I also detected a little bit of citrus fruit in there. It's true, okay. I'm not shitting you. This close up you can smell stuff like that. She pulled out of the hug and put her warm hands on my cheeks and then she leaned forward and kissed me on the forehead.

"I love you, sweet soul," she said as she left.

"I love you, too, V."

Her eyes were bright and dry as she left. That impressed me. I knew she was sincere and that she would miss me like she said she would, but her acceptance of this uncomfortable part of life only added to the respect I had for her already.

Maria came in next. The last of my Florence Nightingales. She took my hand, sat down on the edge of the bed and looked at me carefully.

"We've all known about your friends for a long time. I remember often how you'd try and hide them from us. But they've always been a part of who you are, Janko. And who we've cared for. They are you, just as much as you are them, and I'm going to miss you. All of you."

She reached her arms around me and gave me a hug. I was feeling a lot of love and it was getting tiring. Maybe all this hugging was for their benefit. Things we do to make ourselves feel better about things we have no control over. I was feeling like a kid's teddy. Squeezed and squeezed some more. Don't get me wrong, I liked it, but it sure is tiring. Probably for them, too.

"We've all really liked you, too, Maria. Especially Peter."

"Take care of yourself. Say hi to my mom if you see her."

"I will," I said knowing full well that I had no idea what her mother looked like. What anybody looks like over there.

"Love you, Janko, and you, Peter, and you, Norm, and of course, MJ, too."

"We love you, too," I said, my words following her out of the room as she dabbed at her eyes with a tissue stuck up her sleeve. I think I was in an emotional battlefield. I was shell-shocked. I didn't have any emotion left to use up. I was a tired landscape that could produce no more. My life dug up and tilled and all that was left now was just the dusty soil of my skin, of my soul. But I was warm. The beaming sun of kindness and compassion was beating down on me now. This journey that I would be taking alone would be aided by the thoughts and actions of these people, my friends who had visited me on my last day. And for that I was grateful.

The Antolinis came in. Alfredo carrying a mud brown knitted cap in his hands and Gabrielle carrying her own rosary wrapped around her hand like fighter's tape. She was ready to do battle. Maybe for my soul, maybe against the devil. Or maybe I was just imagining things too creatively now.

"I said the rosary out there for you. And he promised me he'd take you straight into his arms," she said. The crucifix on the end of the rosary swung drunkenly as she brought her hands up to her breast and clutched them into fists. Jesus was getting dizzy, swaying and spinning like he was. I couldn't take my eyes of him. I shared his pain.

"You're a good boy, Janko. God will take you to him. You have nothing to worry about," he said.

He patted my cheeks and stroked my head. His thick rough hands warm on my skin. He was a simple man who didn't quite know what to say in situations like this. But his actions said enough.

"Ciao, Janko. Ciao. Keep a place for me at the table." Those were the last words I heard him say. He then took a couple of steps back to wait for his wife. He wasn't rushing her. She was on a different timetable. She looked up at the ceiling and murmured something and when she looked back down at me, her eyes were welling with tears. She clutched at her cardigan. Her hands balled into fists.

"Mia culpa," is what I thought I heard her say a few times. Whatever that meant. English, please, I can't guess and I'm too tired to try. But clearly it was making her upset.

"Ciao, Janko. We'll see you soon, my son." Those were the last words I heard her say as she reached down and took my rosary, her Jesus and my Jesus kissing. She grabbed my crucifix and kissed it. Then she looked up at me with watery eyes and kissed me on both cheeks and on the forehead.

"Thank you for coming," I said, "you've taught me about decency and kindness. I'll never forget it."

She looked back as she left the room holding her hand up and flapped it once like a broken bird's wing before she brought it to her lips. The beads of her rosary like a noose around Jesus' neck, hanging him in mid-air. Alfredo held his crumpled cap in both of his hands as he left behind his wife. He didn't look at me again. He was looking down at the ground.

It was still a clear sky. It was growing darker. That dark blue before it turns fully into night. There were more stars out now, twinkling and blinking at me from the pinprick holes in the night's gown. I figured they might be the eyes of all the recently departed. Maybe come to check up on me and keep my course steady as I exit this body. Making sure I get to where I'm supposed to be going. I looked down and saw Jesus resting on my navel over my shirt. It looked like he was trying to hug me. His arms outstretched but not far enough, and stuck on that cross. His face smothered into my belly, inhaling belly-button lint.

I couldn't bear it so I turned him around to embrace the night sky. This damn rosary was too realistic. I could feel the little nails, globs on his hand. I wanted to pull them out and help him off the damn thing. What a crappy way to spend eternity, bound up and crucified around people's necks. A sadistic reminder of the kind of world we live in. And he'd been dead hundreds and hundreds of years, and still we're no better off. I'll have to have words with him, if I see him.

Robert came in and stood by my bed. He had a coffee in his hand in a white mug. I looked at him and smiled.

"That sure is a nice rosary you got there, Janko."

I looked down at it and picked up Jesus and brought him towards my face.

"Hard to think that someone so small could do anything for you in this life, let alone the next."

"So you're not a believer, eh?"

"No, I guess not. But it's not that I don't believe, just that I've been shown a different side of life I guess. The side where you can't count on nobody and if you can't count on real people, the last thing you're gonna do is put your faith in some imaginary person."

I let Jesus drop back down onto my belly. He was adamant about trying to hug me. He had turned himself around and plastered his face into my belly.

"That's not going to make a difference, anyhow. You were saved in a church. That's where I found you, so your fate's been sealed from the beginning. You're going back to meet the man. Even if only me and the Antolinis believe. That'll be enough, mark my words. You're going to be okay, my boy. You'll do just fine. Just like you have all these years despite life's best efforts otherwise."

"Thanks, Robert. You've been more influential and helpful than maybe you realize. You checking up on me at times like you did was crucial, on more than one occasion."

He took a sip of coffee and cradled the mug in two big hands. They reminded me of gorilla's hands I'd seen once at the zoo. Only pink and hairless, but still thick and wrinkly.

"I'm just sorry I gave up on you. I figured you were good then, when you met those fine folk. I never thought you'd be taken away from them. I thought you'd found a family for yourself."

I looked down at my lap and my hands folded there. Much smaller than his. Twigs, really, stuck on a small sack of stones.

"Yeah," I said, "I think we all figured that's the way it would go. Me, you and the Antolinis. Problem is, some people don't know how good they've got it. Like that bitch that fucked everything up for us."

I looked up at the night sky. This curtain was drawn now, but still some lights pricked through from the other side. Looked bright over there. Maybe it was a lot more fun. Maybe there was a party happening on the other side. A welcoming party for me. Yeah, I'd like to think so. Nothing wrong with that. I'm tired of this dusty dirt pile, anyway. Time to move on. Robert looked out at the night, too. Holding his mug in two slabs of ham and sausages. Sounded good, but I wasn't hungry, anyway.

"Sure is a nice night out there. A good night to take a long rest. Those stars shining like beacons on a sea, eh? Maybe they'll guide you across."

"That's what I'm hoping. A long rest. I like that. I like that a lot. I could use a long rest."

We sat in silence then for a long while. Robert sipped his coffee now and then. The red numbers on my alarm clock tumbled over each other slowly, and my cigarettes lay inching out of their box, each one trying to offer itself over the next. But I couldn't be smoking anymore. Didn't have the lungs left to breathe let alone smoke. I could hear some voices out in the living room and the front door closing. Sounded like maybe the Antolinis had left. If only dying were that easy. Just close the door behind you and you're there on the other side. In heaven or wherever.

"I think I'll be going now, Janko. It's been swell spending this time with you. I'm glad to have had the opportunity now to have met you, again. I'm really happy with how you've turned out. You're gonna be okay."

He extended his one arm and I clutched at it. He gave me a shake.

"Yup. Still an iron grip just like I taught you. Take care, Janko. Take real good care."

"I will. Thanks for everything. Thanks for coming to visit me."

And then he walked out, his large frame swallowed by the door, and he was gone. It was like he might never have been at all. Except I had the memories.

These postcards I'd like to take to the other side with me. See here, this cop saved my life. Truly he did. Once. Long ago when I was small and the world was a less scary place than it became. Yeah, and check this one out, here. These old folk are the Antolinis, my kin really, if I ever had any kin that weren't blood. See how good they are, smiling at me and waving goodbye. It'd make the introductions easier I figure. Give us something to talk about with the other dead folk. Better than those stupid name tags. Hi, my name is please fuck off. I mean really, what does that get you. Oh, hi, Jane, what an interesting name. Wow, I was just going to say that about yours, Bob. I mean give me a freaking break, okay. How lame would that be? Nah, I'm gonna try and hang onto these little memories of mine. These postcards, if you will.

I heard voices again. I recognized the one as Robert. He was leaving, and the door shut behind him. That easy. Now you see me, now you don't. I wonder if it'll be like that for me. Now I'm awake. Now I'm dead and someone's turned off the lights. Speaking of lights, the stars had me mesmerised. Now they were peepholes made in the toilet stalls of the perverts who got lucky and went across. Shit, it's all speculation isn't it? I'm rambling on. I'll find out soon enough. But I won't be able to tell you, will I? Afraid not, the dead can't talk to the living, at least that's my experience.

MJ came and sat on the edge of the bed. Norm and Peter followed her in and stood like guards on either side of her, peering down at me with their arms crossed over their chests.

"I guess we should be saying goodbye, too, hey?" she said.

I looked at her not sure what to say. I didn't trust the other two.

"Yes, you do," said Peter.

Now they were talking to my thoughts. That was weird. They didn't usually do that. Okay, I know I'm splitting hairs here, after all, they are my hallucinations but still, they used to pretend. We used to pretend.

"Well, there's no more pretending now, J. You're dying. We're dying and we want to make things right without a fight," said Norm smiling at his last rhyme.

"That would be nice," I said.

MJ took my hand in hers and held it gently. Her hand, the same size as mine, but healthy. Not skeletal like mine.

She had some flesh on the bones, or plastic or whatever the hell they were made of now. Still naked as newborns but without the detail, if you know what I mean. You do, I know you do. I've told you about that before. Here's the recap. She sat on the bed next to me, her body warm and naked but neutered, you know.

"I suppose we'll get to go with you, in a way. Seeing as how we are part of you, aren't we?" she said.

I looked into her eyes. She was crying softly. Two streams of tears like worms meandering down her face. I reached up to them and wiped them off. My own eyes were wet, drenched balls of old rags leaking tears.

"Yes, we are. We are all really the same person. So it's not like we'll be leaving each other. We might leave this body, but you'll always be a part of my spirit. Even if you've been difficult before, it's really only me being difficult with myself."

She looked up at me then and smiled. I looked at Peter and Norm. They were smiling, too.

"We knew it. We knew you'd come to your senses. Didn't we, Norm?" asked Peter.

Norm nodded; he was crying too, so was Peter.

"I really have appreciated the many things you guys have done for me over the years. Especially when I was small and needed protection. But also, when I was bigger and needed company. You were always loyal friends even if you didn't really exist. To me you were real and that was the most important thing."

They all came around me then and hugged me. It was touching, okay. We were all crying and clinging onto each other not wanting to lose each other. And we were going to. That much was certain. And it was hard for us, okay. It was hard and painful. These were the most consistent people in my life, ones who had been through thick and thin with me, okay? So I don't care if they're not really real. To me they are and they've been more real on many occasions than some of the so-called real people.

"I knew you'd find your way back to us, J," said Peter, "remember I told you that we knew you when you thought that nobody knew you. Well, we've always known you. You just had to come to know yourself, I guess. You had to come and find yourself and you'd find us and we'd be a family, again."

"Exactly," said Norm, "I might have been an asshole. But I was your asshole. I was you as the asshole. And how you enjoyed it. Especially when we were young and shit disturbers, up to no good. It served a purpose, then. And I guess that I got scared that you were going to ditch me, seeing as how I wasn't that useful anymore for you."

We were still hugging, my friends and me. We love one another. We had been there for one another like no one else had ever been there for me. Even my father is Johnny come lately. They've been important to me and I hope you'll indulge a dying man his last clutch at what has been for him his own kind of reality.

"You are all useful to me. I've needed all of you more than maybe you know. I just sometimes didn't want to let on too much about how much I did need you. I didn't want any of you getting too big for your britches. But that's all behind us now. I can feel the love we have for one another."

We kept holding onto one another, scared that if any of us let go it would be the death of all of us. And we sobbed and I was sad but there was a hint of peace with it. For the first time in my life I had come to accept myself for my hallucinations, my anger, my pain and suffering. And I could hold onto myself and I could love myself for the first time since I can remember. And that's something for a little boy who had always been taught he wasn't wanted, that he was hated and useless. Who was told by so many people that he came to believe the whole world would be better off if he was just dead. And how he came to hate himself for not being able to kill himself and make the world better by his exit. And now I don't believe that, anymore. Now I'm sad to be leaving, but I believe it will be to go to a better place. And I leave this place a better person than when I entered it. And that feels good, okay. That feels free and right and natural and as I sit here propped up hugging onto myself, my soul is buoyed and I feel a lightness in my body that is so unreal and unnatural. And it's good. It's good to be dying not at my own hand but naturally, with peace for myself in my own heart and an understanding of my own intrinsic value as a human being. Will you ever have any idea of what that's like? I hope you do. I really, really hope you get it. Because as I sat hunched over there crying. Us crying. I felt cleansed by my tears like I was being bathed in them and I was being cleaned by them and it felt good. I felt light and ready to leave the heavy chains of this existence.

I came into the room. I had heard Janko crying and I wanted to check up on him. The Antolinis had left and Robert had left and the nurses and Margaret were sitting out in the living room talking a little about nothing of importance and the TV was on a music channel. Just for some background noise. I had heard Janko crying, sobbing really, and I was concerned so I had come to check up on him. He was hunched over slightly, clutching at the blankets. He had pulled them up to his chest and Jesus was being smothered in his fist. His eyes were closed and his sobbing was exhausted, quiet but steadily sustained. I came up and sat on the bed next to him and pulled him into my arms.

"What's wrong, son?" I asked.

He didn't say anything at all at first. And all around me time and space were bunched up and squeezing me. Out in the living room I could still hear muffled voices and the rhythms of the music, and I swayed with him in my arms, back and forth like he was a baby.

"I love you, son," I said to him, "I love you, Janko."

And I was scared now, I was crying, too. Quietly. My pain was burning down my cheeks like hot acid. I didn't want him to go, but I figured it was time. This was his time. He had been called and I was sad. The space and time in the room squeezed me more. It was heavy inside. I could barely breathe. There was nothing for me to fight against and I felt hopeless and insignificant and small and scared and sad. Really, really sad. And the room was closing in on me and time and space had sped up. Each minute as heavy as an hour. I was being smothered. I thought I'd die with him, then. And that wouldn't have been too bad.

He held me tight and his tears fell on my head like warm rain. We were both crying. It was time now, I knew it. But how did I tell him. The crying was wearing me out and I was choking on air. There wasn't enough in the room to fill me up and give me life.

"I love you, too, dad. I was just saying goodbye to my friends. To myself, I guess."

I looked up at him through bloodshot eyes and his were the same.

"Can you help me to lie down, dad? I don't want to fall out when the time comes and I move on."

He helped me into bed and covered me with the blanket. My breath was slow and labored. He kissed me on the forehead and wiped away my tears and his own with a tissue.

"Is it getting close to the time, my son?"

His eyes were still wet and brimming with tears which occasionally fell down his cheeks. He kept dabbing at them but they kept coming. He was a deep well of pain. So was I, but I was tired and too close to the end to dwell on the pain. I was ready. A whole bag of contentment and throbbing pangs of emotional pain. But generally at peace.

"Don't cry for me, dad. Please just think of the good times we've shared these past months. We have lots to celebrate. I mean, we might never have even found each other and what a loss that would have been."

He dabbed at his eyes again and bunched up the tissue into a little tight white ball. It was damp and his eyes were bright in the dim light from my side table lamp. His eyes looked greasy and I could see the red rivers shine in them. There was a shadow of sadness behind those eyes that I had never really noticed before. And that made me sad. I was sad for him. For his pain. And I was moved by it too. To have touched someone, many people I suppose, if you include the nurses, was a blessing that I only now got. Never would I have thought that I'd be dying, with people around me bathing me in their love. It would have been such an outrageous idea to think that I could die having had this effect on someone. And here I was, moved by the anguish of my father. I was sad for him, but I was happy for me. Can you understand that? I was happy, because never before, or hardly ever before had I enjoyed so much tender feeling and good vibes from people. I was ready. In a place like this. In a run-down part of a city that hardly anybody cares or knows about. With hardly anyone aware of my existence or even caring. I was here in this place. A dark, dusty, unkempt corner of the world. And I was ready to die. Fuck, I felt like a king. I felt like this was my time and I was calling it.

My father held my hand and rubbed it and stroked it. He bought it to his lips and kissed the stony back of it. He caressed my forehead and kissed me there. He kissed me on both cheeks and looked at me all this time through his oily, greasy, wet eyes with the red rivers. And I had never felt such love before from anyone. And this was pure love, from a man who was my father but never knew it until just a few weeks ago. I was a feather carried on a warm summer breeze. And that breeze was named love.

"I love you, dad. It's getting real close now for me. Real close."

He blinked and his eyes were brimming but he was trying to be brave. No more tears were falling down his cheeks now. But his cheeks were red and he was choking on pain. Hot pain.

"I love you, son. I love you so much. You've sowed my heart with a garden of flowers that I never knew existed. I'll take care of that part of myself, son, that you've shown me is there. But this pain, this losing you is so hard. The room is stifling me. The air is lead and stuffy. I'm trying not to lose you but I can't help it. I'm impotent now and yet I want to keep you with me. It's selfish I know, son. Forgive me for not being braver."

I was feeling light and unnatural. I couldn't hear my heart beat. I couldn't feel it either, and there was no sensation of breath on my lips anymore. I was more like vapor or steam drifting off of myself. And my father who was looking at me was looking at the body. My spirit was seeing him from infinite angles and through eons of time if that makes sense. It's frigging weird. This dying. But it's not scary when you're not alone. When the room is thick with love and your spirit can feel it. Your spirit swimming through love like it's a warm gel.

"There is nothing to forgive, dad. The veils are closing now across my eyes and I want to thank you. Thank you for your love, for your reaching out, and never quitting on me. I'm dying now, dad, but I've never felt more alive. I've never felt like I've mattered more than I do now. You've shown me love and taught me to love, and I'm so thankful for that. I wouldn't have made it here without love. And now I carry it in my heart and it lifts my soul to heaven. It is my sail and my rudder. And you have been my captain, dad. Thank you. I love you. This ship sails on now, dad. Its sails billowed with your love. I will see you, again. I will feel your love with me through this eternal journey. My father, from your son, I love you. I always have. From that small boy in the cavernous church. I knew you then and I loved you. And now your son a dying man. I've found you. It was love that brought us here together. And it is love that moves me on. Your love. Our love. It's all around us now dad. Can you see it, can you feel it. It is the language of the spirit and you will hear me always through love. And you will be with me always as love."

He leaned down, his eyes streaming and his tears dropping on me like rain, like wet love and he kissed me softly on the lips.

As I kissed him. As my tears fell shamelessly down my cheeks and splashed him on his chest and now his cheeks, I felt his last breath, warm through his nose, caress my cheeks. The last blush of his life. And I wept and I sobbed and I was hot with pain in my soul. My nose pricked and my throat tightened into a lumpy knot and my eyes were blurred and blinded in pain and salty tears and I scooped my hands around him and hugged him to me. I rocked him, holding him tight to the rhythm of the music coming through to me. And I cried into his neck as his body lay limp in my arms on this hallowed night.

"I love you, my son. Go in peace and take me with you. I love you, I love you. In my heart I always have. In my soul I will cradle you close. You will be with me forever in my memories and in my thoughts. My brave boy. My beautiful son, this sensitive soul. Go home. Go to peace. Go in love. Courageous man, your love is with me; I can feel it all around."

I stayed like that for a long time. Rocking him back and forth. Wringing the tears from my soul until it was a dry rag. The moon rotated a hollow orb. And the stars blinked Morse code. The night got darker and quieter and I squeezed him to me till I was hollow bark. And then there was a light hand on my shoulder and a hug around me.

"I love you, Mike. I'm so glad I have you," said Margaret.

And we stayed like that for a while. Margaret hugging me and me hugging my child, and when I turned around to face her I was hollow still, but her eyes were filling me up. She was pouring me back into myself.

"I'm sorry, my love. I'm very sorry."

Then I returned him to the bed and laid him down. I covered him with the blanket, a shroud. I got up and Margaret took my hand and we walked out into the world.

XXX

I was standing by the lake at Blackstrap Provincial Park. Margaret and I had arrived the day before. It was a week to the day I had covered my son with a blanket. Laid him to rest on his bed for the last time. We had rented a motel in Saskatoon and had driven out to the park. It's where he wanted his ashes to be spread. And I thought it was fitting and right. He had come full circle in so many ways. He had found himself and forgiven himself and learned to love himself, again. That was the full circle of the journey of his soul. And now, with me standing on the pebbly beach of this lake, I was going to cast his ashes to the wind. His physical body had now come full circle too. Margaret and I were only going to be spending two nights in Saskatoon and then we'd be driving back to Calgary. This afternoon we'd go back to Saskatoon. I hadn't been here in years. Hadn't come back since I had left the first time. Shortly after I had broken up with Janko's mother.

The breeze was cool on my face as I stood facing the black water. It was sunny and there was the start of new life in the trees. Their grey bark and leafless limbs had started to sprout little buds. If you looked closely enough you could see the green dotted amongst the trees. Little splashes of green. And you'd have to strain to find snow. Only the occasional dirty crust of it hidden behind rocks that didn't see the sun. Margaret was by my side with her hand around my waist. She was slightly behind me.

"This is a wonderful place. So peaceful today isn't it, my love?" she said.

I looked around and across the lake and turned to look behind me. There was not another soul that we could see. No human and no animal that caught the eye.

"Yes, it is. It's perfect for sending him home."

And it was. The weather was a cool, or depending on how you viewed it, a warm fifty-nine degrees. And there were just a few puffy clouds in the sky. I looked down at the black box, just slightly smaller than a shoebox, which held all that was once Janko. It was a few pounds worth. I was taking my time to enjoy this place. A place I hadn't been to in either mind or body in so many years. I remembered the occasional time that I had spent here with his mother when we were young and in love. Foolish but pure of heart. I turned to Margaret and kissed her.

"Thank you for everything you have done for me, honey. I feel so blessed and lucky to have you with me. Now, especially, but also just generally in my life."

She smiled and hugged me around the waist.

"I feel blessed, too. I'm happy and honored to be sharing this moment with you, Mike. I know how difficult and important this is for you."

"It's not that difficult really. It was the dying that was the hardest part. Over this last week I've come to accept his death. I've come to understand the importance of the short amount of time we had together and my role in helping him on to the rest of his journey. It was hard, but I've come to a peace with my role and the part I played. I did my best. I'm happy with that now. In the end, honey, it's only love that matters. And I can say I loved him and I showed him that love. I've come to realize that this life is nothing more than an opportunity for the soul to express love to the best of its ability."

"You're right, my love. Love is what warms us from the cold dark nights of this life. It keeps us going and safe and secure. Love is the currency that we share with one another. The universal language of hope and compassion and truth and honesty. Without love the soul cannot go on."

And it was because of that love that I was looking out at the lake. The black, oily lake with the Mountain, if you could call it that, squatting over my shoulder as I stood in my body with a lightness to my being. I was ready to give him back to the earth. But I was going to keep him on in my heart and my soul as a stamp of love. The memory of one soul seeing the other clearly.

I pried open the box and gave the lid to Margaret to hold for me. I opened up the plastic bag that was inside and I tipped the box slightly towards the sun so I could see into it better. All of him was there and I dug my right hand into his ashes. The grey, speckled grittiness that were his remains. And it wasn't like the smooth, silky ash from a wood fire, it was like coarsely crushed coral and shells that you might find at a beach. And this was very fitting. I paused to reflect on this and looked around me and down at my feet where the pebbly beach was. And some of this beach was coarse and small and gritty like him. But unlike him it was brown. Janko was now more the color of granite rock. I scooped up a handful of him and let him trickle through my fingers back into the plastic bag. I turned to Margaret.

"Would you like to cast some of him to the lake?"

She shook her head.

"No, my love. I think this is something for you and only you to do."

I looked back at my hand and it was dusted lightly with a pale grey residue. I felt for the breeze and it was blowing softly over my right shoulder towards the lake. I scooped up another handful of his ashes and extended my hand out over the lake and watched him pour slowly from my hand and into the lake. I bent down on my haunches and looked at the bigger bits of him, like crumbs of bread, fall through the water and slowly settle at the shallow bottom becoming one with the lakebed. We would all return to our mother this way, eventually. We would all come full circle. Only love would buoy our spirits on to the next journey.

You are gone now, my son. You had love stuffed full in your soul and you are gone now onto another adventure. And I'm happy for you. I will come along in due time to join you on that journey and there will be many people with us. For we are never alone. Life is all around us and love is what keeps it going. From the smallest creatures in the sand to the biggest whales in the sea. This love was what kept us breathing and free. I turned around and admired the mountain, the hill. It was a squat Buddha, peacefully looking on from higher ground. Happy and content with the way things were. The way things had always been. I dug into the box and took a handful and tossed it high into the air. It caught the breeze and was cast over my head and back into the lake. So that's where you want to be, my son.

I turned around and poured some of him out of the box and along the edge of the shore where the water met the land. I wandered down the shore line for twenty or thirty yards, trailing Janko like Gretel crumbs behind me, watching them sink slowly to the bottom of the shallow water just by the shore. I looked around me and saw Margaret watching me smiling. Her hands folded over her chest, her hair ever so slightly tussled by the wind. I smiled at her.

"He's going home, Margaret," I said to her.

"Yes he is, my love. Yes, he is."

I repeated the trailing of Janko along the shore, this time back towards Margaret. I reached her and kissed her on the lips, cupping the black box in my left hand. My dusty hand. Janko was half empty now. And this time empty was the appropriate choice.

"I'm feeling okay with this," I said to her, "I feel that it's right and good that I can send him home this way."

I smiled at her and I did feel good about it. This is what he wanted. I had grieved him, but the parts I cherished I would always carry with me. His life has been an inspiration for me. I looked around again, turning slowly in circles and I relished it all. I relished the slight nip on my nose from the cool air. The slight cold tingling on my hands from where the water had licked them. I was falling in love with Margaret again and I felt like an infant. Alive again, for the first time. The blue sky was beautiful and true and good. The ground was full of wonder and Janko was in my hand, but more importantly he was in my heart. Right there next to my own parents and people I held dear to me. Including the living. Love was all around me and it was a warm embrace of nostalgia and memory and feeling.

I placed the black box down on the ground, grinding it into the pebbly sand to secure it from tipping over. I squatted before it and dug both my hands into it and scooped the ashes out and I held him up in the sun above my head as if in adulation.

"Take him back to you now, great spirit. Eternal Universe, take your son to your bosom."

It felt right, it just came to me, those words, and they seemed to fit. I brought him down under my face and looked at the grittiness of his ashes and then I reached across the black box and poured him into the lake.

I took the chain that was around my neck which I had bought in Calgary for this purpose. It had a sterling silver vial on the end of it as long as the last digit of my baby finger but half as thick. I screwed the tiny lid off of it and scooped some of Janko into the vial. He was in smaller pieces in this last half. Less gritty. I wanted to take some of him with me to be certain that he would always be with me. Forgive me, but I needed something tangible to help me past this point. I placed the chain around my neck again and picked up the box. I stood up and, bending over at the hips like an arthritic old man, I tossed him out of that box back and forth in big swaths. I tipped the last bit out and shook it to make sure.

I gave the empty box to Margaret and she put the lid back on. I squatted down again at the water's edge and rinsed my hands in the cold water. Washing all trace of him from my hands. I shook them off feeling the blood tingle under the cold prickliness of my skin. I rubbed my face with my wet hands. Cold and cleansing. Then I got up and took Margaret's warm hand in mine.

"Good bye, son," I said.

"Good bye, Janko," Margaret added.

I waited for a moment for a voice, a whisper. What I got instead was a robin flying across my shoulder in the direction of the breeze. He squawked once as he passed by me within a few feet.

"That'll do. That'll do just fine," I said.

I turned around and Margaret and I walked hand in hand back towards the car. She held onto my arm with her other hand still holding the box and she nuzzled into my shoulder. We walked slowly and quietly towards the mountain. That stout mountain. That mountain that was content with how things were. With how things had always been.

ABOUT JASON BLACKER

Jason Blacker was born in Cape Town but spent most of his first 18 years in Johannesburg. His thirst for justice and peace for all humanity was formed in the African sun. Currently he lives in Canada.

He writes hard boiled as well as cozy mysteries, action adventure, thrillers and literary fiction under his own name. Jason Blacker also writes poetry and daily haikus at his haiku blog.

You can find his haikus and other poetry at his website **www.haiqueue.com**.

To stay up to date and learn about new releases be sure to visit **www.jasonblacker.com** where you can find more information about his writing and upcoming projects.

If you enjoy space opera in the tradition of Star Trek then take a look at Jason Blacker's pen name "Sylynt Storme". It is under the name Sylynt Storme where you can find both sci-fi and vampire fiction written by Jason Blacker.

"Star Sails" is the space opera series and "The Misgivings of the Vampire Lucius Lafayette" is his vampire series.

www.ingramcontent.com/pod-product-compliance
Lightning Source LLC
Chambersburg PA
CBHW020634020726
47494CB00001B/188